When He Found Me

VICTORIA BYLIN

Scripture quotations taken from the New American Standard Bible® (NASB), Copyright © 1960, 1962, 1963, 1968, 1971, 1972, 1973, 1975, 1977, 1995 by The Lockman Foundation Used by permission. www.Lockman.org

Cover designed by Jenny Zemanek, Seedlings Design Studio

ISBN-13: 9781793192974
Printed in the United States of America

To my husband
A man who lives his faith in the spirit
of the Psalms

I also want to thank the women who made this book possible. Ladies, I can't thank you enough for your input,
encouragement, wisdom, and friendship.

Sara Mitchell
Play the Tape.

Charlene Patterson
Best editor on the planet. Working with you is pure joy.

Jenny Zemanek
Cutest cover design ever and perfect for the story!

Virginia Smith
A huge thank you for the beautiful design work!

Deborah Raad
Thank you for knowing where hyphens go!

Loose yourself from the chains around your neck,
O captive daughter of Zion.

Isaiah 52:2 (NASB)

Chapter 1

Shane Riley yanked his wet Levis out of a grimy wash-ing machine, one of twenty or so in a Laundromat straight out of 1992. Ten years had passed since he'd set foot in a place like this one, but he'd been ambushed by an August thunderstorm while changing a flat tire on a desolate stretch of I-80.

He should have been in Los Angeles, warming up at third base with the Los Angeles Cougars. Instead he was on his way to Refuge, Wyoming, to take a job he didn't want, driving an SUV he didn't like, and worrying about his sister. He also limped when he got tired, the result of the car accident that had cost him the chance of a lifetime.

Given a choice, he would have stayed in Los Angeles and haunted his local gym, but he needed a job. Why it had to be in Wyoming, he didn't know.

Why, God? Mentally, Shane raised a clenched fist to the empty sky. Four months ago he'd been the frontrunner for Rookie of the Year honors—a man with a future and a hope just like the Bible promised. Now his future was uncertain and his hope hung by the fragile thread of his torn ACL.

As he reached back into the washing machine for his socks, the glass door to the Laundromat swung wide. A small boy burst through the door, followed by a woman in her twenties carrying a Spiderman backpack and a grocery bag dripping water. About five-foot-six and rail thin, she had the look of a distance runner—or someone who didn't eat enough. Brunette hair framed her high cheekbones and pretty face, but what most caught his eye was the faded red T-shirt from Venice Beach, his old stomping ground. When his gaze reached her feet, he saw a pair of worn-out Nikes. Next to her, the boy was barefoot.

The kid didn't mind at all, but Shane did. No child should have to go without decent shoes. He'd done it, and he knew how it felt.

The woman led the boy to a row of orange plastic chairs and plopped down the backpack. "Wait here while I get the dryer started."

"But I'm hungry—"

"Shoes first," she said. "Then we'll eat."

"But—"

"Cody, listen." She dropped to a crouch, making eye contact as she smoothed his shaggy blond hair. "It's going to take a while for your shoes to dry. You only have one pair, so you can't go stomping in mud puddles."

The boy frowned. "It was a really big puddle."

"I know, but—"

2

"I *had* to jump over it."

Instead of becoming exasperated, the woman laughed. "I guess you did."

The plastic bag in hand, she headed for the wall of steel dryers just as Shane arrived at the same wall with his wet clothes. She glanced at him, but only long enough to take in his unshaven jaw and the scar above his left eye.

The line marked where he had cut his head in the car accident—a freak crash caused by a deer leaping in front of his new Mustang GT in Malibu Canyon. His other scars—the ones that changed his life—were on his left knee and hidden by gray sweats. Until a week ago he had used a cane.

No one dressed up to go to a coin laundry, and Shane looked particularly disreputable after driving ten hours straight on nothing but coffee and sunflower seeds. She wouldn't notice his first-rate haircut or smell the after-shave that came in a logoed bottle. She'd see road trash— a fitting assumption considering the first fifteen years of his life—but the description no longer fit. Signing with the Cougars had drastically changed his income and overall quality of life.

The woman kept her back to him, a signal she wanted nothing to do with a stranger. Shane wished his sister had as much common sense, but when it came to men, Daisy had no good judgment at all.

He blamed himself for that weakness. After their mother's sudden death, they had been placed together in a foster home run by a high school baseball coach and his wife. While Shane's life morphed into a Disney movie, Daisy stumbled badly. Several months ago, she had dis-appeared completely, so Shane had hired private detective Troy Ramsey to search for her.

In their last meeting, Troy had been blunt. *"Give it up,*

Shane. If she wants to see you, she'll call."

But that was the point. She *didn't* want to see him. He wanted to see *her* . . . He *needed* to see her to apologize for abandoning her when she needed him, calling her terrible names, and for bullying her with his so-called faith.

Frowning, he dug in his pocket for quarters for the dryer. Each coin bought him ten minutes of hot air, a quirk of fate that reminded him of the post-career counseling from Cougar management. Steve Dawes, a retired catcher, had pushed him to apply for the teaching job in Wyoming. Steve thought the change in scenery would do Shane good, and with his BA in history and a minor in education, he could teach with a substitute permit while he tested the waters of a new career.

"What else are you going to do, Riley? Sit around and feel sorry for yourself?"

Self-pity wasn't Shane's style—not at all. In Los Angeles he went to the gym five days a week. He ran until his knee hurt, then did push-ups, chin-ups, stretches, and crunches until his muscles screamed. He'd do whatever it took to return to major league baseball. Until then, he needed a job or he'd race through his savings. When the principal of Refuge High School offered him a one-semester contract, he took it. In February he planned to try out again for the Cougars.

A handful of coins bounced on the floor and rolled in a dozen directions. He turned and saw the woman picking up pennies, nickels, and dimes. Instinctively he bent to help her. His knee protested and he grimaced.

When their eyes met, she recoiled from his scowl, her nose wrinkling as if he smelled bad. "Thank you. But I can manage."

He plucked a nickel from the lint below the dryer and slid it in her direction.

"Really," she insisted. "I don't need your help."

Pain shot from his knee to his spine. Holding in a moan, he answered with a grunt. The woman's mouth tensed, but Shane kept sweeping coins across the floor. Lint made a cloud of scented dust, a mix of cotton and dryer sheets that took him back to the summers he'd traveled with his mother and sister to craft fairs all over the country. He knew his way around a Laundromat, and he didn't see a single quarter among the runaway coins.

"Mommy? Can I eat now?" The boy's voice traveled the length of the storefront. He sounded close to starvation.

"Not yet," the woman answered. Settling on her knees, she peered beneath a washing machine, then reached under it. Whatever she saw, she needed it badly enough to paw through an inch of dirt.

Shane dug in his pocket for quarters. As he put them in the woman's dryer, he saw the boy's shoes, one sole-up and the other on its side. They were canvas sneakers, wet from being rinsed, and the cheapest shoes a mother could buy. Even so, they were worn to the point of sadness. The rubber soles didn't have a speck of tread, and the canvas had faded from black to gray. Only the laces were in good shape. Stark white except for traces of mud, they were brand new. As a boy, Shane had owned shoes just like them.

Jaw tight, he closed the door and dropped a dollar's worth of quarters into the slot. As he pushed the Start button, the woman jumped to her feet. "What are you doing?"

"Turning on the dryer."

Her cheeks flamed pink. "You shouldn't have done that."

"Why not?"

"They aren't your shoes," she said logically. "I can take care of myself."

"I didn't say you couldn't." But he'd been thinking it.

He didn't doubt this woman loved her son, but she had bought shoelaces because she couldn't afford new shoes. How much were kids' sneakers at Walmart? He didn't know, but they couldn't be much.

The woman lifted her chin, a defiant pose, but she had lint on her knees and a handful of dusty nickels and dimes, signs of her poverty. Even more obvious, she was twig-thin. Her leanness, he decided, had nothing to do with running, at least not the kind people did for exercise. She was skinny, defensive, and chasing down pennies. The combination reminded him of Daisy and he wished again he'd been caring instead of critical.

Next to them, the shoes clunked in an uneven rhythm. As the woman turned to the dryer, so did Shane. In the porthole window he saw the reflection of her face, softer now and composed as she turned to him.

"That was rude of me." Eyes wide, she offered him a handful of coins. "I owe you a dollar."

He held up a hand to stop her. "No, you don't."

"But—"

"Help someone else with it."

Suddenly solemn, she nodded. "I will."

He had to stop looking at her face, not because she reminded him of Daisy but because she didn't. Daisy's eyes were blue like his, and he and his sister shared their mother's dark blond hair. This woman's hair was the color of a brown leather jacket, and her eyes, also brown, were large, round, and deer-like. When her gaze flicked to the whitish scar over his left eye, her countenance softened yet again, raising her lips into a tiny smile born of kindness, maybe empathy.

"Mooommmmy!" The boy charged up the aisle made by the washing machines. When he reached the woman, he shoved the backpack into her hands. "I'm *really* hungry. Can I have just the fries?"

She slung the bag over her shoulder and took the child's hand. "How about eating the hamburger first?"

"Now?"

"Right now," she said, smiling at the boy. Her eyes were still filled with love when she looked at Shane. "Thank you again for the quarters."

"My pleasure."

Her son tugged on her arm, half dragging her to the plastic chairs by the front door. With nothing to do but wait for his clothes to dry, Shane went to the opposite end of the row, sat, and checked his phone for messages. He didn't expect to hear from either Daisy or Troy, but he checked dozens of times per day. There was nothing of interest, so he read sports scores.

The woman opened a McDonald's bag. Shane smelled burgers and fries and thought of all the meals he'd eaten on the road with his mother and Daisy. The woman gave the boy the hamburger, admonished him to chew, and ate a french fry. The boy polished off the burger, the rest of the fries, and the carton of milk, slurping to get the last drop. The woman gathered the trash and tossed it, glanced at her watch, and sat back down.

She'd eaten a french fry. That was it. The shoes would need at least twenty more minutes.

"Let's play the alphabet game," she said to her son. "I see a . . ." She glanced around the room. "An appliance."

"What's that?" the boy asked.

"A big word for washers and dryers. It's your turn."

Shane didn't mean to eavesdrop, but he couldn't avoid hearing the woman's playful way with her son. She laughed at his silly jokes, tickled him for the letter T, and praised him when he said Z stood for zipper.

"Let's do it again," the boy insisted.

"Okay, but no repeating."

Silently, Shane played along, stealing glances at the

woman and boy. The game was pleasantly amusing until they got to the letter G. The boy searched the Laundromat for inspiration, then reached inside the backpack and pulled out a baseball mitt.

"Glove!" he shouted.

Shane swallowed hard, his fingers flexing as he savored the memory of soft leather fit to his palm. In high school, baseball had been his escape, his hope for a scholarship and a better life for himself and Daisy. Before the accident, he had called himself blessed. Now he felt betrayed. Frowning, he refreshed the scores on his phone. The Cougars were ahead 3-2. They had a shot at winning their division.

The woman's laugh rose above the clunk-clunk of the shoes in the dryer. "Good job, Cody."

"I'm hungry again."

"We have apples in the room. That'll be dessert."

A french fry. Worn-out shoes. Crawling after a quarter. Yet she had a smile in her voice. Shane liked her and wished they were in Los Angeles so he could ask her to dinner, someplace fun with large portions. But they weren't in Los Angeles. They were in an empty corner of Wyoming, and tomorrow he'd leave early for Refuge. He'd never see her again, but he wanted to do something to help her.

One of the dryers buzzed and the drum stopped turning. As the shoes thumped to a stop, she retrieved them and came back to her son. Shane listened as she wiggled the shoes on to his feet, making yet another game of tying the laces.

As the boy headed for the door, the woman followed him but stopped short of leaving. Instead she smiled at Shane. "Thanks again for the quarters."

"It was nothing."

"It helped." She looked at him a second longer than

necessary, then herded the boy to an old brown Bonneville with oxidized paint, a dented fender, and tires that were unexpectedly new. He'd noticed the car at the motel by the interstate, the same place he'd taken a room for the night. He wouldn't invite her to dinner—he was certain she'd say no—but he could do something else for her. He could buy her son a pair of shoes.

Chapter 2

*M*elissa June Townsend, called MJ by her friends, finished supervising her son's bath, then herded him to the double bed covered with a faded floral spread. Even with the air-conditioning on high, the motel room was stifling. MJ was damp with perspiration, exhausted, and thirsty for a Coke. Thanks to the kindness of a stranger—a man with startling blue eyes—she had a handful of coins in her pocket.

When Cody fell asleep, she'd make her "I'm safe" call to her friend Lyn, then step across the hall to the vending machines. First, though, she had to tuck him in.

"Okay, tiger." She pulled back the covers with a flourish. "It's bedtime for you. We have another long drive tomorrow."

Cody tumbled into the bed as if he'd been tackled. Considering they'd spent two days on I-15 and I-80, the interstates from Los Angeles, she could forgive his rambunctiousness. She endured the same restless urges, and the feelings would only intensify as they approached Refuge. When she'd left home six years ago as a UCLA freshman, she had envisioned medical school. She'd also been ridiculously naïve and had paid a heavy price. She could still hear Nicole Tatum, the junior who'd been her friend and mentor, talking about relationships.

"You can't be independent until you control your own body. Men don't control it. Your mother doesn't control it, and neither does God. You control it."

MJ had taken control of her body the way Nicole advised, but the consequences were unexpected. Pregnancy had been the first shock, but the surprises didn't end with her son. At her postpartum checkup, she'd been diagnosed with the earliest stage of cervical cancer, a condition caused by a sexually transmitted infection called human papillomavirus, or HPV. Five years ago she'd been treated successfully without a hysterectomy, but the virus lived in her system and periodically reared its ugly head.

Nicole had been wrong. MJ didn't control her body; the HPV controlled it. Last month she had gone for her regular pap and received an ambiguous result.

Dr. Hong had been clear. *"It's ASCUS, MJ. We need to do a colposcopy."*

MJ knew all about colposcopies. Dr. Hong would examine her cervix through a high-powered magnifier and do a biopsy. It would hurt.

She also knew all about ASCUS. It stood for Abnormal Squamous Cells of Undetermined Significance. It was better than LSIL or HSIL. Those stood for Low Grade or High Grade Squamous Intraepithelial Lesions, and both were precancerous. In MJ's mind, LSIL and HSIL were pink and red. ASCUS was gray, like the storm clouds she remembered as a child.

Some storms blew over and the sky turned blue again without a drop of rain, but this time the clouds lingered. The biopsy showed moderate dysplasia, and she had undergone another LEEP procedure, her third in addition to a cone biopsy. The abnormal cells had been removed with an electrically heated loop, but they could come back.

A single LEEP was unlikely to affect childbearing, but multiple treatments put her at risk for an incompetent cervix, a condition that complicated future pregnancies. Two months from now she'd see Dr. Hong for a repeat pap. Depending on the result, she could be facing a hysterectomy at the age of twenty-five. She thought again of Nicole saying a woman controlled her own body and sighed.

"Mommy?" Cody was lying on his back, slapping the bed with his palms and waiting to be tucked in.

"Here you go." She pulled the covers up to his chin and kissed his forehead. "Sleep tight."

He swished his feet like windshield wipers. "Tell me about my great-grandpa's house."

"I already did." During the long hours of the drive, she had entertained Cody with stories about the house she loved but needed to sell. Two years ago she had inherited it from her grandfather. A real estate agent tried to keep it rented, but the sporadic income covered little more than taxes and upkeep.

She didn't want to let it go, but SassyGirl, the clothing store she used to manage, had gone out of business. Her severance would soon run out, and so would her health benefits. The situation had forced her to take drastic action, which ironically would open doors. With the money from the sale of the house, she could go back to school. She'd never be a doctor, but she could train to be a medical technician.

Cody kept wiggling. "How big is the house?"

"It has four bedrooms," she said for the tenth time. "You'll have your own room until we sell it."

"And a yard."

"That's right."

His feet swished even faster, a reminder of his worn-out shoes and the stranger who was unknowingly buying her a Coke. Telling Cody to sleep would only inspire him to stay awake, so she told him again about the house. "It's old and big. The kitchen's yellow, and there's a playroom over the garage."

"And there's a Christmas tree in the yard."

"That's right." Her grandparents had planted a blue spruce the day MJ was born. She barely remembered her grandmother, but Grandpa Jake planted a second spruce for Cody. They were her mother's parents, though MJ found it hard to see similarities. She worried about how much to tell Cody about the house. She didn't want him to become attached to a home they couldn't keep, but she wanted him to know he had a family history. Her own mother sent birthday cards to her grandson, but the rift caused by the pregnancy was still wide.

MJ wondered again what Olivia Townsend would say when her prodigal daughter arrived in town. Six years ago when MJ came home pregnant, her mother, a high school principal, had insisted she give up the baby for adoption. When MJ refused, her mother stopped paying her college tuition.

"Be reasonable, Melissa. You can't support a child. I know what it's like."

"But, Mom—"

"No! I won't let you ruin your life."

"Like I ruined your life? Is that what you're saying?"

"Of course not."

Except MJ knew the truth. She'd been the reason her mother married a musician with big dreams and no common sense, a man she divorced after a thousand arguments about money. In spite of her mother's opinions, MJ had returned to Los Angeles naively believing she could support herself and a child. Now she knew little boys wore out their shoes and cars needed tires.

Cody's eyelids drooped. "Do you think Grammie will visit us?"

"I'm sure she will." *Grammie* was how MJ's mother signed Cody's birthday cards. For all her critical ways, Olivia Townsend loved her grandson.

Cody yawned. "Tell me again. What's in the attic?"

"Boxes. More than you can count." Her grandfather saved everything. "We have to get rid of a lot of stuff."

"Maybe Lyn can sell it."

"Maybe." MJ glanced at her watch and figured Lyn would still be at Mary's Closet, the Venice Beach thrift shop she managed. A charitable venture, Mary's Closet was part of Maggie's House, a citywide ministry named after Mary Magdalene in the Bible and dedicated to helping women escape abusive situations. The store provided both funding for a nearby Maggie's House group home and jobs for women starting over.

MJ had met Lyn when SassyGirl made a large clothing donation. With her own finances tight, she enjoyed shopping at the thrift store. Lyn had become her best friend and the person who introduced her to Christianity.

Cody yawned and rolled to his side. MJ rubbed his back for a minute, then tiptoed to the bathroom. She closed the door without a click, drank a glass of cold water, then sat on the toilet lid and bowed her head.

"Thank you, Lord," she murmured. "I don't know what the future holds, but I know you're looking out for us."

What else should she say? Lyn told her to just talk, that God loved her and would listen, but why would God care about a woman like her? She couldn't pay her bills.

14

She lacked an education, and she had an STI, a sexually transmitted infection. She hated the virus, and sometimes she hated herself. This was one of those times, but Lyn's words came back to her. *"It's not about what you've done. It's about what Christ did for us."*

MJ wanted to believe God would help her, but her circumstances had deteriorated terribly since her decision to become a Christian. First she lost her job, then the HPV had come back.

She couldn't pray for herself, but she could pray for her son. "Cody needs shoes, Lord. He needs other things, too." More than anything, MJ wanted Cody to have a father and siblings. Somehow she clung to the hope that God would take away the HPV—that someday she'd have a husband and another baby, and that she'd feel loved. Abruptly she whispered, "Amen."

Steadying herself, she phoned Lyn.

Her friend answered on the first ring. "How's the trip?"

"It's been good." A picture of the man in the Laundromat popped into her mind. She could still see his denim blue eyes focused on Cody's shoes. He'd noticed her, too. His gaze had skimmed her curves, but he hadn't been rude about it. The chance meeting had brightened her day, but the moment was over.

She refocused on Lyn. "We just crossed into Wyoming."

"That's a relief. With that car of yours, I worry."

"Me too."

Lyn made a humming sound. "I'm still looking for shoes for Cody. If I see his size, I'll send them to you."

"Thanks." MJ had been hunting for shoes for her son for a week. Nothing suitable had come into Mary's Closet, though she snagged a snowsuit he could use this winter and a pink ski jacket for herself. She had also checked a couple of Walmarts back in Los Angeles, but they had been ransacked by back-to-school shoppers and were out of his size. Frustrated and eager to get on the road, she had decided to wait until she reached Refuge to shop for him. He was starting first grade and would also need school supplies.

While Lyn chatted about the thrift store, MJ thought back to the man in the coin laundry. She knew better than to make friends with a stranger, but in her imagination he could be anyone. A doctor. A millionaire. A soldier who would understand a woman with some wounds of her own. She constantly spun tales in her head. They were a poor substitute for romance, but how did a woman date when she had HPV? She didn't, at least that was MJ's solution. But a woman could dream about a handsome stranger buying her a Coke without knowing it.

"MJ?" Lyn broke into her thoughts.

"Sorry. I got distracted."

Lyn laughed. "After driving eight hundred miles with Cody, you're entitled."

A groan slipped from her lips. "We've played the alphabet game about a hundred times. He's ready to run around, and I'm ready to sleep."

"Stay strong, honey."

When her mother said things like that, MJ balked. When Lyn said them, she wanted to salute. "I'm trying to be strong, but it's hard. I feel so alone."

"You're not. I'm a phone call away. Do you still have the seagull?"

"I do." The plastic bird was encased in a three-inch glass ball, forever caught in flight and going nowhere.

"Real seagulls are free, and so are you."

"I know." But she didn't feel free.

The women chatted for another minute, then said good-bye. Feeling lost, MJ closed her eyes. Seconds later, her cell phone played the circus music Cody had picked for her ringtone. She saw her Realtor's number and faked a cheerful hello. "Hey, Kim. What's up?"

"We have a problem."

MJ's stomach caved in. "What's wrong?"

"You know how I was gone for two weeks?"

Kim was single and liked to travel. She'd taken a Caribbean cruise. "Of course."

"Anna was covering for me. I must have forgotten to tell her you wanted to sell, because she rented your house through February."

"She *rented* it?"

"Maybe this is better. You'll make money, and you can list the house in the spring. The market should be a lot stronger then."

"I can't wait."

"But—"

"Kim! I told you, I lost my job. I have expenses." Her COBRA insurance cost as much as her rent. If she ended up on welfare, she'd have to rely on Medicaid, which Dr. Hong didn't accept. After six years, MJ trusted her and didn't want to change doctors.

Kim made a humming sound. "It's only six months. Could you stay with your mom?"

"No."

"I understand."

MJ doubted it. Kim had a degree in business and made good money. Her parents were proud of her, and she dated as effortlessly as she breathed. MJ scolded herself for being jealous, then glanced at the ceiling and saw a water stain that fit her mood. "You'll have to break the rental agreement."

Kim hesitated. "Maybe not. I have another idea."

"What is it?"

"How about the apartment over the garage? It has a full bath and it's huge. You and Cody could live there."

"There's no kitchen."

"There's a decent sink, and you could plug in a fridge and a microwave. Of course, we'd have to change the contract to show you'd be living there, and maybe lower the rent since the renter won't have access to that space, but you'd have an apartment *and* an income."

The plan had merit, but MJ's heart ripped in two. She'd promised Cody his own room. And she didn't want to live across the driveway from a stranger. "I have to sell. There's no getting around it."

"But this guy is solid. He's got excellent credit. A job. Money in the bank—"

"I don't care."

"He's the new history teacher at the high school."

That meant her mother had hired him. Knowing Olivia Townsend, the man was cranky and middle-aged. He'd never tolerate Cody running around the backyard pretending to be a fighter jet.

Kim lowered her voice. "I feel sorry for the guy. He was in a terrible car accident. A month ago he needed a cane."

"This happened a *month* ago and you didn't tell me?"

"A month ago he didn't want the place. He called last week and rented it over the phone."

Even with a renter, MJ couldn't wait to sell the house. She had to keep her health insurance. "I need to sell. Even if he agreed to Cody and me living above the garage, I can't honor the six-month lease."

"You haven't asked how much he's paying."

It couldn't possibly be enough to cover her expenses, but she wanted to pacify Kim. "Is it more than usual?"

"I raised the rent to match the house across the street." She named an amount that would cover MJ's health insurance and then some. With her unemployment checks, she could manage. "That's more than I expected."

"So you're willing to think about it?"

"Yes."

"Perfect. He's picking up the keys tomorrow at two o'clock. I'll call him."

"Make sure he knows about Cody." She didn't want to worry about her son disturbing a bad-tempered old man with a cane.

"Will do."

"And make sure he knows I plan to sell. That's important."

MJ said good-bye to Kim and sighed. Knowing the real estate agent, she'd tell the man Cody never made a sound, which wasn't true. The boy bounced off the walls. He needed a yard, a bike, and a place to kick a soccer ball. He *didn't* need a stranger telling him to be quiet. MJ didn't trust Kim to handle the problem, which meant she needed to arrive in Refuge before the man with the cane. That meant leaving the motel at dawn.

Weary to the bone, she pushed to her feet, turned off the light, and cracked open the bathroom door. She didn't move until she heard Cody's even breathing, then she tiptoed past his bed. Leaving the door ajar, she stepped across the hall to the soda machine, bought a Coke, and went back to the room. Alone in the dark, she popped the top and raised a silent toast to the kindness of a handsome stranger.

Chapter 3

"Mommy? Are you awake?" MJ felt Cody's hand patting her shoulder. Bleary-eyed, she looked at the
window and saw a strip of light between the drapery panels. Her phone alarm was set for five in the morning. The
room should have been dark, and Cody should have been
asleep. Groping clumsily for her phone, she knocked over
the empty soda can on the nightstand. She turned on the
light but still didn't see the phone.

Squinting, she turned to Cody. "My phone . . . Do you
know where it is?"

He handed it to her. "It was beeping. I made it stop."

"Oh, Cody." MJ flopped against the pillow. She would
not lose her temper. Her little boy wanted to take care of

her, but he needed to learn about waking up on time. She rolled to a sitting position, took the phone from him, and checked the time. It was eight thirty. If she hurried, she could still be in Refuge by early afternoon.

She set the phone down, then gripped Cody's hands in both of hers to be certain he would pay attention. "Don't ever do that again."

"Why not?"

"We needed to leave early. When I set my phone alarm, it's for a reason. You had no business turning it off."

His brow wrinkled into a scowl. "I don't want to go in the car again. It's hot."

"We're almost there." MJ smoothed his blond hair, a trait he had inherited from his father. Someday her son would ask about that man and she didn't know what to say. The story of Cody's conception was humiliating, but when he asked, she'd tell him the truth in small, age-appropriate pieces. Until then, she didn't want to think about men . . . not even nice men in Laundromats.

She showered, dressed, gathered their things, then walked with Cody to the office to check out. As she pushed through the door, the clerk—an Asian man with thinning hair—greeted her with a wide smile. "Miss Townsend! I have something for you."

"For me?"

"You drive the big, old car, right?"

"Yes, I do."

He went to the back office and returned with two bags from a sporting goods store. Grinning, he came around the counter and set them on the floor. Before she could say a word, Cody pulled out a shoebox and opened it.

"Soccer shoes!" He held up a pair of black cleats that appeared to be his size. Before MJ could close her gaping mouth, her son yanked off his old sneakers and flung them across the room.

"Cody, wait!"

She might as well have been speaking Russian. The boy had the first shoe on his foot and was wiggling into the second. It was pure luck that he put the shoes on the correct feet.

MJ crouched next to him. "I don't know where the shoes came from—"

"I do," said the clerk. "The man who left them was a guest. He said to give you this."

He handed her a piece of notepaper with the motel's logo on it. In bold printing, someone had written, *We met at the Laundromat. Please accept the shoes for your son—S. Riley.*

Was he a creep? MJ weighed the circumstances and decided he wasn't. Finding her would have been easy. He'd seen her car at the laundry and again at the hotel. The old sedan stood out wherever she went. If he had evil intentions, he would have delivered the shoes in person.

Confident of S. Riley's good will, she watched her son enjoy a surprise. He had the soccer shoes on his feet and was trying to tie the laces, something he'd refused to learn with his old ones. She bent down, looked in the bags, and saw four more shoeboxes, three packages of white socks, boys' sweatpants, a hoodie, and a Los Angeles Cougars baseball cap.

Cody looked at her with huge, questioning eyes. "Can I keep the shoes?"

"You sure can."

He kicked his feet with unfettered joy. "Tie them for me!"

"How about we see what else is here? Those are for sports."

With the shoes untied, Cody popped to his feet and together they enjoyed the bounty of leather, laces, and snowy white socks. The socks were brand new. Never worn. Not cast-offs from a family donating to a thrift shop. MJ's eyes misted with grateful tears. She wanted to thank S. Riley in person, but the longings he stirred were too painful. She'd write him a note instead.

Cody opened another shoebox. It held a pair of sneakers. MJ checked the size and grinned. "They'll be a perfect fit."

The next box held a similar pair but a size larger. The third box held yet another pair in the next size up. S. Riley had given her son at least a year's worth of shoes, and there was one box left. She lifted the lid, folded back the tissue, and saw a pair of women's Nikes, white ones with pink stripes in her size. They were the prettiest shoes she'd ever seen, maybe the prettiest shoes she'd ever owned because she needed them so badly. As she took them from the box, a gift receipt fluttered to the floor. On the back she saw his writing and picked it up.

I guessed at the sizes. You can exchange anything that doesn't fit.

MJ wished she knew S. Riley's full name. He'd live in her heart forever. Smiling gently, she put the receipt in her purse, then took the white shoes out of the box. Unable to help herself anymore than Cody, she unlaced her old shoes and kicked them off.

"Mommy, wait." Cody held up a bag of socks. They were white anklets with pink ribbing. "These are for you."

New socks to go with her new shoes. MJ pulled the fresh cotton over her toes, wiggling them for the joy of it. The hotel clerk couldn't stop grinning, and neither could she. She put on the shoes, stood, and spoke to him while she wiggled her happy toes. "The man who left these things—I'd like to leave him a note."

"He's gone."

"Oh." She bit her lip. "So I can't thank him."

The clerk was a stranger to her, but he'd shared the

fun of the shoes and his eyes were bright. "I think he knows what he did."

"I hope so."

At a time when she needed help, a stranger had shown her unexpected kindness. Maybe Lyn was right about her life changing. They'd had that conversation a month ago after MJ became a Christian in the middle of a nerve-wracking night. Sleepless at three in the morning, she had turned on the radio and heard a man ranting about earth-quakes, war, disease, and killer bees. It was all frighten-ing, but the bees scared her the most. She imagined them swarming into her apartment, attacking Cody. Helpless and frightened, she thought of Lyn's simple faith and how her friend trusted the Lord to guide her. In that moment, MJ had prayed. *If you're out there, God. I'm listening.*

Nothing happened.

No voice shouted from the heavens. Thunder didn't clap, and the wind didn't stir. There was only a distant car alarm and the certainty she had done something signifi-cant. When she shared the experience with Lyn, her friend gave her a Bible and told her to get ready for big changes.

Shoes weren't a big deal to most people, but they were big to MJ and Cody right now. She could only hope her mother would show the same mercy when they arrived in Refuge, and that the man who rented her house would be as compassionate.

She needed to get on the road, so she collected the boxes and shoes and spoke to Cody. "Let's put on the sneakers instead of the cleats."

His brow wrinkled. "I like these."

"They're for sports only."

"But I want to wear them *now*." His lip popped into a pout.

Her son could be stubborn. So could she, but this bat-tle wasn't worth fighting. He'd be riding in the car for at least four more hours. If the shoes entertained him even a little, he might not be so crabby. "Okay, but just this once."

Cody barely heard her. He had on the baseball cap and was pretending to swing a bat the way a neighbor, Mr. Davis, had shown him with a plastic toy. A victim of emphysema, Mr. Davis spent his days breathing oxygen and watching ESPN. MJ had adopted him, and in return he had been a substitute grandfather to Cody. Mr. Davis had given her son the baseball glove as a going-away present. The elderly man would have enjoyed this moment.

MJ dropped Cody's old shoes in a wastebasket, paid the bill, and took her receipt from the clerk. Feeling almost giddy, she lifted the bags and headed for the door. "Come on, slugger," she said to her son.

With Cody skipping at her side, MJ hurried to the car. She put the bags in the back seat, checked her son's seatbelt, then turned the ignition. The engine sputtered as always, but it turned over and she headed for the highway that would take her home to Refuge.

Shane wanted to be certain the woman picked up the shoes, so he went to the coffee shop across the parking lot and ordered breakfast. From the booth he could see her car. As he expected, she and the boy went to the office to settle the bill. Minutes later, she emerged with the shopping bags and a radiant smile. When the boy gave her a high-five, Shane signaled the waitress for the check. He'd done a good deed. It wouldn't help Daisy, but he felt right about the shoes.

The woman was putting the shopping bags in her car when his phone chirped. The number belonged to Craig Hawkins, a teammate and friend who shared Shane's

Marina del Rey apartment. It was barely eight o'clock California time, and Craig usually slept until noon.

"What's up?" Shane answered.

"You had a visitor this morning."

"Who?"

"A woman. When I opened the door, she ran. I'm almost positive it was your sister."

Before leaving Los Angeles, Shane had shown Craig a picture of Daisy. Having her show up two days after he left L.A. struck him as a divine joke, a cruel one. "How did she look?"

Craig hesitated. "Not good."

"Was she high?"

"I don't know." Craig lowered his voice. "She was wearing dark glasses, but I saw bruising on her cheek."

So some jerk had given her a black eye. Sick to his stomach, Shane swiped his hand through his hair. "Did she say anything at all?"

"Just 'Sorry, I have the wrong apartment.' She looked—" Craig stopped, but Shane knew what he was about to say. Daisy had looked awful. Battered. Hung over. Maybe strung out. Craig's voice settled into the matter-of-fact tone of a reporter. "She was gone before I realized it was her. She wasn't blond like in the picture. Her hair's red now."

Shane could imagine the brassy tone she would have picked. "Thanks, Craig. Let me know if you see her again."

Next, Shane called Troy, who answered sleepily after four rings. Shane didn't bother with small talk. "Daisy went to my apartment."

"Oh yeah?"

"Some creep gave her a black eye."

Troy swore. "I can check out the shelters again. The best I can do is leave word that you want to see her, but you know the risk."

"She might run."

"Or go back to the creep who hit her."

Shane didn't blame Troy for failing to find Daisy. Shane had failed her first. He blinked and pictured her with the social worker, leaving Coach Harper's house with a ratty suitcase. They'd been with the Harpers for almost two years. While Shane thrived, Daisy had started drinking and hanging out with a bad crowd. Worried she'd get pregnant, the social worker recommended a group home.

Thinking of that day now, Shane gritted his teeth in shame. He should have fought for her, pleaded with the social worker to give her another chance. Instead he'd breathed a sigh of relief and watched her leave.

Eventually she dropped out of school and moved from one low-paying job to another. The last time Shane saw her had been at his college graduation. She'd been wearing a black mini-skirt, four-inch heels, and cherry red lipstick. With alcohol on her breath, she had flirted outrageously with his friends, until he grasped her elbow and half dragged her into a storeroom. He could still see the chairs stacked against the wall, the dim light, and the dust. Blocking the door, he had begged her to clean up her life, until she lifted her chin and told him to go to hell.

Something had snapped inside of him, and he called her horrible names. She started to cry, but he didn't let up. Each lash of his tongue cut deeper until she was hysterically begging him to open the door. When he finally relented, she stumbled in the direction of the guy who'd been the main target of her flirting. They left together, and the next day the jerk bragged about sleeping with "Preacher Boy's" sister.

Shane had been a Christian then. He had prided himself on the nickname, because it proved he walked like he talked. If the car accident had done nothing else, it exposed his hypocrisy as thoroughly as it destroyed his faith.

He needed to find Daisy before she slid deeper into alcoholism, even harder drugs. "Find her," he said to Troy. "She has to be somewhere."

"All right, but you know the odds."

"Yeah, I know."

Shane ended the call, left a generous tip, and paid his bill at the register. In the parking lot he looked for the woman's car but didn't see it. She was gone, but he'd never forget yesterday's encounter.

He drove to a full-service gas station, paid to have the flat tire fixed and put back on, then filled up his truck, a big Chevy Tahoe with four-wheel drive. Satisfied, he pulled onto the highway and set the cruise control. Twenty minutes later, his phone rang. He glanced at the number, saw "Kim Howard" on the caller ID, and decided not to pick it up. Kim was the real estate agent in charge of the house he was renting. They'd had dinner together, though he wouldn't call it a date. She paid for the meal, and he'd been in too much pain to enjoy himself.

She was probably calling to confirm today's key pickup, so he let the call go to voicemail. He had two hundred miles to go. Two hundred miles to wonder about the woman and boy in the coin laundry. Two hundred miles to worry about his sister. In his mind he saw her bruised face and brassy red hair, but in his heart he remembered the girl who clung to his hand when they crossed busy streets. Everything had scared her back then. He wondered if anything still did.

Chapter 4

Daisy Ann Walker stepped into Mary's Closet, a thrift shop three miles from her brother's Marina del Rey apartment. Her insides throbbed with a spongy kind of pain, and so did her head. The sunglasses hiding her black eye turned everything a smoky gray, but they hadn't blocked the sight of a stranger opening the door to her brother's apartment. Shane was never there when she needed him, so why start now?

Her friends were a lot more loyal, especially Chelsea, another waitress at Shenanigan's, the busy Santa Monica restaurant where they had met three months ago. Chelsea shopped at Mary's Closet for her little girl, and she knew Lyn Grant, the woman who managed it.

"If you need help, go to Lyn. She understands."

Daisy hoped so, because she didn't have anywhere else to go. Two days earlier, her boyfriend, Eric, had taken her for an abortion, but then he'd left to audition for the new George Clooney movie. Last night she developed a fever. The doctor prescribed medicine, but it was expensive and she didn't have the money. She'd gone to Shane's apartment to beg him for a loan. If she had her phone, she could have called him. But she didn't . . . Eric had it. Eric had everything—her phone, her bank cards, her heart.

"May I help you?"

She turned and saw a woman with a mane of wavy chestnut hair. "Are you Lyn?"

"No, but I can get her."

As the woman went to the back room, Daisy browsed a shelf displaying beach souvenirs. Among them were a dozen glass balls, each a shade of blue with a seagull frozen in flight. She often watched the real birds at Venice Pier. With the gulls soaring and the waves breaking below her, she gazed at the horizon and imagined falling off the edge of the world. Would she grow wings and fly? Or would she fall?

Today she'd bet on falling.

The tap of heels pulled her gaze to a woman approaching from the back of the store. Tall and slim, she moved with the grace of a dancer, her chin high and her shoulders back. She was wearing a teal-colored suit that set off her ivory skin and made her perfectly cut hair as black as a crow's wing. Silver jewelry twinkled against the blue, a reminder of the sun sparkling on the ocean. Daisy guessed her to be in her early forties.

The woman approached with a smile. "I'm Lyn."

"Hi."

She lowered her voice. "Tina said you wanted to talk to me."

Lyn smelled like dry-cleaned silk. Daisy had last night's martinis on her breath. Where did she start with her story? *I had an abortion and I hurt . . . I'm broke . . . I'm afraid to go home.* The last time she asked Eric for money, he went crazy, maybe because he was high on uppers. Like a fool, she'd shouted back and ended up in an arm lock with Eric's voice hissing in her ear.

"*Apologize, Daisy. Now.*"

"*No!*"

He had pulled her elbow higher, higher still. She begged for mercy and he let her go, but then he cornered her against the wall like those boys in the garage when she was fourteen. When she whimpered, he had hit her.

Daisy's eyes ached with buried tears, but she hadn't cried in a long time. If she started, she might never stop.

Lyn spoke in a hush. "Are you all right?"

She felt as if she were facing the social worker who'd taken her away from Shane and the Harpers. "Chelsea said you could help me."

"I'll be glad to try," Lyn replied. "How do you know Chelsea?"

"We work together."

"At Shenanigan's?"

"That's right." Daisy raised her chin with pride. She liked people and made decent money as a waitress. Thanks to good tips, she earned enough to pay rent and make car payments. But it wasn't enough to pay for Eric's drug habit. She wished she hadn't moved in with him, but he'd lost his job as a bouncer and needed help while he built his acting career.

Moving in with him had seemed smart at the time, but nothing went the way she expected. Instead of finding another bouncer job, Eric slept in and went to the gym. When money got tight, she missed some payments and her car was repossessed. She tried to please Eric, but sometimes he went crazy on her, said things he didn't mean, and hit her. The only thing she did right was dye her hair red. He said it made her look smart and mysterious, not like the dumb blonde she was.

Lyn indicated a door on the back wall. "Let's talk in private."

Daisy followed her into a big room with a couch, two overstuffed chairs from an earlier decade, and a coffee table with a basket holding apples, packaged cookies, and bottled water. She dropped down on the edge of the couch.

Lyn sat next to her, angling her knees in a graceful pose. "You know my name, but I don't know yours."

"It's Daisy Walker." She used to go by Riley but not anymore.

Lyn handed her a bottle of water. Daisy opened it and sipped. A sip turned into a gulp, then another, until she drank more than half.

Hands folded loosely in her lap, Lyn broke the silence. "What can I do for you, Daisy?"

"I need medicine."

"For your eye?"

She remembered the dark glasses and took them off. "It's not my eye. It's something else." Her hand drifted to her middle.

"PID?"

PID stood for Pelvic Inflammatory Disease. A friend of Daisy's dealt with it. "No. I had an abortion."

"I'm sorry."

So was Daisy, but she shrugged. "It wasn't that bad." She'd been awake and it hurt, but a nurse held her hand the whole time. The worst part had been lying on her back with her feet up like an upside-down bug. "The procedure went okay, but I forgot to take the antibiotics they gave me when I left. Now I have an infection."

"Did you call the clinic?"

"Last night," she replied. "The doctor called the pharmacy, but the new pills are two hundred dollars and I don't have the money right now. Chelsea said you might help."

"I will, but I'm also worried about your eye. What happened?"

I walked into a door. If she lied, Lyn would know it. And if she didn't trust Daisy, she might not help her. "Eric hit me."

"Who's Eric?"

"My boyfriend." She tried to look Lyn in the eye, but her gaze skittered to the snack basket. She saw a tiny package of Fig Newtons. She loved Fig Newtons, except they reminded her of Shane buying them for her when she was little. Eric said Fig Newtons made her fat, and he threw them away when she bought them. Daisy could almost taste the gooey filling, but she turned her attention to Lyn.

The brunette plucked the package from the basket and handed it to her.

Feeling shy, Daisy opened it and took a bite. "These are my favorite."

"I like animal crackers," Lyn admitted. "There was a time in my life when eating cookies was the best thing in the world. Sometimes it still is."

"I know what you mean." Daisy chewed the cookie, tasting the sweetness and remembering how Shane bought her a whole package for her eighth birthday. Her mother had given her a bouquet of daisies made out of metal. They'd been pretty, but Daisy had wanted a doll she saw on TV.

Lyn's mouth relaxed into a wistful smile. "Life gets complicated, doesn't it?"

"Definitely."

"Want to compare complications?"

Daisy was enjoying the cookie. "Sure, why not?"

"I'll go first," Lyn offered. "I drove drunk more than once, almost killed someone, and did three months in county jail. I cleaned up my act for a while and got married, but the marriage didn't last. When my ex-husband drank, he hit me. Medical bills led to credit card debt. To cope with it all, I drank even more—"

"Stop!" Daisy stared at her, wide-eyed and frightened.

The woman gentled her voice. "I'm just getting to the good part. I've been sober for nine years now."

Daisy thought of last night's gin and the gin she'd drink tonight. She didn't want to hear Lyn's story. She wanted to get the medicine and go back to the apartment, curl up in bed, and hope Eric would leave her alone.

She took another bite of the Fig Newton, felt it squish, and wished she could stay on this couch forever, but it was her turn to share complications. *My mother died when I was twelve. I was molested by two boys in a garage. I started drinking in high school and I don't want to stop. My own brother hates me.*

Suddenly bitter, she didn't want to tell Lyn anything. Abruptly, she raised her chin. "Will you help me or not?"

"Of course I'll help you." Lyn took an iPhone out of her pocket. "Which pharmacy has the prescription?"

"Save-Rite on Pico."

Lyn connected to the pharmacy, spoke to a clerk, and paid for the prescription with a credit card. Without pausing, she called another number and made arrangements for a woman named Gina to pick up the medicine. She set down the phone and turned to Daisy. "Gina will be here in about an hour. That'll take care of one problem, but I'm concerned about Eric."

"I'm not."

"I know how that is," Lyn said, breathing out the words. "Sometimes he's good to you. Sometimes he's not.

You think about leaving, but you love him. Besides, you don't have anywhere to go. He's bigger and stronger, and somehow he's taken your money."

"How'd you know?"

"I'm describing my ex-husband." Lyn re-crossed her legs. "It's a long story, but he's the reason we're both here today. A friend helped me get away from him, and her church helped us both. Before she moved to Phoenix, we started Maggie's House for women escaping dangerous situations. We have about a dozen houses here in Los Angeles. Mary's Closet is part of that organization."

"My friend Chelsea shops here for her little girl. She told me a little about what you do."

"Would you like to know more?"

No! Except her eye hurt and her insides throbbed with every beat of her heart. She longed to sleep away the pain. Sometimes she longed to sleep forever. Blinking, she thought of the way Shane described heaven. Perfect beauty. Perfect music. People made perfect by the sacrifice of a living Savior. Daisy had no place in all that perfection. But she also liked Fig Newtons, and she couldn't stop looking at Lyn, who had the kindest eyes she'd ever seen.

The woman spoke in a hush. "There's a room available if you'd like it."

"I can't."

"Are you afraid of Eric?"

Daisy shrugged. "He's my boyfriend. I care about him."

"That's not what I asked. Are you *afraid* of him?"

Almost imperceptibly, Daisy nodded yes. When she first met Eric, he was good to her. Sometimes he got a little rough while they were dating, but he didn't hit her until she moved in with him. Her eye hurt, but her belly hurt even more. Eric blamed *her* for getting pregnant, which wasn't fair. She *told* him she'd missed a couple of pills. She thought of seeing him tonight and shuddered.

Lyn took her hand. "I'd like to help you, Daisy."

"How?"

"If you move into Maggie's House, you'll have time to recover from the abortion. You can sort out your life without being afraid."

The offer tempted her. So did Fig Newtons, but they weren't important. Daisy shook her head. "I can't."

"Would Eric come after you?"

Maybe, but that wasn't why she said no. "It's not Eric. It's me."

"What about you?"

"I don't like rules."

"Neither do I. And you're right. We *do* have rules at Maggie's House. The rules keep us safe. If you decide to move in, they'll keep you safe, too."

"I doubt it."

"Why?"

Daisy shrugged. "I grew up in foster care. I couldn't follow the rules even when I tried." Twice she had run away from the Harpers. She knew drinking was wrong for a fourteen-year-old, but she liked it.

She still did, but her thoughts took wing and landed at Maggie's House. What would it be like to wake up and not be afraid? To eat Fig Newtons without someone making fun of her? A pain stabbed her from the inside out, filling the place where for a month a baby had lived. Daisy recalled the morning she did the pregnancy test. Her first reaction, before the fear and the dismay, had been awe at the creation of a human being.

She pressed her hand to her middle. In her mind she heard the suction machine pulling the life from her womb. She hadn't wanted the abortion, but she'd been too weak to fight.

Weak.

It was the story of her life and she was sick of it. She

wanted to shatter the glass balls and set the seagulls free. She could almost see them now—a dozen birds spiraling into flight and leaving through an open door.

She raised her chin. "What are the rules?"

"Most of them are common courtesy." Lyn explained that Maggie's House was owned by a local church. Situated a block from the thrift shop, it had white stucco walls, four bedrooms and two bathrooms that had to be shared. Daisy could live there for free, and she could leave whenever she wanted. She'd have her own room and would help with cooking and cleaning.

To Daisy, it sounded like what a normal family did. It also sounded too good to be true. "What else?"

"You'll need spending money, so you'll work part-time, either at the house or here in the thrift shop. We also provide vocational training."

Daisy liked school. She'd been envious of Shane going to college, but she lost her chance when she blew it with the Harpers. But that was eight years ago. What would happen if she followed the rules? A long time ago, she'd dreamed about going to art school. Maybe she could learn graphic design. "I'd like that."

"Good." Lyn peered into her eyes. "We're a Christian organization. No one will tell you what to think, but we hold regular Bible studies."

A chill shot down her spine. She'd been thirteen when Shane became a Christian. He'd been sixteen, almost seventeen. At first she liked hearing about Jesus and how God loved her. She believed what Shane said and they had prayed, but then she went with the two boys into the garage. Where was God then? Why hadn't he stopped her? Why hadn't he stopped *them*?

She wanted a drink. Badly and right now. A martini, wine, cheap beer. Anything to keep her from thinking about Shane and foster care. She didn't want to go to a

Bible study, but she supposed she could tolerate it. "I guess that's all right."

"That leaves us with just one more rule. For some women, it's a deal-breaker."

Daisy hesitated, unsure. "What is it?"

"No drugs or alcohol."

She'd expected a no-drug policy, but alcohol? She liked everything about it—the taste, the buzz, the escape. She tried to look Lyn in the eye, but her gaze shifted to the side. "This isn't going to work."

"Is it the drugs or the alcohol?"

"I don't do drugs, but I drink."

"Do you want to stop?"

Not in a million years. If she stopped drinking, she might cry. Daisy stared at her feet, saw Lyn's plain ivory pumps, and yearned to be a different person. Could she do it? Could she follow the rules for a change? She thought of the abortion, Eric's fists, and Shane's hateful words. She thought of her mother's death, the social worker taking her from the Harpers, the boys touching her. Until now, no one had given Daisy a real choice. But Lyn just had.

Fear and longing did a wicked march along her spine, stealing her breath until her chest ached. Could she take control of her life? She didn't know, but she wanted to find out. "I'll try to stop drinking, but I don't know if I can."

"You can't. At least not alone."

"But—"

"You're not alone."

Daisy wanted to believe her, but she felt as fragile as the flower bearing her name. Daisies trembled in the slightest breeze, and they burned up in the heat. She gave Lyn a tentative look. "I'll try. I promise."

"That's a good start." Lyn reached out and patted Daisy's knee, reassuring her as if she were a child. "We have some details to work out. Where do you live now?"

"With Eric in West Hollywood."

"Does he own or rent?"

"He rents."

"Are you on the lease?"

"No. The apartment is his. I moved in with him." She hadn't bothered to change her address on her driver's license or bank account. Whatever she needed to do for her maxxed-out Visa, she did online.

Lyn asked a few more questions, and Daisy answered with simple facts. She would call Shenanigan's and quit, then close her bank account, which would end Eric's access to her money. The car she drove to the thrift shop was the clunker he drove to his bouncer jobs, not the red Miata he loved. The old car was in his name, so she would leave it at the apartment. As for her cell phone, she'd have to live without it. For now, she could borrow a prepaid phone from Maggie's House.

"We need to get your things," Lyn finally said. "Is there a time when Eric is gone?"

"He's out now." After the audition, he was having lunch with his agent. He wouldn't return for hours.

"When Gina brings the medicine, the three of us will get your things. There's no reason to tell Eric where you are, but he needs to know you've ended the relationship."

"Should I call him?"

"A note would be safer."

"All right." Inwardly, she cringed. She loved him, and she knew how it felt to be kicked to the curb.

Lyn squeezed her hand. "Would it be okay if I prayed for you?"

Daisy hesitated. Shane, a Christian, had treated her like dirt. Would the women at Maggie's House treat her the same way? What if she couldn't stop drinking? But what if she could . . . Daisy didn't know how, but Lyn did and she had asked to pray. "I guess it's okay."

Lyn bowed her head. "Father God, you know everything about us, yet you love us just as we are . . ."

Daisy listened to every word, but she didn't feel a thing. She could only think about the gin she wouldn't be drinking, the note she'd write to Eric, and Shane and his lectures. She didn't know which hurt more—the bruises that showed or the ones that didn't.

After Lyn said "Amen," Daisy helped herself to a second package of cookies, opened it, and tried not to think about her brother.

Chapter 5

*W*ith Cody napping in the back seat, safely strapped into his booster seat, MJ steered down the off-ramp to Refuge. She passed the visitor's center, taking in a smattering of RVs and a playground with a brown plastic fort. A Best Western announced a vacancy with a pink neon sign, and a billboard advertised the best steaks in Wyoming at Cowboy's Cantina.

She was home.

Inhaling the dry, sunbaked air, she swayed with the curve of the highway that narrowed into Refuge Boulevard. Busy tourist shops lined both sides of the four-lane street, boasting everything from sequined cowboy hats to the finest Western art. Restaurants filled the air with the aroma of barbecue, and the sight of Annie's Campfire Café, famous for its marshmallow-laden hot chocolate, made her mouth water.

Little had changed in the town that mixed Western history with a modern affection for outdoor sports. A gateway to the Tetons, Refuge had a full-time population of ten thousand people, but the numbers swelled in the summer and again in the winter when the snow bunnies arrived. Recalling the change in seasons—something she missed in Los Angeles—MJ indulged in a nostalgic smile.

She shifted so she could see her son in the rearview mirror, still snoozing but starting to stretch. "Cody, honey, wake up. We're in Refuge."

He startled awake, looked out the window, and saw Cowboy's Cantina. "Mommy! There's a horse on the roof!"

"There sure is." A plastic bronco had pummeled the clouds as long as MJ could remember.

She wished again she didn't have to sell the house. Grandpa Jake would have understood, but she expected her mother to protest. In a way, Olivia Townsend had that right. The house could have been hers, but she gave her blessing to the change in Grandpa Jake's will after Cody's birth. Her mother had been extremely gracious about his decision, even enthusiastic about MJ having financial security. Selling the house now would no doubt be another failure in her eyes, one MJ intended to face in person.

As things stood, her mother didn't know anything about MJ's predicament, financial or health-wise. Since Cody's birth, they had managed only polite phone calls and a few visits. MJ knew she needed to forgive her mother for the hurt feelings, but forgiving someone who said "I told you so" at every opportunity was hard. Tonight she'd call her mother, but she dreaded the conversation.

The real estate office came into view. Embarrassed by her car, she parked behind the brown stucco building, turned off the ignition, and glanced at Cody's shoes. She didn't have the energy to wrestle him into the sneakers, so she let him wear the cleats. Side by side, they walked around the corner to the front of the building. The doorbell chimed as they entered.

Kim came down a short hall. "Hey, MJ. You look great."

She didn't, but Kim did. Her hair shimmered with auburn highlights, and the spiky cut accentuated her artfully made-up eyes. Dressed in emerald green and wearing dangly earrings, she greeted MJ with a hug.

MJ hugged her back, then introduced her son. "Cody, this is Miss Howard."

He gawked at Kim as if she were from another planet, then sidled closer to MJ. She was a bit shaky herself.

Kim dropped to a crouch next to Cody. "I bet you were in the car *forever.*"

He nodded.

"How would you like to play with a toy train while I talk with your mom?" She indicated a play area in the corner of the lobby. Walled with carpeted blocks, it held a treasure trove of colorful plastic. After glancing at MJ for permission, Cody went with Kim to a kid-sized table with a Thomas the Tank Engine train set.

When he settled, the women sat on the sofa by the window. Kim set a folder holding the rental agreement on a glass table, then folded her hands in her lap. "So—tell me everything."

They'd been friendly in high school, but MJ had no desire to share the details of her life. Instead she chatted about the drive and how Refuge looked the same. Kim talked about business. Not only did she sell real estate, she owned a bed and breakfast.

She crossed her legs with natural ease, folded her hands, and tipped her head, turning the spotlight back on

MJ. "Cody's adorable."

Kim waited for an answer, but MJ didn't oblige. Being a single mom no longer carried a stigma, but Cody's lack of a father embarrassed her. She hated not having the answer to the question he'd someday ask.

Who's my father?

MJ didn't have a good answer. She had gone to a party with Nicole and met a guy whose name was lost in a fog of rum and Coke. Disposing of her virginity had seemed like the best decision she ever made—until it happened. At that moment, she had felt violated, embarrassed, and alone.

Shaking off the past, she focused on the business at hand. "Did you speak with the renter?"

"He didn't return my call, but he'll be here at two."

MJ glanced at the clock. He'd be arriving any minute, and she wanted to freshen up. "Where's the ladies' room?"

"Down the hall."

MJ stood and called Cody. "Let's make a pit stop."

Her son scrambled over the carpeted blocks and together they went to take care of business. As she washed his hands and face, he squirmed and water splattered her T-shirt. Hoping it would dry quickly, she brushed her hair and dabbed on lipstick. She didn't look like a landlord, but she knew how to be professional. She had done a good job managing SassyGirl. Too bad the chain went bankrupt. She could have taken accounting classes and moved into management.

Sighing, she inspected herself in the mirror, squared her shoulders, and reached for Cody's damp hand. "Let's go, kiddo."

They arrived in the lobby just as the glass door swung wide and in walked a man with startling blue eyes.

Her mouth gaped.

His brows arched.

Yesterday when they met, stubble had covered his jaw. Today he was clean-shaven and dressed in a button-down oxford that matched his eyes. Khakis emphasized his long legs, and his dark blond hair was neatly combed away from his angular face. She couldn't help but notice his broad shoulders and muscular arms, the way he stood tall with an air of confidence. He looked nothing like the middle-aged history teacher she'd been expecting, though she recalled the stiff way he picked up the coins she dropped.

Kim held out her hand. "Shane, it's good to see you."

So *S* stood for Shane.

He accepted Kim's hand and greeted her, but his eyes darted back to MJ. They were full of questions and bright with undisguised pleasure.

Kim gazed at him with her made-up eyes while apologizing for what she called "a little mix-up."

To MJ, the mix-up wasn't little. She was prepared to negotiate with a stranger, not the man who bought the shoes on her feet. She wanted to thank him, of course. But she also wanted out of the negotiations about the house. S. Riley made her want to smile and flirt—and to forget she was facing a hysterectomy. She didn't need a romantic complication in her life and neither did Cody. She had to terminate the lease, but she was sorry about it. He'd been kind to her, and she was repaying him with a big inconvenience.

Kim moved on to the introductions. "Shane, this is MJ Townsend. She owns the house you rented."

"We've met." With a twinkle in his eyes, he offered his hand. "L is for Laundromat."

She clasped his fingers, felt the warmth of his grip, and told her racing pulse to slow down. "S is for Shoes. Thank you. It was a wonderful gift."

His gaze dropped to her feet and her toes curled. He focused back on her face and smiled. "They fit."

"Perfectly."

He turned to Cody, who was staring up at him wide-eyed. S. Riley's face relaxed into a smile. "You have on the cleats."

"I like them best," the boy answered.

"Me too."

Kim interrupted. "So you two know each other?"

"A little," Shane answered.

Kim waited, but neither of them explained further. With a wave of her hand, she indicated the sofa. "Let's sit and I'll clue Shane in to the problem."

MJ needed to tell Kim she had changed her mind about the arrangement. She also had to get Cody settled again with the toy train. When Shane headed to the couch, she murmured to Kim, "I need to talk to you."

"About what?"

"There's a problem."

Cody interrupted in a loud voice. "Mommy, why is that man here?"

She gripped his shoulder in an effort to steer him to the play area. "I'll tell you later. It's time to play with the train."

The boy glared at her. "I don't *want* to." After three days of travel, he was on the verge of a meltdown.

Irritation flickered in Kim's eyes. "So what's the problem?"

Cody pulled away from her. "I want to know *now.* Mommy, who is he?"

MJ gripped both of her son's shoulders and lowered her chin. "Cody, you need to play with the toys while I take care of business."

"No!"

"Hey, Cody." The voice belonged to Shane Riley. "Where's that train?"

His mouth agape, the boy stared at Shane. MJ had

seen that expression before—in grocery stores when they saw families together, in church when a dad carried a child on his shoulders. Cody's hunger for a father was like a baby's desire for milk. No way could MJ let her son get close to Shane Riley. Cody would surely get his heart broken. Until she knew where she stood with a hysterectomy, she and Cody needed to keep their distance from men, especially men who were good-looking and kind.

Cody wiggled out of her grasp and pointed to the play area. "The train's over there. Want to see it?"

Shane grinned. "Sure. Trains are cool."

Cody led the way to the toys with Shane following. Grateful, MJ turned to Kim. "I've changed my mind about using the apartment."

"Why?"

"It's personal." No way would she confide in Kim.

"But it's a good plan."

"Not anymore."

Kim's mouth hardened into a line. MJ's refusal to go along with the strategy made the real estate agent look bad, and Kim didn't like it.

Shane came back to the women without Cody, took in Kim's frown, then focused on MJ. Her cheeks caught fire under his gaze. Bravely, she opened her mouth to speak, but nothing came out.

Shane broke the silence. "So what's the mix-up?"

Kim put on a rueful smile. "I feel terrible about it. Maybe we should sit down." She led them to a sitting area with a sofa and two armchairs. "Would either of you like a soft drink? Water?"

"Water," Shane answered.

"A Coke," MJ replied.

Kim's high heels tapped down the hall. MJ took the couch, and Shane sat in one of the chairs. "You know S is for Shane. What does MJ stand for?"

"Melissa June, but no one calls me Melissa." *Except my mother.* "My last name is Townsend. My mother is the high school principal."

"My boss."

MJ merely nodded.

"Well, MJ," he said, pausing on her name, "what's this problem we have?"

"One of Kim's coworkers rented out my house by mistake. I have to sell it, so I can't honor a six-month lease. I'm really sorry, but you'll have to find another place to live."

He made a humming sound, relaxed back in the chair, and lightly drummed his fingers. Kim arrived with the Coke and the water. She handed out the beverages, then sat on the corner of the couch between MJ and Shane. "It looks like MJ started explaining. I feel just awful."

Shane shrugged. "Mistakes happen."

MJ's shoulders relaxed. "Thanks for understanding."

"Yes," Kim agreed. "I know how much you liked the house. It's too bad the garage apartment didn't work out."

"What about the apartment?" His brows lifted with interest.

"Never mind," Kim said hurriedly. "It's off the table."

Shane turned to MJ. It seemed wrong to leave him dangling. "Kim thought Cody and I could live in the apartment above the garage in exchange for a reduction in your rent, but it would never work."

"Why not?" he asked.

"I want to sell fast," she explained. "You'd have to keep the house neat so Kim could show it. Strangers will be walking through. I'm sure you don't want the inconvenience."

Oh yes, he did. Shane liked everything about MJ Townsend. She'd been gracious about the shoes, a gift that could have been awkward, and she was firm with Kim, who struck him as pushy. The redhead had Hollywood good looks, but MJ had a natural prettiness that combined poise, determination, and genuine caring. She intrigued him in every way.

He saw no reason to break the lease, and he had two good ones to keep it. For one thing, he wanted to live close to the best gym in Refuge. The other reason concerned his guilty conscience. If he helped MJ, he could imagine someone helping Daisy.

All business, he sat forward in the chair. "Let's negotiate."

Kim perked up. "Sounds good to me."

MJ glared at her. "There's nothing to negotiate."

Laughter bubbled from Kim's throat. "There's *always* room to negotiate. Now"—she turned to Shane—"if you're willing to put up with the lockbox, we can show the house by appointment only. Frankly, it needs work before I can list it, and we're near the end of the selling season. I don't expect much traffic."

MJ's scowl deepened, a reaction Shane shared. Kim should have been representing her client's interests, not her own. He decided to get Kim out of the way. "I'd like to know what else is available. Would you pull up some other rentals for me?"

"Of course."

After Kim left, Shane focused on MJ. "Here's what I'd like to do. I'll take the apartment over the garage. You and Cody can have the house and deal with the lockbox and whatever you need to do to sell the house. I figure it'll take some time, right?"

"Yes. Both to prepare it and to sell."

"So it'll be at least a few months before I need to find

Victoria Bylin

another place. If you provide meals, laundry, and house-keeping, I'll pay the full rent."

She huffed. "That's ridiculous."

"Why?"

"You'd be paying too much."

"Not if you factor in what I'd pay to eat out every night. I've done it. It gets old."

She hesitated, then frowned. "You'd still be paying too much."

He didn't care about a few dollars in rent. His future depended on rehabilitating his knee. "Do you know why I picked your house?"

"Why?"

"It's a block from the best gym in town. I tore up my knee in a car accident. I don't need a big house, but I *do* need exercise equipment."

She grimaced in sympathy but still shook her head. "I'm sorry, but the rental agreement won't work."

"Why not?"

"It just won't." Another blush painted her cheeks pink, matching her T-shirt and the stripes on the shoes. He'd been right about pink being her color. If her stubbornness hadn't already given away her awareness of him as a man, the blush would have. He decided to press. "Are you a good cook?"

She arched her brows at him. "Cody thinks so, but he likes hot dogs."

"So do I." Some of his best memories included hot dogs.

She hesitated, then shrugged. "I'm a decent cook, but this doesn't feel right. It's not fair to you."

He knew her needs, but she didn't know his. That omission turned her into a charity case, which she wasn't. "I'm not doing this to be nice. Consider it a business ar-rangement between you, me, and a third party."

"I don't understand."

"It's a long story—one that involves my sister."

Her next breath was soft and tense, the sound a woman made after a kiss, in the moment when she didn't know what would happen next, or what she wanted to happen.

She looked past him through the window to the street, probably weighing her financial needs against her worries. He didn't push. The decision was hers, but he hoped she'd say yes.

"All right," she said in a tentative voice. "But I don't want Cody to bother you."

"He won't."

"And we'll need a schedule for meals."

"That's fine."

"I'll clean the apartment once a week. Would that be enough?"

"Plenty." He kept things neat, and if the bathroom got bad, he knew what to do with a can of Lysol.

"That leaves laundry."

Shane grinned. "Be prepared, because there's a lot of it with those trips to the gym."

Joking, she wrinkled her nose. "Maybe I should charge you more."

"Maybe you should."

He kept his voice light, but talking about household chores reminded him of Daisy. With their nomadic childhood, he knew the value of a washer and dryer. Having met MJ in a Laundromat, he suspected she did as well.

She squared her shoulders. "I guess we have a deal."

They traded a look that lasted a moment too long, then she turned her attention to the hall where Kim was approaching with a handful of printouts. Shane stood as she neared the couch. "MJ and I worked it out. She's taking the house and I'm living in the apartment."

"Excellent!" Kim tossed the printouts in the trash and sat. "I'm glad things worked out. It's best for everyone."

Including Kim, Shane thought.

MJ turned to her. "We need to get the apartment ready."

"I knew we had a problem, so I sent a crew over yesterday. They're painting now, and you're not to worry about the cost. I made a big mistake, and it's important to me to fix it. Tomorrow the crew will bring furniture from the house, and Shane can move in after four o'clock."

"Sounds good." He hunkered forward, ready for anything. "Let's sign the lease."

Kim opened a green folder and removed the rental agreement. As she wrote in changes, he and MJ initialed them. When the signing was over, they made plans to prepare the apartment for Shane to move in.

On his way to the door, he stopped to say good-bye to Cody. "We'll play catch sometime, okay?"

"Okay." The boy's eyes lit up. They were blue, not brown like his mother's, and Shane wondered about Cody's father. Did the guy pay child support? Apparently not.

As he pushed through the door, Kim followed. "I feel terrible about the mix-up. I'd like to make it up to you."

"There's no need."

"But I want to." When they reached his Tahoe, she tipped her face up to his. A sultry gleam shadowed her hazel eyes. "How about dinner? We can talk about decorating the apartment." Laughing softly, she fluttered her hand. "If you leave it up to me, I'll do it in animal prints. You know, something wild and free."

Shane was surprisingly annoyed. He wanted to chase, not be chased. As for being caught, he wanted to do the catching. To his embarrassment, he'd never been with a woman. That was part of the fallout from his Preacher

Man days. He'd been a poster boy for sexual purity, a burden he was now eager to shed, but he wanted a relationship, not something casual, and Kim didn't interest him.

She needed to forget about tiger stripes, so he said, "I like brown." He didn't. He hated brown. He hoped she hated it, too.

She laughed as if he'd told a joke. "Then brown it is. Maybe we can do dinner another time?"

"Maybe."

He didn't mean it, but a flat-out refusal would have been rude. As Kim went into the office, he looked through the window at MJ. She was seated at the play table with Cody, having a serious conversation. He hoped their agreement would alleviate some of the stress in her life, even give her a reason to smile. He liked her, plain and simple. If he had dinner with anyone, it would be MJ. He'd do the asking, and he planned to do it soon.

Chapter 6

Getting the apartment ready in twenty-four hours took all the energy MJ could muster. After the three-day drive, she wanted to collapse on her own soft bed. Instead she joined forces with Kim's crew to turn a drab, dusty playroom into a home for Shane.

The painters worked late into the night, turning the stale white walls to creamy ivory, and another team washed windows inside and out. In the morning, movers carried furniture from the house to the apartment, arranging it while she made the bed and hung bath towels. Last, she wrote out a menu and list of housekeeping questions about Shane's preferences, everything from food choices to laundry soap. He was paying her well, and she wanted to do an excellent job.

Cody was playing next door with his new friend Brandon, a fellow first grader. Brandon's mother, Tracee Anderson, a longtime neighbor, had offered to watch Cody while MJ played landlord.

Enjoying a moment of quiet, MJ watched through her own kitchen window for Shane's arrival. At precisely four o'clock, he pulled into the driveway in a large SUV. Notes in hand, she stepped outside.

He climbed out of the big vehicle and waved. "Hey, there."

"Hi." She hugged her clipboard. "Kim's crew worked fast. I hope you like what we've done."

"Let's see it."

He motioned for MJ to lead the way up the outdoor stairs. She climbed them as easily as she walked, but Shane moved slowly. When he reached the landing, she stepped inside the apartment and swept her arm to indicate the entire room. "What do you think?"

He walked in behind her, removed his sunglasses, and took in décor that mixed the Old West with modern conveniences.

When he didn't speak, she wondered if she'd misjudged his taste. "We can make changes if you don't like it."

"I like it all." His eyes were on the wooden divider that walled off the queen-sized bed. "Those panels look like old saloon doors."

"They are." She stepped to the middle section and pointed at a hole shaped like a nickel. "Do you see that? It's allegedly from a shot fired by Butch Cassidy."

Shane grinned. "True or not, it makes a good story."

"Look around. When you're done, we'll discuss a

cleaning schedule and the foods you like."

"Other than hot dogs?"

She couldn't help but smile. "Yes, but Cody would eat them every day if I let him."

"Where is he?"

"Next door with a friend."

Shane's gaze lingered on her face. "He's a nice kid."

"Thank you." She didn't want to talk about Cody. She wanted to stick to her menus and schedules and the things that made Shane Riley a tenant. "So the place looks okay?"

"It's perfect." His gaze lingered on her grandfather's desk. A roll-top from the 1890s, it was designed for a human being instead of a computer. Furniture from her grandfather's formal living room—a leather sofa, oak tables, hurricane lamps, and a flat-screen TV—filled the living area. She and Cody wouldn't miss any of it, because they would be hanging out in the family room near the kitchen.

"Check out the bathroom." She gestured again like a tour guide and felt silly.

He walked past her and peered into the bathroom with its utilitarian fixtures and faded yellow tile.

"The shower's clean but it's old," she said, raising her voice slightly. "I plan to hire someone to re-grout."

"I'll do it," he offered. "It's an easy job."

"But you shouldn't have to."

"I don't mind."

She didn't want him to do her any favors, but arguing made her seem defensive, even silly, so she swallowed a protest.

Shane returned to the living area. "Did Kim do all this or did you?"

"Me."

He scanned the room again, a faint smile on his face.

"I'm glad. I told her I liked brown."

"Glad?" MJ was confused. She hadn't used any brown. She liked bright colors and wanted the apartment to be cheerful. "If you don't like the colors, I'll change it."

"No," he said quickly. "It's perfect. I wasn't serious about the brown."

She tipped her head to the side. "Then why—"

"I was afraid of tiger stripes."

"Oh." MJ recalled Kim joking about animal prints being sexy when they discussed decorating, then she had called Shane "eye candy" in a tone that made MJ uncomfortable. "No chance of that with me." She had given Shane her grandfather's hardwood bedroom set and selected a homey plaid comforter that brought out the luster of the mahogany stain.

So why hadn't Kim mentioned Shane's color preference? No mystery there. Kim, practically drooling over Shane's good looks, had asked twice about how they met. MJ explained they had crossed paths on the road, but that was all.

Kim had seemed pleased. *"So he's not taken?"*

"Not by me."

MJ fought a fresh wave of envy. What would it be like to date and flirt without the threat of a hysterectomy, or the stigma of HPV? Would she ever know that freedom? Holding in a sigh, she sat on the couch and opened her folder.

Shane dropped down next to her, and they went to work. As if she were meeting with a sales rep at SassyGirl, she quizzed him about his favorite foods. He wanted healthy and lean, whole grains, salads, and veggies. He disliked soggy bacon and rye bread.

"I really do like hot dogs," he added.

"We'll have them sometime."

He lazed back on the couch. "If you have a grill, I'll

barbecue them. That's the best."

She couldn't let that happen. A shared meal could lead to laughter, smiles, and the deep conversation she craved but couldn't risk. "Sorry. No grill."

"Then I'll buy one."

No! No! No! She prayed for ice to form around her heart. Then she wondered if he liked spicy mustard or regular. Scolding herself, she handed him the menu she'd written in a calendar format, seven days a week for the first month. "Does this look all right?"

He studied it for a moment. "Let's leave Friday and Saturday open. I'll be on my own."

He'd be dating, of course. Maybe Kim. Pathetically jealous, she said, "All right."

He continued to read her notes, commenting as he went. "Don't worry about lunches. I'll eat at school."

"I went to that high school." She rolled her eyes to the ceiling. "I hope you like fish sticks."

"My second favorite next to hot dogs."

When she gaped at him, he nudged her with his elbow. "I'm joking, MJ. I just want you to know that I'm not hard to please. Whatever you do is going to be better than eating out all the time."

"Well, good." She tried to feel relieved, but her ribs tingled from the brush of his elbow.

Eventually he saw the note she had written at the bottom. Dinner would be ready at six o'clock, packed in a basket he could take to his apartment. A trace of a scowl rippled across his face. He blinked it away, then set the list on the table. "This is perfect."

"Good. There's just a little more."

She handed him the page about cleaning and laundry. It said she would clean the apartment on Fridays, and he should bring his laundry when he picked up the dinner basket.

"That's fine."

As he handed her the page, his aftershave drifted to her nose. He was wearing Dolce & Gabbana, her favorite scent in the world. Not every man could wear it, but those who could—*Stop it.* She had no business noticing how he smelled—and enjoying it.

With her heart skittering, she handed him a small envelope. "Here's the key." Abruptly she pushed to her feet. "I think we're done."

Shane stood with her. A question seemed to dance in his eyes, one she recognized and feared. *What are you doing tonight? How about dinner together?* Turning quickly, she headed for the door with Shane following her. At the threshold, she faced him. "If you think of anything else—"

"There's just one thing."

Did his eyes have to twinkle every time he looked at her? Did he have to smell like cinnamon, smoke, and a campfire on the beach at dusk? Silently she prayed he wouldn't ask her out. "What is it?"

"Your phone number. If I decide to skip dinner, I'll let you know."

It was a purely practical request, but giving him her number felt personal. He took his phone out of his pocket, and she recited the number.

Instead of entering it in the address book, he called the phone she had left in the house. "Now you've got mine."

She turned to leave, uncomfortably aware of Shane stepping in front of her and leading her down the stairs. It was a gentlemanly thing to do. If she stumbled, he'd catch her. But she couldn't stumble, not in any way. As they neared the last step, Cody and Brandon dashed into the yard. Behind them MJ saw Tracee, seven months pregnant with her fourth child. Tracee waved from the driveway and kept coming.

When the woman reached them, MJ made introductions. "Tracee, this is Shane Riley. He's renting—"

Tracee's eyes turned into saucers. "Shane Riley?"

He held out his hand. "The same."

"Oh my *goodness*! I can't believe it. My husband's a *huge* Cougars fan. So is my oldest son. He's ten, and he thought you were the best third baseman ever. That's the position he plays—well, he tries. He's still learning."

"Give him time," Shane said. "And keep it fun."

"Oh, we do!" Tracee's expression turned from admiring to solemn. "I'm so sorry about your knee."

"Thank you."

MJ was beginning to feel like a bobblehead doll, turning from Shane to Tracee and back to Shane. Somehow her neighbor knew more about her new tenant than she did. Bit by bit, MJ matched the conversation with what she knew from Kim. Apparently the history teacher hired by her mother had been a rising sports star, which meant the knee injury had been more than an inconvenience. It had cost Shane his dream, though judging by his interest in the gym, he planned to return to baseball.

Tracee turned to MJ, speculation plain in her eyes. "Did you meet in Los Angeles?"

"No," they said in unison.

Shane gave MJ an amused look, then turned to Tracee. "I'm teaching at the high school. MJ's my landlord. I'm renting the garage apartment."

"I hope you don't mind if my boys say hello?" Tracee asked. "Maybe you and Cody and MJ could come to dinner sometime? We could barbecue hot dogs like at Cougar Stadium."

Shane and MJ both laughed. It wasn't funny except to them, which made the exchange ridiculously personal— and dangerous. Her laughter withered like grass in a drought. A glance from Shane sobered her even more.

Turning away, he focused on Tracee. "Once I'm settled, I'd be glad to meet your family."

She thanked him, then introduced Brandon, telling him Shane was both a famous baseball player *and* a good role model. When she emphasized *role model*, Shane's mouth thinned to a line. MJ wondered what triggered the tension, but she wouldn't ask. If she asked personal questions, so would he.

Tracee said good-bye and walked Brandon home, leaving MJ and Cody alone with Shane.

Still wide-eyed, Cody tipped his head up to Shane. "Do you really play for the Cougars?" Thanks to Mr. Davis, their old neighbor, Cody had watched several games.

"I did." Shane's mouth relaxed into a grin. "And I hope to play for them again, but I hurt my knee."

MJ's heart broke for him, because she knew far too much about lost dreams. Cody didn't, and his eyes sparkled with excitement. "Can you still play catch?"

"You bet."

"Can we play now?"

MJ interrupted. "Cody—"

Shane broke in. "Not today. But we can play tomorrow if it's okay with your mom."

They turned to her in unison. With their blue eyes and blond hair, eager expressions and a subtle defiance, they could have been father and son. MJ's breath snagged in her lungs, burning and aching because the moment felt both right and wrong. A protective streak told her to keep Cody away from Shane, but he needed to play catch as badly as he needed food and new shoes. God in his confusing wisdom had plopped a famous athlete in her son's path. How could she deny him such a special friendship?

"It's okay," she said to Cody. "But only when it's convenient for Mr. Riley."

The boy furrowed his brow. "Why can't I call him Shane?"

Before she could find the right words, Shane turned to her with a slightly guilty expression on his face. "Back at the real estate office, I said it was okay. I hope that's all right."

"Then it's fine." It had to be.

He held out his hand to Cody for a high-five. The boy slapped it with an intensity that made MJ's chest ache. She needed to clarify one last thing with Shane, so she spoke firmly to her son. "Go on inside. I'll be there in a minute."

Instead of arguing, Cody looked at Shane, who indicated the house with his chin, as if to say, *Do what your mother says.* The boy ran up the porch steps and into the kitchen, leaving the screen door swinging behind him.

Feeling awkward, MJ turned back to Shane. "If Cody bothers you, let me know."

"We'll be fine."

"You don't know him. I'm worried he's going to pester you. He's—"

"MJ?" Shane's voice came out deep and close, like the shadows of dusk approaching.

She raised her chin. "Yes?"

"Kids look up to athletes. I know you're a single mom, and I know little boys can get hurt. I'll be careful with Cody. Does that put you at ease?"

No! You like kids, and I like you. But I might not be able to have kids. And I can't tell you any of this, because it's too personal. Why did he have to smell so good, anyway? His aftershave was driving her crazy. So was his sincerity. She thought of Kim calling him eye candy and wanted to scream because he was so much more than a good-looking man. He was just plain decent.

Her throat went dry. "Thanks for understanding. I better go inside."

She hurried into the house, went to the sink, and filled

a glass with cold water. Sipping it, she peered through the window at Shane hauling a suitcase up the stairs. She forced herself to look away, but she couldn't stop thinking about boys needing fathers, and the ache in her chest— the place where a woman dreamed of love.

A sure cure for her attraction to Shane was to call her mother. With the effort of getting the apartment ready, she hadn't done it last night.

She lifted her phone off the counter, saw a missed call, and remembered Shane sharing his number. A sweet shiver rippled through her, but it ended in dread. Blanking her mind, she added his name in the address book, then called her mom.

A recorded voice spoke with familiar brusqueness. "This is Olivia Townsend. Please leave a message."

MJ disliked leaving a voicemail that would raise questions, but her mother screened all her calls. "Hi, Mom, it's me. I'm at Grandpa Jake's house. Cody and I are fine, but there's a lot going on. I'd like to tell you about it in person. Call me back, okay?"

She set down the phone and sighed. Talking to her mother was like seeing the dentist. MJ wouldn't enjoy the visit, but it was necessary. Just like the dentist told her to floss more, her mother would tell her how to live her life.

Olivia Townsend had her own set of Ten Commandments, and they were etched in stones as hard as the ones Moses had brought down from a mountain. At the top of the list was "Get an education." MJ had failed badly when she dropped out of UCLA.

Next on the list was "Be responsible." Getting pregnant had taken care of that one. She cringed at the vivid memory of her mother's reaction to the pregnancy.

"Melissa, how could you? I taught you to protect yourself. Didn't you use birth control? What were you thinking?" And the hardest question of all—*"Who's the father?"*

MJ had shared the story through choked sobs, including her deep regret. Her mother's reaction was instant and kind. *"You made a mistake, but you can start over. You can put the baby up for adoption. It'll have a stable home, and you can go back to school in a year."*

For three months MJ had cried and ranted, endured morning sickness, and weighed her options. Nicole told her an abortion was easy, but no way could MJ make that choice—not with what she believed even then about human life.

While Nicole counseled abortion, her mother advocated adoption. Under the circumstances, adoption made sense—until she went for an ultrasound. The minute she saw her baby squirming in black and white, she fell in love.

No matter how Cody was conceived, he was hers and she wanted him. Her mother called her naïve and cut off her allowance to prove a point. Instead of surrendering, MJ went to work at SassyGirl, found a cheap apartment, and survived with a little help from Grandpa Jake. She and her mother reconciled shortly after Cody's birth, but only on the surface.

Sighing, she stared at Shane's SUV with the hatch raised to reveal moving boxes. A better Christian would help her neighbor move in. She'd welcome a phone call from her mother, and she wouldn't envy Kim because she could date without complications. As for her attraction to Shane, MJ recognized the feelings as special, but only at the right time, and this wasn't the time. If she needed a hysterectomy, there might never be a time.

She turned from the window and went upstairs. Tomorrow she'd work on the house. She had landscaping to do and an attic to empty. With a little luck, the distractions would keep her from thinking about Shane, at least not too much.

Shane put his clothes in the antique wardrobe, breathing in the dusty scent of cedar as he hung up the sports jackets and ties he planned to wear to school. He was young to teach high school, and a coat and tie would help establish his authority. Teaching had always appealed to him as a post-baseball career. He just didn't expect to be doing it so soon. Classes started in three days. In addition to trips to the gym, he needed to go over lesson plans.

When he finished putting away his clothes, he opened the box that went with him wherever he lived. It held treasures from his past, and he wanted them where they'd remind him of his sister.

Forgive me, Daisy. For I have sinned.

He put a jar full of store-bought pebbles on the nightstand. Just about every tourist trap in America sold the colorful rocks, and they were common at the craft shows where their mother sold her metal sculptures. The rocks in his jar were mostly white, red, black, and gray. Daisy had filled hers with colorful pastels—until their nomadic childhood ended at a rest stop between Las Vegas and Barstow, California, somewhere in the Mojave Desert on a stifling August afternoon.

Complaining of a monster headache, their mother had pulled into the parking lot, then sent Shane and Daisy to the vending machines. When they returned she was slumped over the steering wheel. Shane shouted for Daisy to call 911, pulled his mom from the van, and attempted CPR. But it was too late. She had suffered a fatal brain bleed, an aneurysm.

It was the worst day of his life, but he recovered with love and attention from the Harpers. The old man was gone now, but as Shane lifted a framed photograph of himself and Coach, taken the day Shane signed with the Cougars, he murmured his thanks and set the picture on a bookshelf near the bed.

Baseball mementos came next—a game ball from the college championship, hats from all his teams, and shiny trophies.

Last, he removed a framed snapshot of his mother and Daisy smiling into the camera. He didn't have a picture of his father, or even a name he could trace. He only knew his parents weren't married, and that he and Daisy had different fathers. Shane knew nothing about the mystery man who shared his DNA, and his mother died before he found the courage to ask. Now he felt that loss keenly, though he'd grown up knowing his mom loved him beyond measure. It made a difference.

Shane added a few paperbacks to the shelf, then lifted the last item in the box. His Bible, well thumbed and full of notes, had been a gift from Coach Harper. It was a piece of his history, so he placed it next to the picture of his mother and Daisy.

As he stood, his stomach rumbled. The arrangement involving MJ's picnic basket didn't start until Monday, so he was on his own. He considered inviting her and Cody out for hamburgers, but he was certain she'd say no. Instead he ordered Chinese and ate alone, thinking of her and wondering about Cody's father. Whoever he was, he apparently didn't pay child support. If he wasn't dead, that failing made him a jerk. Shane wondered if his own father was dead or a jerk, then decided yet again that it didn't matter because he would never know. Whoever the man was, he'd let Shane down.

So had God. Enough said.

Chapter 7

$\mathcal{MJ}$ pulled down the stairs to the attic, set the safety latch, and climbed into a room full of junk. The floor matched the shape of the bedrooms below, and the roof peaked in a triangle. Tongue-and-groove knotty pine lined the entire space, a reminder of the 1950s when the attic served as an extra bedroom. A window at the top of the triangle let in a beam of sunlight full of swirling dust motes.

The house was over eighty years old now, and it held the memories of multiple generations. Cardboard boxes were stacked in uneven towers, outdoor Christmas decorations filled a corner, and cheap shelves bulged with books, vinyl records, and movies in obsolete formats.

MJ could have spent weeks digging through the family treasures, but she needed to work fast. The attic offered excellent storage, and Kim wanted it empty before she put up a *For Sale* sign. The junk would go to the dump, but the things MJ wanted to keep posed a storage problem. Her mother's condo had a garage, but it was as neat as a surgical tray. No way could MJ ask her mom for a favor, not with the argument she expected over selling the house.

Sighing, she checked her phone. Her mother hadn't called last night, so MJ expected her to call today. Seeing no messages, she put the phone in her pocket and went to work. Cody was downstairs watching *Star Wars* again, which meant she had about an hour to work.

"Mommy?"

Or less than an hour. He was standing at the bottom of the ladder. "What do you need?"

"Can I come up?"

"No. I'll be down in a minute." She tested a box for weight, decided she could maneuver it down the ladder, then set it by the opening.

"Mommy—"

"You'll have to wait."

"But—" The ladder gave a suspicious squeak.

"Cody, *no.*" Would he ever learn patience? Not anytime soon. She hadn't learned it until she had *him.* When the steps creaked a second time, MJ used her firmest tone. "Cody Townsend, do *not* come up those stairs."

"I'm not Cody."

Shane poked his head through the opening. Next came his shoulders and then the rest of him, long legs and all. Dressed in jeans and a gray plaid shirt, with his hair combed and wet from a shower, he exuded physical confidence.

MJ felt like a dust ball. "Uh—"

He grinned at her. "Cody let me in. I hope you don't mind."

She *did* mind. Tracee's remarks had made her curious, so last night she Googled him. Now she knew his batting average, his exact height and weight, and about the tragedy that landed him in foster care. She also knew what he looked like in a tux. The photograph, taken at a charity ball, showed him smiling straight at the camera—at her, it seemed.

He was smiling at her now, and she didn't like it. "Do you need something?"

"I promised Cody a game of catch."

"I remember."

"If you're free sometime today, the three of us could go to the park."

She couldn't let Cody go alone. The boy had talked about Shane all through breakfast, asking questions about baseball and why Shane lived in Refuge. MJ could answer the baseball questions thanks to Google, but the "whys" of Shane's life remained a mystery, one she had no business unraveling.

"I'd say yes," she replied. "But I have a lot to do."

He glanced at the cardboard clutter. "Is all this coming down?"

"Every bit."

A wistful smile lifted his lips. "One man's junk is another man's treasure."

"I suppose."

"My mother used to say that." He aimed his chin at the box by the opening. "If we do this together, it'll go faster."

"Thanks, but I can manage."

He went halfway down the ladder, braced, and raised his arms. "Slide the box to me."

Irked but grateful for the help, she angled the box into his hands. Balancing it on his shoulder, he went down the ladder and set it on the floor. Working in tandem—MJ moved boxes to the opening and he carried them down— they retrieved eight bulging, dusty cartons. Satisfied with the progress, she called through the opening. "Thanks. That'll get me started."

She navigated the ladder a rung at a time, annoyingly aware of her backside on display. When she reached the carpeted floor, she saw Shane and Cody playing "Rock, Paper, Scissors."

Cody turned to her with a mile-wide grin. "We're seeing who gets to put up the ladder."

On the next round of the game, Shane chose paper and Cody beat him with scissors. Shane groaned as if the contest really mattered. "Scissors cut paper. You win."

"Yes!" Cody pumped his fist, then traded a high-five with Shane.

MJ's heart nearly burst from her chest. Cody didn't just *need* male attention. He craved it. It was a boy's destiny to become a man, and Cody had no one to guide him. No father. No grandfather. No uncles or cousins, or even a family friend here in Refuge.

Shane indicated the ladder to Cody. "Want some help?"

"Okay."

"Here's what we do . . ."

A lump pushed into her throat. She had to get away from two blond heads huddled together, two sets of blue eyes focused on the ladder, so she carried a box into the spare bedroom and opened it. Her gaze landed on a drawstring bag, the watered silk faded and dry with age. Enthralled, she opened it and spread an assortment of keepsakes on the bed—a Chinese fan, an ornate but tarnished mirror, three tortoise-shell combs, and a whiskey flask with the initials *AC*.

In the bottom of the sack she found a newspaper

clipping about the capture of an outlaw named Adam Carter. Presumably he had owned the flask. The women's items were more of a mystery. Had they belonged to a woman in MJ's family tree? It seemed possible, even likely, and the connection made them even more intriguing.

MJ set the treasures on the bed, looked back in the storage carton, and took out a black enamel box sporting a cloisonné rose and a tiny brass latch. She opened it, smelled dust, and discovered a stack of letters with no envelopes. The date on the first one read *September 1, 1894*. Curious, she skimmed it.

> *My Dear Little Miss,*
>
> *I thank our Lord for your safe arrival in Cheyenne, and I pray daily for His blessing on your work at the Broderick School for Young Ladies. Teaching is a noble profession, my daughter. Though I worry you will be exposed to dangerous and immoral elements, I am confident in your good Christian judgment. I am equally confident in the protection and provision of our Lord, though it grieved my heart to bid you farewell.*
>
> *Your mother sends her warmest greetings, of course. So do your brothers and sisters. Thomas, too, sends his regards. He asked my permission to correspond with you. I gave my blessing and pray you will see him for the fine young man he is. A spring wedding would not disappoint me.*
>
> *With great affection,*
> *Your Father*

MJ set the letter on top of the stack, then riffled through the others—about twenty in all. She wanted to read more about Little Miss, Thomas, and Adam Carter, but she had work to do. As she set the letters aside, Shane arrived with a box in his arms and Cody trailing behind him.

He indicated the carton with his chin. "Where do you want it?"

"Anywhere on the floor."

Cody pointed at the antiques on the bed. "What's all that?"

"Our family history." MJ nudged one of the hair combs. "These things might have belonged to your great-great-*great*-grandmother. Maybe even another *great*."

Cody's brows shot up. "That's a lot of greats."

"It sure is." Shane stood behind him, hands in his pockets. "I didn't even know my grandparents."

Had his family short-circuited like hers, with divorce and distance? MJ was a toddler when her parents split up. Her father had called and visited occasionally, but they hadn't been close. When he died eight years ago, she had grieved not really knowing him more than she had grieved his death.

Feeling abandoned wasn't any fun at all, especially when no one else filled the gap. With her mother being an only child, MJ had no aunts or uncles, no cousins. It troubled her to think Cody would grow up the same way, like an isolated vine climbing on whatever trellis it could find. Right now that trellis was Shane.

The two of them were playing another round of Rock, Paper, Scissors. Shane made a fist for a rock and Cody made scissors.

"Ha!" Shane clapped Cody on the back. "I won. That means you give me five minutes to talk to your mom."

"About what?"

"Grownup stuff," he answered. "I'll say good-bye before I leave."

"Okay." Cody left without so much as a grumble.

When he was out of earshot, MJ turned to Shane.

"Thanks for not mentioning the park in front of him."

"That's Rule Number 1 for dating a woman with kids—Mom's in charge."

"Do you date a lot of women with kids?" As soon as she asked the question, she regretted it. Even worse, she sounded flirty.

"Not a one, but my mom was single. I know the drill from Cody's perspective. He doesn't need false hope."

"Thank you," she murmured.

"So, what do you say?" He leaned casually against the doorjamb, one hip cocked and his knee bent. "We can pick up coffee somewhere, then go to the park. You can be Cody's biggest fan."

How did he *do* that? He made her want to say yes without the slightest bit of pressure. There was something trustworthy about Shane Riley, something steady and calming. Instead of telling him no, MJ gnawed her bottom lip.

He watched her for a moment, giving her time to reply. When she remained silent, he filled the gap. "Yesterday I saw a place called the Campfire Café. Is it any good?"

"The best in town." The cinnamon chip muffins were her favorite. "And it's near the park."

"Well, good. It sounds perfect." He smiled at her, then pushed off the doorjamb and stood straight. "I'll meet you downstairs."

Somehow she'd said yes to Shane's invitation without meaning to, but the decision felt more right than wrong. He left to wait with Cody, and MJ retreated to her bedroom. She changed into clean jeans and a red top, then dabbed on lipstick. She was doing it for herself, not Shane. At least that's what she told herself as she checked her teeth for smears. Satisfied, she went downstairs and met Cody and Shane in the kitchen. The boy had his baseball glove in hand.

Shane opened the back door. "All set?"

She snagged her purse off a chair, checked her phone, and scooped up her keychain. "I'm ready."

He held the door for her, stepping aside so she could lock it. When he headed toward his Chevy Tahoe, she explained that Cody needed to be in his booster seat. Shane fetched his equipment bag from the SUV, detoured to the Bonneville, and opened the driver's door for her, making a show of it to teach Cody manners. The boy ate up the attention, and MJ had to admit she enjoyed it, too.

The ride to the café was full of baseball talk. MJ mostly listened until the three of them walked into the Campfire Café and approached the counter. A display case showed off donuts, pastries, and muffins.

Cody tugged on MJ's hand. "Mom, I'm starving."

Shane slipped her a look, silently asking permission to indulge the boy. When she nodded, he told Cody to get whatever he wanted. After pondering the goodies in the display case, Cody asked for hot chocolate and a donut with rainbow sprinkles.

Shane opted for black coffee.

MJ ordered a vanilla latte and a cinnamon chip muffin, plus a children's breakfast sandwich for Cody.

Beverages in hand, they headed to a table in the back of the dining area to wait for the food. As Cody slid into place, the front door chimed. MJ saw her mother and wanted to hide under the table. If she'd been alone, the chance meeting would have been fine. But MJ knew how her mother thought.

What are you doing with Shane Riley? And why are you having breakfast together?

Judging by her appearance, Olivia Townsend hadn't changed a bit. Her suit was one MJ recognized from several years ago—classic lines, navy blue, white piping, no frills. Her shoes were polished, and her short hair was lacquered into the same football-helmet style she'd worn for years, dyed dark brown to hide the gray.

Praying her mother wouldn't see her, MJ slid into the booth next to Cody and hunkered down. Shane sat facing the door. Her mother would recognize him from his job interview, but it was unlikely she'd do more than acknowledge him with a nod.

Leaning forward, Shane spoke in a murmur. "We saw the same person, didn't we?"

"Yes." MJ gave silent thanks Cody was focused on his whipped cream. "I know this is awkward. It's just that I haven't seen her in a while."

They sat in silence with Shane glancing at her mom between sips of coffee and MJ fidgeting until her curiosity got the better of her. "What's she doing now?"

"She just paid for the coffee."

"Is she leaving?"

"Not yet. She went to a table and set her stuff down. Now she's taking out her phone."

"Oh, no," MJ murmured.

Three seconds later, circus music blasted out of her purse. Instead of answering her phone, she kissed the top of Cody's head. "Wait here," she said to him. With an apologetic glance at Shane, she went to speak with her mother.

Olivia Townsend would never understand why people chose annoying ringtones. It was bad enough cell phones rang in public places. To be subjected to silliness struck her as unnecessary. Her own phone played a distinct but unobtrusive two-beat chime. With her brow furrowed, she turned to glare at the owner of the obnoxious phone. Instead of a stranger, she saw her own daughter.

"Melissa!" Gaping, Olivia took in the half smile that had always tugged at her heart, the questions in her daughter's eyes, and the doubt that kept them from sharing the kind of hug Olivia longed to give.

Melissa indicated the phone dangling in Olivia's hand. "You must have gotten my—"

"Voicemail."

When Melissa sighed in irritation, Olivia regretted interrupting. The bad habit came from being in charge and hearing the same complaints over and over. Today she saw her own impatience in her daughter's expression. She didn't mean to exasperate Melissa, but somehow it always happened.

"I was out of town," Olivia explained. "If I'd known you were coming, I'd have been—"

"Ready?" Melissa finished for her, a small revenge.

"I was going to say prepared."

"We need to talk."

Olivia didn't let it show, but she felt a wave of motherly panic. "Are you all right? Is it Cody?"

"We're fine." Melissa fluttered her hand. "I was hoping—"

"Is he with you?"

"Yes."

Olivia spotted her grandson in a booth with Shane Riley, yet another surprise. Her daughter, it seemed, had a man in her life. Had they met in Los Angeles? Probably not. More likely, they had somehow just met in Refuge, which made the cozy breakfast even more disturbing.

Melissa's voice filtered back into her thoughts. "Would you like to say hello to Cody?"

Oh my, yes. But Olivia wasn't prepared. She wanted to have a toy for him, and she wanted to be in Grammie clothes, not a business suit. She also wanted to know Melissa's plans before she greeted her grandson. Was this a visit or a permanent move?

With no idea how to react, Olivia gave her daughter a stern look. "You know how I feel about surprises."

"I know, Mom. I didn't plan to meet like this."

"Obviously not."

"Could we talk tonight?"

Olivia frowned. "I can't. I have a meeting, and now I'm worried."

"I'm okay and so is Cody." Melissa's eyes dulled and she sighed. "I'm here because the SassyGirl chain went bankrupt. They laid everyone off—including me. I have to sell Grandpa Jake's house."

"Oh, Melissa—"

"I know." She held her hands palm out, a helpless gesture that pushed Olivia away. "I don't want to, Mom. But it's necessary."

Olivia hated the idea. The house was her daughter's only financial asset. If she sold it now, she'd squander the money on living expenses. "You can't just sell it. It's not smart."

"I have to."

No doubt a knee-jerk reaction. "There has to be another way."

"There isn't." Melissa clipped the words. "I know school starts in a few days and things are crazy for you. When can we talk?"

Olivia had school meetings every night this week. She hated to put off seeing Cody, but she didn't want to be rushed or exhausted when they met. "Come to the condo on Saturday." She had bought it new when Melissa was in middle school. They had both been thrilled, and for a while it was a happy home.

But now Melissa's mouth tensed, a sign she didn't like the idea. Olivia prepared for a quarrel, but the girl acquiesced with a nod. "That would be nice. What time?"

"How about noon? We'll have lunch."

"That sounds good."

Olivia's gaze went to her grandson. She had a dozen pictures of him in her office, but she wanted to hug the real boy. She considered going to the booth, but Cody was talking a mile a minute to Shane Riley. An uncomfortable awareness made her turn back to her daughter. "It'll be just you and Cody, won't it?"

"Of course."

"I see Mr. Riley." She called all the teachers Mr. or Ms. until they earned her respect.

Melissa's cheeks flushed. "It's not what you think."

"It's not?"

"*No.*" The girl all but rolled her eyes.

Olivia clenched her jaw. She dealt with young people every day, and she was good at it. She offered stability and strength in a world lacking clear rules. Parents, teachers, and students respected her. *Everyone* respected her—except her own daughter, and she didn't understand what she had done wrong.

Melissa gave in with a sigh. "Shane's renting the apartment over the garage. I'll tell you more on Saturday."

"I'll look forward to it." Why did she sound so formal? She wanted to be relaxed with her daughter, not the enemy.

A good-bye called for a hug. Olivia reached out and Melissa hugged her back, but they moved like stick figures, all arms and elbows and rigid backs. When they broke apart, Olivia picked up her purse and coffee and headed for the door.

Through the window, she saw Melissa return to the booth. The smoky glass masked the details of her expression, but she said something to Shane, then shook her head in that eye-rolling way Olivia knew all too well. Once again, she'd been cast as the villain. But why? What had she done wrong? Olivia loved her daughter more than life itself. If only she could make Melissa understand. Determined to find a way, she left for school, the one place where people did exactly what she asked.

Chapter 8

MJ slid into the booth next to Cody and hugged him just because she could. If her mother had hugged her tight, MJ would have squeezed back. Instead they did the awkward dance they always did, the one where they didn't quite touch.

Oblivious, Cody grinned at her with a whipped cream mustache, daring her to notice his silly face.

"You look like an old man," she teased.

She hadn't forgotten Shane, and she turned to him now. "Thanks for watching him."

"My pleasure." He lowered his voice so Cody wouldn't notice. "Is everything all right?"

"It's fine."

"It looked like you surprised her."

"I did, but not on purpose."

She didn't want to talk about her mother, so she took a swallow of her latte. Milk and foam went down the wrong way and she choked. She set down the paper cup, tipping it when she couldn't stop coughing.

Shane grabbed it fast, stopping a spill while she pressed a napkin to her lips and worked to clear her throat.

Cody pushed to his knees. "Mommy! Are you all right?"

She nodded, but fresh hacking knocked her back against the seat.

"Mommy!" He cried again, now on his knees with his bottom lip trembling. He worried about her more than normal, maybe because she was the only parent he had. She needed to reassure him, but she couldn't speak.

She looked at Shane, hoping he'd explain to Cody, but he was studying her with an expression that matched her son's. "Are you okay?"

Nodding emphatically, she took a breath, but the hacking struck again.

"Hey, Cody," Shane said. "As long as your mom's coughing, she can breathe. She's all right. She just swallowed funny."

Brow furrowed, Cody stared hard at Shane. "Are you sure?"

"Positive."

MJ tried to talk but couldn't do more than croak a few syllables.

Shane slid out of the booth. "You need water. Cody, pat your mom on the back, okay? That'll help her."

As Shane passed by, he gave her shoulder a gentle squeeze, a gesture that made her heart flutter like a butterfly in a breeze. She was usually—always—the caretaker. Being on the receiving end flooded her with both sweet relief and a tender longing to roll off her burdens, at least for the moment.

Shane returned with the water and set it in front of her. "They're packing our breakfast to go. Let's eat in the park."

She smiled her thanks, both for the water and the decision to leave. Other customers were waiting for their orders, and she felt like a spectacle. After another sip of water, she cleared her throat and felt a little better. "Thank you both."

Cody giggled. "You sound like a frog."

"Or Darth Vader," Shane added.

MJ laughed and fought tears at the same time. This was what a father shared with a son—and what Cody so desperately needed. Her ears rang with her mother's old criticism. *Your child will need things, Melissa. How will you provide?* Things, she discovered, were the least of her worries. Cody needed stability, someone to teach him how to throw a ball, and when to pat a woman on the back when she swallowed wrong.

Shane indicated the door. "Let's get out of here."

She wiped the whipped cream from Cody's upper lip, slid out of the booth, and picked up her latte and the hot chocolate. The boy scooted past her to walk with Shane, who lifted the to-go bag off the counter.

The three of them stopped at her car to fetch Cody's glove and Shane's equipment bag, then they crossed the street to the park. A winding path led to a sand pit full of plastic slides and hamster tubes. MJ didn't try to talk. Instead she listened as Shane and Cody competed to name the silliest-sounding animal. Cody won with hippopotamus, but Shane fought hard for yak.

When they reached a picnic table, Shane set down the bag. Cody looked at her with the blue eyes that came from his father. "Can I play now?"

"After you eat."

The three of them ate, talking more nonsense about animals and naming their favorite donuts. Cody ate half his breakfast sandwich, gobbled the donut, then politely asked permission to go on the slide.

"Yes, you may," she answered. "But take care of your trash."

He put the wrappers in a nearby metal can and ran off, leaving her alone with Shane and her half-eaten muffin. Her throat felt fine now, but she couldn't seem to find her tongue.

He broke the silence by indicating her empty cup. "Those lattes can be tricky. For a minute there, I thought you'd need the Heimlich."

"So did I." She watched Cody climb the steps to the slide. "If there's one thing I've learned from being a mom, it's that accidents happen."

"Yeah. No kidding."

"Oh—I'm sorry."

"What?"

"Your knee. The way your mom died so suddenly." Too late, she realized he hadn't told her about his mother. MJ groaned with embarrassment. "Well, now you know. I Googled you last night."

A smile lifted his lips. "Learn anything new?"

"A few things."

"Like what?"

Her mind snapped to the picture of Shane in a tux, smiling in that sincere way of his. To clear her head, she focused on baseball. "I know you bat right-handed."

"Correct."

"And you hit five home runs your first month in the majors."

"Close. It was six."

She debated which direction to take. He might prefer

to talk about his batting average—it was .278—but she wanted to know about his life. "Tracee said you were a good role model. I can see why."

He raised the coffee cup to his lips, sipped, then muttered, "Don't believe everything you read."

"No?"

"No."

"What's different?"

"Everything." He tossed the cup in the trash with perfect aim and too much force. Partially full, it clunked to the bottom of the metal can, leaving them with an awkward silence.

What had he meant by *everything*? Was he talking about his career or more personal things? She wouldn't pry. If she asked questions, so would he. Even so, she wanted him to know she cared—not in a man-woman way, but the way Lyn cared for her.

Her next words stumbled off her tongue. "I'll pray for you."

When he didn't reply, she felt stupid. Her words sounded clumsy at best, maybe glib.

Shane stayed focused on Cody climbing up the slide. "Are you a Christian?"

"Yes, but it's only been a month. I'm not very good at it."

"Neither was I."

She heard *was* and waited for more, but he merely glared at a distant cottonwood shimmering green in the faint breeze, his bitterness as evident as the leaves hiding the tangled branches.

MJ had never been hostile to God, but she'd been indifferent until the night of the killer bees. She glanced at Shane, saw the deep creases tightening his mouth, and thought about her friendship with Lyn. There was no criticism, only a steady flow of kindness, like a teapot filling an empty cup.

Was it MJ's turn to be a teapot? She wanted to be Shane's friend—maybe more—but a woman couldn't pour herself into a man without risking her heart, and MJ couldn't take that chance, not unless she spoke candidly about her condition. No way did she want another complication in her life. Nor did she want to be rejected and abandoned by a man she had to see every day.

On the other hand, Shane needed a friend. She broke off a piece of her muffin and handed it to him. "Here."

He took it and held it, waiting for her. She broke off a bite for herself, and they ate. In the distance she heard Cody making airplane sounds as he went down the slide yet again.

To her surprise, Shane gripped her hand. "Thank you."

"For what?"

"Not asking questions."

She could have thanked him for the same thing. Instead she squeezed his hand tight, then let go. "I bet Cody's ready to play catch."

"So am I." He raised his voice over the breeze. "Hey, Cody! Come get your glove."

The next thing MJ knew, the three of them were standing together in a large patch of grass, and she was wearing one of Shane's old baseball gloves. He instructed Cody in the art of catching, then handed MJ a baseball and jogged several yards away.

He positioned himself like the pro he was and called to her. "Give it all you've got."

She threw the ball as hard as she could. It didn't go far, so Shane jogged forward, caught it basket style, and lobbed it to Cody, who instinctively backed away. The boy's face puckered with disgust for himself.

"Don't worry," Shane assured him. "Everyone backs

up the first time."

MJ, too, wanted to back up—from Shane and being a teapot—but she held her ground, listening as he told Cody to use both hands and keep his eye on the ball. After walking Cody through the motion, Shane jogged ten yards away and tossed the ball again.

This time Cody charged forward, and the ball plopped into his glove.

"Good catch!" Shane called.

Cody threw the ball to Shane, who snagged the bad toss as if he were in the World Series. Grinning, he turned to her. "Are you ready?"

"You bet!" She hunkered down the way he had.

"Don't back up," he cautioned.

"I won't."

His eyes matched hers, twinkling bright and full of fun. "Remember to use both hands."

"I will."

"And—"

"Keep my eyes on the ball," she finished for him.

He tossed it straight and true. MJ took one step forward, raised the glove, and caught the ball with a *whomp* against her palm.

Cody pumped his fist in the air. "Good job, Mommy!"

"Nice catch," Shane added with a grin. "Now I know where Cody gets his talent."

MJ didn't have an athletic bone in her body, but Cody's father could have been as skilled as Shane. She had no idea. Faking a smile, she tossed the ball to her son. Someday she'd have to tell him everything, but it wouldn't be today. Neither would she reveal her private thoughts to Shane, but she'd pray for him—for his knee, his secrets, and his troubled soul.

Chapter 9

The daily routine at Maggie's House turned out to be exactly what Daisy needed. She went to bed before midnight and woke up without the stabbing headache of a hangover. Her housemates were friendly, and she enjoyed learning how to cook. Instead of counting calories, she savored every bite of the meals served family-style. She even liked washing dishes, because doing chores made her feel like she belonged.

So did the Bible studies. She heard Shane's voice in some of the verses, but mostly she liked what Kellie, the leader of the study, told the women about making choices. *"God didn't give us a spirit of fear, ladies. The Holy Spirit gives us power, love, and self-control. We have choices—to drink or not. To trust God or not."*

Daisy longed to be strong like Kellie, but she also longed for just one stiff drink. For a week now, she had resisted the urge. Going to AA meetings with Lyn helped, but Daisy felt like a bird huddled on a power line, swaying in a constant wind.

This morning, though, she was safe at Mary's Closet. Humming to herself, she straightened toys left in the children's play area in the far corner of the store. The front door chimed a greeting and she looked over her shoulder. A stocky man with a silver crew cut and a square jaw took off his sunglasses and surveyed the shop, starting with the clothing aisles opposite the play area.

Very few men visited the thrift shop, and those who did came with their elderly mothers. This man was alone, and Daisy didn't like the way he peered down the aisles. Keeping her back to him, she slipped into Lyn's office.

Lyn looked up from a spreadsheet. "A question?"

"No. It's just . . ." Daisy's cheeks heated. Eric said she was paranoid. Maybe she was. "It's probably nothing, but there's a man out there. He's alone."

"A customer?"

"I don't know, but he gives me the creeps."

Lyn headed for the door. "I'll talk to him. Why don't you go through the bags from St. Anne's?"

Relieved, Daisy went to the sorting table, a rickety thing near the opening to the display area but off to the side. She could listen to Lyn and the stranger while remaining out of sight.

Lyn breezed into the store, her heels clacking on the linoleum. Daisy dumped a bag of clothes on the big table and began to separate shirts and pants, eavesdropping while she worked.

"Good morning," Lyn said to the man. "May I help you?"

"Are you Lyn Grant?"

"I am."

"I understand you work with Maggie's House."

Daisy's neck hairs prickled.

"Who are you?" Lyn asked without answering his question.

"My name's Troy Ramsey. Here's my card."

"You're a PI."

"And retired LAPD. I'm one of the good guys, Ms. Grant, not a creep out to make trouble. I'm looking for a woman who goes by Daisy Riley or Daisy Walker."

Daisy stopped breathing. Who would be looking for her? Not Eric. He'd never spend money on a private detective. Was she in trouble with Shenanigan's? She'd done nothing wrong, but last month a hostess had been caught stealing money from the register. Shaking all over, she put a plaid shirt in the sell pile without inspecting it.

Silence hung between Troy and Lyn. Something was happening, but Daisy didn't dare peek around the corner.

"Do you recognize her?" the PI asked. Daisy guessed he was showing Lyn a photograph.

Lyn hummed as if she were considering something. "I've never seen this girl."

"Look again. The picture's five years old."

Daisy would have been seventeen, covered in acne and twenty pounds heavier. The acne was gone, and so was the weight. So was her pretty blond hair. But other things hadn't changed. Her eyes were still blue, and her nose tilted up. Even so, Lyn had told the truth. She didn't know the girl in the picture. Neither did Daisy, not anymore.

Lyn broke the silence. "She looks like a sweet kid. Who's looking for her?"

"Her brother."

Shane . . . But why?

"She's in trouble," the PI replied. "Booze. Maybe drugs.

There's reason to think someone beat her up last week. He's worried and wants to help her."

Daisy knew exactly what Shane meant by *help*. He wanted to shake his finger in her face and make her feel bad. She never wanted to see him again. What she wanted was a drink, and she wanted it now. Even more than a drink, she wanted to tell Shane to go to that particular hot, fiery, awful place he'd told her about, the one for people like herself—bad girls who couldn't obey the rules.

Leave it to her perfect brother to ruin her life again. She could just imagine what he'd say about Maggie's House and the women like herself. What did he want, anyway? To drag her to church? To an exorcist? Probably. His sister the drunken slut would hurt his squeaky-clean image.

The PI's voice drifted through the doorway. "You have my card. If Daisy Walker shows up, give it to her."

"I will."

Trembling, Daisy busied her hands by folding clothes. She heard the door chime and assumed the man had left. After a full minute, Lyn approached her. "You heard?"

"Everything." She tossed a stained undershirt in the rag pile. "Shane hates me. Hiring a detective is just like him."

"You never mentioned your brother. I take it you don't get along."

"That's right." Daisy spat the words. "I don't want him in my life. Thanks for not saying anything."

"You're safe here." Lyn gave her the detective's card.

Daisy stuffed it in her back pocket. She could guess what Shane would say if he knew about the abortion. Deep down, she felt the same way, but she couldn't see another way out—not if she wanted Eric to take care of her.

Her skin felt prickly and she wanted to cry. Only she

couldn't. She needed to stay numb, and gin worked better than anything. There was a convenience store a block away, but she'd left her purse at Maggie's House. She'd have to get it—*no*. She could take money from the register and put it back later.

She needed to get rid of Lyn, so she faked a doleful expression. "I could really use some fresh air. Would you mind if I took lunch early?"

"Not at all."

Daisy wanted Lyn safely hidden in her office, so she indicated the pile of clothing. "I'll finish this first."

Lyn went back to her desk, leaving Daisy to hurry through the bag of clothing. More boy things, then baby clothes—coveralls with an airplane, little striped shirts, and size 3 shoes. A lump bullied its way into her throat. *Stay numb. Don't think.*

Sweeping everything into the rag bag, she glanced at Lyn absorbed in her work with Spotify playing softly on her phone.

"I'm leaving now," Daisy called.

"See you later."

She sneaked to the cash register, opened the drawer, and snatched a twenty-dollar bill. The drawer dinged when she closed it, but maybe Lyn wouldn't hear. Money in hand, Daisy raced out the door.

Seconds later she heard the rapid tap of high heels, whirled, and saw Lyn, her face lost in shadows but her pace ferocious. The convenience store was just across the street, but speeding cars trapped Daisy on the corner. Riled up and bitter, she pulled the twenty-dollar bill from her pocket, turned, and locked eyes with Lyn.

"Take it." She waved the money like bait. "I admit it. I stole it. I'm *done* with Maggie's House. I'm done with your stupid rules."

"That's fine," Lyn replied. "But I'm not done with you."

"Yes, you are—"

"No, I'm not."

Daisy glared at her. "Are you going to charge me with stealing?"

"No." Lyn scowled, either at Daisy or the idea. "I'm not calling the police, but we're going to the pier."

Daisy didn't *want* to go to the pier. She wanted to get blind, stupid drunk. She wanted to stop thinking about Shane, Eric, and baby clothes. "You can't make me."

"No," Lyn answered. "The choice is yours. So is the money."

Daisy pinched the twenty between her thumb and forefinger. How many times had she counted her tips at Shenanigan's, sorting through ones, five and tens? Twenty dollars would buy her a night of oblivion, but she didn't want money from Lyn. She wanted to yell and scream at the empty sky because folding baby clothes reminded her of the abortion. If she'd come to Maggie's House first, maybe she could have kept the baby. Maybe Shane would have helped her. It was a stupid, foolish thought, because Shane hated her.

She didn't want Lyn's money, but she wanted to get drunk so she stuffed the bill in her front pocket. "Thanks." She meant it.

Lyn indicated Washington Boulevard. "The pier's not far, and the exercise will do us good."

Daisy wanted to get rid of her. "But the shop—"

"I locked up."

Lyn would have an answer for everything, so Daisy gave up. "Fine. I'll go to the pier."

Together they walked down the street, breathing in ocean air and car exhaust. As they neared the beach, the stucco buildings changed from dingy offices to colorful tourist shops. T-shirts filled the windows, while clerks stood in doorways decorated with shells and Mylar balloons. It was Thursday morning, not a busy day, and Daisy started to forget that she wanted a drink.

At the foot of the pier, the roar of waves replaced the rumble of cars, calming her as she watched surfers bob with the tide. Wet sand stretched for twenty yards, a sign that the tide was at low ebb and about to turn.

Daisy, too, was at low ebb. Was the shifting tide a sign that her life was about to change? An omen of sorts? She didn't believe in such things, but Shane did. He said God made things work out for the best. She'd seen similar words on coffee cups at the thrift shop, a trivial sentiment when she needed real help.

The only person to offer help had been Lyn. She was a Christian like Shane, but not once had she criticized Daisy for drinking or being with Eric. Neither did she condemn her for the abortion. Daisy had to wonder—what would Lyn say about Shane's idea of the Bible and its rules? No one could live up to those standards.

The pier stretched hundreds of feet in front of them. Lyn, dressed in a business suit, looked out of place among the fishermen and joggers, but she didn't seem to care. When they reached the end, she rested her manicured hands on the railing, fingers laced as she stared out to sea. Gulls wheeled over their heads, squawking and searching for scraps left by fishermen. To the birds, the pier was a place of bounty. To Daisy it was a dead end.

Lyn raised her face to the sky. "I come here to watch the gulls."

Daisy expected her to say more, but she was engrossed in the birds. A gull landed on the railing a foot away from them, squawked a complaint, puffed its wings, and took off.

Daisy laughed in spite of her despair. "I guess I've got his place."

"They *do* speak up."

"Why do you like them?"

Lyn took a deep breath, savoring it. "Seagulls don't worry about what to eat or how they look. They take life a day at a time. They're survivors."

A breeze lifted a strand of Daisy's hair. She hooked it behind her ear, aware of the dryness and the false color. Between her red hair and the weight loss, she looked nothing like the girl in the detective's picture, though that girl lived inside her. Maybe she, too, was a survivor.

She kept her eyes on the birds. "Thanks again for not talking to that detective."

"It's not my place. For all I know, your brother sexually abused you."

"No!" Daisy shook her head hard. "It's nothing like that."

"Then what is it?"

"Shane calls himself a Christian. He thinks he's perfect and everyone else is dirt, especially me."

Lyn winced. "Ouch."

"I embarrass him. He told me to get out of his life until I cleaned up my act."

"Did he use those words?"

"No, but that's what he meant." He had used his faith like a sword and skewered her with it. The pressure worsened after he signed with the Cougars. He called a lot, claiming to be worried about her, but Daisy knew the truth. He was worried about his good-boy reputation, not her. She considered telling Lyn about his baseball career but decided against it. If Lyn was like most people, she'd be impressed and Daisy would feel smaller than she did now—as small as she felt when the social worker took her away from the Harpers.

She smelled the damp wood and felt the push of a wave against the pilings below her. She wanted gin more than ever, but she couldn't drink and stay at Maggie's

House. She'd get caught, and she didn't want to dishonor Lyn.

But neither could she stand the feelings bubbling under her skin. She wanted them to stop *now*. If it meant leaving Maggie's House, so be it. She would be straight with Lyn, then pack her things and go back to Eric.

She turned to Lyn, her chin raised and her fingers knotted on the railing. "I want to be honest with you."

"I appreciate that."

Daisy tried to speak, but before she found the words, something white and gooey fell from the sky and plopped in Lyn's perfectly styled hair. Gasping, Daisy couldn't believe her eyes. "A bird just pooped on you!"

Lyn let out a screech. Twelve seagulls took flight, beating the air into a roar of feathers and wings. She tried to shake the bird poop out of her hair, but it stuck like egg yolk. Neither woman had brought her purse. They didn't have tissues or gum wrappers or even an old receipt. All they had was the twenty-dollar bill in Daisy's pocket. She yanked it free and wiped the mess out of Lyn's hair.

"I got most of it," she said.

"Oh my goodness," Lyn sputtered. "That bird nailed me!"

A wicked smile tugged on Daisy's mouth. It wouldn't be nice to laugh. She tried to hold it in, but then she locked eyes with Lyn.

Lyn's eyes twinkled, then a giggle bubbled out of her throat. The next giggle burst past Daisy's sealed lips. With the seagulls squawking an off-key chorus, the women dissolved into laughter, bumping shoulders and falling into each other, doubling over until they couldn't breathe. The giggles went on and on, rolling like the waves headed to shore, the first signs of an incoming tide.

Lyn pointed at the twenty-dollar bill pinched between Daisy's fingers and covered with slime. "What do you think?" she said between gasps of laughter. "Should we wash it off?"

Daisy saw more than money. She saw a pint of gin, but she also saw Lyn watching her with the kindest eyes she'd ever seen. Daisy didn't need the alcohol, at least not this minute. The twenty dollars had bought her something else, something that felt real even though she couldn't see it or define it with words.

"It's filthy," she said to Lyn. "Let's toss it."

Together they leaned over the railing and released the bill into the breeze. It drifted downward in slow arcs, landed on a swell, and floated under the pier and out of sight. Lyn hugged her, and Daisy squeezed her back. She wouldn't be leaving Maggie's House after all. As for gin, at least for today, she could live without it.

Chapter 10

Shane's first week as "Mr. Riley" ended with Olivia Townsend calling him an idiot. She didn't use that word, but her opinion echoed in her tone. Steering his SUV out of the faculty parking lot, he chastised himself for making a rookie mistake. After track practice, he'd given the key to the equipment shed to a boy he shouldn't have trusted. Somehow Logan Petersen ended up locked in the shed with the traffic cones.

A custodian had heard Logan's cries for help. By the time Shane arrived, the man had radioed for Mrs. Townsend, who sent the custodian for bolt cutters. The incident ended with Logan's liberation and Shane taking responsibility.

Mrs. Townsend showed him no mercy. *"These boys don't need a prima donna athlete, Mr. Riley. They need supervision. Do you understand me?"*

Shane had already owned up to the mistake. The prima donna remark was unnecessary and even mean-spirited. No wonder MJ avoided her mother. Yet the moment had been sadly enlightening. When it came to Daisy, Shane had acted a lot like Olivia Townsend.

Grimacing, he turned down MJ's street, keenly aware of the mental heaviness that had started a week ago in the park. He liked MJ a lot, but her faith stood in his way. As a brand-new Christian, she was a babe in the woods, which made him the Big Bad Wolf, a role he didn't relish.

He didn't need a woman who prayed and fed him muffins. He needed a woman with fewer complications—a woman like Kim. Yesterday she had worked out at the gym he used, and they chatted. After Shane's miserable day, she offered the kind of distraction he wanted. No ties. No promises. Just two adults having a good time. He decided to call her when he got home.

As he approached MJ's driveway, he saw a mountain of trash bags on the curb. Judging by the size, she had made progress in the attic. He climbed out of the SUV and saw Cody near the stairs to his apartment, probably hoping for a game of catch. Shane enjoyed the boy's company, but right now he wanted to call Kim.

Smiling big, Cody pointed to a rubber T-ball stand. "Look what my mom got us."

"Very nice." Shane gave an appreciative whistle.

"She got me a bat, too." Cody lifted a kid-sized Louisville Slugger made of red aluminum. "Want to see it?"

Kim could wait a few minutes. Not only did Shane like Cody, he wanted to get his hands on the bat. It was a toothpick compared to his own, but wrapping his fingers around the black tape would feel good.

Cody lugged the bat and T-stand to the middle of the driveway, then fetched a baseball off the back porch. Shane would have preferred a wiffle ball this close to the house, but the chances of Cody making real contact were slim to none.

Shane judged Cody's height, twisted the rubber to make the stand a few inches lower, then held out his hand. "Let's see the bat."

Cody offered it to him as if it were sacred. Shane took a few easy swings, describing the mechanics to Cody, who concentrated on every motion.

"Your turn." Shane handed him the bat.

Awkward and shy, Cody twisted himself into a pretzel. Hiding a grin, Shane stood behind him, covered the boy's hands with his bigger ones, and walked him through the motions. There was no doubt about it. Shane wanted to be a father. In some small way, it would fill the gap left by the man he would never know.

When Cody found his rhythm, Shane stepped back and put the ball on the T. "Go ahead. Swing for the fences."

Cody hauled back and swung hard. The ball popped high in the air and arced back—straight at an upstairs window.

Glass exploded all over MJ's bedroom carpet. With her heart pounding, she watched a baseball roll to a stop at her bare toes. Groaning, she grabbed two handfuls of her hair and pulled. She had specifically told Cody to save the bat and T-stand for the park. The equipment had been on sale at Walmart, seventy percent off, but still a splurge on her limited budget. Now she had a broken window to repair.

Her son raced into her bedroom, saw the broken glass, and stopped short.

"Cody Townsend." She plopped her hands on her hips. "What did I tell you about the bat and ball?"

"You told me to wait for the park." His bottom lip quivered.

MJ took a step and winced. Balancing on one foot, she wiped a speck of glass off her big toe.

Cody started to cry. She wanted to cry too, but she had to get the vacuum. Then she had to research window repair online and do battle at Home Depot. She hated hardware stores. They were full of tools she didn't understand and things she couldn't afford.

She gave her son another hard look. "We're going to clean up the glass, then you'll tell me why you disobeyed."

Footsteps thudded in the stairwell, then in the hall until Shane arrived with the vacuum. So that was why Cody had disobeyed her. The boy found male attention irresistible, and Shane had unwittingly obliged his disobedience.

Even worse, he had invaded her privacy. She didn't want him to see her bed with its white duvet and seven pillows, some of them heart-shaped and edged with lace, some for clutching to her middle while she slept. She had bought the bedding after the second LEEP, when she needed to feel feminine again. The fluffy covers still cheered her up. So did the candles scattered throughout the room. She loved the mix of scents—vanilla and rose— and sometimes she lit the wicks to chase away a bad day.

Heaving a sigh, she looked from the candles to the window and finally at Shane. Instead of folding laundry, now she had to contend with a handsome man looking charmingly chagrined in her bedroom.

"Sorry." He looked her full in the eye. "I showed Cody how to swing a bat. He's stronger than he looks."

"The ball went *backward*," the boy complained.

MJ focused on her son, not the man with his hand now on Cody's shoulder, as she repeated herself. "What did I tell you?"

"To wait until the park."

"Now you know why."

He looked at his shoes. "I'm sorry, Mommy."

"I'm sorry, too," Shane added. "We'll clean up, then I'll take Cody to the hardware store. We'll replace the glass right now."

She appreciated Shane's offer, but it was Friday. He probably had a date. MJ was having lunch with her mom tomorrow, but she could get up early and fix the window before they left. "If you have plans, it can wait until the morning."

He hesitated. "Now's fine."

"Are you sure?"

"Positive."

When he dragged splayed fingers through his hair, she saw weariness. "Bad day?"

He grimaced. "It was worse for a kid named Logan. He got locked in the equipment shed."

"Oh, dear."

"Bad judgment on my part. The custodian called your mother and the rest was—" He shook his head, speechless.

"Humiliating." Knowing how her mother played drill sergeant to new teachers, she wondered about the rest of his week. She suspected he'd been avoiding her since the park, but now he seemed to need a friend. As badly as she needed to guard her own heart, she couldn't turn her back on him. After all, he'd been teaching Cody how to swing a bat, something MJ couldn't do very well.

The frustration over the broken window receded, and she offered a sympathetic smile. "Would you like to stay for dinner?"

He hesitated.

"You don't have to. I just thought—"

"I'd like that." He stretched the words into a drawl. "I'd like it a lot."

Their eyes locked for what felt like forever, then he lifted one brow, leaving her to wonder if—*no*. Dating was off her radar. But her heart softened like wax in the hot sun.

Inhaling sharply, she smelled the rose, vanilla, and bleach from the laundry. She thought of the lacy pink bra drying in the bathroom, the one she wore when she needed to feel pretty, even desirable. She had to get out of the bedroom now and away from Shane. Unless she told him about the HPV, a dating relationship was off the table.

He indicated the window. "Cody and I will get started. We need paper and a pencil to make a pattern for the new glass."

"I'll get it for you."

He glanced at her feet. "You need shoes."

"It's all right."

She walked gingerly to the door and eased by him, avoiding his gaze but failing miserably to ignore traces of Dolce & Gabbana. She went into Cody's room, fetched the drawing tools, and returned to her bedroom. The vacuum roared to life and she paused in the doorway, watching as Shane gave Cody the handle and pointed to the sparkles on the carpet. When the boy grinned, Shane playfully punched his arm. He was a good man, someone who loved kids and—

Stop it. She set the paper and pencil on the dresser, escaped to the kitchen, and grabbed an onion to chop for the meatloaf. Surely meatloaf would make her forget the scene upstairs. But then her cell phone rang with circus music, and she pictured Cody looking up to Shane with his heart in his eyes.

She lifted the phone, saw Lyn's caller ID, and answered. "Perfect timing. I can tell you about my wretched day."

Lyn gave a light laugh. "What happened?"

"Cody hit a baseball through my bedroom window. Shane's fixing it now."

"I like this guy."

So do I. "He's all right."

Lyn hummed into the phone. "You haven't said much about him."

MJ didn't like to talk about men, not even with her best friend. Concerning Shane, Lyn knew about the shoes and the rental agreement but not much else. "There's nothing to say."

"What did he do before Wyoming?"

"He played third base for the Cougars, but he hurt his knee."

"*The Cougars?*"

MJ's brow furrowed. "You follow baseball?"

"I'm from Chicago, remember? Go Cubs. Now tell me about Shane."

"I already did."

"Tell me more."

"Like what?"

"What does he look like?"

MJ groaned. "You're impossible."

"Just curious." Lyn's voice held a smile. "And you just answered the question. He's good-looking and you're interested."

"All right, yes. But you know the situation."

"I do. But MJ?"

"I know what you're going to say."

"And I'll say it until you believe it." Lyn took a breath. "We all have experiences we regret. Sometimes we bring the problem on ourselves, and other times the trouble finds us. Either way, this is why we need a Savior. Jesus wiped the slate clean for you, me, and all humanity, so stop punishing yourself. You're not the first woman to deal with HPV, and sadly you won't be the last. You know the stats."

Yes, she did. It affected eighty percent of the female population and usually went away on its own. Not everyone got cancer, and not everyone had to be treated. MJ had been stunningly unlucky. She had contracted a high-risk strain, and established treatments had failed to kill it.

For the millionth time, she sighed. "The stats don't mean a thing when it's your own body. I don't want a hysterectomy."

"I'm praying," Lyn murmured. "When do you see Dr. Hong?"

"In six weeks."

"You'll stay with me, right?"

"I'd like that." MJ made a mental note to check airfares. She also needed to ask her mom to watch Cody. It promised to be an expensive, complicated trip, but she trusted Dr. Hong and didn't want to take a chance on a local doctor.

The vacuum stopped. Any minute Shane and Cody would come downstairs. "I better go."

They said good-bye and MJ set down the phone. When Cody and Shane walked into the kitchen, the glint in Shane's eyes shot quicksilver through her veins, warming her and making her shiver at the same time. What had she gotten herself into with that dinner invitation? Cody had disobeyed her because he found Shane irresistible. Looking at him now, MJ feared she had the same problem.

Shane forgot about Kim the instant the window shattered. By the time he and Cody cleaned up the glass, went to Home Depot, and put in the new pane, he couldn't imagine spending the evening with anyone other than MJ and her son. Between the pretty blush on her face and Cody's enthusiasm for Home Depot, Shane felt right at home. He offered to do dishes after dinner, but MJ insisted he was a guest and shooed him into the family room.

Instead he went upstairs to check the window caulking. It looked good, but the toilet was running. The handle needed a jiggle, so he stepped into MJ's bathroom to fix it. As he rounded the corner, his gaze landed on a lacy pink bra hanging over a towel rack to dry.

Shane was no stranger to the battle against lust. As Coach Harper used to say, *"It's not the first look that matters. It's the second."* Avoiding that second look now, he tapped the toilet handle and left the bathroom. His Christianity was in tatters, but he wasn't a jerk like some of his teammates. His feelings for MJ were honest and natural. He liked her, plain and simple. Not only was he attracted to her, he sensed that she, too, needed to heal. Someone—maybe Cody's father—had broken her heart.

"Shane!" Cody called from the bottom of the stairs. "Where are you?"

"Just checking the window. I'm headed down now."

Cody met him halfway down the steps. "Want to stay for Yogi Bear cartoons? My mom found them in the attic. They're super old!"

"Did you ask your mom first?"

"She said yes."

"Then I'll stay."

He and Cody walked into the family room, where MJ was neatening up the coffee table. When she told Cody to go put on his pajamas, he raced upstairs to his room. Within five minutes, Shane and MJ were seated on the couch three feet apart, and Cody was on the floor, a lump in a sleeping bag decorated with dinosaurs.

They watched several episodes, munching popcorn and drinking apple juice while they laughed at Yogi's antics. Shane enjoyed every minute of the silly old show, but it was MJ who captivated him.

But what next? She was a Christian, but that didn't mean she was a wait-until-marriage kind of believer like he'd been. Some couples lived together, claiming to be married in God's eyes while they saved money for a big wedding. Others had sex and considered it equivalent to a white lie, something everybody did. What did MJ believe? He didn't know, but a kiss good night was a safe place to start. If she backed off, so would he.

The credits rolled on the last cartoon. He glanced at Cody, saw he was out cold, and turned to MJ. Eyes closed, she inhaled in the even rhythm of sleep. Shane had never seen her so relaxed, so unguarded. He blinked and thought of the lacy bra, the candles in her bedroom, the soft side of her nature that she kept private and tucked away.

His blood heated with instincts as old as time. Those feelings were strong, male, and natural—but they came with obligations.

MJ stretched her leg until the sole of her foot touched his thigh. A downy white sock, one from the pack he had given her, covered her toes, and he wondered if she indulged in pedicures and bright pink nail polish. Unguarded in sleep, she slid her foot a few inches and took a deep breath. His gaze wandered back to her face. Should he kiss her awake? No. That was presumptuous and a little weird. They weren't living a fairy tale. Real life demanded respect, and respect meant giving MJ a choice about that kiss good night.

He picked up the remote and turned off the TV. The

sudden silence didn't wake her, so he laid his hand lightly on her shoulder. A touch. Not a jiggle. The start of a caress if she nestled against his fingers.

Relaxed and warm, she rolled her shoulder against his hand and sighed contentedly. A caress, he decided.

When her eyelids fluttered, he moved his arm to the back of the couch. "Are you awake?"

"Almost," she said, her voice husky with sleep. "I dozed off."

"So did Cody."

She pushed up on one elbow, glanced at the boy, and smiled. "It's the golden hour."

"What's that?"

"The only time I can relax."

Shane could imagine. The boy talked all the time. "When Cody's asleep, what do you do?"

"I usually check out Instagram and Facebook, whatever catches my eye. Sometimes I call a friend, or—or—" She slid her foot against his thigh, froze, then bolted upright. "I'm babbling. It's late and . . . well, it's late." She snatched up the popcorn bowl and an apple juice cup, then dashed for the kitchen.

Shane picked up the other two glasses and followed. With her hands full, she couldn't turn on the overhead light. The only glow came from the low-watt bulb on the stove hood. She set the bowl and cup on the counter, then turned on the faucet.

He set the two glasses next to the cup, watching as she squirted soap into the greasy bowl and put it under the hot water. Soap bubbles mushroomed like a nuclear explosion.

Striking a casual pose, he leaned against the counter at a right angle to the sink. "I had a good time tonight. Thanks for dinner and cartoons."

She rinsed a glass. "Cody enjoyed it, too."

Shane didn't want to chat about Cody and mischievous bears. Like she said, it was the golden hour—the perfect time for that kiss, except she had her back to him.

Abruptly she turned off the faucet. "I'm thinking of having a barbecue."

"A barbecue?"

She dunked the second glass in the soapy water. "Kim and I went to high school together. I could invite some friends. Kim would come. She's—"

"MJ?" When he touched her arm, she froze. He kept his fingers still, holding her loosely until she turned.

The defiance in her eyes slashed through the dark. "Kim's a lot of fun. You should go out with her."

"You know what I think?"

"What?"

"This . . ." He kissed her then, and it wasn't a peck. Her lips warmed against his, softening into silk as she tested the waters. If she eased back, so would he. But instead she clutched his shoulder blades, swayed against him, and kissed him back with enough passion to light his hair on fire. Both stunned and pleased, he sank with her into the dark water, but then his common sense kicked in. Why the sudden surrender from a woman who so fiercely guarded her heart and protected her son?

Shane didn't know, but it mattered to him, and later it would matter to MJ. For now, kissing her was enough— more than enough because that kiss shimmered with promise.

"Mommy?" Cody called from the family room.

MJ broke out of his arms, pressed her hands to her flaming cheeks, and gulped air. "I shouldn't have done that."

"It's all right." He hooked a loose strand of hair behind her ear. "Stay here. I'll take Cody up to bed. We'll do a story and everything."

"No."

"He'll enjoy it. So would I."

"Mommy? Where *are* you?"

"In the kitchen," she called back, her voice wobbly and too bright. "I'll be right there." Tense and wild-eyed, she faced Shane. "Kissing you like that—I can't— It was a mistake."

"I don't think so."

"It *was*." She pushed away from the counter, away from him, then faced him from the safety of the doorway. "Go," she murmured. "Please."

"Not when you're upset."

"I'm fine." She squared her shoulders, but her voice quavered even more than before. "I got carried away, that's all. It was stupid of me. Just . . . *stupid*."

"Do you really believe that?"

"I can't do this now." Close to tears, she clamped her mouth so tightly that her lips quivered.

In the park she had honored him by not asking questions. He had to give her the same respect. "I'll go, but we're not finished."

"I know." She looked to the side to avoid his gaze, rolled her eyes to the ceiling, then faced him with another defiant lift of her chin. "It's just that my life is complicated right now."

What did that mean? Would it be less complicated later? And if so, why? This wasn't the time to press, but he intended to dig deeper—for MJ's sake as well as his own.

He went to the back door, opened it, and turned for one last look. "I'll see you tomorrow."

"All right."

"And MJ?"

"Yes?"

"I care about you." With that he closed the door,

leaving her wide-eyed, breathless, and more beautiful than she could possibly know.

Chapter 11

MJ put Cody to bed, then fled to her room. Trembling, she closed the blinds to block the shine on the new windowpane, the silver glow of the moon, and the memory of Shane's lips on hers.

"Oh, Lord," she muttered in a desperate prayer. "I don't know what to do."

Either she told Shane about the HPV, or she nipped the romance in the bud. Flopping facedown on the bed, she tried to pray but groaned instead. The duvet warmed beneath her body, filling her with the ache to be in Shane's arms again. Should she call Lyn? Definitely not. Lyn would tell her to be brave, and MJ didn't want to be brave. She wanted to feel safe.

Nerves on fire, she shot to her feet. She needed to do something physical—like vacuum the house from top to bottom. But the vacuum reminded her of Shane. So did the pencil he had left on her dresser. Fleeing the bedroom, she glimpsed Cody's door, pictured Shane teaching him how to throw a baseball, and pressed her hands to her burning cheeks.

Grasping at straws, she escaped into the bedroom holding the boxes from the attic. There were still several to empty—the perfect escape from the present. The first box held old tax records—boring tax records that made her wonder if Shane disliked accounting as much as she did. Groaning, she folded the dusty flaps and shoved it aside.

Turning to the dresser, she spotted the black lacquer box holding the letters to Little Miss. Box in hand, she settled on the bed and lifted the lid.

Dear Little Miss,

I pray for you daily, my daughter. I pray our Lord will protect you and keep you from harm. Though I understand your desire to live boldly and serve others, I am filled constantly with a terrible foreboding. Wyoming is a place of ruffians and outlaws, women of questionable morals, and scoundrels of an ilk beyond your ken.

I pray you have found a suitable church and are attending regularly. My own congregation continues to grow, though not because of my efforts in the pulpit. Young Thomas has proven to be a worthy protégé and is greatly esteemed by all, but particularly the young ladies. His sermons are eloquent and so are his prayers. I am well pleased with his character. Forgive an old man for his meddling, but I encourage you, again, to correspond with him.

With great affection,
Your Father

MJ read five more letters, each written on a Sunday evening. After summarizing his sermons, the reverend reported family news and shared tidbits about neighbors and friends, including Thomas. He wrote often of the young minister, and in a tone that suggested the young man and Little Miss had been childhood sweethearts.

Why had the girl left home? Maybe for the same reasons MJ went to UCLA instead of the University of Wyoming. She had wanted to grow up, and she certainly had. Sighing, she picked up the reverend's next letter.

Two weeks have passed without a letter from you. Your mother fears you have contracted a serious ailment. Living among the pupils at the Broderick School as you do, contagion is impossible to avoid.

Your mother fears consumption. I confess to some concern, as influenza is rampant among our own neighbors. Please advise us of your health. The Lord has put a burden on my heart and I am praying.

MJ skimmed the next three letters, worrying about Little Miss until she found one indicating the reverend had heard from his daughter.

I am grateful for your letter, though your mother complained it was too short. Knowing you are well is indeed a relief, though I remain concerned. The health of one's body is a great blessing, but the safety of one's soul is of even greater import.

Your letter, though comforting, caused me to

wonder why you included none of the details that your mother so cherishes. You mentioned not a single student, not a purchase at the emporium, or an oddity you might have seen. You are precious to us, Daughter. We treasure your letters, as they are windows into your heart and soul.

I never cease praying that God will keep you in his care and look forward to the day you come home to us. Until that joyous reunion, we treasure your letters.

MJ imagined Little Miss starting a letter and balling it up, beginning again, then stopping because she didn't know what to say, probably about Adam Carter. The girl, it seemed, had secrets. Ashamed and maybe afraid, she must have dreaded writing her father.

At UCLA, MJ had behaved the same way. At first she spoke to her mother every day. They talked about everything—except Nicole. Neither did MJ mention parties and her first taste of rum and Coke. In a short time, their conversations degenerated into cryptic weekly reports. The more MJ had to tell, the less she wanted to say.

Six years later, she still had a secret.

Should she tell Shane about the HPV? A kiss could be just a kiss, or it could spark a fire that led to the good things MJ dreamed of—snuggling in bed on a lazy Saturday morning, laughing together at private jokes, siblings for Cody. Shane deserved to be a father, and her body came "as is," like a used car patched up after an accident.

Shane had been nothing but honorable. Surely she owed him the same respect. Little Miss had kept her problems to herself, and so would MJ. Tomorrow she'd tell Shane again that the kiss was a mistake.

In the morning, Shane went to the gym to burn off both the rough first week at school and the lingering pleasure of MJ's kiss. He lifted weights until his biceps felt like cooked noodles, then he stepped on a treadmill for his usual five-mile run.

As the machine pulled him back, he powered forward. Sweat streamed down his spine, his arms pumped, and his shoes slapped the rubber mat in a beat that matched his heart rate. Breathing hard, he ran faster, faster still, until every muscle screamed in protest.

MJ was wrong. The kiss wasn't a mistake. It was human and natural, something to be savored. Why deny themselves? When he had called himself a Christian, Shane viewed sex as sacred, a transcendent bond between a man and a woman. Now he saw it as a drive to procreate, much like salmon fighting their way upstream to a spawning ground. The struggle had a certain nobility of purpose, one Shane admired. Unless MJ slammed on the brakes, the kiss signaled the start of something good between them.

He glanced at the treadmill controls. Four miles down, one to go. The knee felt good today. Not great, but he had time to build up the surrounding muscle. Today he felt like he could do anything. He'd beat the odds and reclaim his dream.

Take that, God!

The verbal punch surprised him. Why fight with a God he no longer believed in? Running hard, he glanced at the mileage counter. A quarter mile to go. The treadmill slowed and he eased into a walk. A moment later his cell phone rang. He stepped off the machine, picked up the phone, and saw Troy's caller ID.

"What's up?" Shane asked between deep breaths.

"I know who gave Daisy the black eye."

Shane cursed. Jaw tight, he struggled to control his voice. "Who did it?"

"Eric Markham. He was a bouncer at Malone's."

"A bar?"

"A dance club in Hollywood."

Shane's lips curled in disgust. A man who used his fists for a living had assaulted his little sister, leaving her bruised and battered. Horrible images flashed in his brain even as he fought them with deep breaths. Nearly puking, he raked his hand through his sweaty hair and collapsed on a bench. "Find her, Troy. You have *got* to find her."

"I'm working on it."

Fury and fright yanked him back to his feet, and he started to pace. When he spoke, the words came out flat, almost detached. "How did you learn about Markham?"

"I went back to Daisy's old apartment. The elderly woman next door was out of the hospital and glad to talk."

Troy detailed the conversation in clipped sentences. Before moving out, Daisy had been working at a restaurant called Shenanigan's and dating an actor named Eric. The neighbor didn't know his last name, but she described him as six feet tall with dark hair and a muscular build. When Daisy left to move in with him, she gave the neighbor a couple of houseplants but didn't leave an address. Troy did some footwork and returned to the neighbor with photographs of wannabe actors named Eric. The neighbor had ID'd Markham instantly.

"I checked him out," Troy finished. "He was arrested for domestic battery about two years ago, but it didn't go to court."

Sweat trickled into Shane's eyes. He scrubbed it away with a towel, but the salt still burned. "Did you check out Shenanigan's? Maybe she's still there."

"No joy. She quit a few weeks ago, picked up her last

check in person, and dropped off the face of the planet. No social media. No new phone. Nothing. The manager didn't know anything, and the serving staff brushed me off. Women can be protective of each other, you know?"

"Keep looking, Troy."

"I'm trying, buddy." The detective ended the conversation with the promise to call again when he learned something.

Shane snatched up his gym bag and strode home, the workout forgotten and his blood on fire. He wanted to smash things, particularly Eric Markham's face. No man had the right to hit a woman—ever. To use a woman and just throw her away was beyond his understanding, yet that's what Eric had done to Shane's baby sister.

Blood still boiling, he stomped down the last block to MJ's driveway. At the foot of the concrete pad, he slowed to a normal walk, the bloodlust controllable though not fully erased.

She came out the back door and approached him, her face tense and her chin high. He knew she wanted to talk about the kiss. So did he. The last of his anger faded into a tenderness that poured a balm over his stinging nerves. He had failed Daisy; he wouldn't fail MJ.

When she stopped three feet away, he sensed her unease and skipped the small talk. "You want to talk about the kiss."

"Yes." She squared her shoulders. "I like you, Shane. But only as a friend. The kiss caught me by surprise, and I reacted. That was a mistake on my part. I'm in no position to start a relationship."

"Why not?"

"I'm a single mom. I have to protect Cody."

Shane knew an excuse when he heard one. They had already talked about Cody becoming attached, and he had promised to be careful—and he would. Cody wasn't the roadblock.

So what was it? His mind shot to Daisy brutalized by Eric Markham. Had MJ been wounded by Cody's father in some way? Or maybe she'd been hurt by someone else. Shane hoped not, but why else would she pull back from something as small as a kiss? In an ironic way, he and MJ were a perfect fit. She needed to regain her trust in men, and he needed to be trusted.

Stepping closer, he gentled his voice. "I meant what I said last night. I care about you."

"You shouldn't."

She raised her chin with an expression that reminded him of Daisy when she was caught drinking beer behind Coach Harper's house. Foolishly, he had badgered his sister until she dissolved into tears.

He wouldn't repeat that mistake with MJ. "It's all right. We'll just be friends—you, me, and Cody."

Relief flashed across her face, but the silvery glint in her eyes faded immediately to tarnished armor. She managed a solemn nod. "Thank you for understanding."

"I get it. But MJ?"

"Yes?"

"I have to wonder if someone hurt you. Whoever the guy was, he was a jerk."

Her eyes flared with emotions he couldn't read. Longing? Hope? Or maybe fear. As much as he wanted to ask, he settled for a respectful pause before heading to his apartment.

As he climbed the stairs, the door to the house flew open. Cody stepped onto the porch. "Mommy, I'm hungry."

"I'll be right there," she called.

Shane waved to him. "Hey, Cody."

"Hey, Shane." The boy turned to his mom. "Can Shane have pancakes with us?"

MJ gnawed her lower lip, a sign of indecision.

"Pleeease?" Cody clasped his hands as if he were praying.

Who could resist? Not Shane. If MJ considered him merely a friend, she could invite him for pancakes. Or he could invite himself. "That sounds good. I'm starved."

She chewed her lip some more, still uncertain, then her eyes twinkled with a hint of mischief. "I guess it's all right. I make them special for Cody, so you're in for a treat."

"Great, but I need a shower."

"I can tell," she said, wrinkling her nose at his sweaty shirt. "You weren't joking about lots of laundry."

He wasn't joking about his feelings for her, either. But he kept that thought to himself.

MJ returned to the house, and Shane went to his apartment. Twenty minutes later, he walked into her bright yellow kitchen. While she cooked, he and Cody set the table. Whatever she was doing involved more than pancake mix, but she wouldn't let them see. After several minutes, she announced, "They're done."

Shane and Cody sat, and MJ put large plates in front of them. A bear-shaped face with two round ears, a strawberry nose, blueberry eyes, and a whipped cream smile stared back at him. The bear looked fierce indeed.

"I have Yogi," Cody declared.

"No," MJ said. "That's Boo-Boo."

Cody grinned at Shane. "Then *you* have Yogi. He takes picnic baskets like you do."

Shane and MJ shared a brief smile. She had closed the door on dating, but with a Yogi Bear pancake she had pushed it back open, if just a crack.

Chapter 12

The trees outside of Olivia's condo clung to their September leaves, but the décor in her living room shimmered with the serenity of a winter day, one full of sunlight and twinkling snow. The white carpet was freshly vacuumed into pristine V's, the glass tabletops didn't have a single smudge or streak, and the Tiffany-style lamp, a replica made of wintry pastels, glowed softly on the end table next to the ice blue couch.

The only out-of-place item was a bright red photo album. Bending slightly, Olivia nudged it to an artful angle, then faced the window looking out to the treelined street in her gated condo community. Homemade vegetable soup, Melissa's favorite, simmered on the stove. A new toy for Cody waited in a corner. Everything was perfect. Or so she hoped.

Maybe, if Melissa felt at home again, she would stay in Refuge and Olivia would have her family back.

She heard the old Bonneville before she saw it. The throaty rumble polluted the quiet and pulled her lips down in a frown as she turned to the window. That car! It had belonged to her ex-husband, now deceased. Olivia hated it just a little less than she hated the devastation of the divorce.

Melissa had been four years old at the time and in a way, so had Olivia's musician husband. He had abandoned them both, more or less. Olivia had recovered. And while she'd done her best to be both father and mother, she would always wonder about the hole he'd left in his daughter's heart.

Outside, the Bonneville sputtered to a stop. Peering through the sheer white drapes, Olivia winced. Oxidized paint blotched the car's hood and roof, and cloudy grime dulled the headlight covers. Her brows knit together in a frown, but then Cody scrambled out of the car, all boy and energy and towheaded charm. Melissa followed, reaching for his hand, then stopping to finger-comb his hair.

The boy didn't look pleased about it, but Olivia grinned through a sheen of tears. Oh, how she had missed these moments!

She flung open the front door, called a greeting to her daughter, and walked toward Cody, deliberately slowing her school stride to a grandmotherly amble. She ached to hug him, but boys could be shy and she didn't want to overwhelm him.

"Hi, Cody," she said with another big smile.

He looked at his shoes, then tilted his chin up and to the side, just enough so he could see her face. Curiosity collided with concern in his denim blue eyes. The concern must have won, because he turned to his mother for guidance.

Melissa nudged a strand of hair away from his eyes. "Cody, this is Grammie."

Olivia bent at the waist, putting them at eye level. When her grandson peeked at her over his shoulder, she smiled so hard her cheeks ached. "I'm so happy to see you."

"Hi," Cody replied.

"I have a present for you. Would you like to open it?"

He looked to his mother for permission, just the way Melissa had once looked to Olivia. Hope for reconciliation snuggled even deeper into her heart, going deeper still when Melissa nodded yes.

The three of them entered the condo. No small talk. Not even about the weather. At Olivia's request, Cody and Melissa took off their shoes in the tiled entry. "White carpet," she said with a shrug.

In their stocking feet they walked down the short hall to the living room. Melissa perched on the edge of the sofa. Cody did the same, dangling his sock-covered feet and kicking slightly. His brand-new socks sparkled as white as Olivia's carpet.

Melissa grazed her hand on the skintight fabric of the sofa, then laced her fingers in her lap. "The furniture is new."

"I bought it two years ago." *Do you like it? Could you feel at home here?* Olivia certainly did. And she wanted her daughter and grandson to feel at home, too.

She lifted a big gift bag out from behind the chair in the corner, set it in front of the coffee table, and crooked her finger at Cody. "Come here, kiddo." Her old name for Melissa. "Let's see what's in the bag, okay?"

Shyness forgotten, Cody scrambled off the sofa and skidded to his knees in front of the bag. His face lit up like

Christmas as he tossed the oodles of tissue paper, and his eyes widened even more when he lifted out a remote-controlled monster truck, a toy the clerk at Toy Town had assured her would be a hit.

The box was as long as one of Cody's arms, but he managed to wrestle it out of the bag. "Wow, Grammie! Thanks. It's really big. Can I play with it now?"

"*May* I." Oliva stifled a groan at herself. Old teachers never died; they just became principals. "And yes, you may. But how about after lunch? I made your mommy's favorite."

"What is it?" Cody asked, turning to Melissa.

Inhaling through her nose, Melissa pretended to ponder the familiar aroma of bay leaf and beef stock. "Do I smell homemade vegetable soup?"

"Yes, you do," Olivia replied. "Complete with goldfish crackers."

Soft laughter spilled from Melissa's lips. "That sounds wonderful. Cody, you're in for a treat. Grammie makes the best vegetable soup in the world."

Olivia glowed from the inside out, her heart pattering as she reached to give Cody's shoulder a squeeze. Before her fingers reached his shirt, he flung himself into her arms and hugged her hard.

Melissa watched from the couch, a poignant smile on her face, the tilt of her lips mixing the same pride and pleasure that Olivia, too, once felt as a mom. The past and present collided in a breath and spun into a dream for a future bright with moments just like this one.

A lump forced its way into Olivia's throat. It was too soon to present her plan to Melissa, so she swallowed hard, set her hope to simmer like the soup, and headed to the galley-style kitchen. Melissa and Cody followed, with Cody chattering nonstop about the truck.

Melissa shushed him with a touch, then glanced at the

big pot of soup and the empty bowls waiting to be filled. "Mom, do you need any help?"

"No. Everything's ready." Olivia had even set the table, though she wished now she hadn't. That had been Melissa's job while growing up. It would have been nice to share that memory.

Olivia served the soup and they ate. Cody did most of the talking. He liked the Minions characters, *Star Wars*, riding his bike, and playing T-ball. He didn't know how to swim, but he was going to learn soon. As for school, he liked math a lot better than reading, but recess was the best. Melissa added she had enrolled him in Mountain View Elementary, and his teacher was Ms. Odenmeyer, a veteran educator whom Olivia liked and respected.

When their bowls sat empty, Olivia gave him an extra cookie for dessert. He fetched the monster truck, went out back to the patio, and happily sped the truck in circles.

With Cody occupied, Olivia guided Melissa into the living room. "I want to show you something."

They sat together on the sofa, shoulder to shoulder. Olivia placed the red photo album in Melissa's lap, and together they turned the pages, smiling at memories and groaning at embarrassing hairstyles.

The album held the best moments of their lives. Melissa's school portraits. A Florida vacation. The snow angels they'd made in matching pink parkas. Middle school pictures ripened into snapshots of a young woman with a sassy smile. The last photograph captured Melissa in a UCLA T-shirt, grinning nervously in front of the Bonneville packed to the roof. Olivia had made the drive with her, helped her move into the dorm, then flown home alone.

The picture was a fitting end to the album. And a fitting place to begin anew.

Melissa closed the book gently, then set it back on the

coffee table. Using her index finger, she nudged it into the exact spot where Olivia had placed it.

Olivia's carefully planned words stuck in her throat. Where did she start? How did they heal?

Melissa hesitated too. She opened her mouth, closed it, then broke the silence with words that pinged like sonar. "Do you remember the last time we were in this room?"

"I remember."

"I told you I was pregnant."

Olivia would never forget that morning. Icy flecks of snow had pelted the windows, while the wind howled and Melissa threw up her breakfast. Suspecting a stomach virus, Olivia had put saltines on a plate and opened the emergency bottle of 7 Up, then checked her daughter's forehead for fever.

"You don't feel hot. Do you think it's food poisoning?"

"It's not food poisoning."

"Then what is it?"

Silence. A sniff. Then the words that changed their lives. *"I'm pregnant."*

Olivia ran a high school. She knew teenagers had sex, and she had spoken candidly to her own daughter about birth control, disease, and especially about love. A single parent herself, she knew the strain of raising a child alone. At the time, she had strongly counseled Melissa to give the baby up for adoption.

When Melissa balked, Olivia had resorted to tough love. *"If you keep this child, you'll do it without my help."*

"That's your choice, Mom. And I've made mine. I'm keeping my baby."

"You're being naïve. How will you take care of it?"

"I'll find a way."

"How? Working for minimum wage? You can't provide for a child. For the baby's sake, give it up."

But Melissa refused, and "it" had turned into Cody. Now here they were, six years later, with the exact problems Olivia had predicted. She hoped Melissa would listen to her now.

Through the window she heard the whine of the monster truck. Her chest tightened into a knot of longing. "You've done a wonderful job raising Cody. You should be very proud of him."

"I am." Melissa scooted an inch to her left, away from Olivia. "I also have to provide for him. I don't want to sell Grandpa Jake's house, but it's for the best. I want to—"

"Melissa, I—"

The girl held up one hand. "Please, Mom. Let me finish."

Olivia felt chastised and rightly so. Would she ever learn to not interrupt? "I'm sorry, honey. Please. Go ahead."

Melissa lowered her hand back to her lap. "I have to provide for him. Being a mom is the biggest job in the world. I know that now. Having Cody opened my eyes to what you tried to tell me. And to everything you did for me. I want you to know, I appreciate the sacrifices you made, how you went back to school, and gave us a home."

Olivia put her hand over her heart. "Oh, Melissa."

"There's more." The girl's eyes misted into a sheen. "I'm sorry for the distance between us. I didn't mean to get pregnant. It was stupid of me. A mistake—"

"But now you have Cody."

"Yes."

"And he's *not* a mistake. He's wonderful." The words rushed past her lips, a torrent of love both for Cody and Olivia's own little girl. "Raising a child is an amazing experience, but doing it alone takes everything a woman has to give. Patience. Love. Going without sleep. It's difficult, to say the least."

"No kidding!"

Melissa rolled her eyes to the ceiling, groaned, and met Olivia's gaze with a tender one of her own. They were thinking alike now. Mother and daughter. Two women woven together by experience and strands of DNA. Olivia had never been prouder.

The tender smile on Melissa's face relaxed even more. "Cody's definitely a handful."

"That's because he's smart," Olivia declared. "He'll need all sorts of things. Piano lessons—"

"If he wants them."

"Space camp—"

Melissa's brow wrinkled into a frown. "Mom, that's expensive."

Olivia had love and money to spare, and she wanted to lavish it on her family. She could already see Cody at his high school graduation. He'd be valedictorian. Harvard would be lucky to have him, or maybe Stanford.

She gripped Melissa's hand. "I want to help you."

"How?"

"Move in with me."

Melissa's jaw dropped. "Live *here*? In the condo?" Craning her neck, she surveyed the living room as if she'd never seen it before.

"You can have your old room. We'll paint it, of course. That rose color has to go. And we'll pick out new curtains and a pretty comforter. Cody can have my office. There's an adorable bedroom set at Martin's Furniture. He'll have tons of bookshelves, a toy chest, but no television. That's not good for his mind."

"Mom?"

"There's more." Olivia could hardly contain herself. "I know how much you wanted to be a doctor. How would you feel about nursing instead?"

Melissa's brow furrowed again. "I'd love it, but I don't

see how it's possible."

"Central Wyoming College offers a two-year nursing program. If you move in with me, you can keep Grandpa's house and rent it out. I'll pay your tuition for nursing school, and you'll have an income of your own."

Melissa gasped. "Mom—it's so much. I never thought—I don't know what to say."

"Say yes."

"It's so generous of you."

"It's the right thing to do." Olivia reached for Melissa's hand, held it tight, and hoped. "Say yes, Melissa. Please. I want the three of us to be a family."

MJ gaped at her mother. Not once had she imagined such an offer. She wanted to shout, "Yes!" and hug her mom hard, but she had learned to be careful. In front of her, the red photo album sat at a perfect angle. It resembled blood on snow, a reminder that her mother had eviscerated her in this very spot. Now they wanted the same things—healing, a fresh start—but kicking snow over a stain didn't make it go away.

The glass tables gleamed, and the white carpet didn't have a spot on it. The vacuum lines made perfect triangles that combined to make perfect diamonds. Most perfect of all, the Tiffany replica glowed with silent, untouchable beauty.

MJ didn't belong in this perfect room. Neither did Cody. With her rambunctious son, smudges and stains were inevitable. So were crashes, bumps, thumps, and broken glass. But oh! The chance to go back to school, have a career, and do more than survive paycheck to paycheck—the opportunity to love and serve women like herself.

She sucked in a deep breath, held it, tried to stop shaking but failed. Before she made a decision, she and her mother needed to talk—really talk—about the practicality of the arrangement.

"It's a wonderful offer, Mom. But I'm worried."

"About what?"

"Cody's on the wild side."

Her mother waved off the concern. "We'll make a few rules, of course. But that's normal."

MJ agreed, but Cody didn't always follow the rules. The broken bedroom window proved it.

The back door popped open. "Mommy? Can I come in?"

"Not yet." She wanted to be sure he took off his shoes again, so she headed for the kitchen in her stocking feet.

The whirring of the monster truck erupted in her ears, followed by the slide of rubber tires on the linoleum. "Cody, no!"

The monster truck, muddy and dripping, jumped to the white carpet. MJ stuck out her foot to block it, but it ricocheted to the left and picked up speed, leaving brown tracks as it headed for the table holding the Tiffany lamp.

Should she run to the lamp or grab the controller from Cody? MJ opted for the controller. Sliding in her sock-covered feet, she lost her balance and nearly fell. Behind her the car smacked into a table. The lamp rattled, but her mother caught it.

Cody stood at the open back door, his feet planted firmly on the concrete step. MJ snatched the controller from his muddy hands. "*What* did I tell you?"

"But—"

"Don't argue. Answer the question."

He raised his chin with the brashness of a six-year-old. "You said to stay outside and I *did*. The *truck* went inside."

She admired his logic but not his attitude. "The truck's dirty. You can't play with it in the house."

"But I washed it. I turned on the hose and—"

"Oh, no."

She stepped onto the patio, turned to the left, and saw the hose running full force, flooding her mother's freshly mulched flowerbeds. MJ sloshed through a puddle and cranked the spigot. When the water slowed to a dribble, she faced Cody, still standing at the back door.

He glared at her from the step. He knew not to touch the hose. That was the rule at home, and it applied here.

She would *not* shout. She had to keep her cool, because Cody would learn from her, and she was the only parent he had. "You know the rule about hoses."

"Yeah."

She lowered her chin. "What kind of answer is *yeah?*"

He smirked, then looked over his shoulder into the house. MJ saw her mother—Grammie—come through the door, holding the truck, now clean from a rinse in the sink.

Grammie scanned the flooded yard from one corner to the other. "Oh, dear."

"Mom, I'm sorry." MJ turned her attention back to her son. "Cody, what do you say?"

With his mouth in a pout, he looked at Grammie. MJ knew that expression well. When it was sincere, the puppy-dog innocence melted her heart. Today it smacked of manipulation. She expected his tone to match the pose. When he apologized to her mother, it did.

"Cody," MJ said, drawing out his name. "You need to change your tone. Say it again. And say it nice."

Glaring at her, he looked ready to stick out his tongue. If he didn't obey, the truck would be off-limits for the rest of the day, maybe a week. MJ started to count. "One—"

Cody smirked at her.

"Two—"

Grammie strode forward, the dripping truck in hand. "Oh, it's all right." She handed the toy to Cody, patting his head and smiling down at him.

MJ's jaw dropped. When *she* was a child, punishment had been swift, fair, and effective. With Cody, Olivia Townsend turned into a marshmallow as white as her living room.

Cody faced her with his nose in the air. "Grammie says I didn't do anything wrong."

"No," MJ countered. "That's *not* what Grammie said. She forgave you for making a mess. There's a difference."

"But Grammie said—"

"Cody!" MJ's hands flew to her hips. "That is *enough*."

Behind him, her mother fought a grin, lost the battle, and cupped her hand over her mouth while her eyes twinkled. MJ saw the humor, but her mother's reaction rubbed her the wrong way. Their eyes met and locked. Silently she willed her mother to go back in the house.

Instead Grammie lowered her hand and laughed. "Oh, Melissa. He's *just* like you."

That tone! It grated on MJ's last nerve. Neither did she like being called *Melissa* as if she were twelve years old again.

"Mom?"

"Yes?"

"Would you please call me MJ? Everyone else does."

Olivia fluttered her hand as if brushing off lint. "You know me . . . I don't use nicknames."

But it's my name. It's my choice. The cry echoed words spoken six years ago about the pregnancy.

The condo suddenly felt like a dollhouse, a perfect place where little girls bossed around pretend people. MJ wasn't a doll. A mother herself, she had a duty to give Cody a loving, stable home. She couldn't stand the thought of bickering with her mother over her son, and the conflicts were certain to occur. Before she made a decision about her mother's offer, as generous as it was, she needed to pray.

She also needed to clean the mud off the carpet. Balancing on one leg at a time, she took off her wet socks. "Is the rug cleaner still in the laundry room?"

Olivia dismissed the offer with a wave. "I'll do it."

Cody looked up at Grammie. "I knew the car was muddy. That's why I washed it before I drove it in the house."

"That was smart." Grammie smoothed his hair, smiling down as if he were the most perfect child on the planet. "Why don't you take off those wet shoes, then go inside and have some more cookies?"

Cody gave MJ an I-told-you-so look, left his shoes on the step, and headed inside with the truck in hand.

She spoke to his back. "Stay at the table." She didn't want crumbs in the living room on top of the mud.

Both women watched Cody through the window. When he was settled at the table, Olivia turned to MJ and smiled. "Don't worry about the yard. It'll dry."

"How's the carpet?"

"Muddy, but I'll use the Bissell on it. So—" Her mother clasped her hands at her waist. "How soon can you move in?"

"It's not that simple." MJ held the wet socks away from her faded jeans. "I need to think about it."

"What's there to think about?" Her mother's brows skidded together and locked. "It makes sense, especially for Cody."

"It's very kind of you, Mom. I'm grateful, but I have some things to sort out."

"Like what?"

"It's been a long time since we lived together. With

Cody in the mix, it might not be easy."

"That's true. But I'd like to try."

"Me too, Mom. But I have to be sure."

"Of course."

Relieved, MJ scanned the yard, decided no real damage had been done, and took two steps toward the house. At the sight of her mother in the doorway, unmoving and stern, she stopped. "What is it?"

"I'm just . . . surprised."

MJ waited for more.

"I thought you'd jump at the chance to go back to school. What could be stopping you?"

MJ did *not* want to argue. Not with Cody nearby and her feet cold and wet. "Could we talk later?"

"You know I don't like loose ends."

"I know, but this is a big decision. I need time to pray—"

"Pray?"

"Yes." She didn't expect her mother to understand. Olivia Townsend went to church occasionally, a different one from Grandpa Jake's, but she had more faith in herself than in God. Rather than get into a debate, MJ kept her answer simple. "I've been going to church with a friend in Los Angeles. Her name's Lyn. She's helped me a lot."

"Helped you do what?"

"Survive, mostly." MJ thought of Lyn and her teapot. Their conversations had given MJ strength, and she needed it now. "Could we talk another time? Cody's in the kitchen, and some of this is personal."

"How personal?"

"Mom, please. It's *not* a good time." Were they really going to argue about this?

Olivia didn't move from the doorway. Silent and stiff, she drilled MJ with her eyes. "You're going to do it again, aren't you?"

"Do what?"

"You're going to squander this opportunity."

"*Squander?*" The word hurt, because she *had* squandered the chance to go to college. Instead of becoming a doctor, she had ended up as a patient, someone Dr. Hong called a "frequent flyer" because of her numerous appointments. Humor helped MJ cope, but the truth hurt. So did the disappointment in her mother's eyes.

Olivia crossed her arms. "You could have gotten an education. Instead you got pregnant—"

"Mom, stop! Cody will hear you."

"You're right. This isn't the time." She spat the words. "I'm just so . . . so surprised."

"I haven't said no. I just need to think about it." How could she live with her mother, when her simplest wishes were disrespected?

Her mother studied her expression for several seconds, sizing her up, searching for the information MJ didn't want to share. Knowing what was coming, MJ braced herself for an inquisition—and wasn't disappointed.

"Something's going on. What is it?"

Irked, MJ rolled her eyes. "Would you *please* stop?"

"What aren't you telling me?"

I have HPV. I might need a hysterectomy. I'm scared and I can't tell you, because you'll badger me with questions I can't answer—and advice I don't want. There's more, Mom. I love you, but please butt out of my life.

MJ swallowed hard. "Let it go. Okay?"

"I can't. I'm your mother."

"It's nothing," MJ insisted. "You know as well as I do—we don't always get along."

"We could if you'd try!"

"If *I'd* try?" MJ's arms flew out to her sides, a helpless plea for understanding, even respect. "You won't even call me MJ."

"It's not your name," her mother said logically. "And besides, you're too smart to throw away this chance over a nickname. It has to be something else."

MJ sealed her lips. Saying nothing was the only way to end the tirade. Or so she hoped.

But she was wrong. Her mother lowered her chin, crossed her arms, and glared down her nose. "Tell me the truth, Melissa. Are you involved with Shane Riley?"

Chapter 13

"*What?*" MJ could hardly believe her ears.
    "Are you involved with that baseball player? Don't be coy. I saw you with him at the café."

"I have no intention of being *coy.*" She didn't deserve this accusing tone. Neither did Shane. "I told you. I'm his landlord."

"Is that all?"

"Of course it is." MJ described the rental mix-up and the agreement they reached. Never mind muffins and tea-pots, Yogi Bear pancakes, and kissing in the kitchen. She and Shane were just friends.

Her mother's lips pinched into a frown. "You took a terrible chance renting to a single man you didn't know."

"*You* hired him."

Olivia sighed. "I suppose I did."

"It's all right." A mother herself, MJ understood the bone-rattling need to protect a child. She also knew how her mother felt about men. The divorce had left her bruised and wary. Instead of dating, Olivia Townsend poured all her love into her daughter, who had just disappointed her yet again.

MJ snagged Cody's shoes off the back step. Her mother opened the door, and they went inside. Seated at the table, Cody lifted a cookie from the serving plate, dropping crumbs as he took a bite. More than a few cookies were gone, a sign he had disobeyed yet again. Sighing, MJ prepared herself for the sugar high of the century.

"It's time to go." She handed him a napkin from the brass holder. "We'll put your shoes on at the front door."

Cody scrambled to his feet, the hose incident forgotten. MJ's own wet socks dangled from her cold fingers, so she asked her mom for a plastic bag.

A minute later she was holding a grocery sack much like the one she had carried into the Laundromat. The women followed Cody into the entry hall. When he plopped down on the tile floor, MJ gave him his shoes and socks. He wiggled his feet into them, she tied the laces, and he jumped upright.

Grammie tousled his hair. "I like your shoes."

He did a karate kick. "Shane got 'em for me. I have cleats, too. I wear them for sports. Shane says—"

"He's a good neighbor." MJ did *not* want her son singing Shane's praises. "Do you need to use the bathroom before we go?"

Cody looked up at the ceiling, considering. "I guess I do."

While Grammie showed him the way, MJ pulled her sneakers on her sockless feet. Just as she expected, her mother returned with her brows arched into question marks. "Cody likes Mr. Riley quite a bit."

"Yes, he does."

"Buying the boy shoes seems rather . . . friendly."

MJ's toes curled in her own new shoes. Eyes down, she tied the second lace and stood, hoping the hot blush on her cheeks didn't show. "Cody's shoes were falling apart. Shane saw them and surprised him with new ones. That's all."

"He likes Cody."

"Yes, he does."

"And he likes *you*."

MJ shrugged. "Like I said, I'm his landlord."

"Oh, honey—"

"What?"

"*Please* be careful. Not all men are trustworthy."

But Shane was. He deserved a defense, especially to his boss, but MJ couldn't protest without giving her mom more ammunition. Cody returned to the entry hall. Oblivious to the tension, he hugged Grammie good-bye, picked up the truck, and went out the door.

MJ hugged her mother, a stick figure as usual, then stood back. "I do appreciate your offer. I'll call you soon."

Not waiting for an answer, she followed Cody to the Bonneville. They buckled up, drove past the gated entrance, and cruised down the road to Refuge.

Cody held the monster truck in his lap, hugging it as if it were a pet. "Mommy?"

"Yes?"

"Do we *have* to go back to Los Angeles?"

An hour ago, she would have said yes. Now she didn't know. Cody needed stability, not indecision. But she didn't have a clear answer. Living with her mom would be difficult, but having a career would be wonderful. If she sold her grandfather's house, she'd lose a piece of her heritage, but she could maintain her independence.

MJ considered her son's question and sighed. "I don't know yet. I have a grown-up decision to make."

"I want to stay here." Staring straight ahead, he hugged the truck with both arms. "I want to live close to Grammie and Shane."

MJ's fingers tightened on the steering wheel. "God knows what's best. Let's pray."

Cody folded his hands and closed his eyes, scrunching them so tight she hurt for him. The sun pressed through the windshield, making her squint as she navigated the ribbon of black asphalt. Blue sky touched the golden hills, and evergreens lined the two-lane road, defying autumn and inevitable change.

The Bonneville took the curves like the sports sedan it still was, and MJ prayed. "Father God, you know what's best for us—Cody, Grammie, and me, too."

Bible verses from thrift store plaques drifted into her thoughts. *I know the plans I have for you, plans for a future and a hope.*

"You know everything about us." *The hairs on your head are numbered.*

"You love us more than we can understand." *For God so loved the world he gave his only begotten son.*

Tears filled her eyes. "We trust you, Lord. Thank you that Cody and I have each other, and thank you for Grammie."

Cody murmured, "And thank you for Shane."

Shane . . . The man whose kiss had awoken her body, her heart. A man with a wounded soul and a heart of gold. How did she pray for this good man who claimed he *used* to be a Christian?

Silently she implored God to be a father to him, to heal his knee and his broken trust, to wrap him in strong arms of love and carry him where he needed to go. She didn't understand the prayer fully, not intellectually, but the power of it gave her goosebumps. As she steered the Bonneville into the driveway, she murmured, "Amen."

"Amen," Cody repeated.

They climbed out of the car at the same time. As she looked up at Shane's apartment, he stepped onto the landing and called down to them. "Hey, Cody."

The boy held up the monster truck. "Look what I got!"

"Wow! Cool."

"Want to see how fast it goes?" Cody asked.

"How about later?" Shane indicated the open door. "The Cougars play in about five minutes. How would you like to watch it with me?"

"Yeah!"

"What kind of pizza do you like?"

"Cheese."

Shane focused on her but spoke to Cody. "How about your mom? What does she like?"

MJ couldn't think of anything better than watching baseball with Cody and Shane, listening to them banter, and laughing at Cody's antics. Her son needed Shane's masculine influence as much as he needed her tenderness. On the other hand, Cody didn't need to see them together, acting like a couple.

She inhaled deeply, exhaled her dreams, then answered Shane. "Is it okay if Cody goes alone?"

"Sure." But he sounded disappointed.

MJ took the truck from Cody, then spoke in a low, firm tone. "Have fun and be good."

"I will."

"And don't forget to say thank you."

"I won't."

He flung his arms around her waist and hugged her. She savored the feel of his thin arms, the tremble of his excitement, but she also ached with guilt for not giving him a father, and for wanting oh-so-badly to tell Shane she liked thick-crust pizza with sausage, mushrooms, and sun-dried tomatoes.

As Cody ran up the stairs, MJ raised her focus to Shane on the landing. Worn denim hugged his long legs, and she recognized the blue plaid shirt from his laundry. It seemed to be a favorite.

He matched her gaze but didn't smile. Instead she saw a challenge, a dare to follow Cody. Would he invite her again? Mentally she weighed her reply. *Yes . . . No . . . Yes!*

But he didn't ask. Instead he said, "I'll send Cody home after the game."

"Thanks."

Her son vanished into the apartment. Shane closed the door, leaving MJ to go into her house alone. She didn't have cable, or else she would have watched the game. Instead she went upstairs to sort through more boxes from the attic.

Shane had been headed to Cowboy's Bar and Grill when the Bonneville chugged into the driveway. He didn't like sports bars, but watching the Cougars game alone appealed to him even less, especially today. A win over the Minneapolis Meteors would clinch a trip to the playoffs, a dream come true for the men on the field, and yet another dream denied for Shane.

He wanted to punch a wall. *He* should have been playing third base today, fighting butterflies and listening to the *Star-Spangled Banner.* Instead he was sitting on the couch with Cody, worrying about Daisy, and watching his team beat the pants off their rivals.

Every time a Cougar got on base, Cody high-fived him. With the team leading 12-3 in the bottom of the eighth,

Shane lost count of the high-fives but not the plays at third. There had been seven—three grounders, a bunt, two line drives, and a pop-up. Could he have made the plays? Six months ago, yes. Today? Maybe.

A commercial for razor blades came on the flat-screen. Cody turned to Shane, started to say something, then stopped.

"More pizza?" Shane asked.

"No, thank you."

The formal tone didn't fit the mood. Shane playfully punched his arm. "What's the matter?"

"I don't want to go back."

"Back where?"

"Our old apartment in California."

Shane didn't like the idea at all. "Is your mom talking about leaving?"

Cody flopped against the couch, his mouth in a pout. "No. I just don't want to go."

The poor kid. He wanted roots. So had Shane at that age. Instead he'd spent long, hot summers in his mother's van, setting up at craft fairs, and leaving just when he made a friend. The school year wasn't much better.

He draped a foot over his knee. "I know what that's like. Moving is hard, but your mom knows best."

"She said we should pray about it, so we did."

"That's good."

Not that it would help. In Shane's experience, false hope collapsed like a building pancaking in an earthquake. It went down one floor at a time, crushing people and their dreams as it fell. His knee hurt today, and the blond actresses in commercials all reminded him of Daisy.

He waited for Cody to ask another question, but the game came back on.

The Meteors' shortstop took some practice cuts, swung at the first pitch, and missed. He took the second pitch for a strike, then hammered a grounder to third. JP Tyler, the man who had replaced Shane, dove for the ball but missed by inches.

Wincing, Shane stretched his bad leg.

Cody looked up at him, worry evident in his blue eyes. "Does your knee hurt?"

"Sometimes."

"You should call my mom. She knows how to make things feel better."

Yes, she does. Shane wished she had come over for the game. "I'm all right."

"You could still call her." Cody sounded a little like a car salesman. "She could bring more Yogi Bear cartoons and we could watch them here. She likes the ones with Cindy Bear."

"Who's Cindy Bear?"

"Yogi's girlfriend."

A casual suggestion? Shane doubted it. Cody was playing matchmaker, a dangerous venture for a boy who wanted a father. The instinct rivaled the drive that sent salmon upstream. Compared to human beings, salmon had it easy. They didn't have to worry about hurting fatherless boys or protecting women from runaway sperm. Neither did the females worry about diseases or sexual assault. He thought of Daisy with Eric Markham and felt sick.

Instead of answering Cody, he took the easy way out. "The game's just about over. Your mom's expecting you to come home."

"Can we bring her pizza?"

"Sure." A single mom could always use leftovers, so Shane had quizzed Cody about MJ's favorite toppings and ordered an extra medium.

The last batter struck out, ending the game and giving the Cougars the division title. As the crowd roared, the players pounded backs and bumped shoulders, jumping and pumping their fists in the air. Shane would have given anything to be in that crowd.

Really?

The thought gave him pause. Would he give up the chance to find Daisy? Would he trade buying shoes for MJ and Cody for a World Series ring?

A handheld camera followed the Cougars into the locker room, jostling in a way that put Shane in the middle of the crowd. Players squirted champagne at each other. He could smell sweat and alcohol, leather, and steam from the showers. Reporters jammed microphones into Manny Jackson's smiling face. As the all-star beamed, Craig Hawkins doused him with bubbly.

Cody, whooping as if he belonged, raised his hand for a high-five. Shane saw the light in the boy's eyes and found his answer. As much as it hurt, today he would choose the shoes.

"High-five!" he said, slapping Cody's hand.

His palm stung. So did his conscience. Before the accident, he wouldn't have given the same answer. Shane the Hypocrite died that day, but the cost was too great—if God was all-powerful, loving, and kind, surely he could have gotten Shane's attention without crippling him. Surely he could handle shoes for a boy *and* a man's dreams? And what about Daisy and her black eye? And MJ . . . Where was Cody's father? Had she been seduced and abandoned, even raped?

Where were you, God?

Champagne splattered the camera lens, dripping like spit, or tears, on the flat-screen TV. Shane blinked and thought of Christ carrying his cross to a skull-shaped mountain, destined to suffer and die for an uncaring world. Why did people have to hurt? Why did Almighty God make dreams come true and snatch them away?

Shane wasn't the only person with holes in his life. Cody had a giant one meant to be filled by the man who gave him half his DNA. In Shane's estimation, God had dropped the ball yet again, and he'd done it to a child.

Why, God? Why?

Lips sealed, he stood and clicked off the television. "Time to go."

"So no Yogi Bear?" Cody chewed his lip in that hopeful way of a worried child.

"Another time." Shane handed him the pizza box holding leftovers "Give this to your mom, okay?"

Cody took the box in both hands and headed for the door. Shane watched him cross the driveway, then went inside the apartment to catch up on schoolwork. God had let MJ and Cody down, but Shane wouldn't. The next move was hers, but he'd be waiting and watching like the good Christian he didn't want to be.

With Cody occupied, MJ went to the bedroom holding the remaining boxes from the attic, opened the next one in the pile, and found her grandfather's vinyl record collection. The old album covers should have enchanted her, but she couldn't concentrate enough to enjoy them. Giving up, she retreated to her bedroom to pray about her mother's offer.

She longed to go back to school, but she couldn't be twelve years old again. If she moved into the condo, she'd have no privacy. Her mother would see her mail, including statements and reminders from Dr. Hong's office. MJ would have to tell her about the HPV, which meant subjecting herself to questions, second-guessing, and her mother's ongoing disappointment.

"Please, God," she prayed. "Show me what to do."

Silence.

Crickets.

Nothing but her own breath scraping in her ears. With her eyes still closed, she recalled Lyn's words. *"God wants you to do more than survive. He wants you to thrive."*

MJ didn't see herself thriving. Surviving? Just barely. But that could change if she moved in with her mom. She hoped God was listening, because she needed an answer that wouldn't make her stomach hurt like it did now.

She opened her eyes and fetched a Coke with the hope that it would calm her nerves, then she went to her room again. Needing a distraction, she nestled against the stack of pillows on her bed and opened the box holding the attic letters. The mustiness mixed with the faint breeze spilling through the open window, and the candles, though unlit, scented the air with a hint of vanilla.

Aware of the fragile, aging paper, she pinched the corner of the next letter from the reverend to Little Miss and started to read.

Dear Little Miss,

Is there a reason you have not written? Three weeks have passed without word from you. Daughter, I am sick with worry. My heart tells me you are in grave danger, perhaps of a moral nature . . .

MJ imagined outlaw Adam Carter taking a swig from the whiskey flask, wiping his mouth with a dark sleeve, and mocking the reverend with his dead eyes and a hollow grin.

Inwardly MJ winced. Just as she had veered into uncharted territory at UCLA, Little Miss perhaps was exploring similar ground in Cheyenne. A crusading schoolteacher and a hardened outlaw made for either romance or tragedy.

Mentally, MJ wandered down the streets of 1890s Cheyenne. She pictured hotels made of reddish stone and dress shops showing gowns with muttonchop sleeves. The day Little Miss arrived from Indiana, locomotives would have chugged into the depot, announcing themselves with gray puffs of steam and high-pitched whistles. Wagons laden with flour, coffee, and tools would have rattled along the cobblestone streets.

MJ took a sip of Coke, then read the next few letters, each full of worry and unanswered questions until a page dated November 19.

Dear Little Miss,

Today my sermon came from the story of the Prodigal Son. When I spoke of the father embracing his wandering child, I could only imagine his joy. Sadly, I know well the weight of his grief.

As you may or may not know, I wrote to the headmistress of the Broderick School. She informed me you are no longer employed but declined to say more. Judging by her discretion, I must conclude you left your teaching position reluctantly and in shame.

My beloved daughter, if you are with child, come home. If you are alone, come home. If you are afraid, come home. If I do not hear from you soon, I will travel to Cheyenne. I will bring you home, my daughter. And if there's a child, it will be embraced by us all

Your loving father

Come home . . . A child . . . Embraced.

MJ stared at the reverend's words, her mind awash in memories of the weeks after Cody's birth. Instead of being embraced, she had been abandoned by everyone.

Exhausted and muddled by hormones, she had paced the floor like a crazy woman, worrying about her job, the rent, colic, diapers, groceries, and more.

Her college friends had visited to see the baby but then stopped calling. Neither could she talk to her mom. The one time she admitted to being overwhelmed, her mother had pushed again for adoption. That memory still hurt. So did being in labor alone. On the way to the hospital, hoping her mother would relent and come to be with her, MJ had called her cell phone.

No answer.

She left a voicemail, labored alone, and gave birth. At midnight her mother finally called back, panicked and apologetic because she received the message hours after MJ had left it.

MJ assured her she was fine. *"So is the baby. Mom, he's beautiful."*

There had been no questions about her labor, no interest in the baby's nose or the color of his hair.

Instead her mother broke her heart. *"It's not too late, Melissa. You can still give the baby to a loving family."*

MJ had murmured good-bye, then cried until an RN brought Cody to nurse. He latched on hard, and her tears had stopped.

The next two months were brutal. She yearned to talk to her mom about bottles and burps but didn't call. The tug-of-war didn't end until Cody's first birthday, when her mom sent a card signed "Love, Grammie" and a stuffed dog Cody still treasured.

MJ barely survived that first year. She took a sales rep job at SassyGirl, a mom-friendly store where the manager kept a crib in the back for her own son. She let MJ use it for Cody, and they traded baby clothes and diaper coupons.

The two women helped each other, but it was Grandpa

Jake who enabled her to provide for Cody. Every month he sent a check and a note that read, *Buy something for my great-grandson—and yourself.*

Now, tearing up with gratitude, MJ took in the paned windows and built-in shelves in her bedroom. She thought of Cody's tree in the yard, almost six feet tall, and the pine her grandparents had planted for her, now mature. How could she sell this house? She didn't want to let it go, but Grandpa Jake would have understood. *"Life has seasons,"* he used to say. *"Be ready for change."*

Leaning back against the pillows, MJ closed her eyes. The offer from her mother glittered like a diamond—or cubic zirconium. Had Little Miss wrestled with a similar mix of hope and dread about going home? Probably. What family didn't have squabbles? But mere squabbles came to an end. The struggle between MJ and her mom was an endless tug-of-war.

She looked again at the reverend's letter. A single line leaped off the page. *If there is a child, it will be embraced by us all.* He was offering his daughter more than a solution to a problem. He was giving her what Lyn called grace. Forgiveness. A clean slate. No veiled I-told-you-so's or taut puppet strings. Those encumbrances cut both ways. MJ, too, needed to forgive and respect her mom.

Could they forget the blood on the snow and start fresh? Her chest ached with a soul-deep longing for home-made vegetable soup, but her stomach churned at the same time. Scars healed, but they didn't disappear.

She lifted the next letter from the box. Instead of the reverend's cursive, she saw an unfamiliar scrawl. Bold, angular, and full of purpose, the words played through her mind in a baritone.

My dearest one,
    I promised to stop loving you, but it is a promise

I cannot keep—a promise I will NOT keep. Your father believes you are with child. He confided to me in a moment of tearful prayer, and I am honored that he did.

I love you, my darling.

I loved you when you told me good-bye. I loved you when you told me you would not marry a minister. I loved you when you stopped writing to me, and I love you still. Come home now and marry me. If you are with child, it will bear my name. I long to be the man who honors you in every way. Come home, my love.

Marry me. Marry me now. Say yes, darling, for I love you with all my heart.

Have I convinced you yet? If not, I'll ask until you are persuaded and pleased to be my wife.

All my love,
Thomas

MJ read the letter again, savoring every word. How would it feel to be loved so deeply that nothing else mattered—neither the past, nor its footprints on the present? The memory of Shane's kiss tingled on her lips and nestled low in her belly. Kissing him had been a mistake, but it was the best mistake she had ever made. For that moment she was free of the HPV and the shame. When his lips first met hers, she had thrived, even reveled, in being desired.

"Mom, I'm home." Cody's shout blasted up the stairs.

MJ put Thomas's letter in the box. She wanted to know what happened to Little Miss, but Cody needed a bath and a story, so she put the letter away and headed down the stairs.

She met him at the bottom of the straight staircase. "Who won?"

"The Cougars." He swung a pretend bat. "Shane said to give you the extra pizza. I put it on the counter."

Her stomach growled. "That's nice."

Cody didn't budge, a sign he had something on his mind. Finally he said, "Can Shane have dinner with us sometimes?"

"I don't think so."

"Why not?"

"Because he rents the apartment." Before he could ask why that mattered, she clasped his shoulders and aimed him up the stairs. "It's bath time. Get started and I'll be there in a minute."

He swept back his arms to make wings like a jet and rocketed up the steps.

MJ went to the kitchen and saw the pizza box. Expecting a few slices of plain cheese—Cody's choice but not hers—she opened the lid and saw her favorite toppings on a thick, doughy crust. Shane didn't know what she liked, but Cody did. He must have quizzed her son. His thoughtfulness touched her to the core. So did the sudden picture of him sitting on her grandfather's couch with Cody, watching his team win without him. It had to hurt.

Tonight he needed a friend. She felt it in her marrow, her heart. But she couldn't go to him. A knock on his door, even a phone call to thank him, would make them both vulnerable to an uncertain future.

She put a slice of pizza in the microwave. Thirty seconds later, the oven beeped, but MJ ignored it. Instead she looked out the window over her kitchen sink, craned her neck, and peered up at Shane's apartment. Plantation blinds, partially open, gave her a glimpse of the lit lamp on his desk.

He passed by with something in hand, stopped halfway, and peered down at her. Her kitchen was dark. She doubted he could see her even in silhouette, but she saw him plainly through the slats.

A prayer took flight in her soul. *Please, God. Heal his knee. Bless him the way he blesses Cody. Amen.* Longing to do more, she blew a kiss to his window. For now, she had nothing else to give.

aisy stood by the cash register in Mary's Closet, tapping her fingernails on the glass counter as she counted the minutes to the end of her shift at five o'clock. When she was free, she planned to meet her friend Chelsea at the coffee shop across the street and pay her back for the abortion money.

A lot had changed in the past month. The abortion was behind her, and tonight she would receive her thirty-day chip from AA, a coin-like token that recognized a month of sobriety. She missed Eric but not his moods. Mostly she treasured her room at Maggie's House, a pastel haven where she slept in peace, munched Fig Newtons, and had heart-to-heart conversations with her new friends. Some of the women were Christians, and Daisy liked them a lot better than she liked Shane. When they talked about God loving her, Daisy listened.

"*God isn't a bully*," one of the women said at a Bible Study. "*He lets us choose for ourselves. Me? I'm trying to choose good things now.*"

Daisy intended to do exactly that. If she could choose not to drink, she could make other good choices as well.

But what were those choices? She had no idea because she was numb inside. When the other women at the Bible study wiped away tears, Daisy sat stiffly on a hard chair. Sometimes she thought about the seagull pooping on Lyn and wished she could laugh like that again, or even cry.

Lyn stepped through the door to the back of the shop, her keys jangling in her hand. "I'm going home to change clothes. Tina is sorting a delivery in the back. Just give her a shout when you leave. I'll be back at six, and we'll head to the meeting."

"Sounds good."

When Lyn left, Daisy glanced at the clock. She had ten minutes to wait, so she leafed through a devotional on the counter. She liked the pretty photographs and upbeat stories, but mostly the book made her wonder about God.

At her first AA meeting, when she admitted to being bitter toward religion, especially Christianity, an old man named Lionel suggested she talk to an empty chair. Daisy had tried it in her room. At first she felt silly, but now she looked forward to those conversations. The chair didn't talk back, but it seemed to listen. That was a lot more than Shane ever did.

A silver Mercedes sports coupe glided to a stop in front of the thrift shop. Anticipating a donation, Daisy closed the devotional and tucked her hair behind her ears.

A woman pushed through the door, approached the

counter, and asked to see the manager.

"She's gone for the day." Daisy hoped she sounded professional. "May I help you?"

Coral lipstick glistened on the woman's overly plump lips, and her hair, long like Daisy's, shimmered with multiple shades of blond. The absence of even the faintest lines around her eyes gave her the look of frozen surprise that came with too much Botox. Daisy guessed her to be in her forties.

Sighing, the woman removed a black watch case from her Coach handbag. "I want to make a donation."

"I'll be glad to take it." Daisy lifted the receipt book out of the drawer.

The woman opened the lid, revealing a diamond watch glittering on white satin. "It's a Rolex."

It had to be worth a thousand dollars, probably more. Daisy had no idea. Lyn would take it to a jewelry store to have it appraised, and sell it somewhere else on consignment.

She couldn't take her eyes off the stones twinkling like captive stars. "It's beautiful. Are you sure you want to donate it?"

"I'm positive. That watch was a big fat lie. My husband's divorcing me."

"I'm so sorry." Daisy wanted to say more, but nothing came out of her mouth. Eyes down, she wrote the receipt in her best printing and handed it to the woman. The woman pinched it between her fingers as if it were filthy, then strode out of the shop without another word. The Mercedes squealed away from the curb as quickly as it had appeared.

The watch sparkled in the fluorescent light, reflecting a million pastel hues. Daisy touched it with tentative fingers, then draped it over her wrist. She had always liked playing dress-up, especially when she was little and her mother let her wear the dangly necklaces in her jewelry box.

Turning her hand, she fastened the clasp. The watch fit perfectly, as if it were really hers. Pretending to be someone she wasn't lifted her spirits, so she decided to show the watch to Chelsea before she placed it directly into Lyn's hands.

Daisy told Tina she was leaving, fetched her purse, and crossed the street to the coffee shop. She asked for a table in the back, then settled in to wait. Every minute or so, she peeked at the watch.

Finally the door opened and Chelsea walked in. Daisy started to wave, saw Eric, and lowered her hand. His gray eyes locked on her face, and he stared in that special way of theirs. When he smiled, his bad-boy grin heated her blood, melted her bones, and turned her brain into mush.

Her pulse tripped once in warning but sped up again. Eric looked so happy to see her, and her heart and body ached for him. A black T-shirt clung to his biceps and broad chest, and she knew it hid six-pack abs. His dark hair was freshly buzzed, but he hadn't shaved. The stubble made him even sexier. But what charmed Daisy the most was being wanted.

Common sense warned her to give Chelsea the money and leave. But Eric had been her friend, her lover, and she cared about him. Surely if she could stay sober for thirty days, she could handle Eric for thirty minutes.

Chelsea slid into the seat across from her, then offered a nervous smile. "I hope it's okay that I brought Eric."

It wasn't, but Daisy was determined to be strong, even confident. She answered Chelsea with arched brows, a silent version of *why?*

"He called me yesterday." Chelsea gave Eric a look to include him, then turned back to Daisy. "He said he wanted to apologize to you—to fix things—and he was afraid you wouldn't see him. I believed him about making things right, so here we are."

Chelsea should have called and asked permission, but she had a good heart and meant well. Mentally Daisy forgave her friend, then mustered her composure and gave Eric a curious look.

"Hey, babe," he drawled. "Mind if I sit with you?"

"Sure. Why not?" She slid toward the window to make room for him.

Chelsea opened a napkin, tucked it in her lap, then stared expectantly at Eric.

He bumped Daisy's shoulder with his bigger one, gently but with purpose. "I have big news, babe."

So did Daisy. Her AA chip meant the world to her. If Eric accepted her sobriety, could they be together again? She didn't want to have feelings for him, to love him, but there was a hole in her heart that Eric filled.

A waitress interrupted with menus and took drink orders. Chelsea asked for water with a wedge of lemon. Eric ordered two beers, one for him and one for her.

Daisy signaled the waitress. "Just coffee for me."

Eric frowned. "You don't drink coffee."

"I do now."

Chelsea's brows arched. "Since when?"

"Since a month ago." Feeling bold, Daisy hooked her hair behind her ear. "I quit drinking."

Eric put his arm on the back of the booth, close to her shoulders but not touching. "Are you all right, babe?"

"I'm fine."

"Then why'd you quit drinking?"

Daisy didn't know how much to say. Eric knew her heart, her fears. But he also had given her a black eye and thrown out her Fig Newtons.

The waitress brought the beverages and they ordered. Eric gulped the beer and signaled for another. Daisy fumbled in her purse, withdrew the envelope with the seven hundred dollars, and handed it to Chelsea. "That's the money I owe you."

Chelsea shook her head. "You don't owe me anything."

"But—"

Eric interrupted. "I took care of it."

Stunned, Daisy opened her mouth to say something, anything. But her tongue locked up.

Before she could untangle it, Eric flashed his megawatt smile. "You're talking to a movie star. I got the part in that new George Clooney movie."

Daisy gasped. "You did?"

"Yeah. I'm playing his son."

His grin tripped every circuit in her female body. She gave him an awkward hug, then put the money back in her purse. Not only was she happy for Eric, she had seven hundred dollars. Tomorrow she could open a savings account.

The food came. While they ate, Eric told funny stories about auditions, dropped big names, and made them all laugh with his dry sense of humor.

Every time he grinned, Daisy relaxed a little more. When he was working, Eric treated her like a princess. He bought her things, and they laughed together. If his career took off, they could have a real future. Daisy had learned a lot in the past month, including how to hope. Hope had kept her sober for thirty days, and tonight she'd get a chip to prove it.

Anticipating that moment, she looked at the watch. "I need to leave pretty soon."

Chelsea grabbed Daisy's wrist and gasped. "Are those real diamonds? That watch is *gorgeous*."

Daisy preened. It wasn't often that someone gushed over her. "It's a Rolex. But it's not mine. I borrowed it."

Eric grunted. "Are you sure it's not from some guy?"

"Of course not."

"Good." He downed the rest of his second beer, stood, and dropped a couple of twenties in front of Chelsea. "Take care of the check, will you? Daisy and I are going outside."

"Okay," Daisy said. "But just for a few minutes. I really do need to leave."

"This won't take long." Eric placed a hand on the small of her back and pressed her toward the door.

She traded good-byes with Chelsea, then walked with him to the parking lot behind the restaurant. A compressor hummed outside the kitchen, and cardboard boxes tumbled out of a packed dumpster, making a brown landslide of trash. Half a dozen cars, most of them shades of gray, filled the spaces painted on the cracked asphalt. Eric's red Mazda Miata stood out like a fire truck.

Roping his arm around her waist, he steered her to his car. "I've got something for you."

"What?"

"Your cell phone."

He opened the door and she slid inside. Just like before, the bucket seat fit her body like a glove. She set her purse on the floorboard, relaxed into the buttery leather, and stole another glance at the Rolex. Four minutes and counting.

Eric climbed in the driver's side, reached in the console, and retrieved her phone.

"Thanks." Daisy took it, their fingers brushing like feathers, then she dropped it in her open purse. When she faced Eric, he cupped her face with both hands and stared at her lips. Her heart leapt in anticipation, then she remembered the AA meeting. "Eric, I can't—"

"I love you."

He had said those words before, and like always, they made her toes curl. So did his breath in her ear and the whisper on her cheek. Eric's temper scared her, but he could also be tender, even sweet. She saw that man now. If he could understand her, they might have a future.

"I love you, too," she admitted. "But I've changed."

He brushed her mouth with his lips. She smelled the beer, tasted the sour residue, and recoiled. *No! Not again. No booze.* She had worked too hard to stay sober for thirty agonizing days. No way would she crack open that door—not even for Eric. Not even to feel loved again.

She jerked away. "Eric, no. I have to leave."

"Come on, babe. Kiss me."

"Eric—"

He silenced her with a hard kiss—a demand that mashed her lips against her teeth. His fingers tangled in her hair and pulled back her head. His tongue invaded her mouth, and again she tasted the beer, milder but just as rancid.

She pushed him away. "Stop it. I can't do this now. I have an AA meeting."

Eric froze. "AA? What for?"

"Because . . ." *I'm a drunk. I need help.* "It's good for me. Tonight I'm getting a thirty-day chip."

He snorted as if she'd told a joke. "I'll give you something better than a silly chip. This role is big, babe. I've got real screen time."

Daisy listened to him brag, but she didn't take in a single word. It was always like this—whenever they talked, it was about Eric. His career. His dreams. His plans. When was it her turn? For once she wanted to talk about herself.

Before she could interrupt him, he squeezed her hand. "I've missed you, babe. Come home."

"I can't. I need time."

"No, you don't."

"But—"

"I can take care of you now." He trailed his knuckles down her cheek, following the caress with his eyes. His hand stopped, but his gaze skimmed to her breasts. She knew that look. He wanted sex, and he wanted it now.

"Don't look at me like that," she insisted.

"You don't mean it."

"Yes, I do." She wanted to talk, not be seduced. "Eric, we had problems—big ones. We have to talk."

"We are talking." His lips trailed along the side of her neck, tickling and teasing until desire took a breath deep in her belly. Dark and primitive, the hunger swept through her. Yet her feelings had another side altogether. She just wanted to be loved. To feel safe and protected.

He pressed her into the bucket seat, his pupils dilated as he kissed her again.

She loved him . . . She hated him . . . She didn't know what she felt, but more than anything else, she wanted her thirty-day chip. Eric knew she had someplace to be, but he didn't care. *He did not care.* The jerk hadn't changed at all.

She broke from his grip, snatched her purse, and flung open the door. "This isn't going to work."

She had one foot on the asphalt when he yanked her back inside. Her purse flew out of her hand and landed upside down on the floorboard. The contents spilled in a heap—her wallet, her phone, the envelope with the seven hundred dollars. "Let go of me!"

Cursing, he squeezed her wrist. The Rolex dug into her skin like a claw. She tried to pull away, but he twisted her arm behind her back. Pain shot to her spine and she cried out.

"Close the door," he said with a growl.

"No."

"Close it, you—" He shouted a foul name.

If she closed the door, he'd drive off. He'd take her away and hit her and rape her. He was out of his mind, raging and hissing filthy words when seconds ago he'd been kissing her. She was a fool to think he had changed—a fool to think she could reason with him. She couldn't outmuscle him, so she had to outsmart him.

"I'm sorry." The words were a lie, but the tremble behind them was true. "Really, Eric. I am. Let go and I'll close the door."

"No one disrespects me, Daisy. Especially not you."

She blinked back tears. "I got a little mad and I'm sorry. Let go of my arm, okay?"

The instant he released her wrist, she bolted from the car. She sprinted as fast as she could, but Eric caught up to her, clamped his hand over the Rolex, and yanked her arm. The watchband broke, setting her free as Eric staggered into a fire hydrant.

She sprinted toward Washington Boulevard, her eyes locked on the Walk signal, counting the seconds until the light turned red. She had six seconds to cross the street, then five . . . four. She sped into the crosswalk, passed the stopped cars, her eyes riveted to the numbers on the signal. Three . . . two . . . one.

The instant she reached the curb, cars surged into the intersection, picking up speed until they passed her in a blur. Across the street Eric paced like a caged animal, his fists knotted as he mouthed curse words.

She ran straight to Mary's Closet, hurried through the door as it chimed, and prayed Eric wouldn't follow her. Turning, she searched for him through the tinted display window but didn't see him. He could be anywhere—in the coffee shop with Chelsea or lurking ten feet from the thrift shop door. She was safe for now, but what about tomorrow? Eric got what he wanted, always. And he wanted her.

Tina come out of the back room, probably expecting a customer. Adrenaline drained from Daisy's body, leaving her chilled and weak in the knees. She turned to tell Tina the ugly story, but her gaze snagged on the receipt book on the counter—and the empty Rolex box under the register. Her hand flew to her bare wrist and she gasped. Eric had the watch. He had everything. Her phone. The money. Her driver's license. She wanted her purse, but more than anything she wanted the watch so she could give it to Lyn. Somehow borrowing had turned into stealing.

Tina tipped her head. "Are you all right?"

"I'm—I'm fine," Daisy sputtered. "Just a bad moment. I'm okay now."

"Are you sure?"

"Positive." She blew a breath that lifted her bangs. "I really am okay. I saw an old friend, and it—it was hard. You know how it is."

"I do." Tina hesitated. "I'm here if you want to talk."

"Thanks. I just need a few minutes. That's all."

"Sure. I'm here if you need me."

To Daisy's relief, Tina returned to the back room. The instant she was out of view, Daisy pressed her trembling hands to her face. *Think, Daisy! Think!* There had to be a way to fix her mistake. Maybe Lyn didn't have to know. The receipts weren't numbered. If Daisy destroyed the page, the problem would go away. She opened the drawer and stared at the brown receipt book. She didn't want to lie, but she had broken the rules. Lyn had been clear. If she broke the rules, she'd have to leave Maggie's House.

No! No! No! A miserable groan clogged her throat. Whimpering, she shriveled into the fourteen-year-old girl who had been taken away from Coach Harper's home by a social worker with big black glasses. *"We don't want to take you away from your brother, but you can't stay here if you don't follow the rules."*

"I'm not doing anything wrong."

"Yes, Daisy. You are. You're sneaking out at night and drinking. We're worried you're going to get pregnant."

After what happened to her in the garage, what

difference did it make? She hadn't told the social worker the truth because she was too ashamed. Now she was ashamed of taking the watch. *Hide the truth.* She could do it easily. But as her fingers grazed the receipt book, guilt swamped her. So did fear and regret, because lies had cost her everything. What if she *had* told the social worker about the boys in the garage? Would she have been allowed to stay with Shane and the Harpers?

The back door chimed and she froze, composing herself as best as she could. After a moment, Lyn approached from the back of the store. "Daisy? Are you all right? Tina told me you were upset."

"I'm fine now." She had to be. "Seeing Chelsea was—a little hard."

Lyn must have believed her, because understanding glistened in her eyes. "Do you want to talk about it?"

"No." *Never!*

"That's okay, honey. Change isn't easy, especially at the beginning." Her voice took on a cheery note. "Just don't forget what's really important. It's not every day you get a thirty-day chip."

To her astonishment, Daisy did something she hadn't done in years. She burst into tears.

Lyn pulled her into her arms. "Honey, what happened?"

"The watch. I—I lost it." Through sobs and hiccups, she told Lyn about the woman in the Mercedes, Chelsea bringing Eric, going with him to his car, and running away. "I was going to put the watch back. Really, I was. But Eric grabbed me and it broke—"

"Oh, Daisy."

"It was worth a *lot* of money. Probably a thousand dollars. I don't know, but it was pretty, and I liked it, and—"

Lyn clasped her shoulders as if she were a child. "Daisy, listen to me. That watch was worth a lot more than a thousand dollars. A diamond Rolex? It was worth *thousands* of dollars."

Daisy tried to pull back, but Lyn held tight. "Do you know what else?"

"No."

"You, Daisy Ann Walker, are worth *far more* than a diamond watch. Jesus Christ died for you, Daisy. He died for me, too. He gave his life for us—for you and me—two struggling women who make mistakes every single day. I don't care about the watch. I care about *you*, and so does God."

Daisy thought of Shane trapping her in the storeroom and berating her. Now here she stood with Lyn, a woman who had every reason to be angry yet offered forgiveness, a gift Daisy didn't deserve. The churning in her gut sped up, but hope for mercy shimmered within reach. Daisy grabbed that hope with both hands.

"I'm sorry," she murmured. "I won't ever borrow anything again. I promise."

"That's good," Lyn said gently. "Because borrowing isn't borrowing unless you ask first."

"I know. I really am sorry."

"It's over now, honey." Lyn handed Daisy a tissue from her purse. "But I'm worried about Eric. Did he see you come into the store?"

"I think so. He watched me from across the street."

Lyn's gaze hardened. "If he decides to find you, he can. Tomorrow we'll go to legal aid."

"Why?"

"To get a restraining order."

Daisy shuddered at the thought. "That'll make him even madder."

"There's some risk, but you have to protect yourself."

Daisy recalled his breath on her face, the punishing kiss, the way he showed interest but didn't care about her.

Fear heated into anger. And anger morphed into courage—not a lot of it, but enough to lift her chin. "He won't fool me again. I'll go to legal aid."

"There's something else we can do." Lyn's eyes shifted to Daisy's hair, both the dry ends and the mismatched roots. "How would you like to be blond again?"

"I'd love it, but I can't afford a salon."

"You can afford this one. The woman who does my hair used to live at Maggie's House. I'll call her tomorrow. Tonight you have something to celebrate."

"I do?"

Lyn arched her brows. "Don't tell me you forgot about getting your chip?"

"No. I just thought . . ." Fresh tears moistened her eyes.

"You thought you'd lost everything."

"Yes."

"You didn't." Lyn spoke with such confidence that Daisy almost believed her. "You found something better than a Rolex. God calls it grace. Now let's get to the meeting."

Grace. Daisy knew from the Bible study that grace was a gift from God, something he gave his children because he loved them. Just last night she had told the empty chair that she wished she could be different, that she wanted to prove she wasn't as awful as Shane thought. Taking the watch had been a mistake, but somehow her failure had turned into a victory.

God, it seemed, had heard her prayers and answered. Stunned, she embraced the unseen power she didn't fully understand. She was an alcoholic. A thief. A whore. How could God love her? Yet he did. She felt it. She believed it.

I'm yours, God. Show me who you are. With her heart bursting, she thought of her perfect brother and felt sorry for him.

Chapter 15

 eated at the wooden desk in his empty classroom, Shane flexed his knee out of habit. It was three o'clock on a cold afternoon in late October, and the halls were empty. He entered the last quiz score into his laptop, gathered his things, and locked the door behind him.

Track practice—he coached cross-country—was cancelled because of rain, so he had a free afternoon. He considered going to the gym, but his knee ached in bad weather. Home appealed to him far more, especially knowing MJ would peek out the kitchen window when he pulled into the driveway.

Over a month had passed since the kiss. She kept Cody safely wedged between them, but Shane didn't mind.

Despite the boy's constant presence, he and MJ had become good friends. He often helped her with yard work, and she had talked to him about her mother's offer. Thanks to the rental agreement, she had some financial breathing room and didn't need to sell the house immediately.

It pleased him to see her more relaxed, and the three of them occasionally grocery shopped and went out for hamburgers. After moving Cody's car seat from the Bonneville to his Tahoe for the third time, he'd bought a booster seat for his SUV.

Shane enjoyed helping her, especially with small emergencies like her car not starting. This morning he had jump-started the old clunker and suggested she get the battery checked. If she didn't step outside when he parked in the driveway, the car trouble gave him a reason to knock on her door.

Work bag in hand, he went to the main office, checked his cubby hole of a mailbox, then headed for the front door.

"Shane!" Cody charged out of Mrs. Townsend's office.

"Hey, there." They traded their standard high-five. "When did you start high school?"

Cody laughed. "I didn't."

"No?"

"My mom's getting the car fixed. It's taking a long time, so she asked Grammie to get me from school."

Mrs. Townsend came out of her office, her spine stiff and straight as always. "Good afternoon, Mr. Riley."

"Good afternoon."

Cody tugged on his grandmother's hand. "Can I go home with Shane?"

The principal's expression remained businesslike, but she ruffled her grandson's hair. "I'm sorry, Cody. But no. Your mom expects you to be here. Plus I doubt Mr. Riley has a booster seat for you."

"Actually, I do." Shane hid a smile. "I'd be glad to take him, Mrs. Townsend. We can hang out at my place until MJ gets home."

The principal's mouth pinched into a tight line, but she didn't voice either displeasure or surprise that he and MJ were friendly enough for Shane to have a car seat for Cody. He expected her to brush him off again, but her secretary interrupted. The district superintendent was on the line with an urgent call.

In a rare show of frustration, Mrs. Townsend sighed, told the secretary she'd take the call in her office, then faced Shane. "It looks like I'll be tied up for a while. Thank you for taking Cody. I'll text Melissa about the change."

Cody pumped his fist in the air. "Yes!"

Mrs. Townsend's face softened into an indulgent smile just for her grandson. "Let's get your things."

The two of them fetched his coat and backpack. In less than a minute, Shane and Cody were dodging raindrops on the way to his SUV in the parking lot.

When Shane opened the back door, Cody scrambled into the booster seat and tried to work the latches himself. Shane tightened the straps, climbed into the driver's seat, and steered out to the street. As he drove, Cody chattered about everything from the rain to peanut butter sandwiches, which he liked a lot more than tuna fish, which he declared to be yucky. Shane tended to agree.

They were on Refuge Boulevard, discussing the merits of ketchup, when Cody called out from the back seat. "Look! That's the tree church. You should come with my mom and me. They give out cookies."

Shane had driven past the log-cabin church almost daily and steadfastly ignored it. Sermons and worship music didn't appeal to him at all. Neither did cookies, because they reminded him of Daisy and her passion for Fig

Newtons. Guilt, like the rain, spat at him. With his sister he'd been the man with the log in his own eye while removing splinters for others.

Cookies were a safer topic than splinters, so he encouraged Cody. "What kind of cookies?"

"All kinds, but my mom's are the best. She makes them with M&Ms. You should come with us."

"No, thanks."

"Why not?"

Shane felt as if Daisy were in the back seat, listening to how he'd explain himself to a trusting child. "I went to church for a while."

"Did you like it?"

"I did then."

Shane glanced at Cody in the rearview mirror. The boy craned his neck to stare at the church. "I like it. I'm learning the Lord's Prayer. Do you want to hear it?"

He lied. "Sure."

"Our Father, who art in heaven . . . Shane?"

"Yes?"

"Where's heaven?"

He could see why children got on people's nerves. "I don't know. Ask your mom, okay?"

"I will," he said with confidence.

"Shane?"

"Yeah?"

"My mom says God's *our* father, but who's *my* father?"

The question hung in the air like a high pop fly. It dangled over Shane's head a solid five seconds, then landed at his feet with a thud. Apparently MJ had told her son nothing about his father, a decision Shane thought was cowardly. Cody deserved answers, facts about his history, all the things Shane would never know about himself. No matter how Cody was conceived, MJ owed her son the truth in age-appropriate doses.

Shane pressed a little harder on the gas. "Ask your mom," he said again.

"She doesn't talk about him. What if she won't tell me?"

"Then ask her again." *Ask her until she answers.* Shane wished he'd found that courage before it had been too late.

MJ had a difficult conversation ahead of her, one that could mark Cody forever. Maybe all three of them, because the more time Shane spent with her, the more he cared about her and her son. Without a doubt, he wanted to be a dad, the kind that coached T-ball and set off fireworks on the Fourth of July. He would never know his own father, but being a dad himself would help fill that void.

When he and Cody reached his apartment, Shane put a video game on the TV, then stepped on the landing and called MJ's cell.

"Hi," she said quickly. "Thanks for taking Cody. I'd be there, but I'm stuck."

"At the mechanic?"

"You were right about the battery, but the alternator was dead, too. The car's so old they had to get the part from a junkyard. The one they found was bad, so now I have to wait until tomorrow. I hate to ask, but could you pick me up? I'm at River Run Auto."

"I'd be glad to. But MJ?"

"Yes?"

"I need to talk to you about Cody."

"Is he all right?"

"He's fine. But he asked me something today. You should know about it."

"Can you give me a hint?"

"He might hear me, and you're waiting. How about dinner at the McDonald's with the playground? We can talk while he runs around."

"Should I be worried?"

"Not at all." He didn't want to alarm her more than he already had. "But you need to know what he's thinking."

She sighed into the phone. "See you in a few."

Shane rounded up Cody, and they dashed back through the rain to the SUV. He picked up MJ, then treated the three of them to burgers, fries, and shakes.

Cody gobbled his food and took off for the plastic jungle gym, leaving Shane alone with MJ. As he opened his mouth to broach the subject of Cody's father, Tracee Anderson and her sons spotted them from across the play area and waved.

MJ waved back politely, then pointedly focused on Shane. "I really hope she doesn't come over here."

"No joy," he said under his breath. Tracee and her kids were already on their way.

They ambushed him at the table. The next thing Shane knew, he was talking baseball instead of fatherhood.

MJ smiled politely but said little. He tried to wrap up the sports talk, but Tracee was a fountain of questions, all designed to show her sons that Shane was a good role model. He felt like a fraud, and he resented the intrusion on his time with MJ. Not very Christian of him, but that's how he felt.

Finally the Andersons left and he turned to MJ. "Sorry. I didn't mean to keep you in suspense about Cody."

"Tracee's nice, but she can't take a hint. Tell me what happened before we get interrupted again."

Shane told her about driving past the church and Cody's interest. "He asked me a couple of questions that you should be the one to answer."

MJ studied him a moment, then glanced toward the plastic jungle gym, presumably to be sure Cody was occupied. Shane followed her gaze and saw Cody scrambling up a corkscrew slide from the bottom just as a much larger boy pushed off from the top.

MJ leapt to her feet. "Cody. Get *down.*"

She sprinted toward the slide, Shane at her heels. They were still five feet away when the older boy's shoe slammed into Cody's face. The boys landed at the bottom in a tangle of arms and legs.

The big kid rolled off Cody unharmed, then glowered at him. "That was stupid. You're supposed to use the steps."

Shane gave the boy a firm stare. "It was a mistake. That's all."

The boy stomped off, but Cody lay crumpled on his side with his nose bleeding all over his shirt. MJ had already dropped to her knees and pulled him into her lap. "I'm here, honey. It's all right."

She wiped the blood off his face with her sleeve, rocking him and crooning to calm him down.

Shane snagged some napkins from a nearby table and handed them to MJ for Cody's nose. From what he could see, the boy's injuries included a bloody nose and a bump on the head, probably a few bruises. He'd be all right—except for his pride. Six-year-old boys didn't like to be seen crying, especially in front of older boys like the one who had called him stupid.

Kneeling, Shane tapped Cody's shoulder. "Hey, there."

Cody hid his face against his mom's shirt, but embarrassing tears dripped down his cheeks.

Shane ignored the tears, giving Cody his dignity. "That was quite a crash, but you're handling it well."

Cody turned to him. "I—I am?"

"You bet."

"My nose hurts," he admitted.

"I bet it does. Your nose will be sore for a few days, but I don't think it's broken."

Cody sniffed to test it. "It still works."

MJ pressed a fresh napkin to his face. "Now blow, but not too hard."

Cody did as she said, with much honking.

MJ laughed, probably more from relief than humor. Shane couldn't take his eyes off her face—the way she smiled reassuringly at her son, the pinch of her brow, the cradle of her arms. Her bloody sleeve said it all. MJ would do anything for someone she loved, but who took care of MJ? Not the man who had fathered Cody. Not her mother. Not God.

Cody finished blowing his nose, inspected the bloody napkin, and made a face. Declaring the contents "gross," he handed the napkin to his mother. Before MJ could pinch the disgusting mess with her fingers, Shane snatched it. "This is quite a souvenir. Maybe we should frame it."

The boy giggled. "Yeah."

"Oh no, you don't!" MJ threw back her shoulders, feigning outrage and adding to their fun. "That's going in the trash right now, and we're going home."

Shane disposed of the souvenir, helped Cody to his feet, then offered a hand to MJ. She took it, and he pulled her upright, tucked her against his side, and hooked his free hand around Cody's shoulder.

The boy looked at him with shining eyes. "I think that kid weighed a hundred pounds."

"Maybe more," Shane agreed.

MJ laughed, but a shudder traveled from her ribs to his. He could imagine how a mother felt when she saw her child hurting. Remembering Cody's question, he whispered into her ear, "Call me later and we'll finish our conversation."

With a little luck, Cody would stay focused on his sore nose and forget the question about his father, at least until Shane could tell MJ what to expect.

MJ oversaw Cody's bath, read him a story, and tucked him into bed. His nose was red and he had a bump on his head, but otherwise he'd forgotten the collision on the slide.

But she hadn't. What if the accident had been more serious? What if someday he needed a blood transfusion? He had his father's uncommon blood type, B-positive. MJ was A-positive and not compatible. She couldn't be a donor to her own son. That kind of uncertainty hounded her. So did whatever question Cody had brought up to Shane. As soon as her son fell asleep, she planned to call him.

Cody lay in bed with his hands laced behind his head and his eyes focused on the ceiling. She glanced at the spot that had his attention, saw nothing, and came to sit with him. "What's up there?"

"Paint."

Smiling, she smoothed his damp hair. "Anything else?"

"Sort of." He chewed his lip, then mashed his pillow into a ball and leaned against it. "I asked Shane something, but he wouldn't tell me. He said to ask you."

MJ braced herself. "What's the question?"

"I know God's my father in heaven."

"That's right."

"What happened to my other father? The one who's supposed to live in the house?"

Please, God. Give me the right words. The question wasn't a total shock. She'd known this moment would come. But how did she explain what happened to a six-year-old? Cody didn't want the biology. He needed a name, a face, the things she couldn't give to him.

"Well," she said slowly, buying time to think. "Your father isn't in our lives anymore."

"Why not?"

"It's hard to explain. He didn't know—I mean—uh—" She had to do better, or Cody would be confused, even hurt. Mustering her courage, she told the truth. "Your father doesn't know about us. But God does. And he loves you. He loves *us*."

"Why doesn't my father know about us?"

"Because I couldn't tell him."

Please, God. Don't let him ask why. She busied herself by tucking the blanket around Cody's lean frame. He didn't look like her at all—not even a hint of her nose or cheekbones. But he'd inherited her curiosity, her easy manner.

Cody made a humming sound, considering the facts. "So he's gone forever."

"That's right."

"I get it." He scooted up on the pillows. Questions burned in his eyes, and he bit his lip, a sign he was working up his courage. "So if you wanted, Shane could be my dad."

Relief softened her bones, but fear stiffened them again with her next breath. Cody wasn't going to quiz her about his father, but he had dangerous ideas about Shane. Hoping to project a casual mood, she tucked the covers even tighter around his legs. "It's not that simple."

"Why not?"

"It's grownup stuff."

Cody's pale brows cinched together. Before he could formulate another question, she stood and kissed his forehead. "It's past your bedtime, kiddo. I'll explain it to you another time."

"Mom, wait."

"What is it?"

"We have to say prayers." Cody's feet swished under the covers, something he did when he was thinking. MJ dropped back down on the bed and clasped his hand. Love for her son squeezed her heart, stole her breath, and left her awed, amazed, and terrified all at the same time.

His earnest tone broke into her thoughts. "Can I ask God to make Shane my dad?"

As much as she wanted to protect him from hurt feelings, she couldn't discourage his childlike faith. "You can ask God for anything, but he decides how to answer."

Folding his hands on his chest, he seemed to consider her answer. "That's what I thought."

MJ covered his hands with one of hers, and Cody prayed.

"Dear God, I want a dad, and I want him to be Shane. I want a brother, too. Amen."

"Amen," she whispered.

Swallowing a lump, she grazed his warm forehead with a kiss. Cody grabbed her shoulders and hugged her. She held him tight until he let go, then she turned out the light. "Sweet dreams, kiddo."

He whispered back, "I love you, Mommy."

"I love you, too."

Tears puddled in her eyes. She didn't want Cody to see them, so she hurried downstairs. By the time she reached the kitchen, her cheeks were damp and she couldn't swallow until the lump in her throat shook loose in a sob. She barely heard the tap on the back door. Only when the knocking became insistent did she raise her head. Shane stood at the door, peering through the lace curtain, worry etched on his brow. She didn't want to talk to him now, not with Cody's prayer ringing in her ears. But the door opened anyway.

He strode across the kitchen, drew her into his arms,

and tucked her head in the crook of his neck. She smelled his warm skin, his soap, the traces of rain in his hair. She didn't dare mold her body to his, but neither could she pull away.

Her will battled with her heart until she couldn't stop herself—didn't *want* to stop herself—from swaying fully into his arms. She leaned into him, borrowing his strength just for this moment. Their breath synchronized into the backbeat of a song, a bass line that was more felt than heard. His arms tightened around her body. She clutched at his back. More than anything, she wanted to pray with Cody that Shane would be his dad.

Finally his lips brushed the shell of her ear. "Cody asked the question, didn't he?"

Chapter 16

"Yes," MJ murmured. "He asked."

Shane rubbed her back with a firm touch. The warmth of her skin soaked through her blouse and into his fingertips. Whatever monsters lurked in the dark, he wanted to slay them for her. She had to face them for Cody's sake, but she didn't have to face them alone.

When her sobs faded to ragged breaths, he handed her a tissue from a box on the table.

Stepping back, she quietly blew her nose. "You tried to warn me. I wish . . ." Shoulders sagging, she dropped down on a chair, her gaze on her bare feet. "I wish a lot of things."

He pulled a chair around for himself, sat across from

her, and hunched forward, his hands loose between his knees. "Cody asked me about his father when we drove by the church. I told him to ask you."

"Yes. Of course."

"He deserves the truth, MJ. Whatever it is."

"That's the problem."

The refrigerator hummed. The icemaker rattled out a few cubes and halted. When MJ still didn't speak, he nudged her foot with his. "I'm not following you."

"I just don't know." She twisted the tissue, turning the cotton until it hardened into a twig.

What didn't she know? How to tell Cody? The *how* wasn't nearly as important as the *who*. "You can't avoid it. Cody needs the truth."

"Yes, but—" She stared into his eyes with the bleakness of an overcast sky. "Like I said, *I don't know.*"

"Don't know what?"

"Not what . . . *who*." The word echoed like the hoot of an owl perched alone in a distant tree. *Who . . . Who . . . Who . . .*

Sitting a little straighter, he studied her face—the wrinkle of her brow, the dull pewter of her eyes, the nervous twisting of the tissue. Suddenly he understood why MJ couldn't answer Cody's question. She knew the circumstances of his conception, of course. But she didn't know the man's name.

Ugly possibilities flashed through his mind, but one leaped out above the rest, leaving him sick to his stomach and afraid for her. "Were you raped?"

"No." She raised her eyelids, met his gaze, and squared her sagging shoulders. "I was willing. Drunk, but willing. It happened at a party in my freshman year. Just one time. How do I explain that to a six-year-old?"

No way would Shane judge her the way he had judged Daisy. "I don't know."

"Neither do I." Her fingers slid out of his grasp, leaving a warm but empty trail behind them. "I was so eager to grow up—and to fit in. Nicole had all the answers."

"Who's Nicole?"

"She lived next door to me in Sproul Hall."

"The dorm?"

"Yes. It's big and social. Coming from out of state, I chose it because I thought it would be easy to make friends, and it was. But it was overwhelming, too."

"Kind of like going from Double AA to the Major League."

"Or from Earth to another planet." MJ sighed. "Nicole was a freshman but a few years older. We talked a lot. You could say she influenced me, but my decisions were my own—especially the one that led to Cody. I wasn't exactly naïve back then. Just . . . curious, I guess. At the time, losing my virginity seemed like a natural thing to do."

MJ stared blindly past him to the back door. "It happened at a party off campus. His name was Brady or Brandon, something that started with a B. That's all I remember. I never saw him again."

Maybe the guy had been drunk like MJ—a naïve kid who made a mistake. Or maybe he was a user like Eric Markham, someone who treated women like the napkin MJ used to wipe the snot from Cody's nose. Either way, Shane wanted to slam his fist into the guy's jaw. "Brady-Brandon dropped the ball here."

MJ implored him with her eyes. "He doesn't even know about Cody. Should I have tried harder to find him? For Cody's sake?"

"It's hard to say."

"I think about it a lot, but that night I knew what I was doing. The guy had a condom. Maybe he used it. Maybe he didn't. I don't remember. There was no obligation on his part, no commitment at all—"

<

"Wrong." Shane refused to let the guy off the hook. "There's a big obligation on his part. The biggest obligation a man can have."

"But—"

"If a guy has sex with a woman, he should have the decency to know her name and to check to make sure she's not pregnant."

She gave him a rueful smile. "According to the women I knew at SassyGirl, that's old-fashioned. Online dating apps changed everything."

Thanks to locker room talk, Shane was no stranger to the hook-up culture. He could only shake his head. "Biology is still biology."

"In more ways than one," MJ admitted wearily. "Cody has his father's blood type, B-positive, which is fairly rare. Mine's A-positive and not a match. What if he needs a transfusion? Or a kidney? What if—"

"MJ, stop."

"I can't." She tossed the twisted tissue in the trash. "I worry all the time."

"You can't change the facts."

"I know, but Cody's going to have questions. Even worse, people will ask *him* questions. I know because they ask me questions all the time. It's natural. But someday he'll be a teenager. I'm terrified he'll be embarrassed or ashamed, or just mad. And bitter. That would be the worst."

Shane said nothing, because her fears were real and likely to come true. After his mother's death, he had searched every inch of the van for a letter, a note, anything with information about his father, in part with the vain hope the man would want him. Grief-stricken and in shock, he had plummeted into a silent rage that sometimes still plagued him. How could his mother have taken such vital information to the grave?

He reached for MJ's hand again. Her fingers were still cold, but she had stopped shaking. "Most secrets do more harm than good. If you tell Cody what happened, he'll be able to cope with it. Anything's better than not knowing."

"You sound certain."

"I am. My birth certificate says 'Father Unknown.'"

Her eyebrows shot up. "You don't know who your father is?"

"I don't even know *about* him."

"Nothing at all?"

"Nothing." The word glided off his tongue with surprising ease. The detachment came with practice. "No name. No pictures. Only the fact I was born in Phoenix."

MJ took a slow, deep breath and blew it out. "You *do* know how Cody feels. May I ask you something?"

"Sure."

"I know you missed having a father, but was it enough to have just your mom?"

"My mom was amazing. And yes, she was enough." More than enough, she'd been everything to Shane and Daisy. "She liked baseball, so we listened to games on the radio while she drove. No matter where we were, she made sure Daisy and I had special birthdays. She loved us and we knew it."

Awash in memories, he told MJ about his unusual childhood. His mother, Jennifer Riley, had left home at the age of nineteen to study art in Paris. When her parents died a few years later, she returned to the United States, bought a van, and sold her work at artisan fairs all over the country. Somewhere in her travels, Shane had been conceived. Later she married a man named Jon Walker and gave birth to Daisy. When the marriage ended, she took her children and went back to the craft fair circuit, where she sold sundials made from scrap metal.

Shane thought of the hours in the van, the boredom

of rural highways. He still wondered about his father, but he also remembered laughter and his mother's spirit of adventure. "There were good times and bad ones, but Daisy and I did all right."

"What about school?"

"We spent most of our winters in Arizona. My mom had friends there. It worked until she died so unexpectedly."

MJ's pretty eyes misted. "I'm so sorry. Did you ever ask her about your father?"

"Once. I was thirteen when she accidentally left my birth certificate in plain view. Until then, I thought Daisy and I were full siblings, that my father was Jon Walker."

"But your last name's Riley."

"We all went by Walker until he left us. After that, we went back to Riley, even Daisy, but she now uses Walker."

"It's confusing."

"That's what happens when kids don't know who they are." Shane recalled the times he'd changed his name and held in a sigh. "When I saw the birth certificate, I asked my mother for the truth. I could see her thinking about it, deciding, but in the end she said I was too young to understand."

MJ nodded solemnly. "I can see why. Thirteen's a sensitive age."

"Yes, but she shouldn't have dodged the question. Don't do that to Cody."

"I won't." She laced her fingers in her lap. "Thank you for listening . . . for everything. You've been wonderful to us both."

MJ's praise warmed him from the inside out. He could be proud of what he'd done tonight, what he'd said to her, and how he had handled Cody's questions. His good deeds were adding up like coins in a bottle, each one shiny, valuable, and a payment toward redemption.

"Cody's a great kid," he said, sharing MJ's pride. "How's his nose?"

"Sore, but he's fine."

They chatted about the slide and the crash, Cody's spelling test, Shane's students, and the possibility of MJ moving in with her mother. She still didn't know what to do, and Shane offered no advice. Working for Olivia Townsend was a challenge. He couldn't imagine living with her.

It was ten o'clock and a school night, so he pushed back in the chair and stood. "I better go."

MJ popped to her feet. "I baked cookies this morning for church on Sunday. How about taking some with you now?"

"No, thanks." Cookies reminded him of his failure with Daisy.

A frown must have rippled across his face, because MJ tipped her head. "What's the matter?"

"Nothing."

"You're upset."

Yeah, I am. "It's nothing."

A lie, and she knew it. "Is it Cody? I know he's attached to you, and he has . . . ideas. If there's a problem—"

"It's not Cody." In his mind Shane saw Daisy dressed in a black leather mini-skirt and strutting on four-inch heels, her lips coated in garish lipstick and her eyes rimmed with heavy makeup. He relived trapping her in the storeroom, berating her in that high-and-mighty tone he now despised.

As if she were a ghost, Daisy spoke to him. *MJ tells you her darkest secret, and you sit there and pretend to be perfect? Well, you're not. You cursed at me when I was hurting. You practically spat on me in that storeroom.*

He owed MJ an equal confession, and he owed Daisy. His conscience squirmed, wormlike and ugly, until he opened his mouth. "Cookies remind me of my sister. I haven't told you much about her."

MJ tipped her head. "Almost nothing."

"She's in trouble, and it's my fault."

In his mind the kitchen morphed into the Harpers' living room. He saw the social worker speaking to Daisy in a hushed tone, then taking her away while Shane eavesdropped from the hall, grateful he didn't have to go with her. He'd been a Christian then, yet he had willfully ignored the promise he made when their mother died. *I'll watch out for you, Daisy. I won't let them separate us.*

He had failed her. Miserably.

MJ brought cookies and milk to the table and urged him to sit. Shane sank back down on the chair, sipped the milk, but couldn't look at the cookies.

She nudged the plate in his direction. "You were in foster care together, weren't you?"

"For a while." He told MJ about living with the Harpers, how his dreams came true while Daisy made one mistake after another. "I tried to stop her from drinking and staying out, but I did everything wrong. I'd been a Christian for a few months, and I had all the answers. Looking back, I bullied her."

MJ winced on Daisy's behalf. "How old were you?"

"Sixteen."

"And scared like Daisy." She nudged the cookies closer to him. "Don't be so hard on yourself. You were grieving your mother and getting used to a new life."

"Yes, but I was older, and Daisy needed me. If I'd asked to leave with her, we might have been placed together in a new home. But I didn't want to leave the Harpers." His eyes dropped down to the sugar cookies loaded with M&Ms. "If I'd left with her, maybe she wouldn't have fallen apart."

"You don't know that."

"True, but I know what *did* happen." He told MJ about

Daisy's promiscuity and drinking. Lastly he described half dragging her into the dark, cluttered storeroom at his college graduation. He couldn't bear to look at MJ, who would either condemn or excuse him. Either reaction would sicken him, but especially an excuse.

He forced himself to look her in the eye. "She wanted to leave, but I blocked the door. I shouted at her about the drinking, the guys. I told her she was ruining her life, and I couldn't stand by and just watch. That's when she told me to go to hell. I lost it and yelled back. She got hysterical, and I still didn't open the door."

MJ gave him a stern look. "You blew it."

"Yes. Big-time." Guilty as charged. But his confession brought no relief—not even a whisper of absolution. "She needed me to look out for her, and what did I do? I told her she needed Jesus, and I wouldn't open the door until she came to her senses. When I finally gave up, she left with a guy who later bragged about hooking up with Preacher Boy's little sister."

Even in the dark, Shane saw MJ go pale. "That's awful. But I don't understand. Who was Preacher Boy?"

He hammered his thumb into his chest. "Me. It's an old nickname. I hate it."

MJ laid her hand on his forearm, but he felt dirty and pulled away.

She allowed him to escape her touch, but not her words. "What you did was awful, but you're sorry." She eyed the little flip-calendar on the kitchen table, Christian-themed, with pretty pictures and a daily Scripture. Until now Shane had steadfastly ignored it.

MJ's eyes lit up. "I like today's verse. It says love covers a multitude of sins."

"Don't go there."

"Go where?"

"To God forgiving my sins. To Jesus dying on a cross

and paying the price. To goodness and mercy following me all the days of my life, because that didn't happen." Sarcasm dripped fire into his belly. He had no desire to torpedo MJ's faith, or to mock it, but neither could he stand a naïve lecture on God's ways.

"Sorry," he muttered. "I was a Christian for eight years. I respect your faith, but I don't share it. Not anymore."

"Why not?"

"A lot of reasons. Let's drop it."

She hesitated. "I won't pry, but I'm wondering about Daisy. What have you done to find her?"

"I've called her a hundred times, but she doesn't answer. Before I left L.A., I hired a private detective." It hurt to think about Daisy's present circumstances, but he needed to be completely honest with MJ. "Last I heard, she showed up at my old apartment with a black eye. My roommate answered the door and she ran. She could be on drugs, homeless, doing anything to survive."

MJ's eyes lit up. "You lived in Marina del Rey, right?"

"In Palm Terrace on Washington Boulevard."

"I have a friend who works with Maggie's House. It's a place for women escaping domestic violence. The organization runs a thrift shop about a mile away in Venice Beach. It's a long shot, but I'll talk to her. At the very least, she can keep an eye out in case Daisy shows up."

"Thanks. The odds are about a million-to-one, but it's worth a try." An old verse echoed in his mind. *With God, all things are possible.* He no longer believed in miracles, but his soul clung desperately to a fraying strand of hope.

MJ carried the plate of cookies to the counter. He picked up the half-empty milk glasses and followed, watching as her hair swished against her slender shoulders.

When she faced him, her mouth slanted in a solemn

line. "You said Cody would forgive me."

"He will."

"I'm telling you the same thing about Daisy."

"You don't know that."

"I do—because of who you are now."

A nice sentiment, but Shane didn't buy it. "I'm no one special." Just a guy who envied salmon.

"You're my friend." Her voice pushed at him through the dark. "I don't know why you lost your faith, but no one else has ever given me the understanding you just did." She looked into his eyes with such caring he wondered if she was about to kiss him—and hoped that she would.

When she didn't look away, he trailed his thumb along her jaw. She inhaled sharply, then put her hands flat on his chest, pressing slightly in a gesture that was either a welcome or a wall. Choosing to see the welcome, he matched his mouth to hers with a tenderness born of their shared confessions.

She kissed him back, but only for a moment. "I can't do this." Except her fingers clutched at his shirt.

At a loss for words, he kissed her forehead instead. She leaned into him with a breathy sigh, then stiffened and pulled back, loosening her grip on his shirt a finger at a time. Breathing out in a gust, she turned and stared out the window with an expression he couldn't read.

Reluctantly, he followed her gaze to the trees dripping with the last of the rain. Why hadn't she relaxed into the kiss? Was she afraid of sex because of Cody's father? Or— Shane's next thought paralyzed him. MJ was thin, almost too thin. Was she HIV positive? Had she come home because she was ill?

His heart jack-hammered against his ribs. "I hate to ask," he began in a voice that didn't sound like his. "But—" He couldn't bring himself to invade her privacy more than he had.

She turned back around. "What is it?"

"Never mind."

"That's not fair. You can't start to ask a question and not finish it."

"All right, then. It's none of my business. But the way you pulled back just now, and before—are you HIV-positive?"

"HIV?" She hugged herself. "No."

"Sorry. I just—"

"It's okay." She lowered her arms, visibly relaxing. "It's smart to ask, especially after what I just told you."

"Even so—"

"Don't worry about it." A tiny smile said she meant it. "We're just friends, anyway. It wouldn't matter."

Shane didn't know what to make of her contradictory reactions, but he knew she enjoyed kissing him as much as he enjoyed kissing her. That meant something else was stopping her, but what? Whatever that mystery was, he intended to solve it. A gentle nudge seemed to be in order. "What are you doing Friday night?"

"Just the usual."

"Let's have dinner together. You and me."

He thought he recognized longing in her eyes, a spark, even hope. But the tension returned with equal force. As much as he wanted her to accept his invitation, he wouldn't rush her.

After several silent seconds, she took a deep breath. "I can't. But if you ask me in a month I might say yes."

"A month?"

She nodded. "My life's up in the air right now. And I have to be careful with Cody. In a month I'll be more settled."

He didn't understand her reasoning, but the wait would give him a chance to romance her on the sly—flowers, compliments, helping with the dishes—all the small acts of caring that would lead to deeper feelings.

"A month it is." Before she could rethink her decision, he kissed her satin-soft lips and headed for the door. It would be a long four weeks, but for MJ he could be patient.

The instant the door closed behind Shane, MJ hurried to the family room where she kept her laptop. In a month she'd have the latest pap smear result. If it came back clear, she could think about dating Shane. Of course she'd tell him about her history. One good result didn't mean she was free of the virus, but a clean test versus a certain hysterectomy was a big step.

She opened the Notepad program and made a to-do list that included scheduling with Dr. Hong, asking her mom to watch Cody, and checking to see if she could crash with Lyn. It was an hour earlier in California, so MJ called her friend now.

They chatted like they usually did, then MJ asked about staying over. "It'll be just a couple of nights."

"You're welcome anytime. You know that."

"Thanks."

"So what's new?"

"Not much." *Except I've kissed Shane and I'm falling for him.* The thought jarred her memory back to the kitchen and his confession about his sister. "I have an off-the-wall question for you."

"Let's hear it."

She told Lyn about Shane losing his mom, being placed in foster care, and now searching for Daisy. "I know the chances she'll show up are remote, but Maggie's House is fairly well known. If Daisy lives in that area, maybe she'll show up. I was wondering if you'd keep an eye out for her."

Silence.

That kind of reaction wasn't like Lyn at all. MJ wondered if the call had dropped, but Lyn's voice came back as clear as before. "I can ask, but you know the privacy policy for Maggie's House. Women have to feel safe here. I can't tell you anything without a person's express permission. That's a hard and fast rule."

"And a good one."

"I'll keep an eye out for her. If this girl needs help, we all want her to get it."

They chatted a little longer about life in general. When they hung up, MJ Googled airfares. The cost—$550 out of the Jackson Hole Airport and even more out of the smaller Refuge facility—nearly made her throw up. She could pay for the trip with her emergency Visa, but just barely.

Being in debt scared her, but she could pay off the balance when . . . when what? When she sold the house? When she moved back home with her mom?

God, are you there?

Uncertainty pummeled her. She loved the idea of becoming a nurse but hated the thought of living with her mother. She loved the prospect of falling hard for Shane but hated the threat of a hysterectomy.

Just tell him.

Why not? What did her pride matter? He could back off now, and no one would get hurt. Or at least *he* wouldn't be hurt. MJ's heart was already an aching mess. She didn't think she could bear a rejection, or worse, the slow withdrawal from their friendship, as if she were a leper.

Or worse still, he'd feel compelled to be kind to her. He'd say a hysterectomy didn't matter, when it really did. If any man deserved to be a father, it was Shane. No way did she want to take away that dream, when he had already lost so much.

What was the loving thing to do? The brave thing? MJ closed her eyes, pressed her fingers to her temples, and tried to pray. When her thoughts ran in circles, she thought of Little Miss. Had she been as lost and confused as MJ was now? That answer, and maybe an answer for herself, awaited in the box of letters on her nightstand.

MJ padded to her room, sat on the bed, and opened the black enamel case. She lifted the remaining letters, nestled against the cloud of pillows, and started to read.

The first letter began like the previous ones.

Dear Little Miss,

Again I implore you to come home. A boardinghouse is no place for a young lady to live, especially when you mention neither work nor church. My dearest daughter, I fear you have become ensnared in a world that lacks honor, morality, and respect for God's laws. Come home, child. Forgiveness awaits.

MJ skimmed the four remaining letters from the reverend but gleaned nothing new. Neither did Thomas write again. Frustrated and curious, she went to the spare bedroom and opened the storage box that still held the whiskey flask and a few other trinkets. She poked through hair ribbons and hankies until her fingers grazed a sheet of paper.

Lifting it, she saw that it was buff colored and folded in half, the crease fraying at both ends. She unfolded the paper gently, saw *Western Union Telegraph Company* in old-fashioned type, and read a handwritten message scrawled by a clerk.

Arriving Jan 10 on UP Overland Flyer (Stop) Bringing Thomas (Stop) Your Father.

UP stood for Union Pacific. Overland Flyer referred to a train route. MJ imagined the reverend and Thomas riding in a crowded passenger car, surrounded by families moving west, businessmen, and politicians embracing Wyoming's recent statehood. The dust would have been thick, the smells of grease and steam heavy in the air.

Where would they look for Little Miss? If she had lost her reputation, no decent shop would hire her. Had she sunk to the life of a laundry drudge? Waitressed in a saloon?

MJ knew her history. The Old West wasn't as kind to women as her grandfather's favorite old movies made it seem. With so few opportunities, prostitution might have been the only way for Little Miss to feed herself. That possibility included everything from the luxury of being a rich man's mistress to the horrors of a hog ranch, the most wretched kind of bordello on the frontier.

MJ imagined Thomas finding Little Miss in such a place—dirty, used, diseased. Would he still want her? The woman's things were in MJ's attic, but that didn't mean Thomas had come to her rescue. Little Miss could have died giving birth to an illegitimate child, or of disease, or at the hands of a violent man.

Was MJ a direct descendent of Little Miss? It seemed possible, even likely. But possible wasn't enough. MJ wanted to know. Multiple generations separated them, but they shared a similar story, one that belonged to every woman who lived with the consequences of a sexual choice.

When MJ asked her mom to watch Cody for the trip to L.A., she'd give her the letters and ask about Little Miss. Maybe her mother could solve the mystery. Setting the letters aside, MJ hoped Little Miss found her happy ending, because MJ very much wanted one for herself.

Chapter 17

With his students taking a test, Shane sat at his desk grading last night's homework assignment. For the third time in an hour, his hand drifted to the pocket holding his phone. He knew better than to check for messages in the classroom. The school enforced a strict policy for teachers and students alike, but sometime today a florist was scheduled to deliver roses to MJ. He wanted to know if they had arrived, so he stole a glance at the screen.

Instead of a text from the florist, he saw a missed call from Ray Blaine, the vice president of player development for the Cougars, the man with the power to restore Shane's career.

There was a voicemail, too.

Pulse racing, he whipped his gaze to the wall clock. Ten minutes to wait before class ended . . . Ten long minutes to speculate and imagine, to hope and . . . No. He wouldn't pray.

While the students finished the test, he tapped his foot, twirled a pencil, and glanced again at Ray's number. The caller ID left no doubt. Ray Blaine had personally phoned him. With five minutes to go, Shane called time and collected the answer sheets. After a final minute of classroom chatter, the dismissal chime played and the students filed into the hall. When the last boy left, Shane locked the door and called Ray.

Amber Washington, Ray's assistant, picked up on the first ring. "Mr. Blaine's office."

"Hi, Amber. It's Shane Riley."

"Oh, good. Ray's been waiting for you."

Ray Blaine—waiting for *him?* Shane's pulse raced like it did before a big game.

Ray picked up the phone. "Hey, Shane. How's it going?"

"Great." He started to pace. "Congratulations on winning the division. Sorry we didn't get to the World Series." The Cougars had lost the league championship in four straight.

"That's the way it goes. How's the knee?"

"Strong again. I work out every day."

"Good. JP Tyler got busted again for cocaine. We cut him loose. Ricky wants to give you a chance."

Shane stopped dead in his tracks between the window and the locked door. Ricky Jordan was the Cougars manager, one of the best in baseball. If Ricky wanted him, Shane had a real shot at a comeback. Six months ago, he would have hit his knees in gratitude. Today he silently mouthed, "Yes!" and pumped his fist in the air. "When do you want me?"

"Ricky just left on a cruise, then I'm headed to Tokyo to do some scouting. How about November 10? That's three weeks from now."

"Perfect."

"Amber will make all the arrangements. We'll send a private jet for you."

"That sounds good." *Good?* It sounded great—better than great.

"No problem," Ray replied. "We're piggy-backing you on a flight out of Denver. Manny's speaking at a cystic fibrosis event, and a couple of guys are going with him. There's an extra seat if you want to bring someone."

A private jet and an offer to bring a guest? Could it get any better? Shane couldn't stop grinning. He'd invite MJ for what he hoped would be an unforgettable first date.

"Thanks," he said to Ray. "There's definitely someone I'd like to bring."

The VP chuckled. "Sounds like Preacher Man has a girlfriend."

"Maybe."

Ray laughed. "Bring her. Amber will set you up with a hotel, a car, everything."

"Thanks."

"Here's Amber. You two can work out the details."

When Amber picked up the line, Shane could barely control his voice. She asked about airports, hotels, and car preferences, then promised to email the details.

The instant she hung up, Shane shouted "Yes!" at the top of his lungs. The Cougars wanted him back! If MJ was up for the trip, their first date would be dinner at the beach, a long walk barefoot on the sand, holding hands while the moon glistened on the ocean.

The Cougars booked VIPs at the Crowne Drake Hotel, a glass-walled tower in downtown L.A. with a legendary view of the city. Possibilities burned in his mind. Playing third base again. Celebrating with MJ. Kissing her senseless, maybe even—he stopped himself from reacting like a salmon, but the thought of making love to her did more than cross his mind.

The next three weeks would be the longest of his life. He wanted to speak to MJ in person, but he had to tell someone the good news now. He scrolled through his phone to Craig Hawkins's number.

His old roommate answered on the third ring. "So how's the school teacher?"

A month ago Shane would have bristled at the jibe. Today he didn't care. He enjoyed teaching, mostly because of the kids. He'd miss the classroom when he rejoined the Cougars. "I'm good," he said to Craig. "Teaching's not a bad gig. I like it, but get ready to have your roommate back. Ray Blaine just called."

"Oh, yeah?"

"Tyler's gone." Shane told him about the arrest. "I'm trying out November 10."

"Excellent." Craig paused, then lowered his voice to the somber tone of a friend who understood. "How's the knee?"

Shane flexed it a couple of times before answering. An ache crept along the ACL, but every athlete lived with some pain. "It's a lot better than it was."

"Glad to hear it. Are you crashing here?"

"No." He mentioned the private jet and the hotel, then went a little further. "I'm bringing someone."

"Female?"

"Definitely."

Craig chuckled. "So is Preacher Man still holding on to his purity?"

Shane loathed his old nickname, but Craig was a good friend. They often poked and prodded each other, always with an underlying respect. In the locker room, however,

Shane had been viewed as a self-righteous snot and rightly so, but no way would he disrespect MJ even with a friend. "Preacher Man's dead and gone, but I still don't talk trash."

Craig laughed. "Yeah, I figured. Anyway, I'll be gone all of November. The place is yours if you want it."

"Thanks. Where are you going?"

"Would you believe through the Panama Canal? I'm taking my parents on a cruise for their thirtieth anniversary, then spending two weeks back home."

"*Ooooh-kla-homa*." Shane sang the famous opening from the showtune. He knew it irked Craig, and that was most of the fun.

As he expected, Craig groaned into the phone. "Good thing you're not teaching music, bro. Your voice stinks, but yeah. that's home. I need some normalcy after this year, and my sisters will make sure I get it."

At the mention of Craig's sisters, Shane flashed to Daisy. MJ had asked her friend Lyn to keep an ear to the ground, but so far Lyn hadn't responded. Troy was still looking, but there was no sign of Daisy.

Shane finished with Craig and headed to his Tahoe. As the engine purred to life, he wished again that he could call Daisy. But there was no way. His stomach plummeted, and he worried she was dead in a ditch. His elation sank into fear, then deeper still into the quicksand of shame and helpless remorse.

A left turn put him on Refuge Boulevard, where the log church loomed on his right. A blast of fury obliterated the shame, even the elation of hearing from Ray Blaine. Spoiling for a fight, he swung the Tahoe into the church parking lot, aimed the hood at the broad side of the building, and jammed the transmission into park. Glowering at a stained-glass depiction of a shepherd and a lamb, he let out a curse at the God who had betrayed him.

Christianity was a lie. God didn't care.

Except Shane felt a Presence in the SUV—as if Jesus himself were in the passenger's seat.

A voice whispered in his mind. *Go inside.*

"And do *what*?" he said to no one, maybe to Someone. "Pray? Ask you to bless the tryout?"

He had told Ray the knee felt good, but the joint crackled like dry spaghetti. It throbbed in bad weather and made him feel like an old man. He had paced himself for a tryout in February, not one in mid-November. If Shane asked for more time, Cougars management would find a new third baseman. It was now or never, do or die.

Mentally he hurled rocks at the green pastures depicted in the window, the still waters he couldn't find.

The voice whispered again, louder and more commanding. *Come inside.*

"What for?" Shane slammed his fist on the steering wheel. "Seek and ye shall find? Ask and it shall be given to you? How do you explain a busted knee instead of a career?"

That internal voice whispered again. *Knock and the door will open.*

"Not the door I want."

The shepherd in the window stared back at him, frozen and silent, as if waiting for an answer.

Shane had heard enough, both for today and a lifetime. He rammed the Tahoe into reverse, made a tight turn, and sped out of the parking lot. He was done listening to imaginary voices, done being taunted by God. The only voice he wanted to hear was MJ's. Did he love her? Maybe. Probably . . . The thought stopped him cold.

She was a Christian. He wasn't.

She went to church. He didn't.

She trusted God. Shane trusted only himself.

Their differences didn't matter in a "for now" kind of

relationship—the kind he had wanted two months ago. But a "forever" relationship needed a solid foundation, one without cracks that would turn into chasms even deeper than the one that had swallowed his career—chasms that could swallow a woman and boy alive.

No way would Shane let that happen. But what kind of foundation did he build? Salmon lived by instinct. Human beings made moral choices, conscious decisions, and sometimes great sacrifices. How did he weigh everyone's desires and needs, including his own?

He inhaled deeply. Once. Twice. Finally his pulse slowed. By the time he pulled into MJ's driveway, his mood had returned to euphoria over Ray Blaine's call. Life was good again, but whatever happened with MJ, he had to take things one step at a time. He respected her and Cody too much to do anything else.

Who would knock on her door at three in the afternoon? MJ hadn't ordered anything online, and the lawn care sales reps had given up on getting her business a month ago. Cody was next door with Brandon, so it wasn't his friend. Curious and wary, she opened the front door to a cloud of pink roses sticking up from a clear glass vase.

A delivery guy met her shocked stare with a grin. "MJ Townsend?"

"That's me."

"These are for you."

He wedged the chilled glass against her palms, gave her a pretend salute, and left with the jaunty step of a man who enjoyed his job.

Eyeing the envelope poking from the center, she carried the flowers to the kitchen, set them on the table, and opened the card.

Six days down. 24 to go. D is for Dinner—Shane

Some of the roses were in full bloom. Others were relaxed and on the verge of opening, while a few of the buds were as tight as fists but alive with promise. Any minute Shane would be home from school. How did she show her appreciation? As long as F stood for friendship, a simple but sincere thank-you was fitting. But a kiss would be more honest. Sighing, she stroked a velvety petal, then sniffed the half-open flower.

A knock sounded on the back door. Shane didn't wait for her to open it, or even nod. He strode straight to her, a grin stretched wide across his handsome face.

He looked like he wanted to hug her, but he noticed the flowers and stopped short. "Good. They're here."

"And they're gorgeous." Her cheeks warmed to a pink that probably matched the petals. "Thank you, Shane. They're my favorite color—and a complete surprise."

"I have another one."

"Really?"

An even wider smile beamed from his face. "A Cougars vice president just called. I'm trying out in three weeks."

Squealing, MJ threw herself into his arms and hugged him as hard as she could. She didn't want to let go, and apparently neither did he. The hug lasted long past the first burst of excitement, stretched to joy, and morphed into hope.

Shane broke the embrace but held on to her hands. "You know that date you promised me?"

"In a month."

"What are you doing November 10?"

Her appointment with Dr. Hong was that week, but she didn't want to tell him just yet. "I don't know."

"How about a trip to L.A.?"

"What?"

"The Cougars are sending a private jet. I'll have a suite

at the Crowne Drake, or two rooms if you'd rather. Either way, you're invited."

"Oh, Shane!"

Her thoughts flew in a dozen directions—some personal, others pragmatic. God, it seemed, had met her need for airfare in an astounding way. A flight to L.A. on a private jet! Never in her wildest dreams had she imagined that answer to her prayer.

She stared into Shane's eyes, her heart brimming and her pulse rushing with every good feeling a woman could have for a man. But with that tug and pull came a surge of fear. She knew his invitation to L.A. came without strings—he didn't expect her to sleep with him. But what would he say about the virus when she finally told him? When did they have that conversation? And if the test came back clear, what choice would MJ make about sex and her own body?

The answer to the last question was surprisingly easy. No matter how wonderfully Shane kissed, or how deeply she cared for him, she wouldn't make love outside of marriage ever again. She wanted to honor God. And being purely pragmatic, she knew the consequences of sex, protected or not.

Serious now, she matched his gaze. "I'd love to go. But instead of the hotel, I'd like to stay with a friend."

"Whatever you'd like."

"I just want to be clear—"

"So do I." He clasped both her hands, warming her fingers as he lightly stroked them with his thumbs. "This is a first date. All I'm asking for is one dinner together. After that, we'll take it a step at a time."

Sweet longings rippled through her, tempting her to waver, but anxiety surged in its wake. In Los Angeles they'd be alone. The Crowne Drake was legendary for beds with duvets like the one on her own mattress. For six years MJ had denied her sexuality. She had stayed a teen-ager, dreaming about movie stars from a safe distance, never venturing from fantasy to the reality of a man's touch.

Until Shane, she had forgotten what temptation looked like, how it smelled or tasted, the way it pushed and pulled like a rubber band, or a beating heart. In Los Angeles they would be alone and accountable to no one but themselves—and God.

Shane gave her hands a squeeze, then let go. "Will your mom watch Cody?"

"I have to check, but I'm sure she'll say yes." MJ had already invited her mom to lunch to talk about the trip and the attic letters. "I'd like to visit a couple of friends while we're there." She counted Dr. Hong as a friend. "Do you remember when I mentioned Lyn?"

"She runs the thrift shop."

"That's who I'll stay with. I'll introduce you in person so you can ask her about Daisy."

The sparkle in his eyes dimmed, and his neck bent as if he were expecting the sharp blade of a guillotine. When he looked up, his eyes were bleak. "Thanks. I'd appreciate it."

"Then it's settled." She wanted to kiss Shane for the joy of it, but she settled for a smile. "We need to celebrate the tryout. Would you like to stay for dinner?"

The smile returned to his eyes. "I'd like that."

While she made chicken stir-fry, they chatted about Los Angeles and their favorite places. They both missed In-N-Out Burger, the ocean, and the air of casual excite-ment that gave the diverse city its personality.

When Cody came home from Brandon's house, he and Shane set the table. The three of them ate like a family, then Shane shooed her out of the kitchen. "Go and relax. Cody and I will handle the dishes."

Feeling blessed, she went to the den, curled on the couch, and listened to the male banter. She asked God to bless them both in the best possible way. For herself, she prayed for patience.

But even as she prayed, she knew her heart had run ahead of her common sense. Shaking inside, she admitted a frightening truth. She had fallen in love with Shane Riley, and not because he had come to her rescue yet again. They were cut from the same ragged cloth. He understood her, respected her, somehow dared her to trust when she was afraid. She hoped she inspired him in the same way.

Laughter echoed out of the kitchen. The faucet went silent, then Cody scampered down the hall, giggling and shrieking about a soap monster. Shane came up behind him and tickled his sides. Her son's laughter filled the air, and she laughed with him.

When her eyes met Shane's, the alphabet game took on a life of its own and became a prayer.

H for healing.

P for purity.

V for victory.

Tomorrow she'd go through her closet and decide what to pack for that date in Los Angeles. In faith, she'd bring her little black dress and highest heels. If she received a good report from Dr. Hong, she'd celebrate by kissing Shane until *his* toes curled. First, though, she had to get her test results. Until then, M stood for Maybe.

Chapter 18

O livia parked her two-year-old Volvo in front of the Campfire Café. Melissa's car was across the street, an eyesore and an embarrassment to say the least. Frowning, both at the car and herself for being eight minutes late, she hurried into the café.

Melissa stood at the counter, waiting. They exchanged a predictably awkward hug, ordered salads and lattes, and commiserated about the cold weather. Trays in hand, they made their way to a booth near the one Melissa had shared with Shane Riley.

Olivia still worried about that cozy picture, but she put her concern aside as she shook out a napkin. Today she had high hopes for a full reconciliation with her daughter.

She and Melissa hadn't argued even once since the muddy truck incident, and Cody loved his Saturday visits. When he called her Grammie, Olivia melted into a puddle of love that spilled on to everyone around her, especially her daughter.

Surely Melissa's lunch invitation signaled she was going to say yes to moving back home.

Olivia could hardly stand the suspense, so she did what she did best. She took charge. "So, tell me. What's new?"

"Not much, but Cody's doing great in school."

Melissa told her all about Cody's good grades and how much he liked Mrs. Odenmeyer. Olivia asked a dozen questions and hugged every answer to her heart. The elementary school wasn't close to her condo, but she could easily arrange for Cody to continue there when Melissa moved back home. "I'm so glad things are going well for him."

"Me too. But I need a favor."

A favor? Not the direction Olivia expected, but she smiled anyway. "Sure. What is it?"

"I have to go to Los Angeles. Could you watch Cody the week of November 10?"

"Oh . . . I see." She didn't mean to sound critical, but disappointment sharpened her words.

Melissa's brows pulled together. "I don't want to impose. If you can't do it, I'll ask Tracee."

"No! I'm glad to watch him. I just thought—never mind."

She lifted her fork, but Melissa left hers on the table.

Determined to avoid a quarrel, Olivia made her voice kindergarten-bright. "I'd love to watch Cody. I was just surprised. I thought perhaps you'd decided to move back home, and we were going to start making plans."

"Mom, I'm sorry—"

"It's all right."

"You've been so patient. I didn't mean to mislead you."
Melissa bit her lip the same way she did on her first day
of kindergarten. "It's a big decision."

"Yes. It is."

"I have to be sure."

"Of course." Olivia meant it. She was disappointed by
Melissa's doubts but proud of her for wanting to be wise.
"I said to take your time and I meant it. But tell me, why
are you going to Los Angeles?"

"I have a doctor's appointment."

"But that's so far." Olivia's brows crashed together. No
one traveled a thousand miles to see a doctor unless
something was terribly wrong. Cancer. A heart condition.
*Dear God, no. She's my daughter. I know I've ignored you,
but not this.* She scrutinized her little girl's face for signs
of fever, illness, any clue at all. She saw nothing and worried even more. "Sweetheart, are you all right?"

"I'm fine. It's pretty much routine."

Pretty much? Olivia wanted facts, not vague reassur-
ances. She stared at Melissa until the girl stopped cutting
the salad and looked up. When their gazes locked, Olivia
lowered her chin. "Something's going on."

Melissa stabbed a cucumber. "My doctor in L.A. knows
me. I want to stick with her."

"What kind of doctor?"

The girl hesitated. "A gynecologist."

"A gyne— Oh, Melissa. *No.*"

"What?"

"You're pregnant, aren't you?"

"No!" She set down the fork with an angry clatter.
"Can't you trust me even a little?"

Olivia felt perfectly justified in her logic. Melissa had
been vague, even secretive, in her reply. She also lived fifty
feet from Shane Riley. Olivia wasn't blind, nor was she

deaf to the gossip around school. The handsome athlete was the talk of the mostly female English department, and he wasn't dating anyone.

In Olivia's experience, nature had a way of asserting itself. "You can see why I'd wonder."

"I guess," Melissa admitted. "But just so you know, I haven't been with anyone except Cody's father. That was just once. Trust me, Mom. I learned my lesson."

"Oh, honey—"

"Let's drop it." Melissa reached for the latte, took a long sip, then resumed eating the salad without saying another word.

The quarrel left them on a road full of emotional ruts waiting to trip them yet again. Olivia didn't want to stumble. She wanted her daughter back, but she didn't know how to act. Like a blind person poking with a cane, she searched for the next step. "Honey, I'm worried about you."

Melissa raised her gaze, her expression soft again. "I know. And I love you for it."

"I love you, too." Olivia longed to squeeze her daughter tight, but the table stopped her.

Melissa bit her lip again. "Please don't worry, but you're right about the visit. It isn't routine. Three months ago I had an abnormal pap."

"How abnormal?"

"ASCUS."

"That's not so bad." Olivia had received an ASCUS result herself. Aging changes, the doctor said. Menopause. Normal or not, Olivia hated it. "Most of the time it's nothing."

"But not always."

"I still don't see the need to travel. Dr. Edwards can request your records."

"Mom—"

"He's an excellent doctor. I've seen him for years." Olivia retrieved her phone from her purse. "I have his number right here."

"Mom, I said no."

Determined, Olivia scrolled through her address book. "There's no need to go all the way to Los Angeles. Airfare is outrageous, and you certainly can't drive a thousand miles in that car of yours."

"I'm not driving."

Olivia lowered the phone. "Then how—"

Her daughter looked her straight in the eye. "I'm flying with Shane Riley on a private jet."

"You're *what*?"

"I'm going to Los Angeles with Shane *as a friend*. And we're flying on a private plane, because he has a tryout with the Cougars."

Olivia's phone plummeted to her lap. She tried to speak, but nothing came out except a dull-witted "Uh..." She tried again and stammered. Olivia never stammered. But she couldn't find her tongue for the life of her.

A faint smile lifted Melissa's lips. "I feel the same way."

"I'm . . . stunned."

"It's amazing, isn't it? I was checking flights when Shane invited me to fly with him to L.A. The timing was perfect, so I said yes. I'll stay with my friend Lyn."

Olivia stated the obvious. "You two are dating."

"Not yet." Melissa paused. "But Mom? I like him. A lot. He's great with Cody. He's thoughtful and funny and just . . . good. We laugh at the same things. He understands me in a way no one ever has."

"Oh, Melissa." Olivia pushed her salad aside.

"What is it?"

"Men are . . . It's just . . . I can't . . ." More stammering. Olivia hated being unprepared. And worse, confused. And maybe wrong. As badly as she wanted to find fault with

Shane, she couldn't. His colleagues liked him, and his students respected him. The best character reference came from Cody, who adored him.

Olivia had to admit she liked him too. He was a younger version of Richard Connor, the one man she had loved since the divorce. She had met Rick three years ago when he joined the counseling staff. They'd been colleagues first, then friends. A widower with a passion for motorcycles, he dared her to test the limits of life, love, and her own courage.

Whirlwind memories spun through her mind. The motorcycle ride to Yellowstone, that first kiss, the words that followed.

"I love you, Livy."

"You can't love me! I'm seven years older than you."

"So what?"

That night they made love, a first for Olivia in twenty years, and she felt as if she were seventeen again. With Rick's encouragement, she didn't think past the moment, but in a few months her nerves were frayed. Her Christian faith was almost nonexistent then, but she had felt a vague unease about sex outside of marriage, especially with a man so different from herself. Rick drove too fast and dreamed of African safaris. She had no interest in seeing lions except at the zoo. When he asked her to marry him, she said no. Shortly after the break-up, he moved to Alaska. Sometimes late at night, she imagined calling him.

She still hurt because of that break-up, and she longed to protect her daughter now. "I just want you and Cody to be happy."

"I understand, Mom. I do. It's not easy being a parent."

"Definitely not." Olivia could hardly breathe. "I remember when you were little. I felt terrible that your father left. But we were still a family, weren't we?"

"Yes."

"So are you and Cody."

"We are." She hesitated, her brown eyes misty. "But I'd still like to find someone special and fall in love."

Thinking of Rick, Olivia dug for what little courage she had left. "I hope that happens."

"Thank you, Mom."

Pleased with her daughter's shy smile, Olivia dared to take the next step. "Cody would love a little brother." She imagined Star Wars toys and bicycles under the Christmas tree. "Or maybe a little girl. Wouldn't that be fun?"

Melissa paled, then took a ragged breath. "I have to tell you something else."

Olivia's stomach plummeted yet again. "What's wrong, sweetheart?"

"This isn't the first time I've had an abnormal pap. I have HPV. Five years ago, the pap came back positive for the earliest form of cervical cancer."

Olivia's hand flew to her heart. She couldn't breathe, let alone form words. "Oh, no."

"I'm okay. The cancer's gone."

She sucked in a single breath of air. *Take control. Ask questions.* But she couldn't move her mouth.

Melissa sighed. "Unfortunately, the virus keeps coming back. We're at the point where I *might* need a hysterectomy. That's the real reason I'm going to Los Angeles. I want to see Dr. Hong because she knows my history."

Olivia's whole body turned to stone. What did it say about a mother when her daughter chose to face cancer alone rather than confide in her? Was Olivia that demanding? Tears pressed behind her eyes, but they stopped short of the surface. Later she'd cry. Now she needed answers. "Tell me everything."

Melissa described the tests and treatments she'd undergone, including the most recent result. "That's why I have to see Dr. Hong. If she says a hysterectomy is necessary,

I can believe her."

Olivia wasn't so confident. "Where did she go to medical school? What's her training? There's so much at stake—"

"Mom, I know."

"We need a second opinion."

"She sent the last biopsy to a special research lab, and she consulted with other doctors in the practice."

Olivia heard the logic but couldn't process it. "There has to be more we can do."

"There isn't." Melissa paused, letting the words sink in. "Dr. Hong specializes in HPV. I trust her. Other doctors send their patients to *her*."

"Even so, you should see someone else."

"Mom, *please* don't start."

"Start what?"

"Second-guessing! Telling me what to do!" Melissa's hands flew into the air, her fingers as stiff as twigs. "I've lived with this a long time. Different pathologists have looked at the biopsies, and I've had the tests more than once. The sad truth is that I have a strain of HPV that causes cancer and is hard to remove. There's not a doctor in the world who can change that fact."

Olivia sputtered. "There could be new treatments. Another physician might have a completely different opinion."

"I'm seeing Dr. Hong. I trust her." Melissa's eyes blazed with defiance.

With her daughter's happiness, even her life, on the line, how could Olivia hold back? "At least consult with Dr. Edwards."

"No."

"Melissa—"

"It's my body, my decision."

"Of course, it is! But you're *my* daughter. I'm right

about this."

Melissa leaned forward, eyes blazing as she whispered, "Like you were right about giving up Cody?"

Olivia gasped.

"You pushed for adoption. Hard. What if I'd given him up? I can't imagine life without him. And if I need a hysterectomy—" Pressing her spine hard against the booth, she sealed her lips, a sign she was about to cry.

Olivia felt terrible. "Honey, I'm sorry."

Blinking furiously, Melissa forced words past her tight lips. "Cody might be my only child."

"Oh, honey."

"I know, I know." She shook her head, grimacing. "Adoption made sense at the time. It did. I know that, but something told me to keep him. To trust for the best. And I'm so glad I did."

"Oh yes, Melissa. Yes."

"I'm just as certain about seeing Dr. Hong."

Olivia studied her daughter's face. Instead of a stubborn girl or a rebellious teenager, she saw a younger version of herself—a woman facing the future with courage in spite of her fears. Olivia couldn't make Melissa's problems disappear the way she had when her daughter was three and afraid of caterpillars, but she could help in one small way.

She rummaged in her purse, then slid a Visa card across the table. "Take it."

"Why?"

"Because you're going to Los Angeles." Olivia couldn't verbalize her feelings. She'd only stammer again.

Melissa's eyes shone with pleasure. "Thank you, Mom. It's good to have in case of an emergency."

"And for fun. Buy something for Cody."

"I will."

"And for yourself." She yearned to do more, but what?

"Buy some fun clothes while you're there." A safe topic. "The shopping's much better in L.A. than here in Refuge."

"That's really nice. Thanks, Mom." Melissa slipped the card in her wallet. "I'm down to two pairs of jeans."

Normalcy returned in talk of clothes, shoes, and Olivia's hard-to-fit narrow feet. When they finished the meal, Melissa set a bulging manila envelope on the table. "I have something for you."

"What is it?"

"I found some letters from the 1890s. They're from a father to a daughter he called Little Miss. I'm wondering if she's in our family tree, maybe your great-grandmother. Have you heard of her?"

"The name's not familiar." Olivia resisted a comment about insipid nicknames. "I'll see what I can figure out."

"That would be nice. If I'm related to her, I'd like to know."

Olivia had taught social studies for ten years, but Melissa didn't usually share her interest in history. "Any particular reason?"

"Read the letters. You'll see."

"I'll be glad to." Olivia glanced at her watch. "I have to go." If she didn't hurry, she'd be late to a staff meeting.

Melissa piled their trash on the tray and dumped it. Olivia gathered her things, including the letters, and led the way to the sidewalk. A cold wind blew between them and mussed Melissa's hair but not Olivia's. Every strand stayed in place just the way she wanted, but today the style Melissa once called a "brown football helmet" felt heavy and old.

Maybe it was time for a change. Time to call Richard Connor, or do something shocking like travel to China.

Or maybe not. Olivia didn't like change, and Melissa's news threatened the worst changes a mother could imagine. With her eyes on Melissa and her windblown hair,

Olivia decided her football helmet fit just fine. After exchanging another awkward hug, the women went their separate ways.

Chapter 19

The day of the flight to L.A. dawned clear and bright. There wasn't a cloud in the November sky, only a cold, steady wind that chilled Shane to the bone as he carried his suitcase down the apartment stairs. Shivering, both from nerves and the cold, he put the luggage in the Tahoe next to his equipment bag.

MJ stepped onto the porch with a tote bag on her shoulder and her rolling suitcase in hand. "Good morning!" she called as she locked the door.

With her hair up and her eyelashes sporting mascara, she didn't look at all like Cody's mom. Instead of blue jeans, she wore black ones tucked into leather boots and a little zip-up jacket. His thoughts wandered to the pink bra he'd seen in her bathroom, but he forced the picture out of his mind. The tryout came first, then dinner to celebrate. He also planned to meet briefly with Troy and to talk to MJ's friend Lyn about Daisy.

He met MJ between the car and the porch, lifted the tote from her shoulder, and gripped the long handle of the suitcase.

"Are you nervous?" she asked.

"About flying? No."

"I meant the tryout." She tipped her face up to his. "I hope it's not bad luck to ask?"

"It's not." Luck and God had nothing to do with tomorrow. "I worked hard for this. I'm going to knock it out of the park." Confidence was half the battle for an athlete. His knee felt good this morning. Mostly.

On the way to the airport, they bantered about the trip. A valet parked his SUV and a skycap took their luggage. The pilot himself welcomed them on board, and they climbed into a cabin that resembled a living room. The eight overstuffed seats were arranged in two groups of four, with the front seats facing the tail and the rear seats facing the cockpit.

Shane and MJ took the seats closest to the tail. Minutes later they soared into the Wyoming sky. During the short hop to Denver, they sipped sparkling water, nibbled brunch-style hors d'oeuvres, and enjoyed a smooth flight.

In Denver the pilot taxied to a private terminal. He explained they'd be leaving immediately because of an incoming storm, so Shane and MJ stayed in the two back seats while the new passengers boarded.

Second baseman Dwight Allen climbed in first, saw Shane, and came over to shake his hand. Shane introduced MJ, and Dwight returned to the front. Next came Todd Rankoff, a relief pitcher with straight brown hair and beard scruff. A womanizer and a fan of Jack Daniels, he ignored Shane until he spotted MJ. A half-cocked smile pulled his mouth into a leer, and he ambled toward her.

Instinctively, Shane stood in the aisle. "Hello, Todd."

The pitcher swallowed a belch. "Whadaya know. It's Preacher Man."

Shane ignored the taunt. He'd have to get used to the digs, because they were sure to start up again during spring training.

But right now Todd was ogling MJ. "Hey there, beautiful."

Jerk. Shane would have enjoyed stuffing the words back down Todd's throat. Instead he rested a hand on MJ's shoulder. "Todd, this is MJ Townsend."

"Hello, Todd." She offered a mild nod. No handshake.

Todd waggled his brows at her. "What are you doing with a kid like Riley?"

The jerk's breath reeked of alcohol. If Todd thought Preacher Man would turn the other cheek, he was dead wrong. Shane's hand slid from MJ's shoulder and he stepped fully into the aisle, his eyes never leaving Todd's face. "Do you need help finding your seat? I believe it's up front."

The pitcher chortled, lurched to the front end of the cabin, and sat across from Dwight.

MJ leaned into Shane and whispered, "He's obnoxious."

Shane smiled at her until a deep voice boomed through the cabin. "Shane Riley!"

Manny Jackson, all-star center fielder, strode toward him, a megawatt smile on his dark face. Manny's wife, Rebecca, and their seven-year-old daughter, Kaylee, boarded behind him. Kaylee had cystic fibrosis and was the reason Manny, Dwight, and Todd had attended the CF fundraiser. Finding a cure for the disease was Manny's passion. For Dwight and Todd, the trip was an off-season junket.

A giant of a man, Manny hauled Shane into a back-slapping hug. "God bless you, brother. I'm praying for you."

"Thanks." He knew Manny was sincere, but Shane didn't want anyone's blessing, much less their prayers.

The Jackson family settled into the middle section. Rebecca and Kaylee took the seats directly in front of MJ and Shane. Manny sat across from his daughter in a seat facing the tail, which allowed for eye contact with Shane but no conversation.

Shane appreciated the distance. He wanted to concentrate on MJ and the tryout, not Manny and his prayers.

The first hour of the flight was as glorious as the leg from Refuge to Denver. They soared over the Rockies and skated over the Utah desert. Everything was perfect until the pilot's Texas drawl came over the PA.

"Sorry, folks. We expected to beat the storm to Burbank, but it picked up speed. We're in for some turbulence. Stay in your seats and buckle up."

MJ turned to Shane. "I hope it's not too bad."

"Scared?"

"Not really. Just . . ." She laughed. "Let's just say I'm well aware that we're 30,000 feet in the air."

"We're only at 24,000."

She waved her hand. "Well then, never mind. If it's only 24,000—" The plane hit an air pocket, a big one. They dropped like a runaway elevator.

Manny called out, "Whoa, there."

Whimpering, Kaylee reached across the aisle for her mother. Rebecca Jackson gripped her daughter's hand and held it.

When the plane swayed from side to side, Shane turned to MJ with an apologetic smile. "Make that 22,000 feet."

"Or twenty," she said drily.

The Learjet dipped and banked to avoid the thunderheads billowing all around it. Rain pelted the windows, and lightning flashed between the gray clouds, filling the sky with jagged prongs of light. Both beautiful and terrifying, the storm tossed the plane as if it were a toy.

Todd cursed at every bump. Kaylee's frightened shrieks rose above the drone of the engines, and Rebecca and Todd used their airsickness bags. Between their gagging and the stench of vomit, Shane felt a tad bit ill himself—more than a tad.

MJ moaned. "I'm not feeling so good."

"Me either." Nausea humbled a man. Shane resented it, both the sickness and the humbling. Refusing to give in, he sat ramrod straight.

MJ took her airsickness bag out of the seat pocket and laid it in her lap. "Just in case."

The plane shuddered and plummeted yet again. Everyone screamed—man, woman, and child. Cold sweat slicked Shane's skin. He glanced at MJ and saw her pasted against the seat with her eyes closed and her mouth moving in what he assumed was a prayer.

A flash of light strobed through the cabin, followed by a deafening boom and long rolls of thunder. The interior lights flickered but stayed on.

The captain's brusque voice droned over the loud speaker. "Lightning strike, folks. We're fine."

The plane dipped yet again.

"Daddy!" Kaylee pleaded. "Make it stop."

"I can't, baby." Manny's voice cracked. "God knows I would if I could."

Todd dropped an f-bomb, then broke out in drunken laughter. "Hey, Preacher Man? Why aren't you praying for my soul?"

Manny glared over his shoulder at Todd. "Shut up, Rankoff! I got my kid with me."

Todd cursed again.

Shane knew exactly how the pitcher felt. He wanted to curse at the turbulence, the fear, the stench of vomit. Mostly he wanted to cry out at the suffering of seven human beings, infant-like in their need, each afraid of death and puking, and helpless to change their fate. What kind of Father did this to his children? *What is the point?*

MJ gripped the airsickness bag, her face pale and her mouth rigid. Kaylee's sobs bounced off the rounded walls of the fuselage. Over and over, she begged her daddy to make the plane land right now.

"Riley!" Manny's voice boomed. "Pray with me."

The outfielder didn't know about Shane's loss of faith. MJ did, but she looked at him with a plea in her eyes, her face ashen and tight. Shane didn't want to be a hypocrite—not again. But Kaylee's terror crawled into his chest, and he chose hypocrisy over the cruelty of denying comfort to a child. He signaled Manny with a nod, then bowed his head.

The outfielder prayed first. In a big, booming voice that rose above the noise, Manny confessed his weakness, begged God for mercy, then claimed victory and grace with a statement of faith. "You control the wind, Lord. You control the stars and seas. Lord Jesus, we trust you with our bodies, our souls, and our loved ones." Manny ended the prayer with a loud "In Jesus' name," a sign for Shane to begin.

He forced familiar words through his clenched teeth. "Father God, in a storm like this one, you calmed the waves for your disciples." *So why didn't you stop that deer in Malibu Canyon?* "You kept them safe." *But you didn't keep me safe—or Daisy, either.* "We ask you to calm the storm now, especially for Kaylee." *A child . . . a sick, helpless child. How could you do this to her?*

Shane's jaw throbbed, but he managed the final

words. "Lord, we ask for peace of mind, mercy, and a safe landing. Amen."

MJ, Manny, Rebecca, and Kaylee echoed him. Shane tasted bile and snatched the airsickness bag from the seat pocket in front of him. He managed to control the nausea but not the rage. Eyes forward, he didn't see MJ reach across the aisle to cover his hand with hers, but he felt the warmth of her touch. He didn't want her to comfort him. He wanted to be the strong one, so he turned his hand to cradle her fingers, claiming control he didn't have.

The dips eased. So did the nauseating horizontal sway. Rain continued to spatter the windows, but gradually the flight leveled out.

The pilot came on the P.A. "The worst is over, folks. We'll be on the ground in twenty minutes."

No one spoke as they banked toward Bob Hope Airport in Burbank. Eventually the jet dropped out of the clouds, wobbling occasionally until it touched down with the grace of a ballerina, then taxied through the rain to the terminal. The Jackson family exited with Manny carrying Kaylee and Rebecca clutching his muscular arm.

Todd followed the Jacksons without giving Shane a glance, but Dwight stopped to clap him on the shoulder. "Good luck tomorrow."

"Thanks."

Dwight picked his way down the steps, leaving Shane alone with MJ. "How are you feeling?"

"Not so hot."

"Nauseated?"

"Yes, but mostly I'm just—" She shook her head. "Let's get out of here."

She walked to the door, then down the steps where a steward waited with a big black umbrella. Shane took her hand and together they hurried into the terminal.

Manny was hugging his wife and daughter in a far

corner of the waiting area. Todd had disappeared, and Dwight was on his phone bragging to someone that he had just cheated death.

MJ indicated the ladies' room. "I'll be right back."

Shane squeezed her hand and let go. As she passed the Jacksons, Manny set Kaylee down and walked over to Shane.

They traded remarks about the miserable flight, then Manny let out a low whistle. "There's nothing like a brush with death to make a man count his blessings."

"I guess."

"You guess?" Manny drew up to his full height. "That doesn't sound like Preacher Man to me."

"I'm all right."

Manny's dark eyes burned a hole in him. "I don't want to hear that fake happy talk, Riley. How are you doing really?"

"The knee's good." Shane put extra confidence in his voice. "The tryout's tomorrow."

"I didn't ask about the knee."

Shane considered dodging again, but Manny's middle name was persistence. "Things have been tough since the accident. Preacher Man retired."

"*Retired?*" Manny's big right hand clamped down on Shane's shoulder. "What kind of nonsense is that? Christians don't *retire*. They get lost, and they get found. They get knocked to their knees, and they stand up again."

What could Shane say to that? Manny got knocked down every time his little girl went to the hospital, and he always stood back up. Shane's bad knee, even his career, were petty compared to a child with a life-threatening illness.

"So," Manny said, lifting his hand, "what's got you in a twist?"

A man's voice came from the side. "Mr. Jackson?"

Shane and Manny turned to the team representative, an intern named Jeff, who advised Manny his limo was waiting. Manny nodded, then turned to Shane. "I wouldn't let this go, but my little girl needs to get home. Call me anytime. Day or night."

Shane nodded but said nothing.

Manny guided his wife and daughter to a Lincoln Town Car. A few minutes later, MJ emerged from the ladies' room, steady on her feet and wearing fresh lipstick.

"Feeling better?" he asked.

"Much."

Jeff approached them with a key fob. "I have your car, Mr. Riley."

Shane planned to take MJ to Lyn's apartment in West L.A., then drive back across town to the Crowne Drake. He accepted the key fob from Jeff. "We're headed to Santa Monica. How's the traffic?"

"At a standstill. A mudslide closed the 405."

MJ laid her hand on his arm. "It'll take hours to get to Lyn's. I'll rent a car and drive myself."

Shane saw a far better solution. He asked Jeff to give them a moment, then he focused on MJ. "Stay with me at the Drake. Two rooms, just to be clear."

She made a small humming sound, a sign she was thinking about it. Not a yes or a no. A maybe.

"There's no way I'll let you drive alone to Lyn's. It'll take hours, and you have to be exhausted."

"I am." Her voice came out shaky. "I'm okay with the hotel, but I have to be somewhere in the morning."

"What time?"

"Nine o'clock."

"Where?"

"Santa Monica."

He wondered where in Santa Monica but didn't ask. The tryout was at one o'clock, so he had plenty of time to take her. "If I drop you off, can Lyn pick you up?"

"Let's find out." She called Lyn, made new arrangements, and smiled at him when she finished. "It's all set. I'll pay for my room."

"No, you won't." If the Cougars didn't spring for it, he would. Before she could argue, he signaled Jeff.

Phone in hand, the intern approached. "Yes, Mr. Riley?"

"Would you add a second room to my reservation?"

While Jeff made the call, Shane went to the men's room. When he returned, MJ was on the phone to her mother saying they'd landed safely.

Jeff approached him. "I texted your confirmation numbers, sir. You have two rooms on the same floor compliments of the Cougars."

The intern led them to the front of the terminal, where Shane saw a red Dodge Challenger. The sleek lines put his SUV to shame, and for a moment he recalled happily cruising through Malibu Canyon in his Mustang, blasting music, and replaying that night's game in his head. But then the deer leaped in front of him and he'd instinctively swerved.

The past and present kaleidoscoped into flashes of light, rain, breaking glass, and the crunch of metal. His stomach did a flip, rattling nerves still frayed from the flight.

Get a grip, he told himself.

Inhaling deeply, he waited while Jeff loaded their bags in the trunk, then helped MJ into the passenger's seat. Shane slid behind the wheel and pressed the Start button. The engine roared with muscle car power, and his nerves settled.

MJ ran her hands over the leather seat. "This sure beats the Bonneville."

"Let the fun begin." Grinning, he adjusted the mirrors,

put the radio on a rock station, and accelerated into traffic. The tires hissed on the wet pavement, and palm trees swayed in the gusting wind. The storm showed no sign of letting up, but he didn't care. They were together on the ground in a fast car, headed to a first-class hotel and a night alone.

MJ rested her hand on the center console, her fingers tapping to the pulsing beat of the music. Shane covered her hand with his, warming away the chill, then warming even more when she matched their palms and laced her fingers with his. They rode like that—touching and close— for several minutes.

"Shane?" Her voice came out husky.

"Yeah?" His came out even huskier.

"What you said on the plane—that prayer—it was beautiful."

Acid flooded his stomach. That prayer had been a lie. "I did it for Kaylee."

"It helped me, too."

If she had been comforted, fine. But his back teeth clenched so hard that his jaw throbbed. He gave the car a little more gas, but the traffic kept him in check. Frustrated, he looked for a break between the cars and found it. "Let's cut through Griffith Park."

"Good idea."

A mile later, he steered into an oasis of trees and shrubs in the middle of the city, the home of the L.A. Zoo and a world-famous observatory. Animals and the cosmos—a paradoxical tribute to the mysteries of nature— mysteries he wanted to explore with MJ without God telling him what to do and what not to do.

Shane's nerves started to settle. But two miles into the park, a box truck sped around a curve and rode the double yellow line. The headlight beams smacked Shane in the face, and a thick fan of water slapped the windshield, blinding him.

MJ gasped and pushed back in the seat. Shane cursed under his breath and swerved to the right, just missing a ditch as the car fish-tailed. Once. Twice. Finally it steadied.

Pulse pounding, he snapped off the radio. "Are you okay?"

"I—I'm fine. It's just—just—"

"Too much."

"Yes."

Bile burned in the back of his throat. "I've had enough."

"Me too."

A sign indicated a picnic area, and he turned onto a winding road that led to a grassy circle filled with ghostly tables and black trash cans. Eucalyptus trees blocked most of the wind but not all of it. Leaves rattled and a branch snapped.

Shane cut the engine, slumped against the bucket seat, and squeezed the back of his neck.

MJ touched his arm. "Shane?"

"I'm all right."

He heard the click of her seatbelt, the scrape of her denim-clad legs on the seat. She touched his jaw, urging him to face her. When he did, he wanted to kiss her— needed to kiss her to chase away the fear, his vulnerability, the weakness of being human. Rain pounded the roof of the car. Thunder rolled in the distance—and in his chest. With their gazes locked, he cupped the back of her head, splayed his fingers in her hair, and kissed her deeply, without hesitation or doubt.

MJ matched him breath for breath, taste for taste. The windows fogged to make a cocoon of sorts, hiding them from the world. Slowly, very slowly, giving her time to tell him to stop, he trailed kisses down her jaw to the silky skin of her neck, then to the soft throb at the base of her throat. His hand touched the zipper of her jacket. To unzip or not?

She jerked away, her eyes wide and her breath coming in puffs. "I can't do this. I'm not— I can't—"

Shane battled through a thick sexual fog. "I thought—"

"I am *so* sorry." She buried her face in her hands.

Why had she apologized? She'd been eager, even encouraging. If she had hesitated at all, he would have taken her lead and eased off. She turned to the passenger window, giving him her back. He let her hide but stroked her arm. "What's wrong?"

She turned back to him, her eyes bleak.

Her remorse didn't make sense—unless she was full of Christian guilt over being tempted. Shane knew that kind of guilt well. What he didn't understand was why God made sex so desirable, then told human beings to control themselves. The battle wearied every man Shane knew, married and single. It certainly wearied him, especially now—with MJ's kiss on his lips.

He'd endured all the mystery he could stand, so he simply asked the question. "Is this because you're a Christian?"

"Yes."

He forced himself to sound matter-of-fact, not disappointed, though he was. "Like I said, I respect your faith. You're being honest."

"Oh, Shane—" She stared at him like a trapped animal. "I'm *not* being honest. I had a plan, but it's too late."

"Too late for what?"

She squared her shoulders in a way that reminded him of Cody holding a baseball bat. "This is hard to admit, but after that kiss, you need to know. I have HPV."

Shane's teammates joked about HPV in the locker room. They made crude remarks about women who had it and secretly visited dermatologists to seek treatment for themselves. Tongue-tied, he stared at her. "Are you saying you have—uh—"

"I have human papillomavirus. It's incredibly common. As common as a cold. It causes—" Her eyes closed as if to hide her shame.

"Warts," he finished for her.

"Some strains do. Not all." She looked up, her shame naked and exposed by the sheen of tears. "The worst strains cause cervical cancer. I don't have warts, but I have the worst kind."

"You have *cancer*?"

"I *had* it," she clarified. "I was diagnosed right after having Cody. Dr. Hong caught it early, but it keeps coming back. That's where I'm going tomorrow morning—to follow up with Dr. Hong."

Shane couldn't think, couldn't move. Then it hit him. MJ had a serious health problem, one that affected every breath she took. "Are you okay?"

"Maybe."

"I don't understand."

"A few months ago, I had another abnormal pap result. Dr. Hong's repeating the test tomorrow. If it's positive, she'll recommend a hysterectomy."

In all his salmon-like desire, not once had Shane imagined infections, cancer, even infertility. Repulsed and angry at the unfairness, he took a slow breath. "I don't know what to say."

"It's all right." The words rushed off her tongue. "I understand. For Cody's sake, I hope we can still be friends."

"Of course."

"Well. Now you know."

She refastened her seatbelt; so did Shane. He started to drive away, but how could he leave with so much unsaid? Churning inside, he jammed the transmission into park and faced her. "I want you to know, I heard everything you said. I just don't know what to say back."

"You don't have to say anything. It's all right," she said for the second time.

"It's *not* all right."

"It has to be."

"It's *not*." His voice rose to a near shout. "It's so *wrong* I don't know where to start."

"So don't."

"But—"

"I want to go to the hotel." Lips tight, she faced forward, hiding her face from his stare but not her clenched jaw. She blinked hard and fast, no doubt fighting tears.

If she started to cry, he'd have to hold her, comfort her. She didn't have leprosy or AIDS, but he had to be honest. The thought of warts, especially warts *down there*, disgusted him. At the same time, he cared about her. And Cody—Shane adored the boy.

"All right," he finally said. "We'll go to the hotel, but we're not done. There's more to this than you know."

"Like what?"

"I don't know exactly."

She stared through a porthole on the windshield, the work of the defroster. "You don't have to be *nice* about it. If I were you, I wouldn't want anything to do with me. I'm a single mom. I have an STI—"

"MJ, stop."

"My life's a mess."

"Stop it. Please." She was killing him. "The tryout's tomorrow. I can't do this right now."

"So let's drop it."

He couldn't stand the hurt in her eyes, the bitter words, or the self-hatred in her voice. Needing to fix things, at least a little, he brushed a tender kiss on her cheek.

MJ jerked her head to the side as if she'd been slapped.

Defeated, he put the car in gear and made a wide turn. The headlights swept through the trees and illuminated picnic tables that resembled lifeboats, out of reach and in danger of sinking. He cleared his throat, then realized whatever he said would make the situation worse. Trapped in silence, they drove to the Crowne Drake and went to their separate rooms.

Chapter 20

*D*aisy couldn't go to the pier in the pouring rain, so she entertained herself in Lyn's office, editing the seagull pictures she had snapped yesterday. The used camera she'd bought from Mary's Closet delighted her. She didn't have to think or plan when she took pictures at the beach. She simply waited for something to catch her eye.

She liked being spontaneous in that way. Making decisions upset her, and so did the prospect of seeing Shane. He was in Los Angeles and wanted to see her.

Three weeks ago, Lyn had asked Daisy into her office and closed the door. "Do you believe in luck?"

Daisy said no.

"Neither do I." That's when Lyn had told her about the call from someone named MJ, who lived in Wyoming and knew Shane. Lyn called it serendipity. "I have to wonder if God's trying to tell you something."

God . . . Her Higher Power . . . The empty chair that listened to her and somehow made her feel loved.

Was Lyn right? Was it time to face her brother? In an hour or so, he'd step through the door with the woman named MJ. Daisy had to decide—surprise him or avoid him. Lyn said the choice was hers. *"Too many people have robbed you of the right to choose. Whatever you decide, I'll support you."*

But that was the problem. Daisy hated making decisions, because she always made the wrong one.

Lyn walked into the office, her phone in hand. "That was MJ. You have a reprieve."

"What happened?"

"A mudslide closed the 405. She's staying at the hotel with your brother, so you have another twenty-four hours."

Daisy slumped against the chair. "So I don't have to decide right now?"

"Not yet."

Sighing, she studied the seagull on the screen. Perched on a wooden rail, the bird stood with its wings spread wide, ready to take flight. She cropped an inch from the bottom, decided it was too much, and undid the change. "I wish I had an undo button for my life."

"In a way, we do." Lyn pulled up a chair next to Daisy. "Christ wiped the slate clean for us."

Daisy didn't know what to think. She liked going to the Bible study at Maggie's House, but the talk about sin and forgiveness sounded too much like Shane. Why should she forgive him? He'd been horrible to her. As for needing forgiveness herself, Daisy knew she was trash. What she didn't understand was why God cared.

She stared at the seagull but didn't really see it. "You think I should see him, don't you?"

"What I think doesn't matter, but I have to wonder if God's nudging you to talk to him."

But what if Shane acted all superior? How would she feel? Would she fall off the wagon and drink? But what if he had changed? She knew about his knee injury, but until Lyn heard from MJ, Daisy assumed he had rejoined the Cougars. Nothing ever went wrong for Shane—until now. Daisy almost felt sorry for him.

Shuddering, she thought of the boys in the garage and focused back on the seagull.

"Finish your picture." Lyn stood and patted Daisy on the shoulder. "Then we'll go to a meeting."

Daisy printed the photograph and framed it. Mary's Closet sold her work on consignment, which Lyn said made her a professional photographer, a dream that had begun when she was a little girl visiting artisan shows with her mom. Should she confront Shane? Maybe, but she wanted a drink so bad her hands shook. *A day at a time . . . A minute at a time when necessary.* She carried the photograph into the thrift shop and displayed it among the souvenirs.

Lyn came up to her again, her gaze on the picture. "I wonder if that's the gull that pooped on me."

Daisy laughed. "Maybe."

"I'm still trying to forgive that stupid bird. It's not easy when someone does that to you."

"No. But the bird didn't mean it."

"Exactly."

They were talking about Shane and Daisy knew it. The bird hadn't meant to poop on Lyn, but Shane had deliberately hurt Daisy. He had betrayed her in that filthy storeroom, and he'd let the social worker take her away. He'd stopped surprising her with Fig Newtons and started pelting her with Bible verses that made her feel weak, dirty, and unloved.

Like right now. She couldn't think straight. "I just don't know what to do."

"This decision is yours," Lyn repeated. "But God just might be opening a door for you."

"I just don't know," she said yet again. Thinking about Shane made her feel stupid. Now she sounded stupid, too.

"Do you trust me?"

"You know I do."

"Then let's do this. MJ expects to introduce me to Shane. I'll meet him first and tell you what I think. It's your job to pray about it. How's that?"

Daisy gave a rueful chortle. "Right now I just want a drink, but I guess that's all right."

Lyn looped an arm around her waist and hugged her. "Let's go to the AA meeting."

While Lyn locked her office, Daisy dawdled in front of the display of seagull paperweights like the one in her bedroom. She and the plastic birds were trapped, but the real ones lived a day at a time. She'd keep that in mind as she considered what to do about Shane.

Shane stood at the window of his room at the Crown Drake, his arms crossed over his chest. The rain had stopped hours ago, and the clouds had departed, leaving behind a velvet black sky. Twenty-nine floors below, headlights reflected white on the damp pavement. Across from him, skyscrapers formed a glittering mosaic of silver, black, and white. The stars were pinpricks and pale by comparison.

He needed to hit the sack, but he couldn't stop

thinking about MJ. They hadn't exchanged a word since the elevator ride when he suggested dinner together. She had declined with a polite, "No, thank you," and escaped to her room down the hall.

Should he call her? Send a text? Knock on her door and . . . what then?

"Idiot," he muttered. If he didn't get his mind off her, he'd bomb tomorrow for sure. She wouldn't want that for him, and he sure didn't want it for himself.

If he held his glove, maybe he could focus. He crossed the room to his equipment bag, opened it, and smacked into a crayon drawing of two stick figures wearing Cougars blue baseball caps. Cody's printing leaped off the page. *Dear Shane, good luck. Your frend, Cody.* "Friend" needed an "i," which made the picture even more endearing.

If the tryout went as Shane hoped, he'd tape the drawing inside his locker and treasure it every day. But what about MJ? His gaze shot to his phone charging on the nightstand. *Pick it up. Say something. Anything.* He scrubbed his jaw with his hand, searched for words, but couldn't come up with a thing.

Later, he promised himself. After the tryout, he could focus solely on her.

He reached back in the bag for his glove. Instead of leather, his fingers grazed the edge of an envelope. Lifting it, he saw his name in MJ's loopy cursive and opened the card. The front showed a cross-eyed cat in a baseball uniform, hanging by its claws from a chin-up bar. Inside was a joke about cats having nine lives, plus a note from MJ:

Dear Shane,

   I hope you find this before the tryout. Cody and I are your biggest fans—and not just because you play baseball. You've been a wonderful friend to both of us.

Cody's needs are simple. Pizza. Playing catch. Just hanging out. My life is more complicated. That's why I asked you for a month before we went on an official date. When we have dinner tonight, I'll tell you why I needed the extra time. I hope you'll understand. The situation is painful to me.

You're going to do great today! I wish I could be there to cheer for you.

Hugs, MJ

If he'd read the card before that moment in the car, he would have been prepared. Instead he had squirmed away from her like a worm. But who could blame him? Warts were disgusting, and hysterectomies were forever.

He dropped the card in the bag, sat on the fluffy bed, and hung his head. HPV repulsed him, which meant a piece of MJ repulsed him. What did that say about the new and improved Shane Riley—the man who didn't judge people? Not much. And nothing good.

Manny's words echoed in his mind. *"Christians get lost and they get found."*

But Shane didn't *want* to be found. He didn't want to calm down and pray. He was *stinking* furious at God— mad enough to snatch the TV remote in his throwing hand and hurl it against the wall. It hit hard, broke into pieces, and scattered across the brown carpet. Still furious, he paced back to the window, thumped his palms against the glass, and stared down at the cars crawling in a preset pattern of right turns . . . or wrong ones.

"Why?" The word scraped at his throat.

Nothing made sense to him. *Nothing.* Not the accident, not HPV. If God was listening, Shane wanted answers.

"Why the accident, the pain, and every *stinking* minute at the gym?" He spat each word. "You destroyed my career. I can't find Daisy. She could be an addict, selling her body, even dead!"

An oath shot off his tongue. He was on a roll and complained about everything, even ending up in Wyoming, the emptiest state in America. Except he'd met MJ in Wyoming—a woman who cheered for him, believed in him, and somehow filled him with hope. She was beautiful inside and out. He'd been blessed—*blessed*—by a woman who cared about him and a boy who thought he walked on water.

He didn't. He knew that now. His breath steadied, and his thoughts raced to the next step. *Father, forgive me. I have sinned.* And harder still to say, *Thy will be done.*

If he spoke those words, his career would be on an altar much like the one where Abraham had offered Isaac. Shane knew the story well. When Abraham departed for the mountain, his beloved son at his side, he told Sarah, "We'll be back."

We. Abraham had trusted God to make it right, but Shane had no such trust.

"I can't do it," he muttered. "*I just can't.*"

A knock sounded on the door. Startled, he crossed the room and opened it. MJ stood there waiflike in jeans and that cute jacket, her expression guarded as she gripped the handle of her suitcase. "I'm leaving. Lyn's meeting me downstairs."

"MJ, I—"

She shook her head. "Good luck tomorrow."

"But—"

"I have to go." She turned and fled down the hall, her suitcase rolling behind her and reminding him of Daisy leaving the Harpers. He grabbed his card key and followed, barefoot in his lucky sweats and a white T-shirt, but he didn't feel lucky. He stepped in front of her, blocking her way to the bank of elevators.

She looked at him with those hollow, empty eyes.

"What is it?"

Kiss her . . . Hold her close. But what then? Until he figured out where he stood, both with God and her condition, he had nothing to offer except a toxic brew of self-pity, anger, and confusion. Disgusted with himself, he stepped out of her way. "I'll call you tomorrow."

"After the tryout."

"Yes."

She headed down the hall, the suitcase rolling behind her. As he watched her go, he wanted more than anything to love her the way she deserved. But he couldn't—not when he hated himself and couldn't find God. Head down, he went to his room and closed the door.

MJ stepped into the elevator and faced forward. She didn't expect to see Shane as the doors closed and she didn't. She saw only herself in the mirrored panel, pale and grim in spite of washing her face twice. She slumped against the back wall, bracing herself as the elevator plummeted to the lobby. Her stomach didn't keep up, and she thought of the awful flight, the awful drive, and that awful kiss on the cheek.

The elevator slowed. The doors slid open, and she spotted Lyn. They hugged tight, and in minutes they were in Lyn's Camry and headed for the Santa Monica Freeway.

MJ slouched against the seat. "Thanks for picking me up."

"Do you want to talk about it?"

"No." She didn't even want to *think* about what had happened.

Tomorrow she'd visit Dr. Hong, get her test results late in the day, and fly home alone using her mother's credit card. The ticket would be expensive, but she didn't care.

All that mattered was avoiding Shane, that disgusted look in his eyes, and the pain of being oh so gently kicked to the curb.

Chapter 21

E quipment bag in hand, Shane strode into the club house at Cougar Stadium. Even empty, the locker room smelled of wood and leather, bleached towels, sweat, and traces of expensive aftershave. He recalled Craig pranking him with shaving cream in his hat and smiled.

The discipline of being an athlete kept him from thinking too much about MJ, but as he walked to the locker that used to be his, he thought of Cody's drawing and winced. Blowing out a slow breath, he set his bag down, eyed the practice jersey waiting for him, then walked down the hall to Ricky's office.

The manager came around the desk and offered his hand. "Good to see you, Shane."

"Likewise."

Ray Blaine, tall and slightly balding, rose from his seat in front of Ricky, and they moved to a sitting area with comfortable leather chairs. Steve Whittie, the head trainer, joined them.

Ray got down to business. "We want you back, Shane. But we're worried about the knee."

"I understand."

Steve relaxed in the leather seat, his fingers steepled over his chest. "You and I worked for three months, and the knee didn't regain the stability you need for third base. How is it now?"

"It's strong, and I have full range of motion. Though I'll admit it aches in bad weather."

As Shane hoped, the men chuckled at the familiar lament of anyone with an injury. He relaxed, but just a little. At Steve's request, he described his workout regimen. The trainer told him that if he did well today, he'd be sent to a sports medicine specialist in Century City for motion analysis.

No surprise there. But at the mention of a specialist, his mind wandered to MJ seeing Dr. Hong.

The men rose from their seats. Shane went to the locker room, put on the practice uniform, and laced up his cleats. Glove in hand, he jogged to the field where Ray and Ricky waited with Javier Rodriguez, Tom Kenner, and Bart Alberts, members of the coaching staff.

Ricky indicated home plate. "Let's see you sprint to first."

Shane hustled to the plate. Eyes straight ahead, he ran for his life to first base. The knee felt good—very good. He sprinted to first again, rounded the corner, and headed for second, third, then home. In a gutsy move, he went into a slide. Red dirt flying, he jumped to his feet and turned to Ricky and the coaches, all watching him with raised eyebrows.

He barely held in a grin. "What next?"

Ricky tossed him his glove. "Take third."

Shane and the coaches assumed their positions. Julio, a retired Hall of Fame pitcher, selected a ball from a bucket on the mound. Shane hunkered into a crouch at third, his eyes on Tom at the plate, as the pitch smacked off the bat. Shane snagged it one-handed and threw with pinpoint accuracy to Bart at first.

For the next half hour, he dove for grounders and leaped for line drives. He threw bullets to first base as effortlessly as he breathed. Ricky and Ray watched every throw, every step, every bend of the bad knee. Shane didn't hesitate. Not once. But every time he crouched, his knee hurt a little more.

Ignore it. Pain is part of the game. But the joint started to wobble. Three plays later, the wobble morphed into a steady shake. If he wasn't careful, the knee would collapse and he'd fall, possibly injuring the ligaments all over again.

He signaled Ricky that he needed a break, took off his cap, and wiped the sweat from his brow. He smelled the red clay and lush grass. He relived the cheering crowds and the satisfaction of a perfect throw. He thought of friends, locker room jokes, and the thrill of a close game. A lump shoved into his throat and refused to budge.

Ricky's baritone broke the spell. "You look great, Shane. Let's see you hit."

He jogged to the plate, his knee throbbing. In his mind he heard the announcer call his name. *"Number 17 . . . Shaaaaaaane Riiiiiley."* And in his heart, he accepted the bitter truth.

No way could he play nine full innings.

This at-bat would be his last.

Home plate gleamed white against the clay. He

imagined the stands filled with cheering fans, picked up his bat, and took some practice cuts. Savoring every detail—the balanced swing, the power in his chest and legs— he walked to the plate, dug in his spikes, and stared hard at Javier on the mound.

The pitcher met his stare, wound up, and sizzled a fastball right down the middle. Wood smacked cowhide, and the ball flew like a bird, high and out of sight, until it dropped into the centerfield bleachers, counting for nothing but giving Shane the dignity of a noble end. He longed to run the bases but couldn't. His knee hurt too much.

Head high, he walked over to Ricky and Ray, giving in to a limp. "Thanks for the chance, but my knee's shot."

Ricky jammed his hands in his back pockets. "Man, I'm sorry. You looked great out there."

Ray offered his hand. "You've got skills, Shane. I wish it had worked out."

"Yeah. Me too."

After a final look around the stadium, he retreated to the locker room, iced his knee, and popped ibuprofen. After a quick shower, he dressed in the khakis and blue oxford shirt he often wore in the classroom. On Monday he'd be Mr. Riley again, a thought that brought more solace than he expected.

Keys in hand, he climbed into the Challenger, drove to the Crowne Drake, and checked out. He didn't want to be there without MJ, so he drove toward his Marina del Rey apartment. It was a fitting retreat—the place where he had licked his wounds after the accident. But he didn't want to go back to that time. He wanted to go forward—*needed* to go forward—so he drove past the white stucco apartment complex to Venice Beach at the end of Washington Boulevard.

He paid the attendant to park, found a space that faced the wide expanse of sand, and cut the engine. The ocean rumbled in the distance, wave after wave, echoing the pounding in his chest. What was the point of the past six months—except to break him? It had worked. All that remained was to bury the old Shane once and for all.

He yanked off his shoes and socks, shoved his wallet and phone in the glove box, then hid the key fob in the wheel well. With the breeze ruffling his hair, he headed for the water, the warm sand sifting between his toes until he reached the water's edge.

A wave crested, broke, and raced toward him. Chilly water washed over his ankles, tugging at his khakis and drawing him forward as it receded. The next wave engulfed his knees, reversed itself, and dragged him past any sign of solid ground. Ninety feet away—the distance between third base and home plate—a wave higher than his head gathered momentum. It rose higher, higher still. And the water pulled him closer, closer still.

Arms raised, he finished the prayer he'd started in the hotel room. "Father God, your will be done."

The wave knocked him back and he went under. Water whooshed in his ears, lifted him, and spun him around in slow motion.

Seven years ago, he'd been dunked in a church baptismal, a hot tub really. The pastor had reminded him to hold his nose, then lowered and raised him in one smooth motion. That day, Shane had come up sputtering and full of joy. Today there were no strong arms to lift him, and he'd forgotten to hold his nose. But he broke the surface exactly as he had in the church baptismal—full of joy.

Staggering to his feet, he pumped his fists in the air and shouted "Yes!" Laughter bubbled out of him as he sloshed to the shore and kicked through dry sand to the car. In about five minutes, he'd be an itching mess because of the salt. As for the sand, well, it was everywhere.

He retrieved the key fob, spread a towel from his gym

bag over the driver's seat, and drove to his apartment, mulling the things he wanted to do. First, a hot shower. Second, a text to Manny to thank him for his prayers. And third and most pressing, a face-to-face apology to MJ for failing to love her the way Jesus loved them both.

After the shower and the text to Manny, he scrolled to MJ's caller ID, savored the smiling photograph, and prayed she'd forgive him. Ready to grovel, he called her.

She answered on the second ring, her voice both dull and stern as she said hello.

He didn't waste a breath. "I messed up so bad yesterday I can't believe it. Forgive me. Please."

"There's no need. You were honest. That's all." Her voice came out flat and impersonal. "I only took the call to tell you I'm flying home alone."

"MJ, no."

"It's for the best."

"No. It's not—not for you *or* for us." He paced in front of the couch. "I am so sorry for how I reacted in the car. I was an idiot. If I'd thought for two seconds—"

"Forget it."

"I can't. Where are you?"

"With Lyn."

"Let me pick you up. We'll have dinner."

"No." Her chilly voice shivered through the phone. "I have things to do. You're off the hook."

No way. If salmon could fight their way upstream, so could he. "I don't want off the hook. And you promised me one dinner, remember? Please, MJ. I need to talk to you. It's been a . . . a crazy day."

"The tryout—"

"I bombed. My playing days are over, but that's not why I have to see you. This is about us—and God."

She paused for six beats of his heart. "All right. You can meet Lyn. We're at the Denny's on Washington."

"I'll be there in ten minutes."

Before she could argue, he ended the call and drove to the coffee shop in record time. When he pushed through the glass door, he spotted MJ and a woman he presumed to be Lyn in a booth by the window.

"Is that him?" Lyn asked.

MJ glanced over her shoulder just as Shane whipped off his Ray-Bans. They locked eyes, and in a single blink, that soul-stirring kiss in the car pulsed back to life. She wanted to hate him for what had followed but couldn't. Who wouldn't be repulsed by an STI? Even MJ was repulsed—and it was her body.

She moved to Lyn's side of the booth, being careful to put her purse on the seat where Shane wouldn't see her phone lying on top. Any minute Dr. Hong would call with the test results—a biopsy and not just a pap because of a suspicious spot. Dr. Hong, aware of MJ's travel situation, had ordered the results stat from the in-house lab.

Shane strode past the empty tables to their booth in the back. MJ almost stood and hugged him, but common sense—and self-preservation—prevailed. For Cody's sake, they needed to remain friends. For hers, they couldn't be anything more.

He laid his hand on her shoulder, forcing her to look up. The determined glint in his eyes softened into a sheepish twinkle that begged her to smile. "I really am sorry."

"I know you are." But it didn't matter now—not with the biopsy hanging over her head. "And I'm sorry about the tryout."

"Thanks. It was quite an experience." He turned his attention to Lyn and offered his hand. "Shane Riley. You must be Lyn."

"I am." She accepted the handshake at an awkward angle.

Even more awkward for MJ, Lyn's tone could have frozen water, a surprise because Lyn typically made everyone feel welcome.

Shane indicated the empty seat. "May I?"

"Of course," Lyn replied.

Just as his hips hit the vinyl, MJ's phone blasted circus music. She saw Dr. Hong's ID, leaped to her feet, and hurried away from Lyn and Shane without bothering to explain. Heart pounding, she accepted the call.

Chapter 22

D r. Hong wasted no time. "I'm sorry, MJ. The biopsy showed moderate dysplasia."

"Oh, no."

"It's still precancerous. But as you know, I'm concerned. Are you with someone?"

"A friend." She meant Lyn, not Shane. No way did she want him involved in whatever came next, though her heart broke as much for his loss on the field as it did for her own bad news. Shaking inside, she dropped down on a padded bench by the front door. "I'm all right." A small lie. "What do you recommend?"

"We both wanted to avoid a hysterectomy, but—"

"Oh, no." *Please, God.*

"We can save your ovaries. That will help with some of the hormonal issues."

Her mind jumped onto a runaway merry-go-round, each thought more blurred than the last. Her breath came in shallow pants that left her dry-mouthed, and her foot tapped nervously. She barely heard Dr. Hong explain the benefits of a hysterectomy. No more risk of cervical cancer, only a slight risk of vaginal lesions. Routine paps instead of being a frequent flyer. She'd be normal again—but at the cost of her fertility.

Footsteps alerted her to Shane's approach. She looked up and shook her head, scowling as hard as she could. He sat next to her anyway and laid his hand on her knee. Consoling her. Caring for her. Making her hurt even more.

If he weren't in her life, would she say yes to the hysterectomy right now? She was weary of the fight, the worry, and especially the interminable waiting. Most important of all, she had Cody to consider, and the threat of cancer was real. Her thoughts buzzed like those killer bees when she first believed in God, but she ached to hope that maybe he would be kind to her.

Holding back an ocean of tears, she chose to hope just a little longer. "Dr. Hong?"

"Yes?"

"Could we try one more LEEP?"

The doctor said nothing, a sign she was weighing science against hope, the facts against the unknown. This was why MJ trusted Dr. Hong, and why she closed her eyes with the fervent prayer the physician would agree to one more try.

Dr. Hong finally spoke. "Cervical cancer is usually slow growing but not always. There's some risk in waiting."

"I know."

"Why don't you take a few days to think about it?"

"I *have* been thinking, and I'm sure about the LEEP. If you could do it while I'm here in L.A., that would be great."

"Hold on. I'll check the schedule." Silence echoed until Dr. Hong came back on the line. "Tomorrow's a short day. I can add you at the very end. How about two o'clock?"

"Yes. Thank you."

"We'll hope for the best and move on from there."

After they said quick good-byes, MJ slumped against the cool paneled wall. She dreaded the procedure, the discomfort, the bleeding. But she'd done it before and could do it again. But she was a breath away from dissolving into a puddle of tears.

Instead she took a deep breath and faced Shane. "Bad news. But I guess you heard."

"I did." He shifted his knee so that it pressed even tighter against hers. "Are you sure there's no risk in waiting?"

"I'm not sure of anything." Except that she didn't want Shane to have a front-row seat to this highly personal part of her life. She gave him a stern look. "I meant what I said about flying back alone. You're free to go."

"No way. I'm staying with you."

"Really, you don't have to—"

"MJ." He waited until she blinked—the start of her heart caving in—then he seared her with a gaze that sizzled as hot as the one in the car. "I'm here." He ran a finger along her jaw. "And I'm *not* leaving."

She longed to lean on him but couldn't. For all Shane's good intentions, the threat of infertility lurked in her future. He wanted to be a dad—needed and deserved to be a dad. Even if he could accept MJ as-is, she couldn't accept herself as anything but a used car fighting to stay out of the junkyard.

Love and honor made her strong. "You're a good man, Shane. I value your friendship, but I don't want your help."

"But you need it. Let me drive you tomorrow."

"No." She gave him a slightly patronizing look. "This isn't like going to the dentist. I'm a lot more comfortable with Lyn. Let's go back to the table."

"All right." He stood and offered his hand. "But I'm not leaving L.A. without you."

"You should."

"Well, I won't."

A familiar stubbornness burned in his eyes, the same look he used to get when he talked about rejoining the Cougars. MJ's heart hitched on the bad news he'd delivered earlier. He had told her quickly, like ripping off a Band-Aid, but it had to hurt. "The tryout—what happened?"

"Later." He tugged her gently to her feet. "Let's get you taken care of first."

Together they walked to the booth where Lyn waited with a fresh cup of coffee. Concern creased her brow. "So what did Dr. Hong say?"

"It wasn't good." MJ dropped down on the seat. Shane sat next to her, holding her hand under the table while she told Lyn about the call. "The procedure's at two o'clock tomorrow. I hate to ask for another favor, but could you take me?"

Lyn made her "uh-oh" face. "I have to be in court. But I can find someone else."

"That's all right." MJ didn't want to inconvenience a stranger. As much as she dreaded accepting Shane's offer, she saw no other choice. Trying not to grimace, she faced him. "I guess I need that ride after all."

He gave her knee a reassuring squeeze. "Riley Limousine Service, at your beck and call."

MJ's mouth twitched at his joke, and even Lyn seemed pleased. The three of them arranged for Shane to pick up MJ at Lyn's house and to drive her to the appointment.

The procedure would be quick, but Dr. Hong usually ran late. MJ dreaded the entire experience—the waiting, the chilly exam room, being naked from the waist down. Her feet would be placed in the stirrups, and she'd be aware of the instruments, the smells, every sound. Even if she experienced no pain at the time, later she'd feel somehow violated.

When the procedure was finished, she and Shane would go to his apartment. Lyn would call after her court obligation, and MJ could decide how to spend the rest of the evening.

With the logistics in place, she felt steady enough to face the next hurdle in her day. Her mother had texted twice in the past hour, both times with a long row of question marks. MJ sympathized with her worry, but those question marks—and her impatience—added to MJ's own anxiety.

She nudged Shane to let her out of the booth. "I need to call my mom. You can ask Lyn about Daisy while I'm gone."

A pained look flashed in his eyes. Standing, he let her out of the booth.

Lyn rose, gave her a hug, and whispered, "Stay brave."

MJ eased by the waitress approaching with a coffee-pot, stepped through the glass door, and recoiled at the traffic noise on the busy boulevard. Turning to her left, she walked down a side street lined with old apartment buildings and towering queen palms.

She expected the solitude to settle her nerves, but her thoughts boomeranged back to Shane. The shoes on her feet were the ones he'd given to her. She felt as if she could fly in them, but HPV marked her body like initials carved in wet cement. It was only right she pay the price for a bad decision, but Shane deserved better.

The dried palm fronds rustled in the ocean breeze. A

car honked. Another zoomed past her. She hadn't planned to go this far down the street, but she couldn't escape the noise—both the mental clutter and the city roar. Her steps lengthened until she was almost running and had a hitch in her side.

Short of breath, she ground to a halt. Tears pressed into her eyes—unwanted tears but they were unstoppable. A sob burst out of her throat. Hands on her knees, she hunched forward and gave in to the tears that she prayed would wash away her misery. In the midst of the storm, her phone played circus music.

No doubt, her mother was calling.

A police helicopter whipped through the night sky, hovered over Daisy's head, and aimed the spotlight into the trees on the far side of the park. The AA meeting had ended ten minutes ago, and she was waiting for Lyn to pick her up at the rec center. With MJ in town, Lyn had skipped tonight's meeting but promised to pick up Daisy afterward. Any second Lyn would arrive with news about Shane.

"I met him," Lyn had said on the phone.

"You didn't tell him about me, did you?"

"Of course not." Lyn's voice had been soft but scolding. *"Shane doesn't know that we're friends, but he knows about Eric."*

"How?"

"The detective he hired." There had been a pause, a long one. *"Shane gave me a message for you—in case we ever met. I'll bring it tonight."*

The helicopter zoomed overhead, turned, and aimed a spotlight at a row of eucalyptus trees. Two black-and-whites sped past the park, sirens blaring until they halted in front of a shop with bars on the windows. A third police car blocked the intersection where a crowd had gathered. An ambulance arrived next, followed by a lumbering fire engine that glided to a halt.

Someone had called 911.

Daisy's vision tunneled into black and white. Dizzy and helpless, she tumbled into the abyss of the past—her mother parking the van because she had a headache. Shane walking with Daisy to the restrooms, then buying her a Snickers because she whined for it. As they headed back to the van, Shane noticed something and broke into a run. Daisy followed, but she couldn't keep up. By the time she reached the van, he had pulled their mother out of the front seat and laid her flat on the asphalt.

Daisy remembered the shock, the tears. *"Shane? What's wrong?"*

"Call 911."

"But—"

"Call now!"

Somehow she found her mother's cell phone and made that call. Shane didn't stop CPR until the paramedics arrived twenty minutes later, then he went behind a bush and threw up. Daisy had stayed by the van, a twelve-year-old girl with a melted candy bar and her brother's promise to protect her, always.

The beat of helicopter rotors yanked Daisy back into the present. Paramedics were sliding a gurney out of the ambulance, a reminder of the times Eric punched her, the night he threatened to choke her. The restraining order was in place, but twice he had cruised by Mary's Closet, and once he'd stuck his hand out the window and made an obscene gesture.

Lyn's Camry cruised into the rec center parking lot. Daisy hurried to the edge of the sidewalk, expecting to be picked up, but Lyn parked and climbed out of the car. "I had to beg a cop to let me through. Do you know what happened? I counted eight police cars in two blocks."

"I don't know. But the helicopter's been going crazy."

Lyn clasped her arm and steered her into the building. "Let's wait inside."

They stepped into the meeting room, where three men were talking. Daisy recognized one of them as a newcomer with the shakes so bad he had spilled his cup of coffee. Earlier she had welcomed him with a smile, mopped the floor with napkins, and given him a half-full cup.

She whispered to Lyn, "Let's wait in the car."

They retreated to the Camry and locked the doors. The fire truck rumbled to life and rolled down the street without lights or siren. Daisy noticed two more police cars and an unmarked sedan like the ones used by homicide detectives. Someone had wrapped the building in yellow crime scene tape.

Lyn dug into her coat pocket and removed something. Daisy glanced down and saw a wallet-sized photograph. "What's that?"

"A picture of you. The same one the detective had. Shane wrote a note on the back."

Holding it by a corner, Daisy angled the photograph toward the window. In the glow of the streetlight, she saw a frightened girl with acne, a fake smile, and lifeless eyes. "I hate this picture." She flipped it over and read, *Please forgive me.* Shane had signed it with a big S like he used to sign her birthday cards. Below the initial, he'd written his phone number and *Please call*, both underlined three times.

Daisy slipped the picture into her pocket, then stared at the emergency lights across the street. Again they carried her back in time to Shane giving their mother CPR. He'd tried hard to save her life, but later they learned she had died instantly from a cerebral hemorrhage. For twenty minutes, her brother had given CPR to a dead woman. Maybe he wasn't as awful as she thought. On the other hand, he'd thrown Daisy to the wolves.

"Are you going to see him?" Lyn asked.

"I don't know."

"The choice is yours, but I have to say—I like him." She told Daisy everything about the conversation with Shane. It had lasted fifteen minutes, long enough for Lyn to hear his story and form an opinion. "I believe he's sincere about wanting to apologize."

"Shane's always sincere."

Daisy thought of the fight in the storage closet and the ugly names he'd called her. He'd meant every one. Eric had *sincerely* blackened her eye, and he would have *sincerely* raped her at the coffee shop if she hadn't pulled free from his grasp.

She stared at the police cars across the street, the flashing light bars, and the yellow crime scene tape. Criminals were sincere, too. So was Lyn. The Harpers, the social worker, the awful boys in the garage—*everyone* was sincere. How did she know who to trust?

Daisy balled up her fist. "I hate Shane."

Lyn said nothing.

"I mean it. I hate him. I hate Eric, too."

Across the street the coroner arrived in a large white van. Someone, it seemed, had sincerely committed a murder.

Lyn heaved a weary sigh. "When I see things like this, or I hear about abused children, or terrorism, or sex trafficking, I wonder why."

So did Daisy, but not about bombs or terrorism. She wondered why God had let her go into that garage with those boys, why he let Eric hit her. And Shane—her own brother had called her a whore. It all hurt, but she hated Shane most of all because his words had hurt more than Eric's fists.

Daisy stared hard at the activity around the coroner's van. Two police officers were talking to each other, one man dark skinned and the other pale. A petite woman in a different kind of uniform carried a toolbox into the building, and a news team arrived. A man set up lights, while a female reporter tried to buttonhole one of the detectives.

Lyn shook her head. "God sees all this evil—our cruelty and failings. Everything. Yet Jesus still died for us."

Daisy frowned. Just who was this Jesus? Thanks to the empty chair, Daisy could believe that a higher power loved her, but he didn't have a name other than *God.* He gave her the strength to stay sober, but what did she do about Shane? Was she supposed to forgive him with a snap of her fingers? And Eric—did she have to forgive him, too?

And what about the boys in the garage? The oldest boy, the brother of her best friend, had tricked her. *"Hey, Daisy. Our cat had kittens. Want to see them?"*

Pleased to be invited, she had followed him into a garage that reeked of paint and grease, then to a back room where a boy she didn't know was drinking beer. He made her nervous, but the kittens were adorable, especially the one that licked her face. One of the boys had shoved a beer in her hand. She sipped it and laughed with them, because that's what the popular kids did. The oldest boy told her cool girls did other things, too. They let boys see their breasts. The coolest girls let boys touch them.

Memories assailed her—awful ones. Her hand flew to her mouth, but she couldn't hold in the moan that vibrated against her fingers.

Lyn squeezed her shoulder. "Daisy, what's wrong?"

She shook her head hard and fast. She couldn't go back there, not even with Lyn at her side. But then the EMTs came out of the building, pushing a stretcher with a body draped in a white sheet.

Victoria Bylin

Sobs erupted from Daisy's mouth. "I let them! *I let them.* I should have run away, but I didn't. I went back again because—because—I don't know why."

The story gushed out in fragments as sharp as broken glass. By the time she finished, she had told Lyn everything about high school, boys, drinking, and getting in trouble. The worst was the night she sneaked home at dawn and encountered Shane on the back porch, furious and full of dire warnings. *"You can't do this, Daisy. You'll get in trouble, and they'll send you away. You need to give your life to Christ."*

"What for?" If Shane's perfect God knew the truth, he wouldn't want her.

"I'm warning you, Daisy. I won't go with you. I like it here."

She had tried to straighten up but failed miserably to follow the rules. Not even Shane could help her.

Lyn handed Daisy a tissue. "Do you think Shane was scared for you?"

"I guess." She stared out the passenger window.

"Daisy?" Lyn touched her arm.

"What?"

"Look at me, please." Lyn waited for Daisy to turn back around. "If you were *my* sister, I'd have done *anything* to keep you safe, even things you didn't like. Shane made mistakes—bad ones. But I believe he truly wants to make things right with you. For your sake—not just his—I hope you'll try to forgive him."

Daisy stared bitterly through the windshield. Yellow tape glowed in the bright lights, the only color in a grim world, and a flimsy barrier between good and evil.

A familiar trembling invaded her body. She drew a breath to fight it, but the air refused to leave her lungs. One dry gasp led to another until she was panting like a little dog running from a bigger one. She'd been running her whole life, or hiding, because she didn't know how else to stay safe. Unable to stand up for herself, she'd done the tricks—sit, roll over, take off your clothes, play dead.

Why couldn't she fight?

"I'm weak." Tears stung her eyes. "I brought everything on myself. Everything that happened—it was my fault."

"Daisy. Stop." Lyn spoke with all the authority Daisy lacked. "You made a mistake when you went in the garage to see those kittens—an innocent one. You were what? Fourteen?"

"Yes."

"What those boys did was criminal. They should have been arrested for sexual molestation of a minor. They tricked you, and they manipulated you."

Fresh tears gathered in her eyes. "I guess."

"I *know.*" Lyn took Daisy's cold hand in both of hers and rubbed gently to warm her fingers. "You made a mistake. Don't compound it now by blaming yourself for what happened."

"But I—I didn't say no."

"You didn't know *how* to say no. It's time to forgive, Daisy—both yourself and others. We can forgive, because we've been forgiven. Jesus paid the price for all of us, even Eric and Shane."

Jesus . . . Lyn's God with a name. Daisy couldn't make that leap. "I don't know how."

"Talk to God. He'll meet you right where you are, and he'll answer your prayer."

"Really?"

"Yes." Lyn paused. "Forgiveness is yours for the asking. It's also yours to give to others—including Shane."

Daisy shook her head. "I can't. It's just too hard."

"Harder than staying sober?"

The question burrowed deep into Daisy's heart, curled up, and stayed there trembling. She carried her thirty-day chip everywhere, and soon she'd add a sixty-day chip to her collection. She was powerless over alcohol, and the chips reminded her to lean on God, not herself. Lyn's logic was obvious. "You're saying I can't work things out with Shane on my own. I need God's help."

"Exactly."

"Right now, I don't even *want* to forgive him."

"That could change."

Daisy didn't know what to think. She could talk to the God in the empty chair, but Lyn's God with a name—the one who offered mercy—was bloody, messy, and confusing. Even more difficult, he seemed to want something from her, namely her trust.

Across the street, a policeman climbed into a patrol car and drove away. The helicopter was gone now, and so were the rescue vehicles. Only the detectives and coroner remained at the scene. And the victim. And the gawkers waiting for a glimpse of the body.

If Daisy had stayed with Eric, she might have been in a scene just like this one—and on her way to the morgue.

Pieces of a puzzle snapped into place. As misguided as Shane had been, he had bullied her out of love. He'd been trying to save her from forces of evil like the ones walled off by the yellow tape. He hadn't meant to hurt her any more than Daisy had meant to steal the watch. Lyn had forgiven her, and now Daisy was in the same position to show mercy to Shane.

Still wounded and furious, she forced the words through gritted teeth. "I forgive him. I forgive my brother." Her heart rebelled, but for Lyn's sake, she tried to smile.

"You can call him right now." Lyn held out her iPhone. "I put his number in my contacts."

Daisy stared at the black screen, her chest tight and her foot tapping the floor mat. How much did Shane know about her life? Had the detective told him about the abortion? Would he call her a murderer? She tried not to think about the baby, but she'd forever wonder if it had been a boy or a girl.

Tears stung her eyes. "I'm not ready for that."

Before she confronted Shane, she needed to talk to the empty chair. She wanted to know if her God had a name, and if that name was Jesus, because her life was as bloody, messy, and painful as his.

Chapter 23

The building that housed Dr. Hong's clinic was a far cry from the Beverly Hills high-rise where seven months ago Shane had consulted a team of knee experts. A fresh coat of yellow paint covered the chipped bricks that formed two stories, but nothing could disguise the 1970s architecture. Junipers spilled onto the cracked sidewalk, and the wood shingles curled like the prongs of a dried pine cone.

Not that a building mattered. All the wisdom in the world had failed to repair Shane's knee. Like Humpty Dumpty, he'd had a great fall. Unlike Humpty Dumpty, God had put him together again, albeit with a few cracks to keep him humble.

The nursery rhyme remained in his mind as he stepped with MJ into Dr. Hong's waiting room. In the car she had thanked him three times, but after five minutes, they had lapsed into an awkward silence that followed them now.

While she checked in at the window, he riffled through a stack of women's health magazines, then eyed a table with a toy made of wire and beads. On the other side of the room, two very pregnant women happily complained about kicks to their bladders, while a trio of toddlers wrestled with each other.

When MJ finished at the reception desk, she sat a chair away from him and picked up an old copy of *People*.

The seat—as well as his understanding of her nature—stopped him from slipping his arm around her. MJ didn't want to be coddled any more than he did. She had a job to do today, a battle to fight. Admiring her fortitude, he scrolled through sports news on his phone. The time to fight—either for her heart or at her side—would come later.

After ten minutes, MJ closed the magazine and sighed. "I'm sorry you have to wait."

"I don't mind." *Good, she's talking.* He put his phone in his pocket. "How are you doing?"

"Okay, but I'd rather be at the beach." Her toes tapped in a nervous way he recognized.

"So let's go." He leaned back in the chair and draped a foot over his knee. "How about an imaginary drive up the coast?"

MJ gave a soft hum. "I'd like that."

For the next ten minutes, they mentally traveled up the Pacific Coast Highway to Big Sur, with Shane describing places he had visited but MJ had not. He wanted to make that trip with her in real life, but for now the game provided a welcome distraction until a medical assistant stepped into the waiting room.

She glanced at her clipboard. "MJ Townsend?"

MJ launched to her feet, took a few quick steps, then turned back to him. A smile graced her face. "Thanks for the drive up the coast. I had a good time."

He answered with a nod, his heart brimming as she left with the assistant dressed in maroon scrubs.

Settling in to wait, he lifted his phone from his pocket and saw a missed call from Troy. Surprised, he stepped outside to call the detective back. But when Shane reached the sidewalk, he hesitated.

Lyn had impressed him over that cup of coffee. She would neither confirm nor deny knowing Daisy, but she'd been blunt about Shane honoring his sister's wishes. *"Confidentiality is pivotal to our program. As long as a woman is safe, what she needs more than anything is respect. The decision to speak with family and friends is hers alone."*

"In other words, you're saying it's up to Daisy to call me."

Lyn merely smiled. But she also had quizzed Shane relentlessly about his motives, the past, and what he wanted from his sister. In the end, she had counseled him to give God time to work.

Was it time to cut Troy loose out of respect for Daisy? Or was he right to continue the search for her? Still weighing the facts, he called Troy.

"So what's up?" Shane asked.

"I met Markham."

"Where? When?"

"I staked out his apartment last night. Around ten o'clock, he went to a bar and I followed him inside. He must be a regular, because a female server called him by name." The detective described sitting a few stools away and listening while Markham bragged to the bartender about being in the new George Clooney movie. At that point, Troy buddied up to him. Markham didn't mention Daisy, but the bartender made a crack about Markham's girlfriend dumping him for Clooney.

"The joke set him off on a rant," Troy said. "Apparently Daisy filed for a restraining order and got it."

Good for you, Daisy. "Did he make threats?"

"Nothing direct."

"Troy, you have to find her." Pacing, Shane spoke over the traffic noise. "A restraining order's a public document. It has to have an address."

"Yes, but not hers. She filed through a legal aid office in Santa Monica. I called and explained the situation to one of the attorneys. If Daisy's a client, he'll relay the message."

"Good." Daisy was close. But so was Markham. And so was Lyn Grant. Santa Monica and Venice Beach were just a few miles apart. A coincidence, or God's providence? Shane considered his conversation with Lyn and her questions. Did she know Daisy? Very possibly. But Shane wouldn't pressure her. As Lyn had said, it was a matter of respect. But that didn't mean he couldn't speak with her later.

As long as Daisy was in danger, the detective had a job to do. "Keep on it, Troy. Ask if anyone at the bar has seen her lately."

"I plan on it."

"And keep an eye on Markham, okay?"

"I will." The detective paused. "There's one more thing."

"Yeah?"

"Have you seen this guy's website?"

"Unfortunately." Shirtless pictures showed off Markham's six-pack abs and a tattoo of a serpent wrapped around his torso. His biography made him out to be the next Robert De Niro, but at least a few of his movie credits sounded like porn. Shane had been disgusted when he first saw the website, and he was disgusted now.

Troy's tone stayed professional. "With his priors, we have to be careful. If you ask me, the guy's a powder keg."

"I can see that." Lyn's last bit of advice came back to Shane in a whisper. *"Give God time to work."*

But what if Daisy didn't have time? His skin crawled at the thought of Markham hunting her down and hurting her, punishing her for standing up to him with that restraining order. What if she was scared and hiding, even wishing someone would help her? And what if God had called Shane to be that person?

No way could he back off now. "Keep a low profile, but stick with it. We have to find her before Markham does."

"Will do."

"And Troy?"

"Yeah?"

"Work fast. I have a bad feeling."

Shane put away the phone, squeezed the back of his neck, and considered changing the travel plans for the return to Refuge. He and MJ had first-class seats booked for Sunday morning, but he didn't want to leave Daisy. On the other hand, what could he do? A misstep on his part could inspire Daisy to run again.

Shane also had track practice and a classroom waiting, and MJ had a son who needed her. There was only one logical thing to do—go home to Refuge and leave the search to Troy and Lyn.

He returned to the waiting room and sat. A newborn wailed until the mother offered a bottle. A couple in their thirties sat with their hands locked on the armrests, their eyes hopeful. Behind the closed door, MJ was having a procedure that shouldn't have been necessary.

And somewhere in Los Angeles, Daisy was hiding from

Eric Markham—and from Shane.

Troy would help with Daisy, but Shane was on his own with MJ. He had to convince her that he loved her, and that the effects of HPV made her no less desirable. It wouldn't be easy, but he wouldn't quit until he found a way.

The LEEP was harder on MJ than she'd expected. Even without general anesthesia, she felt wobbly as Shane helped her into the rental car. With the sun nearing the horizon, they picked up Chinese food to take to his apartment. When Shane went into the restaurant, MJ called her mother. Olivia didn't answer, so MJ left a voicemail saying everything went well and she'd call that evening.

Thirty minutes later, she was seated next to Shane on the couch in his apartment, a two-bedroom boasting a massive flat-screen and sports memorabilia belonging to Shane and his roommate. Plates of cashew chicken, beef and broccoli, and white rice sat in front of them. MJ nibbled at her meal, but Shane devoured his like a starving man.

Neither of them said much. The plan called for Lyn to pick up MJ after her evening AA meeting.

In the meantime, MJ was stuck here with Shane and his good intentions—a painful blessing, because he knew just what she needed. He didn't hover or nag like her mother, or worry like Cody. Today he had simply driven her to the appointment, bought her dinner, and acted as if taking a woman for a LEEP was something he did every day.

But it wasn't. She needed to keep the friendship line firmly in place, even make it thicker, but her body took priority.

She set down her plastic fork and pushed the plate away. "Thank you. That was good."

He glanced at her half-eaten food and raised an eyebrow. "Mind if I finish that?"

"Not at all." Except sharing food on a plate was something a couple did, not two people who were merely friends. She needed to use the bathroom, so she lifted her purse off the floor and pushed to her feet. "I'll be right back."

"That way." He indicated the left half of the apartment.

She walked down the short hall. The bathroom was on her right, but her gaze went to the bedroom on the left. One of Shane's shirts hung over a treadmill, and the king-sized bed was rumpled, a sign he had slept in it last night—and a reminder that he'd had a life before moving to Refuge. MJ had never asked about past girlfriends. As long as they weren't dating, it wasn't any of her business. But now she was curious. And a little angry that he knew all her intimate secrets and she knew none of his.

Sighing, she went into the bathroom and took care of business. Disposing of the sanitary pad embarrassed her, but that was silly under the circumstances. The cramps she anticipated were starting, so she took a couple of ibuprofen. Needing a pick-me-up, she brushed her hair and rubbed some color into her cheeks.

When she returned to the living room, the table was clear and Shane was standing by the sliding glass door with his back to the room, hands propped on his hips and feet planted wide.

She longed to approach him, to lean her head on his shoulder, but instead she dropped down on the couch. "Thanks again for dinner."

"My pleasure." His voice came out soft, but she didn't hear pity.

Her middle hurt more with each beat of her heart. She

wished the ibuprofen would kick in, but so what? She wished a lot of things but settled for hugging a throw pillow to her middle.

Shane turned slowly, head first, then shoulders, then chest and hips until he was fully facing her. An odd look clouded his eyes. "We have to talk."

"I'd rather not." She hugged the pillow tighter. "But I really do appreciate what you did today."

"MJ?"

"Yes?"

"If you thank me one more time" —he clipped each word but let his eyes twinkle—"I'm going to howl like a dog."

Relief flooded through her. Maybe they could keep the evening light after all. Her lips quirked upward. "Now that I'd like see. So thank—"

"No." His eyes blazed into hers. "I feel like howling, and not just because of the thank-yous. How are you feeling?"

I hurt. I'm worried. I love you, but I can't tell you. "I'm all right. The pain's about what I expected." A little worse than last time, but she didn't want to share the details with him.

He studied her face for several seconds, maybe taking in the color on her cheeks and gauging her recovery. "If you're feeling okay, there's something I need to say."

Another apology? Something about the tryout? Curiosity got the better of her. "What is it?"

"I love you."

Her heart hitched into her throat. Why would he say those words now, when her insides were a mess and she felt like damaged goods? She longed to say the words back, but instead she shook her head. "Shane—no. Please don't say that."

"Why not?"

"You know why." A cramp seized her abdomen. She

wanted to run out the door and never come back. But she knew Shane as well as he knew her. He'd follow her, lagging behind at a safe distance until she exhausted herself. Then he'd scoop her into his arms and carry her forward. No way did MJ want to be followed down this road. HPV was her cross to bear. Not his.

Let the battle begin. If she had to play rough, so be it.

She set the pillow aside, squared her shoulders, and sat with her spine rigid and not touching the back cushions. "I have feelings for you, too. You know that. But right now I have to look out for myself."

His eyes flashed as if she'd tossed down a gauntlet. "True, but you don't have to do it alone."

"Yes, I do."

He stayed on his side of the room, eight feet away. "Have you heard of a Hail Mary pass in football?"

The sports talk took her by surprise. "The quarterback throws the ball as far as he can and hopes for the best."

"Exactly. It's a last-ditch effort. Today's LEEP was a Hail Mary, wasn't it?"

"Yes."

"The ball's just been thrown." He faked a pass. "It's going to hang in the air for months, maybe years, before we know the results. I'm willing—make that *determined*—to be at your side while this plays out. I love you, MJ. Game over. I win."

"You didn't *win* anything." She jumped to her feet, ready to fight. The ache in her middle swelled like a water balloon, but she refused to sit, or even let the pain show. "I've talked to Dr. Hong about all this. It's unlikely I'd pass this strain of the virus on to you, but those are just statistics. Who knows?"

"I could also get hit by a bus," he countered. "I'll take my chances."

"Fine, but what about kids? Be honest, Shane. Do you

want children of your own?"

"You know I do."

"With me, that's a big question mark. I have to live with whatever happens. You don't. You have choices."

"Exactly. And I know what I want. I want you and Cody."

MJ's heart melted into a puddle of hope. Would adopting Cody be enough for Shane? She wanted to believe that it would, but she also knew how much he wanted—even needed—to be a dad.

She made her voice strong. "That's easy to say. It's a lot harder to live with disappointment. You don't know what that's like."

"I think I do." His eyes skimmed the apartment walls—the sports posters, the Leroy Neiman print of a batter in full swing, the massive you-are-there flat-screen television—then he focused calmly on her face. "I just spent six months working my butt off for a dream that died yesterday."

MJ hadn't forgotten about the tryout, but her own needs had consumed her. If Shane was ready to talk, she would be more than glad to listen—especially if it meant taking the focus off her, off them. "You still haven't told me what happened."

"There's not much to say." One shoulder hitched up in a shrug. "I gave it my best shot, but the knee isn't stable enough for nine innings. What matters more is what happened afterward. God and I had a little talk yesterday. I'm still angry. Bitter, too. I'm not sure I'll ever be able to trust God fully, but I'm willing to try."

"That's wonderful." She meant it.

"And it's why I can tell you now—and mean every word—that I'm okay with uncertainty, even disappointment. God knows what the future holds. As hard as it is, we need to trust him."

"I do trust him," she insisted. "But faith doesn't change the facts."

"No. But it gives us the strength to cope with them. I once believed that faith and my love for God trumped everything else in my life. I found out that it didn't, but I want to trust that way again."

She yearned to believe him, but her deepest fear snaked up from her aching belly, wrapped itself around her ribs, and squeezed until she could barely breathe. As much as she loved Shane and longed to trust God with their future, there was one fact she couldn't ignore. It concerned Shane and his past—the one part of his life she knew nothing about. It was time to face *all* the facts. Not just the ones about *her*.

She propped her hands on her hips, assuming a pose as confident as his. "I'm going to be blunt here."

"Please." He held out a hand, inviting her questions.

She raised her chin, daring him to be as truthful as she'd been with him. "You know all about my sexual past. But I don't know anything about yours. Even if you've been with only a couple of women, you could have a dangerous strain of HPV and not even know it. If you've been with a lot of women, the odds increase. No way do I want to risk being infected again."

"Of course not." His eyes glinted silver in the fading twilight. Hard and shiny, they made her think of the foil shields that protected cars in the California sun.

"So—" Even more determined, she drilled him with her eyes. "Before things between us go any further, I need to know about your past."

"Ask away."

"How many?"

"Women?"

"Yes."

Shane paused for several seconds, a delay MJ

understood. Some secrets were harder to tell than others. When he spoke, his voice came out low. "I'll tell you what you want to know, but I want you to promise me something."

"What?"

"That you won't hold anything against me."

It seemed that Shane, too, had a confession to make. Christian or not, he'd been a professional athlete—famous, wealthy, virile, and as handsome as a man could be. She didn't care about his past on an emotional level. Who was she to judge anyone? But she was truly worried about the virus.

Chin high, she spoke like a diplomat negotiating a peace treaty. "I need a number. How many?"

"Zero."

Her mouth gaped.

"I was—and am—a Christian waiting for marriage. I'm still waiting . . . for you." He held up his hand and made the universal victory sign. "You're safe with me, MJ. Because V is for Virgin."

Chapter 24

S hane watched as MJ looked away, hung her head, and dropped down on the couch. He didn't regret surprising her in the least. Saying *I love you* now, in his bachelor apartment after the LEEP, wasn't his most romantic moment, but she needed to hear it—and to believe it. He couldn't do anything about the D words like *dirty* and *damaged*, but he could go to war against the most formidable D word of all—*doubt*. Doubt in her own worth. Doubt in his commitment.

As for shocking her with the V word, he had simply told the truth.

He strode to the couch and sat next to her, their hips touching as the cushions sank with his weight. "That's not how I planned to tell you."

"Then how?" Her head jerked up. Planting her hands on the soft cushions, she shifted a foot away from him.

"I thought we'd have a conversation about awkward first dates, first kisses. That sort of thing."

"Well . . . we just did."

"So that's it," he said, matter-of-fact, hoping to calm her. "You don't have to worry about HPV with me. We're equal here, MJ."

"Equal?" She gaped at him. "You're"—she made air quotes—"'as pure as the driven snow.' And me? I'm the woman you couldn't get away from fast enough back in the car. You apologized and that's over, but it doesn't change the facts."

Before he could reply, she stood, went to the kitchen, and opened a cabinet. "I need a glass of water."

Shane followed her, opened the fridge, and handed her a cold bottle, opening it first with a twist of his wrist. "Do you need ibuprofen?"

"No," she muttered. "I just took some."

"Let's get you off your feet." He was tempted to scoop her up and carry her, but she needed to be strong on her own. Instead he nodded toward the couch. "You have to be hurting. Let's sit back down."

Leaving her, he went down the hall to his bedroom to fetch a pillow and a fleece throw. When he returned, MJ was still in the kitchen, standing but slightly hunched, sipping water and looking sullen. He knew all about pain, both physical and mental. It made some people angry—and stubborn.

He set down the pillow but held the blanket, waiting for her.

She still didn't budge. "I feel like an idiot."

"Why?" He had hoped she'd be happy about his confession.

"For how I reacted." She took a long swallow of water, then another one. "I was surprised. That's all. Here I am— a mess. And here you are." She shook her head, maybe unsure of what to say. "I think it's really nice that you waited."

Nice? There wasn't anything *nice* about the battle against sexual temptation. Every day he waged an internal war between his faith and natural desires. In college, he had dated a lot, mostly Christian women who struggled the same way he did. Resisting temptation as a professional athlete had been even more difficult.

Still holding the water bottle, MJ ambled into the living room. Her eyes lasered to the television. "How about a movie?"

"A movie?" He couldn't have heard right.

"Something light. How about a comedy?" She stayed on her feet, a good ten steps away from him. "There must be something on Netflix. It'll pass the time until Lyn calls." She lifted the remote and aimed it at the screen.

Shane reached her side in three strides, clasped his hand over hers, and stopped her from pushing a single button. "It won't work."

"What?"

"You're trying to avoid this conversation."

"There's nothing more to say."

He matched her angry glare with a strong one of his own. "Let me understand this—we were talking about *us*. And about sex. And there's nothing else to say?"

"That's right." She stalked to the slider facing a garden, keeping her back to him as she stared through the glass.

Shane followed, stood behind her, but didn't touch her. In front of them the courtyard was verdant with jasmine, spiky junipers, small palms, and giant ferns. A serpentine path led to a hot tub bubbling in a secluded corner, and soft green lights turned the spot into a manmade Garden of Eden.

MJ glowered at the tangled leaves and soft shadows, her arms crossed and her index finger tapping her biceps. "You're right. I'm avoiding this whole conversation. It's just—I didn't know what to say. But I really do admire you for your choice. It couldn't have been easy."

"No, it wasn't."

"Especially being a professional athlete."

He refused to be placed on a pedestal. "It's not easy for anyone. We can't turn off what God put into us."

"No." She paused. "I've tried because of the virus, but those feelings—the ones I have for you—they won't go away."

"Would you want them to?"

"No," she said, breathless. "But I'm scared. I'm not ready for what's happening between us."

"I am."

"Shane, I—"

"MJ, listen. Please."

She paused a long second. "All right."

"We have something special here. I want sex to be a part of it—a strong part. That means doing things God's way. Between a husband and wife, making love is sacred—and fun, too." He paused to let that part sink in. "But our culture has twisted hooking up into a hobby, even a sport. You were a victim of that."

She shook her head hard, annoyance evident in the swish of her hair. "I wasn't a victim. I made a choice that night."

"Yes, you did. But you also went along with the crowd. I'm not shaming you or anyone else. I just think people are settling for the fun and sacrificing the sacred."

MJ thought a moment, her face reflected in the glass. "The fun part stops being fun when someone gets hurt."

"Someone like you." Ever so gently, he clasped her arms. "Or someone like me. I'll never know my father. That hurts."

She chewed her lip, probably thinking of Cody. "So what kept you strong?"

"I wanted to live my faith, but don't think for a minute I haven't thought about crossing the line." *Full confession time.* "I had high hopes for this trip—you and me. I won't apologize for wanting to make love to you. I still do—just not yet."

Her eyes misted again, and she crossed her arms over her middle. "I just feel so damaged."

"You're not." He wrapped his arms around her waist and tugged her against his chest, urging her to lean on him. It was time to demolish, destroy, and debunk the D words, and to embrace new ones that started with the letter B. "You're beautiful and brave. Big-hearted. And bold, too."

"Bold?" She sighed. "I don't think so."

"You just threw a Hail Mary pass. That's gutsy." He turned her in his arms, peering into her misty eyes as she lifted her face to his. "When I look at you, I see the woman God created just for me. A strong woman who's caring, wise"—he ran a finger down her cheek—"and *very* desirable."

Yearning flared in her eyes. Bright and alive, the spark gave him hope. But the ember died in a blink. "I feel it too, Shane. I do. But it's not fair to you."

"Since when is life fair?" He stroked her back, his touch firm and commanding. "I love you, MJ, exactly as you are. That's why I'm sorry I pushed things in the car. If I had been a better man, you wouldn't have gotten hurt again."

She managed a rueful smile. "You got a rude surprise."

"So did you just now."

"Your choice wasn't rude. Just a surprise." Her voice trailed off to a wistful silence. Sighing, she stared down at her feet.

He couldn't stand seeing her defeated—yet another obnoxious D word. "You have to stop punishing yourself."

"I wish I could."

He studied her lips, his breath slow and light. If she wanted to forget her pain, he'd be more than glad to make that happen. Fingers gentle, he tunneled his hands through her hair, tipped back her head, and was on the verge of bliss when two words trembled off her lips.

"But why?"

He stopped but didn't back away. "Why what?"

"Why me?"

"Because of this." He matched his mouth to hers, savored her silky lips, and claimed her with a kiss that foreshadowed the deepest commitment to come. She kissed him back just as passionately, molding her body to his, but then her lips tensed, trembled, and she pulled away.

Knowing he'd taken her as far as she could stand, he brushed a kiss on her temple. "Let's watch that movie."

"I'd like that."

He guided her back to the couch, where he sat in the corner, giving her room to lie down with her head in his lap. After flipping through the movie choices, they settled on an adventure flick set in the Amazon jungle, complete with a touch of romance.

Twenty minutes later, MJ was sound asleep, breathing evenly and free from doubt, worry, and pain from the LEEP. Shane watched the movie, but mostly he considered the future.

When the film ended, she was still out cold. He knew it was Cody's bedtime and that she needed to call her mom. Rather than wake her, he decided to call Mrs. Townsend himself. He didn't have her personal cell number in his phone, so he borrowed MJ's, eased off the couch, and went out to the patio to make the call.

At eight o'clock, Olivia cajoled Cody into bed by promising him an extra story. She loved reading to him, and he'd selected one of her favorite Dr. Seuss books. Her grandson was as smart as a whip. He could read *Red Fish, Blue Fish* by himself, and they both laughed at Thing One and Thing Two in *The Cat in the Hat*.

Olivia expected Melissa to call any minute to say goodnight, so she had placed her phone on Cody's nightstand, part of the camp-style bedroom set she had purchased last week. Whether or not Melissa moved in, this would be Cody's room when he visited Grammie, and Olivia wanted it to be filled with books, toys, and love.

Cody opened a book about dinosaurs and promptly named every single one. Olivia was beaming when her ringtone chimed.

She checked the ID, smiled at her daughter's photograph, and snatched the phone to her ear. "Melissa, honey. How are you?"

"It's Shane Riley, Mrs. Townsend."

Something had to be wrong—terribly wrong. For Cody's sake, she controlled her voice. "This is a surprise."

"MJ's just fine," he assured her. "She fell asleep, and I didn't want to wake her."

A thoughtful thing to do. The kind of thing Richard Connor would have done. Rick had been on her mind ever since Melissa handed her the attic letters. Twice now Olivia had reached for them, and twice she had returned the unopened envelope to the back of the photo album.

Cody tugged on her arm. "Is that my mom?"

Olivia moved the phone away from her mouth. "No,

honey. Your mom's asleep. It's Shane."

"I want to talk to him!"

Shane's chuckle filled her ear. When she heard male laughter at school, it always reminded her of Rick. Hearing it in her condo unnerved her to the point that she gave Cody the phone without speaking again to Shane.

While her grandson babbled, Olivia succumbed to memories—riding on the back of Rick's Harley, her arms clinging to his waist as the motorcycle tipped and swayed; trying to love it the way he did despite the fear squeezing her heart. Where had she found the courage to ride with him in the first place? Maybe because he had pushed her. *"You're brave, Livy. Braver than you think."*

She wasn't brave at all. If she was brave, she'd call Rick just to say hello.

Disciplined as always, Olivia forced herself back to the present. Cody was babbling to Shane about his spelling test, how kite started with K and not C like cat, and did Shane know sometimes K was silent? Occasionally Cody stopped to listen, and once he said, "Can we play catch when you get home?" Shane said something, and Cody grinned. "I'm glad you're coming back."

So was Olivia. She had sincerely wished Shane good luck before the tryout, but she'd been terrified he'd lure Melissa and Cody back to Los Angeles.

"Okay, Shane. Bye." Cody shoved the phone into Olivia's hand. "He wants to talk to you."

She raised the phone to her ear but hesitated. Did she call him Shane or Mr. Riley? Undecided, she skipped the greeting. "Thank you for taking care of Melissa."

"It's a privilege."

His voice rang with confidence, a tone Olivia recognized. Shane Riley had some fight in him, and he'd just staked a claim on her daughter. Rick had spoken in that same tone when he asked her to marry him. *Oh, Rick . . .*

Why couldn't she have been brave? But she knew why. The divorce had shredded her courage along with her heart.

"Mrs. Townsend?"

Belatedly, she cleared her throat. "Yes. I'm here."

"If you don't mind, I have a work question for you."

"Go right ahead." She far preferred her professional world to her personal one.

"My contract was for one semester. If you have an opening, I'd like to come back for the spring. I need to be fully credentialed in Wyoming, but that shouldn't be a problem."

"You're hired."

A low chuckle came across the phone. "That was fast. Thank you. I appreciate it." Pleasure echoed in his voice, and maybe relief, because after all, a man needed a job.

"You're an excellent teacher, Mr. Riley. I'm sorry the tryout didn't go the way you hoped, but I'm delighted to have you back. I mean that sincerely."

"I'm glad to be back."

"In fact, Coach Hardin asked about you this morning. He'd like you to coach the JV baseball team."

"Definitcly. I'm in 110 percent."

Olivia didn't quite know what to say, so she told him to give her love to Melissa and ended the call.

She couldn't help but respect Shane. He was a good man, a hard worker, responsible, and well liked by his colleagues. Her daughter could do worse than marry him, though Olivia wondered how he felt about having—or not having—children.

She glanced at Cody, saw his closed eyes, and kissed his forehead the way she used to kiss Melissa. With her heart brimming, she ambled to the living room and turned on the Tiffany lamp. Pale light sparkled on the glass tabletop where she had left the photo album. She would have put it away, but Cody liked the pictures of his mother as a little girl. So did Olivia. Her grandson didn't have Melissa's brunette hair, but mother and son shared a certain smile.

Wistful, she trailed her fingers across the slick red cover. She'd put off reading the attic letters long enough, so she sat and removed them from the back of the album. Even photocopied, the father's handwriting reflected an era when penmanship showed class, artistry, and self-discipline. Olivia couldn't recall the last time she'd received a handwritten letter, though earlier today she had read and deleted at least seventy emails, none of them worth keeping.

After cleaning her glasses, she read the first letter. The words sucked her immediately into life in 1895. She pictured Little Miss at the Broderick School for Young Ladies and imagined the father's pride—until his tone changed to one of worry. Little Miss, it seemed, had a secret. The next several letters described a situation Olivia knew well. A daughter left home and made a mistake; a parent grappled with what to do.

Reading on, she slipped deeper into the father's skin— the worry, the fear, the shame. It burned in her stomach until she couldn't read another word. The letters sat in her lap, the words a blur until her eyes bobbed up to the watercolor landscape of winter hanging on the wall. She craved the serenity of that frozen place, but the ache in her gut drove her to read the next letter.

The father's deep voice came to life in her ears. *"If there is a child, it will be embraced by us all."*

Cody . . . Olivia couldn't imagine life without him. She nodded in full agreement, until her gaze locked on the father's final words.

Come home, child. Forgiveness awaits.

Chills raced down Olivia's spine, each one an echo of

the cruel things she had said the morning Melissa revealed she was pregnant. Olivia had gone to war for her daughter. But somehow fighting *for* Melissa had turned into fighting *with* Melissa. Oh, the cost of that battle!

Her hand flew to her chest, fingers splayed as she bowed her head in regret. She had missed her daughter's pregnancy, missed rocking Cody to sleep, giving him bottles, those first baby smiles. And why? Because she'd been stubborn and angry. And, if she was going to be completely honest, she'd been embarrassed, even humiliated, to be a high school principal with a pregnant teenage daughter.

Come home, child. Forgiveness awaits.

The reverend's voice whispered to her again. Only this time the words were for *her.*

What kind of mother shunned her daughter when she needed her most? Never mind Olivia's good intentions. She'd been stubborn and prideful—a middle-aged know-it-all who had forgotten how to love others, even her own daughter.

Through a sheen of tears, she turned to the last picture in the photo album. Looking at Melissa's face—the scared smile, her courageous eyes—Olivia vowed to fix what she could.

"MJ," she said a few times. "MJ." From now on, she would use the name her daughter preferred.

Whether or not MJ moved into the condo, Olivia would offer to pay for community college.

And last, the Bonneville had to go. Surprising her daughter with a new-to-her car would be better than Christmas.

A weight flew off Olivia's shoulders. She could hardly wait to see Melissa's—MJ's—face! Eager to have the car by Sunday, she Googled car dealerships on her phone.

She couldn't help but think of Rick again. He had

loved anything with tires and an engine, the bigger the better. Did he still live in Alaska? Or had he moved again? It was late here in Wyoming, but he'd always been a night owl. Why not call him and satisfy her curiosity? Maybe then she could delete his number once and for all. In a burst of courage, she made the call.

His phone rang once, twice. A nervous prickle raced up her neck. What in the world had she done? Maybe he wouldn't answer. The third ring brought some relief. She'd leave a message saying she had called by mistake, something businesslike. Breathing deeply, she steeled herself for his voicemail greeting.

"Livy?" The shock registered across the miles, wherever he was.

"Hello, Rick." She dragged her hand through her stiff hair, no doubt ruining the style. "I—uh—I was just thinking about you."

"It's great to hear from you." He paused for a breath, maybe to recover. "I mean it."

They talked like the old friends they were, sharing stories about friends, work, and their families. He was living in Denver and teaching at a community college. She told him all about MJ and Cody, and how much she loved being Grammie.

When they hung up, Olivia had yet another surprise for her daughter. In three weeks, dear old Mom had a date with a handsome younger man who rode a Harley and somehow made her brave.

Chapter 25

Three days after the LEEP, MJ and Shane flew first-class back to Refuge courtesy of the Cougars. The jet didn't hit a bit of turbulence, but the smooth flight only intensified the churning in MJ's mind. Physically, she felt fine. Mentally? Not so much.

Falling in love with Shane challenged her in all new ways. To love meant to trust—to believe that he loved her as-is. Maybe he did, but at what cost to himself? It also meant embracing her female self—the part of her that she had walled off in her bedroom. Embracing her sexuality meant being vulnerable. And so far, being vulnerable had meant being abandoned and hurt.

By the time the plane touched down in Refuge, MJ was

tied in knots and ready to go back to simply being Cody's mom. Shane collected their luggage, and they headed to her house, where her mother would meet them with Cody.

MJ could hardly wait to hug her son. She and Shane had presents for him, and she had bought a seagull paperweight for her mom. The blue glass, pinkish sand, and white seagull matched her mother's living room to perfection. MJ had picked it out after a long talk with Lyn about whether or not to accept her mother's offer to move back home. The strings still gave MJ pause. Was she being selfish or wise? She truly couldn't decide.

Shane steered down her street. The trees were barren now, but the late-autumn sky was high and blue with just a few wispy clouds. As they approached the house, she saw her mother's Volvo parked on the street, but the little red SUV in her driveway wasn't familiar.

"I wonder who that is," she said wearily.

"I don't know." Shane parked behind her mother's Volvo, and they climbed out of his Tahoe. "I'll get the luggage later."

They were halfway up the driveway when the front door burst open and Cody barreled toward her. "Mommy!"

MJ hugged him so hard he complained he couldn't breathe. He wiggled out of her grasp and ran to Shane. Grinning, they exchanged their trademark high-fives.

"MJ!"

Her mother's voice—but the wrong name. Confused, MJ turned and saw her mother hurrying in her direction. She braced for their usual stick-figure hug. But before she could stiffen, her mother wrapped her tightly in her arms and squeezed hard—as hard as MJ had hugged Cody, even harder.

Laughter bubbled into MJ's throat. She couldn't recall the last time they'd hugged so freely. But why now? She remembered the red car—a Ford Escape—and wondered who was here and if something bad had happened. She pulled back just enough to see her mother's face. Brown eyes that matched her own glistened with tears. Olivia Townsend never cried, at least not in front of other people.

MJ's heart jumped into her throat. "Is everything all right?"

"It is now."

"I don't understand. You seem . . ." *Different. Happy.* MJ shook her head. "I don't know."

Olivia took both of MJ's hands in hers. "I read the letters from Grandpa Jake's attic. They changed everything. I should have asked you to come home. There are so many things that I regret—"

"Oh, Mom—"

"Can you forgive me?"

"Of course!" MJ hugged her mom again. They cried happy tears and shared apologies and regrets until MJ sensed Cody and Shane watching them. Worried her son might be confused, she turned to him. "Don't worry. Everything's fine."

Cody turned to Shane, a knowing look on his six-year-old face. "You were right."

"About what?" MJ asked.

Shane's eyes twinkled. "I told him girls sometimes cry when they're happy."

"We do," the women said in unison.

Turning to share another smile, MJ recalled the first word out of her mother's mouth. "You called me MJ."

"Yes, I did," Olivia replied, sounding proud. "I'm sure I'll forget now and then, but I'll get used to it."

Hearing it once was enough. "It's okay, Mom. You can call me Melissa."

"I do like that name, but—oh! That reminds me—I don't know if Little Miss is your great-great-grandmother or not. It's quite a story, and my own mother never breathed a word of it."

MJ tucked away the disappointment. "I guess we'll never know."

"Probably not, but the letters did their job." A fresh sheen dampened Olivia's eyes. "Now I have two more surprises for you."

"Two?" MJ was too stunned to think.

"The money I put aside for UCLA is sitting in the bank. Whether you move in with me or not, I'd like to pay for community college."

MJ's jaw dropped. An education! A career with a future! Best of all, the gift came with no strings, only love. Her hand flew to her galloping heart. "Mom, that's amazing of you. I'm—I'm speechless." She lifted her arms for another hug, but her mother raised both hands to stop her.

"Wait. There's one more surprise."

Cody chimed in. "I know what it is."

MJ glanced at her son, then at Shane. The next thing she knew, her mom was pressing a key fob into her hand. "I hope you like the car behind you, because it's yours."

"*Mine?*"

"Cody helped me pick it out." Grinning, she tousled his hair into a little boy mess. "We did a good job, didn't we?"

"Yeah!"

MJ couldn't stop gaping. "A *car*? You bought me a *car*? Mom—" A sob burst out of her throat. Never in her wildest dreams had she imagined a moment like this one. She didn't deserve her mother's generosity—not by a long shot. Humbled and stunned, she might have collapsed if Shane hadn't looped his arm around her waist.

The strain of the past three days—the past three months, the past six years—melted into joyful tears. They flooded her eyes and spilled down her cheeks, leaving glistening trails. Shane had told Cody the truth—women cried when they were happy. She needed to blow her nose, but her purse was in Shane's SUV.

Seeing the need, her mother reached in her own pocket and handed her a tissue.

MJ accepted it gratefully, smiling to herself because she felt like a little girl again. "Mom, I can't thank you enough. The car is perfect. I don't know what to say—"

"Just enjoy it." Olivia hugged her again. "And drive safe!"

"I will." Laughing now, MJ finished blowing her nose, then held up the key fob. "Who wants to go for a ride?"

"Me!" Cody shouted.

Olivia beamed another smile at her grandson. "Your mom will be driving you to soccer practice, piano lessons—"

"Piano?" Cody pretended to gag.

"Hey." Shane play-punched him on the shoulder. "Music is cool. Take the lessons."

Cody wrinkled his nose, then laughed at himself.

As the four of them walked around the Ford Escape, Olivia shared details about the purchase. "It's three years old, but it's low mileage. I bought the warranty, of course."

MJ hid a smile. Her mother *always* bought warranties. Even her toaster had a warranty.

When they reached the car, she opened the driver's door and oohed and ahhed. All the newest electronics! Heated seats! Power windows that worked! She said "wow" over and over, until Shane tapped on the roof.

"How about that ride?" he asked.

She settled in the driver's seat and adjusted the mirrors. Shane offered the front seat to her mom, but Olivia chose to ride in the back next to Cody in the car seat already installed. She climbed in, and Shane took the front.

As he latched his seatbelt, Olivia leaned forward.

"Shane? When we're not in school, please call me Olivia."

"Thank you. I will." He traded a pleased smile with MJ, then surveyed the dashboard and grinned. "I bet you won't miss the Bonneville."

"Not a bit!" But a lump wedged in her throat. The old sedan had been a good car for a lot of years, the one thing her father had given to her. She'd miss it—but just a little.

She started the engine, then turned to her mom and Cody in the back seat. "Where to?"

"Let's just take off and see where we end up," Olivia replied. "A friend of mine calls that a joy ride."

Shane hung his elbow out the open window. "Sounds good to me."

"Me too," Cody chimed in.

MJ backed out of the driveway and headed for the hills. In the distance, mountains wore a crown of early snow. Even in November, a month caught between the brilliance of autumn and the tedium of winter, the land-scape offered a serene beauty that embraced the inevitability of change. With her hands on the steering wheel, she listened to Cody banter with Shane, her mother praising the landscape, and the steady purr of the engine.

A joy ride. Yes. Tomorrow and its worries could wait.

A week later, Shane drove himself to the Sunday morning service at the log cabin church, also known as Refuge Christian Fellowship. MJ, who had arrived earlier to help with hospitality, was already seated in a middle row. Cody was in the children's program, so they were alone together but surrounded by familiar faces. In just a few months, Refuge had become home to him.

The worship music watered the seeds in his soul, while the sermon nourished those seeds with wisdom. In a booming voice, the pastor quoted words from Isaiah. *"Who is among you that fears the Lord, That obeys the voice of His servant, That walks in darkness and has no light? Let him trust in the name of the Lord and rely on his God."*

Shane held tightly to MJ's hand as the pastor taught. They had no light when it came to a potential hysterectomy, but he had no difficulty at all trusting God to guide them. They already had Cody. If they couldn't conceive, why not adopt? And even if they could conceive, he still liked the idea of adoption. There was more than one way to make a family, another advantage humans enjoyed over salmon.

When the congregation left the sanctuary, Shane sought out the minister, an older man with a shock of white hair and a gravelly voice. They found a private corner and prayed for Daisy, then Shane joined MJ and Cody in a community room buzzing with activity. She declined his lunch invitation with the excuse that she needed to pick up groceries, so he drove home and busied himself with grading papers from his world history class. Two hours later, he finished the last one, stood to stretch, and peered down at MJ's new car. He hadn't heard her return.

He hated to see her living out today's words from Isaiah—walking in darkness with no light. He ached to give her a flashlight, at least. But the rest of the sermon had been a warning to him. If he pushed her instead of waiting for God, they'd both be miserable.

The back door to her house burst open. Cody, his brow furrowed, charged full speed toward the stairs to Shane's apartment, shouting as he crossed the driveway. "Shane! You have to come *right now.*"

Shane bolted for the door, flung it wide, and pounded down the steps—never mind his bum knee. "What's wrong?"

"My mom's in the attic—"

"Did she fall?" Those pull-down stairs—but why would she be in the attic? They had emptied it weeks ago.

Cody halted at the bottom of the steps. "She's fine, but the mouse isn't."

"What mouse?"

"The one in the ceiling. She bought traps, but I think we should catch it and keep it in a box. Brandon has a dog, and his brother has an iguana." Excitement gleamed in Cody's eyes. "A mouse would be cool."

MJ wasn't in mortal danger, so Shane hunkered down in front of Cody. "Field mice don't make good pets. You can buy tame ones at the store, but I can tell you from experience, they stink."

"They do?"

"Yeah." At least the males, who marked territory. He'd learned that lesson when he was a little older than Cody.

The boy's face puckered with determination. "I don't care. I want a pet."

Shane was in over his head, so he opened the back door. "Come on. Let's go help your mom."

With Cody in the lead, they jogged up the stairs. The ladder to the attic was down, and MJ's footsteps drummed over their heads. Shane wondered if she had set the traps a while ago and was replacing them, or if this was a first assault. Either way, he needed to prepare Cody for the spoils of war.

The boy had one foot on the ladder when Shane clasped his shoulder. "Have you ever seen a dead mouse?"

"No."

"It's gross. And kind of sad."

Cody thought for a moment. "But we have to save the mice." He lowered his chin and charged up the ladder. At the top, he yelled, "Pee-yew" and scooted down as fast as he could. "I don't want a mouse anymore!"

Shane hid a smile. "Good call."

"Want to play catch?" Cody could turn on a dime.

"Maybe later. I'm going to help your mom." He climbed into the attic, empty now except for MJ, a pile of wooden mouse traps, and a jar of peanut butter. A beam of light poured through a high window, capturing dust motes and illuminating the dim space. The dead mouse smell, while obnoxious, didn't bowl him over.

Even in baggy sweats and an old T-shirt, with her hair in a high ponytail and no makeup on her face, MJ was beautiful to him. When he thought about it, she'd been living in sweats since the LEEP. Not that he cared about what she wore, but he wondered why.

She gave him a dull look, then went back to baiting the trap in her hand. "Cody must have gotten you. Thanks, but I have things under control."

He jammed his hands in his pockets. "I'm not here to help you."

"Then why?"

"I'm here to save the mice."

Her mouth gaped. "You are *not*—"

"No." Grinning now, he indicated the remaining four traps. "I'm with you on the war on rodents. But Cody wants a pet. Fortunately, he got a whiff and changed his mind about a mouse."

"Well, that's a relief." She rolled her eyes, then dipped the knife in the peanut butter jar.

"Need help?"

"No, I can handle it. I found a few old nests when I took down all the junk, but something new has been running across my ceiling. It probably came from there." She pointed to a piece of plywood blocking the crawl space above her bedroom.

Shane picked up the hammer at her feet, crouched in front of the panel, and started to pry out a nail. Cody's talk about a pet gave him an opening to mention an idea he'd considered all week—adoption. He'd spent his evenings visiting websites and mentally filling MJ's house with foster kids.

He pried out the first nail. "I always wanted a dog."

"Most kids do."

He pulled a second nail. "What about you? Any pets?"

"A fish." Laughing softly, she placed a trap in the far corner of the room. "Her name was Goldie and she lasted a month. My poor mom—we had a funeral in the backyard. But after that, no more pets. My mom's allergic to cats, and we didn't have a yard for a dog."

Shane saw his chance and took it. "Lots of animals need homes. So do kids. I've been researching adoption."

He pulled three more nails before MJ approached him from behind. He pushed to his full height and faced her. Bluish shadows fanned from her nose, a sign she wasn't sleeping well. Neither was he.

She placed her palm on his biceps, imploring him with her eyes. "Please don't do this."

"Do what?"

"Get ahead of me. I'm not ready for—for us." She spun away from him, her head down and her shoulders rounded.

He set the hammer on the floor, came up behind her, and wrapped his arms around her waist. She slumped against him, her spine to his chest, and gave a weary sigh.

Holding her close felt both good and right, but her silence threw up a wall between them. Words couldn't break it down, so he inhaled deeply. Savoring the scent of her, he grazed her temple with a kiss. "I love you, MJ. Whatever happens, we can handle it together."

Her spine snapped straight, jerking her from his arms. Catlike, with her back arched, she turned and glared at him. "I told you. I can't do this now."

"Then when?" And why not? No way would he back

down. "I'd like to have kids the ordinary way, but adoption is a real possibility."

"I know you mean it, but—"

"I do."

"It's not that simple!"

"It is for me." Especially after seeing pictures of children on websites. "I was a teenage foster kid. That's the hardest kind to place. Adoption is in my DNA."

Her mouth quivered with a faint smile. "So is being a knight in shining armor."

"What's wrong with that?"

"Nothing." She turned away from him, again, and went back to the pile of mouse traps.

Shane caught up in three strides. Before she could crouch down, he caught her elbow. "MJ—"

She froze at his touch. "Shane, stop it. This isn't a fairy tale."

"No, it's real life."

"That's right." Chin high, she glared at him. "You don't know what it means to give up the hope of having a child of your own. I do. I've lived with the possibility for a long time, and I have Cody. You've thought about it for barely a week."

"A week's long enough."

"No, it isn't." Her voice rang with gentle confidence, the tone of a wise woman who saw below the surface of things. "I've seen you with Cody. I've heard you talk about kids, even your students. I *know* you want children."

"I want a *family.*"

Why was she pushing him away yet again? For a week he'd spent evenings alone, grading papers when he wanted to hear about her day, Cody's latest antics, and anything else on her mind. He had resisted the urge to break down her door and kiss her senseless. He'd stayed strong with the belief that she needed to work through her doubts herself. Now he wondered if she needed something else—an ally in an all-out war on those D words, a real-life knight to fight at her side.

Stepping forward, he lifted her hands. Chin down and eyes on fire, he put authority in his voice. "You're right. I want kids. But I don't care if they come from your body, or China or Africa, or from social services. As for being just friends, I'm sick of it. We're already a lot more than friends. We're this—" He drew her into his arms, slanted his lips over hers, and kissed her as if she were already his wife, savoring every sensation until something wet touched his cheek.

A tear. MJ's tears.

He lifted his lips from hers, but only so he could hold her tighter. His mouth grazed the shell of her ear, and he whispered again that he loved her.

She clung to him like a woman needing a life preserver. "I want to believe you. But I can't do this—not yet. It's not fair to you."

"Who says?"

"I do." She lifted her hands from his neck, stepped back, and wiped her eyes with the back of her wrist. "First you bought us shoes, then you paid too much rent. I can't count how many times you've helped me. You're doing it again."

His brows snapped together. "Doing what?"

"Rescuing me." She squared her shoulders, then made quotation marks with her fingers. "Poor MJ is all messed up. I'm going to ride to her rescue—yes. I'll save her. I'll—"

"That's not fair."

"It's true."

How could she be so blind? *She* was rescuing him. A man needed a mission, and nothing—*nothing*—called to him more than being MJ's husband—her lover and best friend, her protector, provider, the hunter of mice and driver of the family car.

He didn't see her as needy in the least, or as damaged, but that's how she saw herself. He got a whiff of self-pity and didn't like it. "Do you really think I feel sorry for you?"

"You do!"

"Do you know what?"

"What?"

"I *do* feel sorry for you. Yes, you need rescuing. So do I. Every human being on this planet needs rescuing. But hey—if you're so perfect that you don't need anyone to care about you, fine."

"That is *not* what I'm saying."

"Then what?"

"I—I'm saying—" Her mouth quivered with the threat of tears. "I just don't know."

Every muscle in his body tightened, ready to fight for her. But the spiritual man in him, the one who had suffered and wrestled with God, knew a simple truth. MJ had to find her own way to the light. If he carried her, she'd never develop a strong faith of her own. He'd be the rescuer she didn't want, not the Rescuer she needed.

Please, God, help her.

The prayer echoed in his mind. So did the desire to fight for her. Mentally, he surrendered to both God and to MJ's needs, but he was human, and he wanted the last word.

"Fine," he ground out. "But if you think you don't need rescuing, you're dead wrong. Now—" He picked up the hammer. "Let's finish this and go where it doesn't stink like dead mice."

MJ would not break down again. *She wouldn't.* But

the tears behind her eyes were as thick as motor oil. No way did she want to talk to Shane about the future when she felt as attractive as a blob of mud. When they finished with the traps, she'd take Cody to the movie about talking dogs. Except Cody wanted a pet, and now pets reminded her of Shane's insistence that he had adoption in his DNA.

Did she? A leap of her heart said yes, but she couldn't shrug off the weight of failure, or feel pretty, much less desirable.

While Shane pried nails from the plywood, she slathered peanut butter on three traps for the crawl space, listening as the nails plinked to the floor.

When only two nails held the board in place, he offered her the hammer. "You pull. I'll lift the board."

Her fingers brushed his on the rubber grip. Shivers shot through her—both cold and hot, a mix of fear and the longing to be pretty and desirable, the woman he deserved, instead of a blob in sweatpants.

He gripped the plywood and braced. MJ pulled the last two nails, and the wood gave way. Muscles flexing, Shane lifted the board and leaned it against the wall.

Foul air spilled into the main attic. Wrinkling her nose, she picked up the flashlight she'd brought up earlier and aimed it into the alcove. A dead mouse was the first thing she saw. "Yuck."

"I'll get that." Shane retrieved the Ziploc bags she had brought up and took care of the problem.

While he double-bagged the dead mouse, MJ aimed a flashlight into the dark corners. Cobwebs hung from the rafters and covered a stack of furniture—a four-poster bedstead, a matching bureau, a vanity with an attached oval mirror, and an ornate chair with a cushion that had turned to dust. A cedar chest faced forward, its latch undone.

Shane peered over her shoulder. "I wonder why this

stuff is in here. It seems odd to board it up."

"My grandfather and his cousins slept up here during World War II. Maybe someone shoved these things out of the way, then boarded it up to keep four boys from getting into it."

"We need to check for nests."

He swept away the cobwebs with a broom, then braved the dust and grit to manhandle the cedar chest into the main attic. He picked up the flashlight and pointed it under the remaining furniture. "I don't see any more mice. I'll haul the furniture out later."

"Thank you. It's gross in there." Her gaze drifted to the cedar chest. Even covered in dust, it exuded a romantic charm. "I wonder what's inside."

"The sooner we look, the sooner we can go downstairs." He picked up a rag and wiped the top clean with strong, swift strokes.

When he finished, MJ opened the lid. The first thing she saw was a lavender dress faded nearly to gray. The fabric matched the swatches in the storage carton where she had found the letters. "Little Miss! I wonder if these are her things?"

All else forgotten, she lifted the fragile garment by the shoulders and saw a vintage 1890s style. Time had left its mark, but the cedar chest had protected the garment surprisingly well from light, insects, and mice. "I can't believe it! If this belonged to her—"

"Who's Little Miss?" Shane peered down into the chest.

"The letters we found up here. Do you remember? They were with a whiskey flask and some hair ornaments."

"I remember."

"Little Miss's father wrote the letters. My mom and I don't know for sure, but we think she's my great-great-grandmother. Maybe there's something here."

MJ riffled through fabric scraps until her fingers

brushed a leather-bound journal. With the greatest care, she lifted it and opened the shriveled cover. An ornate title page read *My Diary* and below it, in artful penmanship, was her great-great-grandmother's name, Margaret Jane Abbott.

A different name, but another MJ. Her heart skipped a beat as she read the first lines.

> *I love Papa dearly, but I am eighteen years old. Why must he call me Little Miss instead of by my given name? I deplore silly nicknames!*

MJ bounced on her toes. "She's definitely related to my mom and me." She hugged the book to her chest. "This is so special. I can hardly believe we found it."

The patient look in his eyes melted her heart. So did the timbre of his voice when he finally spoke. "Read it now. I'll take Cody to a movie."

"You don't mind?"

"Not a bit." He glanced down at the book with a hint of awe. "I teach history. A diary like this is a real discovery. Enjoy it."

"I will."

He went down the stairs first, took the diary from her, and set it on the dresser in her bedroom. MJ was halfway down the folding stairs when he returned and stood at the bottom, ready to catch her if she fell.

In her mind she pictured him in ten years, then twenty, even fifty years with more silver in his blond hair than sun-kissed gold. She wanted to grow old with him, but she didn't want to be a damsel in distress, or a disappointment. She wanted to make his dreams come true. And hers.

Shane gave her a quick kiss good-bye and went downstairs to round up Cody for the talking dog movie. The instant he backed his vehicle out of the driveway, MJ lit her candles, nestled against her mountain of lacy pillows, and started to read.

Chapter 26

ear Diary,
I love Papa dearly, but I am eighteen years old.
Why must he call me Little Miss instead of by my
given name? I deplore silly nicknames! Margaret
suits me far better than an endearment meant for
the child who cuddled in his lap. I am the youngest
of his four daughters, but I am by no means incom-
petent as my mother and sisters seem to think!

Only Papa believes in my abilities, though I re-
gret to admit he is not pleased with my plan to leave
home for the purpose of teaching.

I do not expect Mother to understand my ambi-
tion, nor do my sisters have a fervent call to seek

more from life. They do not understand me; but Thomas does. A similar yearning for purpose—to bring the message of the gospel to the world—led him to our small town and Papa's tutelage.

Papa is full of stories about his travels as a missionary in western America. He still speaks of those days with the greatest passion, and I am quietly envious of such an adventuresome life. So is Thomas. Sometimes he complains that he is planted like a cornstalk when he wants to soar like an eagle.

Papa wants me to be a cornstalk too, but how can I put down roots when I believe that I am destined for a grander life?

I am determined to be a New Woman, one who rides a bicycle in bloomers. Ha! I refuse to be imprisoned by corsets and billowing skirts that confine the use of my legs. God gave me legs! Certainly He expects me to run and leap and even dance on those legs! The Almighty gave me a sound mind and a noble purpose. I, Margaret Jane Abbott, am determined to fulfill that purpose by sharing my passion for the education of girls . . .

For the next several pages, Little Miss wrote fervently about women's rights. MJ admired her determination to do something with her life, a passion that drove Little Miss to get on a train for Cheyenne just as MJ had driven the Bonneville to Los Angeles with an eye on someday going to medical school.

Some of the passages were social commentaries that rambled for pages. Others remarked on the weather. Most typically she wrote about her search for a teaching position that would take her to "a place where women are considered equal to men in intellect and ability." When she received an acceptance letter from Miss Adele Broderick, Little Miss rejoiced for pages and thanked God for the chance "to bring enlightenment to a dark world."

MJ wanted to celebrate with her, but she knew what lay ahead. A mistake. Heartache. Fear. And very possibly, shame and self-doubt. With her own chest tight, she read on.

I do not know where to start! I expected Thomas to celebrate my acceptance as a teacher at the Broderick School for Young Ladies. Instead he dropped to one knee and proposed marriage! He told me he loved me and had great plans for us—plans that will take us to places unseen and faraway, plans to take the gospel to the world.

Before I could gather my wits, he drew me into his arms and kissed me fully on the mouth. I am . . . stunned.

I am more than stunned.

I am awake to feelings my mother would call improper, but how can I believe such feelings are wrong when God made our bodies? Did He—or did He not—give us desires that are as natural as breathing? Oh, Diary! Thomas's kiss made my body cry out with longing—or was it Lust? I do not know. The kiss was most unexpected, but I cannot say it was unwelcome.

I care for Thomas, but I am committed to my Season of Discovery. We bickered like little children until he reluctantly agreed that I should accept the position in Cheyenne with the understanding that I return home at the school year's end. At that time, I will give Thomas my answer to his proposal of marriage.

Do I love him? I do not know, but I know this: I

love my dream more.

With dust tickling her nose, MJ wondered when pursuing a dream crossed from a noble cause to selfish ambition. Shane knew the answer. He'd found it when he walked off the field at Cougar Stadium.

The next entries described the five-day train trip to Cheyenne in excruciating detail—every meal, the heat, the idiosyncrasies of her fellow travelers. Little Miss arrived grimy and disheveled, but Miss Broderick herself met her at the station and whisked her to the school, where she shared a room with Miss Annalisse Petty, a pious spinster whom Little Miss found "pedantic" and "small minded."

Little Miss had opinions about everyone and everything, and she didn't hold back. She criticized the curriculum at the school as "too domestic" and waged a battle to introduce a biology class. She also wrote praises for each of her students and knew the tender details of their lives.

In September, about the time the reverend's letters began to express worry, Little Miss made a confession.

> *Today I met a man unlike anyone I have ever known. If I had crossed his path anywhere but Cheyenne, I would have been compelled to turn my back to avoid his blatant stare! He came out of the Lancer Hotel just as I crossed the street. I was so distracted that a carriage nearly ran me down. When I dropped my reticule, he bent to pick it up.*
>
> *Oh my stars and garters! I have never seen such a handsome man. His hair was as black as a raven's wing, and his eyes were the color of the sky at dusk. Blue, I thought. But I looked again and I believe they are indigo. He wore trail clothes—a black duster and dungarees—but they were clean*

and his freshly shaved jaw shone in the afternoon sun.

I believe he had been to the barber across the street, because he smelled like Papa smells on Sunday mornings—of bay rum and soap. Such good smells!

But oh! This man is a rogue. When I offered my gratitude for retrieving my reticule, he gave me a look I shan't ever forget. With one eyebrow raised, he invited me "to share a proper cup of tea at a proper café with a not-so-proper gentleman."

Why not, I thought to myself. I am a New Woman. Miss Broderick would skin me alive if she knew, but I will keep this adventure a secret. Adam—his full name is Adam Carter—must understand my situation, because he asked for a table in a secluded back room.

We chatted for two hours about all the things I hold dear. Adam agrees that women should vote, and he paid me the greatest compliment. "Miss Abbott, you are both brave and wise, a woman with a maturity far beyond your years. I am honored to make your acquaintance, and I hope we can meet again."

I said yes, of course. And New Woman that I am, I invited him to use my given name.

This coming Saturday I am meeting Adam at four o'clock. Miss Broderick expects me to attend a music recital for our older girls, but I will tell her the truth—part of it. I have a dress fitting and promised to spend the afternoon with Ruby Dearborn, the dressmaker. Ruby supports education and equality for women just as I do, and we have become fast friends.

Saturday cannot arrive soon enough, but Diary,

I must confess that I am troubled. My father would not approve, and I am quite sure Thomas did not intend my Season of Discovery to include supper with Adam Carter. But I cannot resist! I must learn more about him!

MJ scanned the next entries and gasped at the lies spewing from Adam Carter's mouth. The newspaper clipping she'd found with the reverend's letters tied Adam to an outlaw gang known for train robberies. He told Little Miss he was in the railroad business and let the foolish girl draw her own conclusions. In the diary she marveled at his success in business and the abundance of his fortune. He lived at the Lancer Hotel, though "business" often took him to Laramie, or so he said.

The rest of the story was sadly predictable. Within a month, Little Miss had accompanied Adam Carter to his hotel room.

Last night branded my heart and soul. I wanted it to happen and it did. Yes, I lied to Miss Broderick about staying the night with Ruby, and I would lie again. I would do anything for Adam. He needs me, Diary. He is a lonely man and gentle of spirit, a man without a family or love. He is a strong man yet broken inside. Last night at supper he leaned across the table, his face lit by candles, and he told me how we could fix the brokenness together.

"You are beautiful, Margaret," he said. "I want you in my bed."

Diary, I confess to you—Ruby told me about sexual relations. Adam did not pressure me in any way. He said the decision was mine, and I willingly chose to give myself to him in this way. I find it abominable that females are so sheltered that they are not allowed to enjoy the same sexual freedoms as men. My mother sought to keep me ignorant. She would not speak of procreation at all except to promise a talk on my wedding day.

Diary, I love Adam. I do. He has not spoken of marriage, though surely he will after the bliss of last night.

I must go now. I am sadly behind in my correspondence to my family, and my father is sending letters full of doom and worry. He need not fret. I am confident my future is here in Cheyenne as Adam's wife. Yes, I know I have not mentioned Thomas. I have broken my promise and cannot bear to think of him.

MJ skimmed several pages, frowning constantly as she lived the next few weeks with Little Miss. She typically used Ruby the dressmaker to cover her clandestine meetings with Adam, and her diary entries complained of Miss Broderick questioning her whereabouts.

From what MJ gleaned, Ruby was in her mid-thirties and dreamed of designing costumes for theater companies. Her interest in women's rights had nothing to do with politics and everything to do with growing up poor and hungry, marrying an older man, and suffering abuse until he died.

MJ skimmed through a dozen entries that praised Adam with schoolgirl gibberish and overblown poetry. Finally she found the passage about Little Miss being dismissed from her teaching position.

Annalisse Petty is despicable! We have shared a room for nearly three months now. I tried to befriend her, but she is critical, old-fashioned, and pea green with jealousy! She spied on me and told Miss

*Broderick she saw me take the elevator with Adam
to an upper floor.*

*When I returned to school the next morning,
Miss Broderick ordered me to leave immediately. I
was denied even the simplest good-byes. She
treated me like a prostitute, which I am not. I love
Adam and he loves me.*

The remaining entries described a downhill slide. Little
Miss took shelter with Ruby in a boardinghouse, where
she anxiously waited for Adam to return from Laramie. A
week passed, then two. Little Miss's careful penmanship
degraded into a panicked scrawl.

*Where are you, Adam? I need you. This morning
Ruby heard me retching into the washbowl and confronted me. Yes, I am with child. Come home to me,
darling. I need you, and so does our baby.*

A dried tear smeared "baby" into a blur, but a pregnancy in 1895 couldn't be so easily erased. MJ imagined
Little Miss clutching the pen and dipping the ink, as frantic as MJ had been over a home pregnancy test. The next
entry shrieked the same plea.

*Adam, where are you? I blink and see you lying
injured, even dead. I cry and wonder if you were
drowned in a river. Worst of all, my love, are the
doubts about your love, the fear that you don't— No,
I cannot say it.*

*You love me. You said so. You will return and
marry me and provide a good home for our baby,
who makes his presence known with unrelenting
sickness. I can barely leave my bed, but I must earn
a living. Ruby allows me to help with piecework, but*

my funds have dwindled to a meager sum.

Diary, what should I do? My father's letters arrive and I cannot bring myself to reply. He knows I was let go from the Broderick School, and he rightly suspects I am with child. My mother is hysterical with worry, and though my father does not mention Thomas, I am riddled with guilt for all they are suffering.

MJ skimmed the next two pages, then read the entry that matched the date on the newspaper clipping.

Adam is dead. What am I to do?

The rest of the page was blank, a testament to Little Miss's grief. Hungry for the details, MJ retrieved the newspaper article from the other room and reread the story about the train robbery. The crime had resulted in the deaths of four members of an outlaw gang, among them Adam Carter.

Three days passed before Little Miss dipped her pen again.

I am so ashamed! I cannot bear to leave my bed. I was a fool! Adam lied to me about everything. When I read about him in the newspaper, which I have done until I am blind with tears, it is as if I am reading about a stranger.

Did he love me at all? I want to believe his pursuit of me was born of mutual admiration, but I fear—oh, this hurts to write—I fear he used me as if I were a sporting woman. Or worse, he played with me the way a cat toys with a mouse.

Yesterday an actress from the theater company came to see Ruby about a costume. The woman saw me and smirked. "You did not believe what he said, did you?"

But of course I did. I was a fool. And now I am with child. I cannot bear it.

I have not written to my father in three weeks. I cannot face him. I cannot! And my mother—I fear the shame will cause her heart to seize.

There is only one hope of escaping the shame, but I cannot bear to consider Ruby's advice. She knows a woman who would give me herbs that would bring on my monthly. Ruby will loan me the money if I so desire, and I am considering it. It is as if I never existed to Adam. I am left to grieve and cope alone with a child who will be shunned by society.

As I will be shunned.

I think of Thomas's letter and his insistence that he could love this child. I want so desperately to believe him, but how can I accept such a gift knowing I do not love him the way I loved Adam, or the man I thought Adam to be?

It is all too much. I cannot believe Thomas truly loves me as I am.

And there it was—MJ's own heart bleeding on the page. Cradled by the pillows and fluffy duvet, she felt the ache of the LEEP all over again, the shame of telling Shane about HPV.

He had convinced her that he didn't care about the virus itself, even about adopting if she couldn't conceive, but what did she do with her feelings about her body? She believed Shane loved her. And she loved him, but like Little Miss, she was riddled with doubts. And yet here she was—aching to tell the girl to take a chance.

If MJ had the faith to believe in love for Little Miss,

shouldn't she have it for herself?

Her cheeks burned as she read the next pages in the diary. When Little Miss received the telegram announcing the arrival of the reverend and Thomas, she mustered her courage and met them at the train station. There she fell into her father's arms and begged him to forgive her.

> *My father welcomed me with open arms even as I sobbed that I was with child. He held me tight as if I were small. When he called me Little Miss, I wept harder still. A child's name, yes. But I am, and always will be, my father's daughter.*
>
> *Thomas looked on, a slight smile hidden under his dark mustache. I could not meet his gaze and we did not embrace. If by a miracle of grace, he still wants to marry me, I must tell him everything. I have come to love this innocent life in my womb, but my shame grows with my thickening middle.*

Several entries described Thomas courting Little Miss, who experienced all the confusion MJ experienced with Shane. Yes. No. Yes. A kiss. Fear. Regret. More fear. Then a tantalizing hope that demanded a leap of faith. After a month, Thomas won the war.

> *Tonight Thomas asked me again to marry him and I said yes. How my earthly father and future husband can forgive me is beyond my comprehension.*
>
> *I have shared many talks with both Thomas and my father, and I have come to know the simplest of truths: I am a sinner saved by grace because the Son of God paid for my sins. The old things have passed away; I am a new creature in Christ.*

MJ stared at those words a long time before she turned to the last page in the diary. A sepia-toned photograph, its surface dry and cracked, slid into her lap. Pinching the corner, she turned it over and saw the words *Mr. and Mrs. Thomas Monroe, August 22, 1895.*

A serious Thomas stood next to a chair, where Little Miss sat with his hand on her shoulder and a bouquet in her lap. She wore the stoic expression deemed proper for the time, but neither time nor a photographer's slow exposure could hide the happiness in her eyes—or the quiet confidence.

Little Miss had made peace with herself. Could MJ make that same leap? More than anything, she wanted Shane to be truly happy. How could she be sure that he wasn't riding to her rescue out of some misplaced need to redeem himself?

No answer came, but she relived the reverend welcoming Little Miss—and MJ's own mother welcoming *her.* The gift of the letters—hope for prodigal daughters everywhere—deserved to be shared. Tomorrow she'd photocopy everything and send the package to Lyn for the women at Maggie's House.

The decision pleased her, but she couldn't shake the envy she felt for Little Miss. Was it time for MJ to take a step of faith on her own? To put on lipstick, a pretty outfit, and let herself feel those feelings for Shane that terrified her?

Fear collided with excitement, then electricity shot from her head to her heart, or maybe it went from her heart to her head. Or—it didn't matter. She was tingling all over, blushing, and determined to take a chance.

Before doubts assailed her and she changed her mind, she called Tracee and asked if Cody could come over for a while.

"Sure," Tracee replied. "What's up?"

"I'm going out tonight."

Tracee's smile echoed through the phone. "With Shane? It's about time."

"It's just dinner." *Not a date.* But it was.

"How about a sleepover? The kids will love it, and you won't have to rush home."

"Thanks. I'd like that."

The dog movie was about to end, so she put together clothes for Cody, then popped into the shower, washed her hair, and wrapped herself in her fluffy white robe. The cotton caressed her skin, but as she blow-dried her hair into feminine waves, she wondered if she was out of her mind. Shane could do so much better than her—he deserved better.

"Stop it," she ordered herself.

But she couldn't control her fears. Her insecurities mushroomed until she opened her top dresser drawer and spotted the pretty pink bra and matching panties. Why not wear them? Shane wouldn't see the pearlescent silk, at least not tonight. But MJ would know, and the womanly things made her feel brave. Beautiful too. Maybe even bold.

Five minutes later, she was dressed in black leggings, a flashy tunic top from her days at SassyGirl, and the cute boots she'd worn to Los Angeles. Eye shadow, mascara, and a dash of lipstick finished the look. Not quite satisfied, she added a pair of dangly earrings and swept her hair up into a messy bun that showed off her neck. Still nervous, she made a flirty face in the mirror. The silly look made her laugh and she relaxed—almost.

Shane's Tahoe rumbled into the driveway. As she stepped into the hall, Cody bounded up the stairs. "Mommy! We're back."

In little-boy fashion, he gaped at her. "Why do you look

like that?"

"Because I do." She jammed his backpack into his arms and steered him back to the stairwell. "You're going to spend the night with Brandon."

"I am?"

"Yes, you are." *Please, God, don't let him argue.* "You can tell him about the movie."

"Okay, but can we get a dog?"

"Maybe." She turned Cody around and marched him back down the hall.

He tromped down the stairs, said something to Shane, and slammed the door behind him. MJ took a breath to compose herself, placed her hand on the polished rail, and paused at the top. With her eyes on Shane at the bottom, she navigated the stairs one slow step at a time.

His eyes popped when he saw her. Not the least bit shy, he took in every inch of her. "Oh man. I'm dying here."

"Oh, yeah?"

"Yeah." His voice deepened to a rumble. "You're beautiful."

She feasted her eyes on his handsome face, his wide shoulders, the confident gleam in his eyes. When he looked her up and down again, for the first time in her life she experienced the sexual force of being a woman—the power to captivate a man and enjoy it.

Maybe she could pull this off after all—or maybe not. It was a lot easier being a mom in jeans than a woman with a vulnerable heart. She ambled down the stairs, slowly, enjoying the moment as much as she could, loving the look on Shane's face, yet scared to death that the look wouldn't last.

Courage made her voice strong. "I thought we'd go out to dinner. Just you and me."

"A date?" He quirked a brow.

"Yes, a date."

"I'm in."

Shane whipped out his phone, made reservations for two at the Riverbend Steakhouse, and told MJ he'd be back as soon as he showered and changed clothes. Twenty minutes later, freshly shaved and wearing a sports jacket, he trotted down the apartment stairs with a grin on his face. Instead of going to the back door as usual, he went to the front door and knocked. This was a real first date, and he wanted MJ to feel special.

When she opened the door, he brushed a kiss on her cheek and told her again that she was beautiful. This time she accepted the compliment without blushing, and he offered his arm. Something had changed—something big. They made small talk on the way to the restaurant, slipped into a booth with a view of the river, and ordered steaks with all the trimmings.

MJ smiled shyly. "I want to tell you about the diary."

"Did it answer your questions?"

"Most of them."

For the next several minutes, she talked about Little Miss, Adam Carter, and Thomas. Shane wanted to punch Adam Carter in the nose, but he was deeply moved by the reverend's love for his daughter. As for Thomas, Shane gave him a mental high-five for being a good guy. He also admired the man's persistence, and he knew intuitively that was what MJ needed from him now.

Time. Persistence. And maybe some gentle persuasion.

When they finished the meal, they lingered over a decadent chocolate dessert, relaxing with each other, laughing quietly, just being together. He didn't want the evening to end, and apparently neither did she. They hung out until the restaurant closed, which he covered with a big tip for their servers.

When they arrived back at the house, he walked her to her door. "I had a great time."

"Me too." She raised her face to his, a kiss poised on her lips.

Taking his time, he matched his mouth to hers and told her without words exactly how he felt. The kisses were long and slow. Hungry but patient. Generous, command- ing, yet as tender as a man could be with a woman. In unison they took deep breaths and eased back. Like a wave returning to the ocean, the attraction retreated to something bigger, stronger, deeper. That place was love. The heart of God. A gift to them both.

Shane gave silent thanks for the attic letters and the diary, and for the all-loving, all-knowing God who had put them in MJ's hands at just the right time. He hoped to- night was the start of a new phase in their lives—one that started with the letter F for Forever.

Chapter 27

Daisy didn't want to get out of the car after Lyn parked in front of Maggie's House following the Wednesday night AA meeting. A full moon cast an umbrella of light over the tan stucco house, but claw-like shadows stretched across the sidewalk to the porch. She imagined Eric lurking in the bushes and cringed.

Earlier today, he had parked in front of Mary's Closet in violation of the restraining order. Lyn called the police, but he left before they arrived. An hour later, he called the store. Before Daisy had the good sense to hang up, he chewed her out—something about a guy showing up at Eric's favorite bar and asking questions about her—and about Eric.

"Who is he, Daisy?"

"I don't know."

"Why is he asking about me now?"

"What do you mean?"

"If he makes trouble, you're going to pay. The movie starts filming next week. I don't need some jerk sniffing around me like a pit bull."

Daisy didn't know anything about a man looking for her, unless Shane was still paying a detective. The urge to see her brother quickened her pulse, but the old numbness turned her blood to sludge. In spite of Lyn's belief that Shane was sincere, Daisy had remained hidden during MJ's visit. Now she wanted to go to sleep and pretend Eric hadn't called; to forget Shane; and even to ignore the God in the empty chair.

Lyn reached into the back seat. "I have something for you."

Daisy hoped it was a photography magazine. Sometimes people donated old ones to the thrift shop.

Instead Lyn handed her a manila envelope. "MJ Townsend sent copies of old letters and a diary she found in the family attic. They're about a woman in 1895. She could have used a place like Maggie's House."

Daisy peeked in the envelope, saw the old-style penmanship, and held in a sigh. History bored her to tears. "I'm not really interested."

Lyn smiled in that calm way of hers. "Give them a try."

"Why?"

"Because three women have read them, and we each experienced something different. For MJ, the letters were about faith. For her mother, forgiveness."

"And you?"

Lyn squeezed Daisy's hand. "I saw the reason I started Maggie's House. I saw healing."

Daisy didn't expect to find anything special, but she

wanted to please Lyn. "I'll read them tonight."

They hugged good-bye with Daisy holding Lyn a little longer than usual. Knowing her friend would be watching, she held the envelope against her chest, braved the shadows, and hurried into the house. She chatted a few minutes with a friend, then went to her room and tossed the letters on the bed.

After a bath, she put on her favorite pajamas—the purple ones with rainbow unicorns. Safe in her room, she settled into bed and half-heartedly skimmed the first few letters. Her bored expression soon deepened into a frown. Little Miss had a family who loved her, an education, and a career as a teacher at a time when women didn't have careers. She possessed everything Daisy dreamed of having, yet she walked away from it for adventure and a cause.

"How stupid could you be?" Daisy muttered.

If Little Miss had been in this room, Daisy would have told her to stay with her parents and to love them. Didn't the girl know that people died? Mothers disappeared, and fathers . . . Daisy didn't know what fathers did, because she didn't have one.

She read a few more letters from the father, then a letter from Thomas—a love letter so full of commitment and passion that Daisy's heart fluttered.

"You had everything," she muttered to Little Miss. "A mother and a father. A home. A man who loved you."

Daisy would give anything for just one of those blessings. She thought of the father coming for his little girl, loving her enough to travel a thousand miles. Who would love someone enough to do such a thing?

Shane.

Her breath caught in her throat. Her brother had come to Los Angeles to find her. He'd hired a detective and come to Lyn for help. He knew all about her mistakes—the choices the Bible called sin—and he was still looking for her.

He knew she hated him. And still he loved her enough to search for her.

Little Miss had been a fool, but was Daisy a bigger fool for not calling Shane right this minute? She stared at her phone for several seconds, her chest tight and her lungs burning. She wanted her brother to be proud of her, not embarrassed. What did she have to show for herself? Nothing at all—except her sobriety.

Air hissed through her nostrils, then her spine weakened until she sagged like a deflated balloon. She couldn't do this by herself. Just like when she was little, she wanted someone to hold her hand and help her across the street. That person used to be Shane.

He'd let her down, but Daisy still wanted to be rescued as if she were a child. Was that bad? Or weak? She had already admitted she was powerless over alcohol. Only God could help her stay sober. But who exactly was God?

Her gaze narrowed to the empty chair against the wall. In a rush, she popped to her feet, pulled it close to the bed, and sat back down on the mattress. Like a little girl in church, she folded her hands in her lap and pressed her knees tight.

Lyn's God helped Lyn every day. He made her strong and kind, and he had a name. Daisy wanted what Lyn had.

"Who are you?" she said to the chair.

Silence.

She felt stupid and ignored, but she wanted answers now. Closing her eyes, she bowed her head and concentrated. In her mind she saw a seagull flying over the ocean, soaring higher and higher, until it vanished in the glare of the sun. In a moment of gleaming mental light, Daisy saw the horizon—the vanishing point—and she thought of the

Bible study about God's forgiveness stretching as far as the east is from the west.

She started to cry, because the bird was flying higher, farther, taking her regrets with it. Her mistakes. The miserable choices the Bible called sin.

Her eyelids flew open and she stared again at the chair. With her insides quivering, she came to the unmistakable knowledge that God could sit in the chair because he had once walked this earth in a human body. He knew how it felt to be Daisy. To hurt. To cry. To want and to yearn. God had come to earth as a man named Jesus, the man in the Bible who loved the world enough to die for fallen women and failed men, human beings like herself and Shane.

Daisy slid to her knees, folded her arms on the seat of the chair, and laid her head on top of her arms. Tears rushed into her eyes, a torrent of them. When she cried out for grace, she spoke not to an empty chair but to her Lord. Over and over, she said, "Thank you, Jesus, for loving me. Thank you, Lord."

MJ had found faith in the letters.

Her mother discovered forgiveness.

Lyn embraced the Healer.

Daisy met her Savior.

Wiping her eyes, she knew exactly what to do. Calling Shane wasn't enough. She wanted to see his face when she told him her good news, and that meant surprising him in Wyoming. She had money saved from working at the thrift store, enough for a plane ticket. She could hardly wait to see his expression when his prodigal sister hugged him tight and thanked him for his prayers.

Chapter 28

On a cold but sunny Friday morning, MJ and her
mom arrived at Dr. Edwards's office for MJ's two-
week checkup after the LEEP. Knowing her mother would
have questions, MJ had invited her. But mostly she just
wanted her mom with her.

The physician was of average height, slightly rotund,
and gray around the temples. Laugh wrinkles fanned from
his eyes, but he was all business when it came to taking
her history. MJ liked him a lot. He performed the exam,
and now she and her mom were waiting in his office to
hear his opinion.

The doctor had said very little during the exam itself,
which took longer than MJ had expected. A good sign or a

bad one? She didn't know, and though her stomach was in knots, they weren't as tight as usual.

A tap sounded on the door. Dr. Edwards came in with an iPad—a far cry from the raggedy paper files in Dr. Hong's office. He greeted MJ, exchanged a smile with Olivia, and got down to business. "Everything looks good, Miss Townsend. You're healing nicely."

"I'm glad to hear it." She felt fine, too. In fact, better than fine. Her body practically glowed with a sense of healthy newness—and with her feelings for Shane.

On the other hand, she'd seen his face when Tracee's husband handed him a cigar with an "It's a Girl" label. She believed he was telling the truth about adoption, but what would happen if that belief was fully tested? She felt compelled to protect him—and her own heart, too. For now, it was wise to let their relationship grow slowly.

Dr. Edwards laced his hands on his desk. "I spoke to Dr. Hong yesterday. She filled me in on your history, and we agreed on the next step. How does a six-month check sound?"

"That's just what I expected."

Her mom sat straighter in the chair. "Dr. Edwards?"

"Yes?"

"Do you think the virus is gone for good?"

MJ knew better than to ask that question. The virus didn't "leave," but her immune system could suppress it for the rest of her life. For the next several minutes, Dr. Edwards patiently answered her mother's questions—at least twenty of them. When Olivia was satisfied, they thanked Dr. Edwards and left the office.

Stepping into the sunshine, MJ inhaled deeply to clear both her mind and her lungs. She and her mom walked across the parking lot, chatting about how nice Dr. Edwards was, until they reached the Volvo and the Escape, parked side by side in the back row.

"How about the Campfire Café for lunch?" Olivia suggested. "There's something else I'd like to talk about."

"That sounds good. But now I'm curious." MJ took her phone from her purse and turned the volume up. There were two missed calls and a couple of texts. Hoping it wasn't the school calling about Cody, she opened her messages while speaking to her mom. "What's up?"

Olivia pursed her lips in a way that wasn't like her at all. "In case something comes up, you should know I can't watch Cody the first weekend in December."

"No problem. Are you going somewhere?"

"Maybe. I have a date."

"A *date*?" MJ forgot all about her phone.

"Well, yes."

She tried to stifle her shock, but she gave up and did a little happy dance. "Mom, that's great! Who is he? How— Never mind. Let's get to the bakery so we can talk."

"Oh, all right!" Her mom sounded annoyed, but she was grinning crazily as she unlocked the Volvo. MJ turned to the Escape, stealing a glance at her messages. A text from Lyn read *CALL ME 911*.

"What in the world— Mom, hold on. I have to make a call." Frantic, MJ started to call Lyn. The two missed calls were from her, too.

Her mother laid a hand on her arm. "What's wrong? Is it Cody?"

"No. It's Lyn. She left a 911 message."

The call connected without ringing. Lyn's voice shot straight into MJ's ear. "I need Shane *now*. He's not answering his phone. Is he with you?"

"He's in the classroom. But why—"

"It's Daisy. She's hurt."

"*Daisy?* His sister? How— What—"

"She came to Mary's Closet for help. She's been here for two months."

All this time, Daisy had been safe while Shane worried. It didn't seem right. But that wasn't Lyn's fault. "You mean—"

"Yes. But she's hurt." Lyn's voice fractured into a sob. "Her ex-boyfriend came here. I don't know exactly what happened, but the ambulance just left. It's . . . it's bad. Shane needs to get on a plane *now*."

Her mother was already unlocking the Volvo, motioning for MJ to get inside.

She gripped the phone tighter. "I'm with my mom. We're on our way to the school to find him."

Heart pounding, MJ silently pleaded with God to save Daisy's life.

For Daisy, Friday morning dawned pure and bright. She ate a bowl of Honey Nut Cheerios for breakfast, then asked one of her housemates for a ride to Venice Pier. Camera in hand, she walked to the end of it, drinking in the serenity of a sunny winter day.

"Thank you, Jesus," she whispered out loud.

Three months ago, she had stood here and imagined falling off the horizon. Now she was flying to Wyoming on Sunday afternoon. Later today, Lyn would call her friend MJ to help arrange the surprise for Shane. Daisy could hardly wait.

Smiling, she remembered the gull that pooped on Lyn and how they cleaned up the mess with a twenty-dollar bill. She had more than twenty dollars in her pocket today. She earned decent money at Mary's Closet, both clerking and selling her photographs. Today she planned to shop at the store for fun new outfits for her trip. Lyn had offered to give her the clothes and shoes, but Daisy wanted to pay, both as a matter of pride and to give back a little of what she had received.

She took a few pictures of seagulls, thanked God for her new life, and walked the six blocks back to Mary's Closet. The thrift shop didn't open for ten minutes, so she went to the back door and knocked. Lyn let her in, and they looked at some jeans and tops Lyn thought Daisy might like.

"I love them all!" She could hardly wait to see Shane's face when she hugged him.

At ten o'clock, Lyn went into her office to do payroll. Daisy went to the display area, unlocked the front door, and busied herself dusting shelves. Humming quietly, she crouched in front of a rack of shoes in the front corner of the store.

The doorbell chimed and she stood. "May I—" *Eric.* The greeting shriveled on her tongue.

"Hello, Daisy." His dark eyes fixed on her face, the pupils dilated in spite of the bright lights, a sign he was high on something. Staring hard, he flexed his fingers into white-knuckled fists, relaxed them, and flexed them again. And again.

Daisy shifted her balance to the balls of her feet and prepared to run, but Eric had her cornered. Lyn was alone in the back and as vulnerable as Daisy. Somehow Daisy needed to warn her without alerting Eric to her friend's presence, then trust Lyn to call 911. But anything she said or did—except submission—would light Eric's short fuse.

Daisy refused to submit.

If she couldn't convince Eric to leave, she'd run for the street. A busy convenience store was a block away. If she reached it, she'd be safe.

"Do you need something?" she said in a soothing voice.

Eric lowered his chin. "I want to know what the"—he dropped an f-bomb—"is going on."

"I don't know." She faked concern, anything to cool his temper. "What's up?"

He prowled around the store, touching things, smirking at her, daring her to tell him to stop.

She inched toward the front door, but he lunged at her. Before she could scream, he clamped his left hand over her mouth and twisted her arm behind her back. She stomped on his foot and kicked his shins, but the drugs made him numb to pain.

Effortlessly, he dragged her toward the front door. The shelf of seagull paperweights loomed on the right. She swiped at it, grabbing one as the others crashed to the floor. Surely Lyn would hear the noise and know something was wrong. And maybe Daisy could smash Eric's head with the leaden glass.

He dragged her kicking to the sidewalk. Furious and starved for air, she tried to bite his hand.

"You—" A filthy name.

He flung her against the hood of his Miata. She rolled off and ran, but he grabbed her from behind. Whirling, she smacked him in the jaw with the hand holding the paperweight. He jerked back and she tried to sprint, but he caught her again. Her arm nearly came out of the shoulder socket and she screamed.

"Shut up!" He hurled her with even more force against the trunk. Her chin banged on the cold metal. Pain shot through her chest and lungs. And worst of all, through the rear window she saw a girl with red hair in the passenger's seat—her replacement.

"Run!" Daisy cried as she pounded the glass.

The girl climbed out of the car. Not fast. Slowly. Her pupils were as dilated as Eric's, and on her wrist was the diamond Rolex. Daisy couldn't escape Eric, but she could help this girl. As he pulled her off the car, she shoved the paperweight into the girl's belly.

Startled, the girl took it.

"Keep it," Daisy cried. "Remember this place."

Eric's fist slammed into her jaw. Her feet flew out from under her, and her head smacked against a brick planter. Pain exploded in her brain, blinding her. She tried to curl into a protective ball, but her body refused to move. Eric's boot slammed into her ribs. The crack of bones—*her bones*—echoed in her ears.

The door to Mary's Closet flew open, and through a haze she saw Lyn's pretty shoes. Fighting for consciousness, Daisy tasted blood and smelled burning rubber as Eric's car squealed away from the curb.

Lyn dropped to her side. "Hang on, baby. Hang on."

Daisy blinked once. Twice. Somehow the sidewalk turned from blood-soaked concrete into blue sky, where a single gull flew toward the horizon.

Friday afternoons in the classroom had a special kind of buzz. Students and faculty alike eagerly anticipated the pep rally and football game, and the coming weekend promised sleep and relaxation. Shane was particularly pumped up. Tomorrow he and MJ were taking Cody to the nature center north of town—an official family date.

But first, he had to finish the school day, particularly the review session with his fourth period American history class. He was standing at the dry erase board, blue marker in hand, when a startled hush settled over the classroom. Turning to the door, he saw Mrs. Townsend striding toward him, her expression carefully blank.

Shane lowered his arm. Something was wrong. *MJ.* She'd seen the doctor this morning.

Olivia spoke in a muted tone. "Get your things and go. MJ's in the hall."

"Is she all right?"

"She's fine. So is Cody."

"But—"

"Just go. Please. MJ will explain."

Confusion steamrolled into panic. What— Who— He couldn't think of a single good reason Mrs. Townsend would take over his class. Stuffing down the fear, he grabbed his coat and work bag and strode into the hall.

As the door swung shut, MJ laid her hand on his arm. "I have news about Daisy. It's not good."

Blood drained from his brain. The hallway spun until he pressed a hand against a locker to steady himself. "Daisy? But how—"

"She's in the hospital. Lyn called. Shane, I'm so sorry." She squeezed his arm hard. "Her ex-boyfriend beat her up. It's bad. We need to fly to Los Angeles now. The next flight is in three hours, so we have time to pack a few things. I'm going with you. My mom will watch Cody."

They took off for the parking lot, his pulse pounding with questions as they ran for his car. Between gulps of air, MJ told him as much of the story as she knew. Markham had beaten Daisy unconscious at Mary's Closet, and she'd been rushed to Centennial Hospital. Lyn was with her and would call the minute there was news.

They sped away in his Tahoe, shooting through yellow lights and taking turns hard and fast. At home they broke apart to throw things into carry-ons, leaving Shane alone with horrible pictures flashing in his mind—Daisy lying bloody, bruised, and limp on the sidewalk. Markham speeding away.

So Lyn had been Daisy's friend as he'd suspected— and hoped. That knowledge brought some comfort but not enough.

In less than fifteen minutes, he met MJ at the SUV and they drove to the airport.

Victoria Bylin

"I have to see her," he mumbled to himself more than to MJ. "I have to tell her I'm sorry."

MJ laid her hand on his knee. "She knows. I'm sure of it."

"How?"

"From Lyn."

Shane's jaw clenched until it ached. All these weeks his sister had been within his reach, and now she lay near death. He might never have the chance to talk to her, to apologize, to start over. The guiding light that had returned to his life—his faith—disappeared as if someone had flipped a switch. Darkness blinded him. Doubt assailed him. Bitterness churned in his belly and soured his mouth.

Grimacing, he waited for his spiritual eyes to adjust to the dark. But they didn't. He couldn't see a thing, but did blindness mean God had abandoned him?

No. It did not. Just as turning off a lamp didn't change the shape or contents of a room, neither did a human tragedy change God's nature. God—the great I AM—was loving, sovereign, and wise. No matter what happened, Shane vowed to cling to those words. But he was still just a man. And it hurt.

Why, God? Why?

A jet roared overhead; another taxied to the end of the runway and made a fast turn. Comings and goings. Hellos and good-byes. A life-and-death dance choreographed by a man in a tower who presumably saw everything in the sky. Faith . . . Human beings couldn't fly or drive without putting faith in other people. As a Christian, Shane needed to place that same kind of trust in his Lord.

More than anything, he wanted Daisy to live. To recover and be happy again. To forgive him. He glanced at MJ riding shotgun. Her calm presence didn't erase his burden, but it eased it. He needed her—today and always.

A light turned red. There was no choice but to stop. Shane gritted his teeth until MJ reached over and rubbed his shoulder. "We have plenty of time."

"Do we?" She meant to catch the flight, but he pictured Daisy, pale and lifeless.

The traffic light flashed green. Shane veered into the parking structure, snagged the ticket, and took the first spot he saw. With MJ at his side, he grabbed both carry-ons and hurried to the terminal. Mercifully, they passed through security fairly fast and reached the gate with time to spare.

He tried to call Lyn, but she didn't pick up. Not knowing what the future held, he gripped MJ's hand and held tight.

Chapter 29

The instant their flight touched down in Salt Lake City for the connection to LAX, Shane and MJ reached for their phones. While MJ texted her mother, Shane called Lyn for an update. Daisy was out of surgery and alive, but her injuries were extensive—internal bleeding, broken ribs, a skull fracture, and diffuse brain trauma.

"She's in very critical condition," Lyn told him in a shaky voice. "I wish—I wish a lot of things."

So did Shane, mostly that he could have taken the violence in Daisy's place. MJ seemed to know how he felt. She remained quiet, her arm pressed against his on the narrow armrest, their feet touching from toe to heel.

Next he called Troy, who told him that Markham and

a girl were in custody on drug and assault charges. Additional charges of attempted murder, or God help them all, homicide, were pending. The instant he ended the call, Shane broke out in a cold sweat. Every minute counted now; every second mattered. He needed to see Daisy— needed to be with her while he begged God to spare her life.

Time crawled as he and MJ changed planes, soared back into the sky, and landed two hours later at LAX. With the brakes screeching and the momentum pulling him forward, he called the ICU, gave the privacy code from Lyn, and was connected with Nina, Daisy's nurse.

"How is she?" *Please, God. Please.*

"She's extremely critical." Nina paused. "Does your sister have an advance directive?"

"A what?" He knew what the words meant. He just couldn't bear hearing them.

"An advance directive," Nina repeated gently. "It's a legal document that expresses a person's wishes in the event they're unable to speak for themselves."

Also known as a DNR. *Do not resuscitate.* Shane's vision tunneled into black and white. Fresh chills erupted with a fiery vengeance, and acid singed the back of his dry throat. The pilot made a sharp turn on the taxiway, causing him to lean against MJ.

She gripped his free hand, worry and dread written all over her face. Nina's words had reached her ears, too.

He swallowed back the bile in his throat. "Please tell me that's a routine question."

"It is." A long pause stretched into the unknown. "Your sister's neurologist is on call tonight. It's best if Dr. Sethi talks to you in person."

Shane choked out a thank-you and ended the call. He hated being helpless, but there was nothing else he could do. The plane lurched to a stop at the gate. Passengers crowded into the aisle as if this were an ordinary day. But it wasn't. MJ sought his gaze but didn't speak. There were no words, only the keening hope that Daisy would survive—and heal.

He hoisted their bags from the overhead bin, then he and MJ surged with the crowd until they broke free. They dashed through the terminal, caught a taxi, and told the driver to hurry to Centennial Hospital. In minutes, they were on the 405, mercifully moving at a decent clip.

Shane silently pleaded with God all the way to the hospital, MJ quiet and respectful beside him, her hand light on his knee as the driver wove through traffic. Somehow her strength poured into him, steadied him, though it seemed to take eons to reach the hospital. Once inside the sprawling building, they followed the signs to the ICU on the second floor. He spotted Lyn in the waiting room, seated on a worn brown couch, her head bowed.

MJ called out to her. "Lyn!"

Lyn launched to her feet and ran to them, her face stained with tears.

"Daisy—" His throat locked tight.

"She's hanging on." Lyn hugged him hard, then squeezed MJ even harder. "I'm so glad you're both here."

Questions buzzed in Shane's brain, but they could wait. "I need to see her."

"Of course." Lyn pointed down a short hall that ended in a T intersection. "The ICU's on the left."

MJ touched his arm. "I can wait here, or—"

"Come with me." He gripped her hand and held tight. God seemed very far away, but the Almighty had kindly sent MJ in his place.

Leaving their bags with Lyn, they walked down the corridor to a closed wooden door. Without its small plastic sign, it would have resembled a closet, or a storeroom on a college campus. He pushed the intercom and identified himself. A buzz signaled he could enter.

He held the door for MJ, and together they walked into a world of fluorescent lights, glass walls, and twitching monitors. A nurse in her late twenties, wearing maroon scrubs with her straight black hair in a tight bun, nodded at MJ, then greeted him.

"Mr. Riley? I'm Nina Martinez, your sister's nurse. I'm sure you're eager to see her."

"I am."

"I'll take you right in. Dr. Sethi will be here shortly."

Holding tightly to MJ's hand, Shane followed Nina to a glass-walled room with a drawn curtain. The nurse paused at the closed door. "Daisy isn't fully conscious yet after the surgery. Her head has been shaved, and her face is swollen and bruised. You might not recognize her. Be prepared."

Shane nodded, but how did a person prepare to see a loved one bloody and broken? He blinked and imagined Christ on the cross, and the Father seeing his Son suffer. Christ's blood had a purpose. What purpose did the attack on Daisy serve? None that he could see now.

Nina opened the door, led the way inside, and greeted Daisy as if she were fully alert, cheerfully telling her that she had visitors.

Could she hear? Maybe. Desperate to hope, Shane opened his mouth, but nothing came out. He could only stare at Daisy motionless on the high bed, her face the color of a plum and unrecognizable, her head bandaged, and her pretty hair nowhere to be seen.

Nina checked what nurses check, then left them alone. Shane gave MJ's hand a squeeze and let go. She stayed near the door, while he approached Daisy.

Barely breathing, he stared at his sister's battered face until the shock subsided and he saw the woman beneath the bruises. His little sister . . . the child who looked up to him. He had failed her too many times to count, but most condemning of all, he had failed to show her the grace and forgiveness he so desperately needed for himself now— from her.

How many times had he lectured her about Christianity? Dozens. Sometimes she listened and prayed with him. But not once had he really listened to *her*.

Shane finally found his voice. "Hey, Daisy. It's me." Her fingers lay limp in his grip, neither warm nor cold. He squeezed lightly, praying for a response—but none came.

Whether Daisy could hear him or not, Shane needed to speak. "You deserve far more than an apology for how I treated you, but it's all I have to give."

Again nothing. Not even a twitch.

The old bitterness toward God squeezed his belly, a coiled snake about to strike. MJ dragged a chair to the bed, indicating he should sit, then she dragged one up for herself. Together they sat at Daisy's bedside, silent and devastated, until Nina stepped into the room.

"Dr. Sethi's ready for you," she said to Shane.

When he stood, MJ slid to the chair closest to Daisy. "I'll stay with her."

As Shane followed Nina, MJ introduced herself to his sister as if they were going to be best friends.

The nurse guided him to a small room with a desk pushed against a wall. A short, dark-haired man in a rumpled suit stood and introduced himself. After indicating Shane should take the side chair, he swiped the mouse to wake up the monitor, then pointed to an image with a ballpoint pen. "This is your sister's CT scan."

To Shane's untrained eye, Daisy's brain resembled a black-and-white butterfly. But the sides didn't match. Black speckles, a white crescent, and white splinters indicating bone fragments showed the damage to the left lobe.

The doctor aimed the pen at the screen and outlined the damage. "This was taken prior to surgery. The white indicates bleeding between her brain and skull—in other words, a subdural hematoma. Our biggest concerns now are swelling and stroke."

"Stroke?" Shane's mind jumped to physical paralysis, loss of speech, memory problems, and more.

"Yes. We will know more in twenty-four to forty-eight hours."

His accent made the words singsong, softening the blow, but Shane couldn't take his eyes off the white crescent on the left side of Daisy's brain. "How bad is it— I mean—" *Brain damage.* He couldn't bring himself to say the words. "If she survives, what can we expect?"

"We simply do not know."

Shane grabbed for hope, even a shred of it. "But she could recover, right?"

Dr. Sethi held out his hand, palm up. Not a sign of indifference, but an acknowledgment of the unknown. "Anything is possible, Mr. Riley. But you can see the CT scan for yourself."

Only God knew what the future held, but Shane knew what *he* wanted as a hurting human being—and as Daisy's protector. He wanted his sister to live—and to live well.

Dr. Sethi reached for a clipboard wedged in a vertical file. "Your sister does not have an advance directive. Is that correct?"

"Yes."

"And you are her closest relative?"

"Yes, that's also correct."

"And do you know what her wishes might have been?"

There was no doubt—Daisy wouldn't want to be kept alive with a feeding tube. At the same time, Shane was desperate to fight for her life. His voice came out in a choked whisper. "There's still hope, right?"

Dr. Sethi replied with a slow blink. "There is always hope, Mr. Riley. Are you familiar with how a DNR is followed?"

"Not exactly."

"Allow me to explain."

The doctor handed him a clipboard with a form and a pen dangling from a string. Just like that—a stroke of a pen on a preprinted form—and Daisy's life was in Shane's hands.

"With a DNR, if your sister's heart stops beating, no medical procedure to restart the heart will be initiated. However, the order will not prevent her from receiving other medical care she may need."

Shane stared at the form for several seconds, lifted the pen and tried to sign it, but couldn't. He wanted—*needed*—to fight for her. But what was best for Daisy?

Shaking his head, he laid the clipboard on the desk. "I need to think about this."

"Of course." Dr. Sethi stood. "If you have questions, please ask Nina to call me."

Shane strode out of the office. As much as he wanted to return to MJ and Daisy, he veered to the outer door. At this point, Lyn knew Daisy far better than he did. What would his sister want? As for his own need for absolution, he'd have to live with whatever happened—and so would Daisy. That last thought scared him to death.

The worn carpet muted his steps as he walked into the waiting room, empty except for Lyn hunched and praying on the couch. He murmured her name.

Her head snapped up, worry evident in the deep lines around her mouth. "How is she?"

"The same." He sat down on the couch. "Her neurologist showed me the CT scan. It's bad. He asked about a DNR. I don't know what to do."

Lyn shifted on the cushions, facing him as best as she could. "That's an awful decision to have to make."

"The worst." Shane drew a breath. "I was hoping you could help me. I don't know anything about her life now. Is she happy?"

A faint smile put light in Lyn's eyes. "Yes. I believe she is. A lot changed in the past few months."

At last, the story he was desperate to hear. "Tell me everything."

Lyn described his sister's arrival at Mary's Closet, her fight for sobriety, and finally about witnessing a 911 call and how Daisy revealed and confronted her own abuse. "I don't know if she would have shared that with you, but you should know."

His fingers knotted into a helpless fist. He wanted to punch the wall, all of Daisy's abusers, and especially his own smug teenage self. Instead he ground the heel of his hand in his eye. "I hate myself for not realizing she'd been hurt."

"You were young, too."

"Even so—"

"Shane. Stop it." Lyn's voice crackled with authority. "We all have regrets. Suck up the guilt and move on."

He looked at her, incredulous. "I wish it were that simple."

"It *is* simple—simple but not easy. You're a Christian. You know what the cross means."

Did he really? He knew the right words to say, but could he fully surrender Daisy to the God who sometimes said no? A two-headed beast rose up in him—one head called Pride and the other Fear. The beast roared like a dragon spitting fire, its spine writhing and its hot breath on his neck, a reminder of how helpless he was to fix anyone— Daisy, MJ, or himself. Lyn saw the pride in him, and she had swung for the fences. Shane could only shake his head.

"I'm talking to myself, too," she admitted. "If I'd been quicker, I might have saved her. I could have—"

"Lyn, don't. You've done more for Daisy than anyone."

"All I did was share what I've been given. MJ did the same with those old letters and the diary. Daisy read them. Two days ago, she became a Christian."

"Really?" He nearly wept.

"Yes."

"I'm—I'm glad." More than glad. No matter what this day held, he'd see his sister in eternity. God had said yes to that prayer, but Shane's heart still ached.

"She forgave you, Shane." A wistful smile fluttered across Lyn's face. "In fact, she was planning to surprise you in Refuge. We were going to call MJ and—and—" The words broke into fractured syllables until Lyn composed herself. "She had come so far. All she wanted was for you to be proud of her."

"I am." Whether Daisy could hear him or not, he needed to tell her now. He pushed to his feet. "I need to get back."

"Of course. And Shane?"

"Yes?"

"I'm truly sorry I couldn't tell you about her sooner."

"It's okay. It was Daisy's call, but I'm here now. Why don't you go home and get some rest? I'll call if anything changes."

They hugged and went their separate ways, Lyn to the bank of elevators and Shane back to the ICU with the luggage in hand. He entered Daisy's room, shoved the bags against the back wall, then approached the bed.

MJ, seated at Daisy's side, looked over her shoulder. "She's hanging in there. What did the doctor say?"

"He asked about an advance directive."

"Oh, Shane."

"It's bad." He told her about the CT scan and Dr.

Sethi's assessment. "I didn't sign the DNR. I just can't. Not yet."

MJ rose to her feet and hugged him hard. He clung to her, drinking in the kindness and strength that were uniquely hers.

After a minute, she leaned back and looked into his eyes. "There's still hope, right? We believe in a big God. He answers prayers. He hears us."

"Yes. But sometimes God says no."

A soft breath leaked from her lips. "Do you want to talk about it? I mean, the DNR?"

"No. Just pray for me—and for Daisy. I'm staying all night. If you'd like to get some sleep, you can Uber to my apartment."

She gave him the same strong look she used on Cody. "There's no way I'll leave you now." But then her eyes flared wide with doubt. "Unless that's what you want."

"No!" He hauled her into his arms and held tight. "Stay. Please. I need you." Love for her swamped him, strengthened him, and made him brave.

The two of them kept up the vigil all night long. Sometimes they talked to Daisy, and sometimes to each other. Shane told his sister he loved her and was proud of her, but he doubted she could hear him. He and MJ prayed, dozed, and talked about hope, heaven, and everything in between. No matter how hard he tried to face the facts, he couldn't bring himself to sign the DNR.

Was life worth the fight, when heaven promised bliss in the presence of a loving God? On the other hand, God was in the business of healing. Shane wanted that healing for Daisy in the here-and-now.

Shortly before dawn, Nina asked them to leave so that the staff could take care of Daisy's physical needs in private. He and MJ wandered to a room full of vending machines. Front and center, Fig Newtons sat at a jaunty angle on a metal curlicue. Choking up, he bought them and put them in his pocket. He and MJ wolfed down sandwiches, then returned to Daisy's room.

She was alone, propped on the bed raised to a 45-degree angle, and covered with a white sheet. A serene expression graced her bruised face, but she hadn't moved or opened her eyes. Afraid, he glanced at the monitors. The blood pressure numbers were the only ones he understood, and they were 88/57—low and dropping fast. His gaze went to the cardiac monitor, where he saw uneven changes.

Nina pushed through the door, a vial of medicine and a syringe in hand. She went straight to Daisy's IV. "This is for her blood pressure." She pushed the liquid into the plastic line, then watched the monitor.

The numbers went up a bit and stabilized, and the heart rhythm settled into a regular pattern. But for how long? Shane's heart wedged high in his throat and stayed there.

Nina checked wires and the IV bags. Before she finished, Daisy's blood pressure plummeted a second time.

Shane grabbed MJ's hand and squeezed. *No! No! No!* He tried to pray, but no words formed. All he could do was watch the amber numbers on the monitor flash a warning, then turn red.

A man in maroon scrubs strode through the door with a second vial. He administered the medicine while speaking to Nina. "I called Dr. Sethi. He's on his way from the ER."

Shane stared hard at the blood pressure numbers, half listening as the nurses used words like pneumothorax and embolism. Daisy was either fighting for her life or preparing to surrender forever.

Shaking all over, he pulled MJ tightly to his side. "Should I sign it?" He meant the DNR.

Turning, she laid a hand on his arm. "I've been thinking—no, praying—about it. No one can decide for you, Shane. If it were my mom, I'd sign it. It's what she would want. But if it were Cody, I don't think I could."

The blood pressure numbers were higher now—a lot higher. Maybe too high. The male nurse left, but Nina stayed.

A rivulet of drool spilled from Daisy's swollen lips. MJ checked with Nina, then dabbed at his sister's mouth with a tissue, talking to her as if she were Cody.

Shane dug his hands into his pockets, a helpless gesture, until his fingers collided with the Fig Newtons. A small offering, but it was all he had. Stepping forward, he laid the cookies in Daisy's palm, curled her fingers around them, and willed her to open her eyes. "Daisy, talk to me. *Please.*"

No answer.

He covered her limp hand with his. "I am so sorry for how I treated you. Lyn said you forgave me. I don't see how, but I'm grateful." He rambled a little more, telling her what Lyn had shared with him. "I love you, Daisy. And I'm proud of you."

Her fingers twitched on the Fig Newtons.

"Daisy?"

Her eyes popped open, but could she see him? Her pupils were huge and black. She blinked and he thought he saw recognition. Or was it merely a reflex? He couldn't tell, but her fingers tightened on the cookies. The plastic wrap crackled, and she looked at him—really looked at him. In slow motion, her mouth formed a smile. She tried to say his name, but nothing came out of her dry throat.

"Daisy! It's me. I'm here." Tears ran down his cheeks in a flood of blessing. *Hope . . .* He clung to it, savored it, dared to believe that Daisy would live.

He glanced at MJ, expecting to share the glory, but her

eyes were wide and riveted to the monitors. Nina hurried past him to the door, opened it, and shouted something he couldn't take in.

And then it happened—the moment he feared in the depths of his soul. The cardiac monitor flatlined.

Chapter 30

$\mathcal{S}$ hane's blood seemed to freeze in his veins. To have hope given and then snatched away was a cruel hoax. Who wanted to worship a God who would do such a thing? The DNR flashed in his mind.

Nina raced back into the room, lowered the bed to make Daisy lie flat, knelt on the mattress, and started CPR.

Dr. Sethi strode into the room with the male nurse on his heels. A woman in royal blue scrubs arrived with a cart holding vials of medicine, needles, patches, and a defibrillator.

The doctor's gaze stayed on Daisy's slack face. "Epinephrine one milligram, please."

Fearing someone would tell him to leave, Shane pulled MJ into the far corner of the room. Huddled together, they watched like flies on the wall.

Nina, still kneeling on the bed, counted the compressions out loud. With each push, Daisy's feet jerked off the mattress. The male nurse intubated her and squeezed air into her lungs with a balloon of sorts. A third nurse arrived and went to the side of the bed opposite Nina. Words flew around the room, yet the atmosphere remained controlled and oddly calm.

Shane held MJ tight, shielding her face against his shoulder while he stared at the activity around Daisy's bed, his mental chaos and their professional calm colliding as the staff did their jobs. After two minutes, Nina stopped the CPR at Dr. Sethi's command.

Nina and the other nurse each took Daisy's pulse. The cardiac monitor blipped once, twice, then flatlined again. The male nurse took Nina's place and restarted the compressions. He was tall and didn't need to kneel on the bed. Instead he loomed over Daisy, pressing hard and fast on her broken ribs, crushing them even more.

Shane buried his face in MJ's hair, but he still saw Daisy's body under assault. "I just can't let her go. Is that wrong?"

MJ clung to him, squeezing hard as if she could infuse him with fresh hope, maybe peace. But she couldn't. He dragged his gaze to the heart monitor. When the nurse paused the compressions, the flat line jumped on its own and didn't stop. But even to Shane's untrained eye, the pattern looked wrong.

"We have V-tach." Dr. Sethi spoke like a robot. "Defibrillator, please."

A female tech pulled up Daisy's gown, revealing the black-and-blue mottling covering her torso. Shane blanched at the sight of the bruising, and though it was impossible, he wished he could take her place.

A tech put two large white patches on Daisy's middle. Dr. Sethi shouted, "Clear!" and everyone stepped back from the bed. The defibrillator beeped a warning, then her body jerked as if she'd been kicked. The cardiac monitor went dead again, blipped once, twice, a third time. The lines were ragged now, different sizes, and too fast.

"We have V-fib," Dr. Sethi announced. "Clear!" The monitor blipped for a minute, then flatlined.

Dr. Sethi looked straight at Shane, waited three seconds, then gave the order to continue CPR.

The third nurse pulled out a stool from under the bed, stood on it for leverage, crossed her hands on Daisy's chest, and pumped hard and fast. With each compression, Daisy's body jerked like a rag doll. The medical team spoke in calm tones—words about lab results, medications, procedures, things that could mean life for Daisy—or more suffering.

Time mattered. And it was running out.

Shane thought of her broken ribs and bruises, the damaged butterfly of her brain, and in his heart, he knew what he had to do. It was time to let her go. If she lost this battle, heaven awaited—that better place where there was no more suffering.

Calm beyond all reason, he broke from MJ's arms, faced the bed, and spoke in a clear voice. "Stop. Please. My sister's been hurt enough. I'll sign the DNR."

The medical staff looked to Dr. Sethi, who nodded. Someone handed Shane a clipboard and he signed the DNR form. The medical team filtered out of the room, but Nina and Dr. Sethi remained.

Shane reached back for MJ's hand, and they approached Daisy together. The monitor blipped once, twice, then stopped and started again. No one moved. No one breathed. Shane clung to Daisy with one hand and MJ with the other. The decision was made, and he was at peace. No one would bully his little sister back to life.

He let go of MJ just long enough to wipe away his tears, clung to her again, then spoke the only words that remained. "I love you, Daisy. I want you to live. But if it's time for you to leave, I understand. The decision to fight is yours alone."

Somehow Daisy could see herself on the bed. Her face was a mess. Not pretty at all, but she felt utterly beautiful on the inside. She wanted to dance and laugh and even sing, something she never could do very well. A joy unlike anything she had ever imagined flooded her entire being.

She saw Shane standing at the side of her bed. Next to him was the woman Daisy knew to be MJ. They were clinging to each other and sobbing. Daisy felt bad about that. If Shane knew how wonderful she felt, he'd be happy for her.

A male voice came out of nowhere. "Daisy?"

In the corner of the room she spotted the empty chair from her bedroom at Maggie's House—except it wasn't empty anymore. A man sat in it. His eyes defied being labeled a single color, or maybe they were all colors. His clothing, though, was ordinary, the kinds of things she sorted at Mary's Closet—worn Levis, a white shirt with long, rolled-up sleeves, and a pair of brown leather flip-flops.

Her eyes riveted to the scars on his feet. As she looked up, he turned his hands to display the nail marks on his palms.

Somehow her body coalesced into a flesh-and-blood woman, and she landed on her knees at the foot of the chair, her neck bent, and her hair falling to make a curtain of sorts. She wanted to soak in the splendor forever—to blend into it, to become it. *Heaven . . .* She was going to see it!

The man in the chair touched her chin with his index finger, gently lifting her face.

The light was too strong, too revealing . . . too *good*. She didn't deserve to gaze into the ocean of his eyes, let alone to dive in and swim. But somehow she felt welcomed, as if unseen angels were rejoicing on her behalf.

The hospital ceiling dissolved into a perfect blue sky. A seagull circled overhead, spiraling higher and higher. Daisy's soul soared with the bird, but then she looked down and saw Shane. He was seated next to the bed, head down with his fingers pinching the bridge of his nose. A tortured moan crawled out of his throat, a sound she hadn't heard since their mother's death. MJ stood slightly behind him, her hand on his shoulder, weeping with him while she kissed the top of his head.

The man in the chair—Jesus, she knew that with certainty—cupped the back of her head. An indescribable light flooded through her, wordless, yet conveying that she stood on the edge of eternity. Was it her time to leave this life? She yearned to bask in the bright light, to step deeper into the glory, but then she recalled Shane and MJ grieving for her, clinging to each other. Somehow she saw Lyn driving back to the hospital, pleading with God for Daisy's life. More prayers reached her ears. Her friends at Maggie's House were begging for her life as well.

Daisy felt loved, cared for, and most of all, *wanted* by people she loved now and people she would love in the future.

Humbled, she raised her face to her Savior. An ocean of love washed over her, and she realized there was nothing to fear. Her life was in his hands and she was safe.

Heaven promised eternal bliss, but living meant love—for Jesus, her family and friends, and countless others she had yet to meet.

Yearning to please her Lord, she bowed her head in joyful surrender to his will. There were no decisions to be made; nothing to do except rejoice as his hand came to rest on the left side of her head, his fingers splayed over the wound. Tinging heat poured into her skull, swirled between her ears, then eased into a gentle warmth that stopped short of touching her cheeks. As the heat faded, Daisy raised her head and looked up. The blue sky morphed back into ceiling panels, and somehow gravity pulled her to the bed.

Her hands and feet warmed up first, then her legs, her shoulders, and finally her chest. Her heart took a beat, then settled into a strong, steady rhythm. Pain skewered her, but her head didn't hurt at all. Her thoughts were perfectly clear, including the vivid memory of the radiant light.

She pried her eyes open, blinking to focus until her gaze narrowed on Shane's face. He was on his feet, staring down at her, calling her name just like when she was small and wandered too far. MJ stood next to him, her mouth agape and her eyes brimming with tears.

Dr. Sethi took her pulse, while the nice nurse named Nina, the one who had prayed for her when they were alone—Daisy knew that now—pressed her hands to her cheeks in shock.

Daisy blinked again, reached for Shane's hand, and stared into those blue eyes that were the same color as hers. "You found me."

"Oh, Daisy—"

"I'm back," she whispered. "I'm—I'm alive, right?"

"Yes," Shane said through his own tears. "You're alive."

Overwhelmed, she let out a shuddering sigh. The journey ahead wouldn't be easy, but she wouldn't be walking the road alone. Jesus would be with her every step of the way, and so would Shane and MJ.

MJ couldn't believe her eyes—or her ears. Daisy had spoken in a voice as clear as her own. Dr. Sethi stepped to the side of the bed, checked Daisy's pupils with a penlight, then asked her if she knew her name and where she was.

Daisy answered both questions, though she had no memory of the assault or the day prior to it. Dr. Sethi assured her that was typical. When he asked about her pain level on a scale of one to ten, she answered with eight. Nina left to retrieve pain medicine. The doctor stayed at Daisy's side, talking to her and assessing her, until Nina returned and administered the medication. A minute later, a man in scrubs arrived with a portable CT machine.

MJ watched with Shane as the tech performed the scan. Dr. Sethi checked it, then motioned them both over to view it.

"What do you see?" he asked.

MJ didn't know much about CT scans, but the sides of Daisy's brain looked identical.

Shane squeezed her hand hard, then answered the doctor. "What I don't see is that white crescent."

"It's gone." Dr. Sethi turned to Daisy. "I cannot explain what happened just now, except that the human body possesses a remarkable capacity to heal."

Daisy just smiled. The pain medicine was making her groggy, but she whispered a few words. "Call Lyn, okay? Tell her I'm all right. And thank her . . . for everything."

With that, she dozed off.

Dr. Sethi urged them to let Daisy rest. As he departed, Shane told Daisy that they'd be back soon, squeezed her hand, then turned away and suggested to MJ that they go back to his apartment.

A little rest sounded wonderful after all they'd been through. When she nodded, Shane fetched their luggage from the spot against the wall. At the door, MJ turned and saw Daisy sleeping peacefully. She shared a smile with Shane, and they left the ICU together.

MJ was reaching for her phone to call Lyn, when the elevator doors slid open. Lyn stepped out, saw them, and pressed her hand to her chest. "Daisy. How is she?"

"Alive." Grinning, Shane let go of the suitcase handle but kept his duffle bag on his shoulder. "She's awake and talking."

Lyn's jaw dropped nearly to the floor.

"It's true," MJ added. "I can hardly believe what just happened." Daisy, though, was only part of the miracle. In the middle of the fear and Shane's uncertainty, MJ had made a discovery of her own about the man she loved. She had something important to say and could hardly wait to say it.

She listened and nodded while Shane told Lyn the story—everything from Daisy flatlining to witnessing the return of her healthy heartbeat. "She has a lot ahead of her, but she also has us." He looped his free arm around MJ's waist.

She leaned against him, cherishing every word.

Lyn glanced down the hall to the ICU door. "Would it be all right if I stole a peek at her?"

"Definitely," Shane replied. "You're family."

They said their good-byes, and Lyn walked down the hall, her heels clacking as always.

Shane moved to push the elevator button, but MJ gripped his hand, took her own suitcase, and tugged him down the hall. "This way."

He gave her a curious look but followed her to the waiting room. Another family was present, so she led him down the hall to the first open door she saw. It turned out to be a large linen closet. No one was around, so she led him inside and closed the door. When he set down his duffle, she wrapped her arms around his shoulders.

As he drew her close, her body molded to his. Relaxing into him, she raised her face and gazed into his eyes. "I just needed to hold you."

He kissed her temple, her cheeks, finally her quivering lips. In Daisy's hospital room, MJ had witnessed Shane making the hardest decision of his life. The man she cherished knew when to fight for someone he loved—and when to let go of an impossible dream. The three special words she had yet to speak danced on her tongue. Easing back, she looked into his startling blue eyes.

"I love you," she said.

A roguish smile lifted one corner of his mouth. "Do you realize that's the first time you've said it?"

"Yes," she admitted. "But it won't be the last."

"It better not be." A low rumble echoed in his throat. His eyelids gave a languid blink, then he kissed her long and slow, telling her without words that he would love her always, just as she was. Full of joy, she kissed him back with equal commitment, staking a claim on his heart and baring hers. Vulnerable yet unafraid, she rejoiced in being the woman God had made just for Shane.

Chapter 31

Six weeks later, Shane was behind the wheel of his Chevy Tahoe, with MJ riding shotgun as they cruised up I-15 from Los Angeles. A Laundromat wasn't the most romantic spot to propose—unless it was where you met the woman who restored your heart and soul. The diamond ring Shane had purchased in L.A. a few days ago was burning a hole in his pocket, but he kept the speedometer at a reasonable seventy-five on the deserted interstate. MJ was holding his free hand, humming along to a song on the radio.

With school out for winter break, they had driven to L.A. to clean out his apartment and to help Daisy pack for her move to Refuge. She'd be flying with Lyn in a few days and moving into MJ's house. Daisy didn't have much, but what little she owned would be waiting for her when she arrived.

The past week had been a blast for everyone, including Olivia and Cody, who had flown in for a family trip to Disneyland. Olivia had become good friends with Lyn, and Cody had hit it off with Daisy instantly. He already called her Aunt Daisy, and the two of them had played about a hundred games of checkers, Candy Land, and Hungry Hungry Hippos.

A sign marked the turnoff for the town with the Laundromat. MJ gave a loud yawn. "I can't wait to get home."

"Me too." He pretended to check the fuel gauge. "We better stop for gas."

"Sure. Whatever." She yawned again, then wiggled her feet into the shoes he'd given to her four months ago.

His nervousness mounted as he steered down the off-ramp, stealing glances at MJ as he turned up the hill toward the Laundromat.

At the sight of the hotel, she bolted upright. "This is where we met!"

"Wow, what a coincidence." *Not.*

Grinning, she pointed up the road to a row of stores. "There's the Laundromat. Let's go inside."

"Sure. Why not?" Perfect! He wouldn't have to make up a lame excuse, or sound all sentimental, which he was when it came to MJ and Cody.

The instant he parked, she jumped out of the SUV and headed for the door. He reached it first, held it wide, and followed her inside, noticing with some relief that they were alone. Nothing had changed. The space still smelled of dust and laundry soap, and he was sure there were a few stray coins under the washing machines, maybe even the pennies MJ had dropped.

His pulse revved up to a spin cycle. "I'll never forget

that day."

"Me either." She laid her hand on a washing machine, took a few steps, and faced him. "So much has happened since then."

Playing it cool, he reached into his pocket for the ring. "Do you remember the alphabet game?"

A sweet smile lifted her lips. "Of course. L is for Laundromat."

"It's also for Love." As if he were going down for a ground ball, he dropped to one knee and held out the ring. The diamond caught a ray of sunlight and sparkled with an intensity that far exceeded the lights of any baseball stadium. Shane's pulse rocketed into double-time. "I love you, MJ. You're beautiful, kind, and the missing piece of my heart. I love you with everything in me, and I love Cody like a son."

"Oh, Shane—"

"Will you marry me?"

"Yes!" MJ answered, her voice loud and clear. "Yes!"

Shane slipped the ring on her finger, stood tall, and drew her into his arms for a kiss she would never forget. Some kisses affirmed life. Others celebrated it. And a few like this one gave birth to new beginnings.

Four months ago, MJ had stood in this very spot with only faith to sustain her. Some of their dreams had died, like Shane's baseball career. Others, like finding Daisy, had come true. Thanks to the attic letters, MJ and her mother had reconciled, and MJ was completely comfortable with her own body. They wouldn't know about the HPV for a while, but she and Shane were committed to trusting God for a family.

Shane brushed kisses on her cheek, her temple, finally

her soft lips. "Life is short. And it's fragile. I don't want to waste a minute of what we have together."

"Neither do I."

He kissed her again, then they hugged until Shane broke the silence. "You know who'll be happy about this?"

"Cody."

"And your mom?"

"Definitely."

Arm in arm, they walked out of the Laundromat. Shane helped her onto the front seat of his SUV, and they took off for the interstate. MJ reached for his hand and squeezed. The diamond glistened in the sunlight and she couldn't contain her joy. An idea surfaced, and she decided to run with it. "Let's play the alphabet game."

"Sure. You first."

"W is for Wedding."

"I like that." He thought a moment. "How about the letter U?"

MJ came up blank. "Tell me."

"U is for Us."

Grinning, she played the letter she had in mind. "What does H stand for?"

Shane drummed his fingers on the steering wheel. "House? Home?"

"No." She dragged out the word. "Try again."

He shook his head. "I give up."

"How about Hawaii? As in Honeymoon?"

"Oh yeah, I like that one." He waggled his brows at her until she laughed and waggled hers back at him.

What a joy to anticipate M for Marriage! God—the Alpha and the Omega—had come up with the perfect end to the alphabet game. With her heart brimming, MJ held tight to Shane's hand and dreamed of their future.

Next in the Road to Refuge Series . . .

A Gift To Cherish

By Victoria Bylin

A woman's scream cut through the night. Sharp. Penetrating. It stabbed Rafe Donovan's eardrums and sent him running down the dark alley toward the shrieks. Three stories above, laughter tumbled out of a tenement window backlit by a dull pink bulb. The old brick walls stank of urine and grease. Dumpsters overflowed onto cracked asphalt, and rotting garbage clogged the gutters.

The woman screamed again, louder this time.

No. No. No. He couldn't let Kara die. He ran harder, faster. The soles of his black uniform boots slapped the pavement, each stride a hammer blow. His Glock rode tight on his hip, his badge heavy and bright on his chest.

She screamed again—a heaving plea for him to save her.

He ran toward the scream, his arms pumping and lungs straining. But instead of growing louder, the scream faded, as if Kara were being dragged away from him.

He imagined her bare heels repeatedly hitting the concrete. He blinked and saw her pale arms flailing, her skin mottled with track marks from the addiction she couldn't shake. She had tried. Rafe knew that better than anyone. But the pills and later the needles had a grip so tight no one—not even wannabe superhero Rafe Donovan—could drag her from those fire-breathing demons of addiction. He tried and had ripped her in two.

A third scream cut through the night. Vile laughter poured out of the windows above him, like bubbles from a child's bubble machine, only the bubbles were huge and had horrible faces.

"Kara!" He shouted at the top of his lungs. "Kara! I'm coming for you!" His legs bicycled despite his exhaustion. Sweat poured off his body and he smelled his own stink. A cry ripped out of his throat, and then—

"Rafe!" A deep voice sliced through the fog. "Rafe! Wake up!"

"No!"

"Come on, bro."

The voice belonged to Jesse, Rafe's older brother. Somehow it called to him as if they were kids again, and the monster in the house was their dad. Rafe's stepdad but Jesse's blood father.

"Wake up. You're having a nightmare."

A bright light popped on but dimmed to a tolerable glow. Rafe's head cleared with the shift. He was in Jesse's house in Refuge, a log cabin with dimmer switches on every wall, hardwood floors that didn't squeak, and almost no furniture because his brother was too busy building houses to furnish them.

Rafe swung his feet over the side of the bed, scrubbed his face with his sweaty hands, then raked his fingers through his hair. His head didn't feel like his own. He'd been off the job for a week now and hadn't bothered to get a haircut. Shaving was optional, something else he had ignored. When he was in uniform, he kept his hair short and shaved at least once a day, sometimes twice.

Jesse stayed in the doorway. "That sounded like a bad one."

"Yeah. Stupid, too."

"Wanna talk about it?"

"No." Rafe snatched up his phone. "What time is it

anyway?" The blue numbers told him it was 2:58 a.m. "Crud." Too soon to get up. Not enough time to calm down and go back to sleep. It was early Sunday, so he didn't need to think about getting to work. It was an easy job, anyway. Just pounding nails for Jesse's construction business but Rafe took it seriously.

He took everything seriously.

Jessie didn't budge. "Coffee?"

Rafe swore. "Go back to bed. I'm fine."

Except they both knew he wasn't. A few days ago Rafe had pulled his brand new red Camaro into his brother's driveway, hauled his duffle out of the trunk, and rapped on the door like the cop he'd been until last week—the cop he wanted to be again, but first he had to shake the nightmares. As for that panic attack in a Cincinnati alley, only Rafe's supervising officers and the department shrink knew about *that*, and no one else would know if he had anything to say about it. To hide it from his friends and fellow officers, he had made up a story about his brother needing help with his business, then hightailed it to Wyoming. A few friends asked why, but no one was surprised. The daily battle against crime, drugs, and ugliness took a toll on everyone.

But leaving put Rafe in a Catch-22. Police work gave him a purpose. He was protective by nature, which meant he needed people to protect. Strangers on the street filled that bill just fine. But then he had suffered the panic attack, or whatever it was, while responding to a call about a woman screaming. Just like that, he flashed back to Kara Howard, his high school sweetheart and the love of his life—the beautiful girl next door who had somehow loved the troubled boy whose stepfather drank too much. He had tried to save Kara when the pills told their lies. He'd done everything—

"Rafe?"

"Yeah, yeah." He wished his brother would leave him alone. Standing abruptly, he snatched yesterday's Levis off the back of a chair, the belt dangling in the loops. "Go back to bed. I'm all right."

"Sure you are."

"I am." Now they were both lying. "Get out of here. I'm going for a drive."

"It's almost three in the morning."

"So what?" Rafe scowled out the window. He would have preferred a long, hard run, but the half moon cast only a dull glow and Jesse's house was nestled low in a canyon. No sidewalks. No streetlights. If he went running, he'd be running blind. No way would he risk tripping on a rock and busting his arm again. Been there, done that. Took the pain pills for a day, then dumped them in a can of stale coffee, duct-taped it shut, and buried it in a Dumpster.

He wished he'd done that for Kara. Icy fingers of sweat dripped down his spine. "I have to get out of here."

Jesse stepped back. "Go for it. Just—"

"I know. Be careful. You sound like Mom."

"Sorry." Jesse grimaced, maybe more at himself than at Rafe. Shaking his head, he ambled back down the hall to the master bedroom, leaving Rafe to cinch his belt, punch into a shirt, and snag his key fob.

Two minutes later he was behind the steering wheel. The engine purred to life at his touch, and the headlights slashed through the darkness as he cruised down Jesse's street, a narrow road lined with homes set back in the trees. Only an occasional porch light, left on to scare away raccoons, hinted at civilization.

He didn't belong here. His heart beat to an urban rhythm—convenience stores open 24/7, the dull hum of cars at all hours, early morning delivery trucks.

Jaw tight, he shot up the last hill and headed toward

downtown Refuge—if it could be called *downtown*. When he reached the six square blocks of restaurants, shops and businesses, every window was dark and buttoned up. Not a single electric sign lit the night, so he decided to cruise to the interstate fifteen miles away. He'd grab coffee somewhere and drink it in his car the way he did when he was on patrol back in Cincy.

Or better yet, if Angie was working graveyard at IHOP and her tables were slow, maybe she'd sit with him. Rafe liked everything about Angie—her sense of humor, her olive skin and shiny black hair, those dark eyes made up to seduce truck drivers into leaving big tips. He didn't know about the truck drivers, but he'd been generous just for the pleasure of it.

Or maybe Krystal at the Denny's would like some company after work. Rafe didn't smoke, do drugs, or drink more than an occasional beer, but when it came to women, he was far more open-minded.

Anticipating female company, he cruised the highway until his gaze snagged on a car stopped on the other side of the road. The passenger door was open, and the dome light cast a dull glow into the interior of a late model Hyundai. The trunk was raised, and the car was listing on the driver's side thanks to a flat tire.

Adrenaline chased away whatever gloom remained from the nightmare. Someone needed help, and he was in the right place at the right time.

Using one hand, he pulled a U-turn just short of a fishtail and parked twenty feet behind the Hyundai. If the driver was a woman alone, he didn't want to scare her. And if this was some kind of weird set-up, he didn't want to be a victim.

The Camaro headlights lit up a Hyundai Elantra with Wyoming plates. So the driver was a local, perhaps someone headed to Refuge. Whoever he or she was, they were staying out of sight. Rafe retrieved a mini Maglite out of the console. The flashlight wasn't much bigger than a felt-tip marker, but it could light up the night. Ready for anything, he climbed out of the car, pushed to his full height, and used the flashlight to scan the darkness on the periphery of the headlight beams.

"Hello there," he called out as he took a couple of steps. "Looks like you need some help."

"Get back! Now!"

Whoa. No doubt he'd ridden to the rescue of a woman alone. She just didn't know it and was wise not to trust him. He didn't bother to say he was a police officer back in Ohio. Ted Bundy had used that line too.

Still holding the flashlight, Rafe raised his arms to shoulder level. The beam of light shot skyward, leaving the woman in the dark until footsteps scraped on the sandy apron of the highway. She remained in the shadows, but she appeared to be a white female in her twenties, about five-foot-six, and average weight. Her blond hair was in a waitress-y bun, and she was wearing a uniform of some sort. If he wasn't mistaken, she'd assumed a combat stance and was holding a can of pepper spray.

"Don't move!" she said again. "Get in your car and leave."

"Miss—"

"I said *leave.*"

"I can't."

"Yes, you can."

Of all the things in life Rafe couldn't do, abandoning a woman in trouble was at the top of the list. He'd rather get pepper-sprayed, even shot, than read about a woman murdered on the side of the highway when he could have saved her. No way could he abandon this woman, which meant he needed to win her trust.

Books By Victoria Bylin

Contemporary Romance
Until I Found You
Together With You
Someone Like You
The Two of Us
When He Found Me

Inspirational Westerns
The Bounty Hunter's Bride
Kansas Courtship
"Home Again" in In a Mother's Arms
"Josie's Wedding Dress" in Brides of the West

The Women of Swan's Nest Series
The Maverick Preacher
Wyoming Lawman
The Outlaw's Return
Marrying the Major

Harlequin Historicals *
Of Men and Angels
West of Heaven
Abbie's Outlaw
Midnight Marriage
"A Son is Given" in Stay for Christmas
"The Christmas Dove" in The Magic of Christmas

* These stories have Christian themes, but they were
written for the mainstream market. They contain scenes,
situations, and language some readers will prefer to
avoid.

A Word from Victoria . . .

This may sound crazy, but I was driven to write romance by giant bugs and killer rabbits. I just couldn't take it anymore. My husband and two sons would be camped in front of the television watching a movie about spiders the size of bowling balls, and I'd be wondering when the handsome scientist would get around to kissing the spunky woman with the bug spray. When it didn't happen, I decided to write my own happy endings—without the giant bugs.

I made that decision in January 1999 after a cross-country move from southern California to northern Virginia. A job change for my husband made the relocation a necessity, but it wasn't easy. I grew up in Los Angeles, attended both UCLA and UC Berkeley, and lived for eight years in a mountain community just south of Bakersfield. I'm happiest at the beach and have ridden out earthquakes. I know Interstate 5 like the back of my hand. I'm addicted to sunshine and can tolerate smog.

Packing up and moving to the east coast was like yanking a palm tree out of the sand by its roots. Our adventure started with a cross-country drive. I'll never forget cruising down I-40 with my husband and sons in our old Dodge Ramcharger, our hearts full of excitement and nervous anticipation. Somewhere in Arizona, a thunderstorm struck fast and hard. When it cleared, we saw a double-rainbow arching over the highway. Like Noah in the days of old, I took at as a sign of a promising future and new opportunities.

For me, that meant writing a novel. As soon as we settled into our new routine in Virginia, I sat in front of the computer, named the heroine Susan because it was the first name that popped into my head, and promised myself that I wouldn't edit a word until I'd written "The End." I had no idea who Susan was or how the story would unfold. I just stuck her in a barn with a dead body and a grief-stricken rancher.

The writing wasn't very good, but something wonderful happened. Ideas came. My characters developed personalities, and I wanted to know what would happen next. That effort is under the bed gathering dust, but my second manuscript turned into Of Men and Angels, my first sale to Harlequin Historical.

Writing is a challenge and a joy, but the things in life that matter to me the most are faith, friends and family. I'm bone-deep grateful for a wonderful husband and two terrific sons who are married and on their own. I have beautiful grandkids, too! The promise of that double-rainbow in Arizona has been more than fulfilled. Life is good, and best of all, there's more to come.

Visit my website at www.victoriabylin.com

About the Author

Victoria Bylin is known for tackling tough subjects with great compassion. In 2016, *Together With You* won the Inspirational Readers Choice Award for Best Contemporary Romance. Her other books, including historical westerns, have finaled in the Carol Awards, the RITAs, and RT Magazine's Reviewers Choice Awards. A native of California, she and her husband now make their home in Lexington, Kentucky.

Made in the USA
Coppell, TX
19 January 2024